SHARON SALA

'TIL DEATH

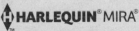

HARLEQUIN® MIRA®

Recycling programs
for this product may
not exist in your area.

ISBN-13: 978-0-7783-1427-1

'TIL DEATH

Copyright © 2013 by Sharon Sala

Printed in U.S.A.

"At all costs" is a commonly used phrase in our culture,
but rarely do we consider that the true meaning
often encompasses the worth of a human life.

It's what drives us to excel
when by all accounts we should actually fail.

It's what pushes us beyond physical strength to a refusal to let go.

It's what makes one person a survivor and another a victim.

And it's inherent in the vow in a wedding ceremony
that holds the most meaning...'til death do us part.
And is often the first one broken.

I believe in a forever kind of love—the kind that still endures
after death, the kind with a spirit so strong that it refuses to
acknowledge separation and still finds a way to communicate.

I dedicate this book to forever loves
and to the people who hold on to their dreams at all costs.

One

The sweet, soulful voice of a blues singer spilled out into the room from Meg Lewis's radio, sharing a message of unrequited love as old as time.

I can't make you love me....

Meg looked up from the fabric she'd been cutting and caught a glimpse of herself in the mirror on the other side of the table. Just for a moment she saw herself as a stranger might: tall, mid-thirties with dark hair below her shoulders and a heart-shaped face with eyes as green as new grass.

She frowned and then returned to the cutting table.

The last thing on her mind was finding love. Her high school sweetheart had gone to prison for killing his dad, and when she took a chance on love again and married at nineteen, within two years her husband had killed a man over drugs and gone to prison for life. She wound up divorced at twenty-one and shamed in the eyes of the residents of Rebel Ridge by association alone.

Her saving grace had been a family who didn't believe in quitting. Her grandfather Walker, who was in his last days in a nursing home, gave her his house. Having a place to call her own and a family that always had her back saved her. They were fiercely protective of each other, and she was grateful every day for her brothers: Ryal, a master carpenter, James, who farmed and was the mail carrier on Rebel Ridge, and Quinn, an army vet and a Back Country Ranger in the Daniel Boone National Forest.

The only real skill she had was sewing, which was what she turned to in the dark days after her divorce. She went back to quilting during that self-imposed exile because it was a solitary task, and when she had finished the first quilt, in a way, she'd finished grieving for her failed marriage, as well.

Her father died a short while afterward, and her mother, Dolly, gave up their family home to Ryal, the oldest son, and moved in with Meg. They were together for the next fourteen-plus years, until just over a year ago, when Dolly remarried and moved out to her new husband's home. For the first time in her life, Meg Lewis was finally living alone.

These days the sad song's message had no place in Meg's world. She didn't have an unrequited love and wasn't looking for a new one, although there were times when the loneliness of living alone got to her. The song ended just as a gust of wind popped the screens on the outside of the house.

Though the window shades were down and the curtains drawn, she quickly glanced toward the window. For her own peace of mind, she had to make sure there was no one outside. She laid down the scissors and, without turning on more lights, went into a darker part of the house to look out, remembering the odd things that had been happening around the place.

The first time she'd noticed something was wrong was when she went to feed the chickens and the feed bucket was not in the shed where she'd left it. At first she'd blamed herself for being absentminded, but when she finally found it sitting outside near the water faucet, she was shocked. Because of the small pinholes in the bottom, she never carried water in that bucket.

The next incident happened days later, just before dawn, when she was awakened by thumping and banging outside her window. When she got up and looked out, she saw her milk cow grazing in the yard. She grabbed her bathrobe and a flashlight, slipped on a pair of tennis shoes and headed outside, muttering beneath her breath.

The cow looked up, recognized Meg's voice and then took another bite of the sweet green grass underneath the old tire swing.

"Daisy! Get!" Meg shouted.

The cow lowed softly before ceding to Meg's insistence and headed back toward the barnyard at a jog with Meg right behind her, yelling and waving the flashlight to get her through the gate.

The unsettling part for Meg was discovering the loop of rope used to fasten the gate had not broken as she'd assumed. The moment she saw the clean-cut ends, she remembered the bucket that had gone missing. She stared in disbelief, then, in sudden panic, swung her flashlight into the darkness, but she neither saw nor heard anything unusual.

Her hands were shaking as she pulled the belt from her bathrobe and used it to tie the gate shut, then hurried back toward the house. Once inside, she grabbed her daddy's rifle and a handful of shells and headed back out to the porch. She loaded the gun, then sat watch in the porch swing until the sun came up, wishing old Blue were still alive and lying at her feet.

Once she could see, she got dressed, made herself some breakfast, then went outside, still carrying the rifle, and began looking for tracks.

She found them coming out of the woods behind the barn and then going back the same way. From the size of the shoe print, it was hard to decide whether it was a teenager or a small man. She wanted to believe it was some stupid kid thinking how funny it would be to bug her since she now lived alone.

The problem was that there weren't any teenagers within five miles of her place, which shot a big hole in that theory. She didn't know of a one who would willingly trek through five miles of forest in the dark just to play a trick. Drive, yes. Walk, no.

Later, as she was doing the morning chores outside, she kept trying to decide what to do. Once she told her family, her brothers would raise hell until this was solved. She hated to disturb their lives over something that most likely didn't amount to anything, but, at the same time, she didn't like feeling uneasy in her own home. By the time she took the fresh milk into the house to strain up, she'd calmed down and convinced herself it was nothing to bother anyone about.

Still, when dark came she put the loaded rifle near the headboard of her bed, just in case. The next four nights came and went without incident, and she convinced herself that whatever had been going on was over.

Now she wasn't so sure. She hated that just the noise

of the wind had rattled her sense of security. She looked out through all the windows but saw nothing that seemed to warrant concern.

The yard was as dark as the night sky No moon. No stars. Just an occasional flash of distant lightning—a promise of the storm to come. She paused to watch as a possum waddled up the steps and onto the porch, sniffing around the pots of plants and then checking beneath the porch swing before waddling back down the steps.

She smiled. The swing was her favorite site for a retreat from work, the place where she often drank her iced tea and ate a snack, which was usually a couple of her homemade cookies. The possum was obviously looking for cookie crumbs. After a final sweep of the yard, she felt confident that all was well and went back to the sewing room with an easier feeling, anxious to finish what she'd started before going to bed.

A few days ago she'd been digging through some old quilt patterns and found one called Storm at Sea that had belonged to her granny Foster. She'd never seen that pattern made into a quilt and was anxious to see what the top would look like once it was pieced together.

The fabrics she had chosen were washable cottons— a plain, bright white, two different shades of solid blues and three different shades of blue prints to give the wavelike imagery needed for the design. The feel of fabric in her hands was, for her, the equivalent of running her fingers through jewels.

She picked up a length of fabric with tiny navy blue flowers on a pale blue background and unfolded it, sliding it onto her cutting table, smoothing it out, folding it just so, methodically laying on the pieces of pattern.

Over the years her fascination with color and texture had garnered her a reputation as a craftswoman of some note, and now her name among quilters was synonymous with quality. But it had come after years at the task. She had four special orders finished and waiting to be shipped, and one still on the quilting frame.

The wind popped the screen again. She shuddered but made herself focus. She'd never been afraid to be alone and wasn't going to start now. After cutting out the last of the pieces for the new quilt top, she locked up the house, took a shower and crawled into bed.

Meg woke just after daybreak but lay in bed with her eyes still closed, thinking about the day ahead. She was considering the idea of rolling over and catching another hour of sleep when she heard a board creak. She'd lived in this house long enough to know that the only time that sound happened was when people walked just behind the kitchen table.

Someone was in the house!

Panic shot through her so fast she almost lost her breath as she threw back the covers and grabbed the rifle. She ran out into the hall in her nightgown and bare feet, carrying the rifle waist high and ready to fire. All of a sudden she heard the sound of breaking glass and then the back door slam.

Whoever it was had heard her coming and was making a run for it!

She ran down the hall, through the living room, into the kitchen, then out the back door as fast as her long legs would carry her. She caught a glimpse of movement at the edge of the tree line and fired, then leaped off the porch, firing as she ran, until the rifle was empty and her heart was hammering against her rib cage so hard she thought she was going to pass out.

The sound echoed within the quiet of the morning, sending the milk cow racing toward the pasture and the chickens flying about inside the coop.

"Run, you coward, run!" Meg screamed, and then stopped near the fence and began to shake.

It wasn't until the bottoms of her feet began to burn that she looked down past the hem of her nightgown and saw blood between her toes.

"Just what I need," she muttered, then gave the trees one last look and headed back to the house, limping from the pain.

As soon as she stepped up on the porch she saw that the lock on the back door had been jimmied. Once inside, she shoved a chair beneath the doorknob, then turned to scan the mess the intruder had left behind. The floor near the dining table was scattered with water, wildflowers and broken glass.

What the hell? He's breaking into my house to leave flowers? What's next...climbing into my bed?

She'd run right through the debris without feeling a thing, which said a lot for what a surge of adrenaline could do to a body. But this time there was no question of whether she would call for help. She hobbled across the floor with the rifle, leaving bloody footprints as she went. Her fingers were still trembling as she picked up the phone. Her mother and her new husband, Jake Doolen, were too far away to be of immediate help. James and Quinn would already have left for work. That left Ryal, who worked from home.

She made the call, then closed her eyes and took a

deep breath, willing herself not to cry. But when she heard his voice, her best intentions were not enough.

"Hello."

"Ryal, it's me. I need you. Can you come over now?"

Ryal heard the fear in her voice. "What happened, Meggie? Are you hurt?"

"A little."

"Do you need to go to the hospital?"

"I don't know...maybe."

"I'll be right there, honey. Hang on."

"One more thing," she said.

"What's that, Meggie?"

"Bring your gun."

She heard a swift intake of breath, and then there was a growl in his voice that made the hair rise on the back of her neck.

"What the hell happened to you?"

"I'll tell you when you get here," she said, and then hung up the phone.

Ryal's heart skipped a beat as he disconnected. "Beth! Beth!"

His wife came out of the kitchen drying her hands. "Ryal, what on earth?"

"Something's happened to Meg. Get the baby and our first-aid kit."

"Oh, my God. Oh, no...should we call Dolly and Jake?"

"Not until I know what to tell them," he said, and started out of the room.

"Where are you going?" she asked.

"The last thing Meg said was to bring my gun."

Beth's face paled, but she spun into action. She filled

the diaper bag with stuff she might need, grabbed their toddler, Sarah, who was still in her high chair, eating breakfast, and picked up the first-aid kit on the way out of the house.

Ryal took the baby out of Beth's arms and buckled her in the car seat as Beth tossed the other stuff onto the floorboard of their SUV. The baby was unhappy at being separated from her food and started to cry, stopping only when Beth handed her a cookie.

Ryal drove as fast as he dared. He couldn't imagine what the hell had happened, but he knew it was serious. Meg was the oldest of his siblings and not the kind of woman who panicked.

He glanced at Beth. She was tight-lipped and staring out the windshield. He knew she was remembering a time when she'd been in danger and on the run. His family had come through for her then, and they would come through for Meg now, whatever was going on.

"Do you want me to call Dolly now?" Beth asked.

"Let's find out what happened first, but call Quinn."

"What about James?"

"He's on his mail route, and his cell phone only works intermittently out there. We'll talk to him later."

"Got it," Beth said, and quickly put in a call to Quinn, hoping it would go through.

Moments later she heard him answer.

"This is Walker," he said shortly.

"Quinn, it's me, Beth. Hang on. Ryal needs to talk to you."

She handed the phone to Ryal and turned her attention to the baby in the back.

"Hey, Quinn, where are you right now?"

"Just leaving headquarters, why?"

"Meg called me a few minutes ago. She's hurt, and Beth and I are on the way there now. I don't know what happened, but she sounded rattled as hell, and you know how much it would take to make that happen."

"I'm in the truck. I'll meet you there."

"Uh...one more thing," Ryal added.

"What?"

"She told me to bring my gun."

He heard Quinn grunt, and then the line went dead in Ryal's ear. He tossed the phone into the console and accelerated as much as he dared. He had precious cargo riding with him, and on the narrow winding roads of Rebel Ridge, driving too fast could get them killed.

It seemed that the drive took forever, but it was actually less then fifteen minutes. He pulled into the driveway and braked hard only a few feet from the front porch.

"I'll get Sarah," Beth said. "You take the first-aid kit and the gun. We'll be right behind you."

He nodded. Moments later he was running across the yard. The front door was locked but, being family, he had a key. He quickly unlocked it, then left it ajar as he ran inside, calling Meg's name as he went.

Meg was dizzy and beginning to get sick to her stomach from the pain. The hem of her nightgown was soaked with blood, and she had moved from the chair to the floor and was leaning up against a wall for fear she would pass out. Her feet were still bleeding, and she couldn't quit shaking. She knew it was shock, but knowing why didn't make it stop.

When she finally heard her brother's voice her vision suddenly blurred. At last! Now she was safe.

"I'm in the kitchen!" she yelled.

Ryal burst into the room and took one look at the chaos and blood. He dropped to his knees beside her and grabbed her by the shoulders.

"What the hell happened here?"

"Someone broke into the house. I heard him and grabbed the gun. I guess he heard me coming down the hall and ran out."

"Did you get a look at him? Could you tell who it was?"

She shook her head. "By the time I got to the porch all I saw was movement inside the trees. I followed all the way to the fence, shooting as I went, and didn't stop until the rifle was empty."

"Son of a bitch."

Ryal sounded like she'd felt at the onset: mad and frustrated. But she didn't feel that way now. She was scared, and her feet were hurting. She shoved a hand through her hair, unaware that she'd just smeared blood across her forehead.

At that moment Beth came hurrying into the room. "I got the playpen out of the back bedroom and put Sarah in the living room." Then she saw the broken glass and Meg on the floor bleeding, and she went into action. "Do you know if there's any glass in your feet?"

"No. I was running and shooting, and didn't even know I'd cut myself until the gun was empty and the guy was gone."

Beth rocked back on her heels. "What? Someone broke into the house?"

"It's a long story," Meg said.

"Save it for when Quinn gets here," Ryal said. "Right

now we need to see what you've done to your feet and whether or not we need to take you to the doctor."

Meg groaned. "You called Quinn?"

"Yes, and I'm about to call Mom and Jake," he said.

"Oh, my Lord," Meg said.

"We'd never hear the end of it if we didn't," Beth said, and gave Meg's arm a quick squeeze. "I'm going to get a pan and some water so we can see how bad the cuts are, okay?"

Meg nodded, then leaned her head against the wall and closed her eyes. There was no need to be afraid anymore. Her family was here. Everything was going to be all right.

A few minutes later Beth came back over, carrying a basin of warm water with a couple of towels and a wash-cloth. Ryal was cleaning up the blood and broken glass. Beth knelt beside her and proceeded to wash Meg's feet to assess the damage.

"I'll try not to hurt you," she said softly.

"It's okay," Meg said. "I'm just glad you're here."

Ryal was still sweeping when they heard Quinn drive up.

He came inside on the run, calling Ryal's name.

"In the kitchen!" Ryal called back.

Quinn was in his ranger uniform—and armed. He quickly eyed the room and what his brother was doing, and then got down on one knee beside Meg, touching Beth's shoulder as he knelt. The cuts on Meg's feet were obvious, but not how they got there. His voice was gruff with emotion.

"What happened, honey?"

Meg sighed. Quinn was the brother who'd been to war. From the look in his eyes, he was ready to go back.

"Someone broke into the house," she said.

"She couldn't see enough to tell who it was, but she emptied the rifle at him just the same," Ryal said.

"Which direction did he take when he ran?" Quinn asked.

Meg wasn't fooled by the soft tone of his voice. The family all knew that the quieter he got, the angrier he was.

"The first time he was here, he came and went behind the barn, but this time he went left of the house into the trees."

"What the hell do you mean, *this time?*" Ryal asked. "You didn't say this had happened before."

Meg's eyes welled with tears. "I didn't think it amounted to much. From the size of the first footprints I found, I thought it was a teenager just messing around, trying to rile me up because I'm alone."

"I didn't mean to raise my voice, Meggie. Don't cry," Ryal said. "Just tell us what's been happening."

Beth put a clean towel under each of Meg's feet and went to pour out the bloody water while Meg began to explain, telling them about the bucket going missing in the barn, then the cow getting out and the rope latch being cut. By the time she got to what had happened that morning, she couldn't stop shaking.

"Shock," Quinn said. "Hey, Beth! Bring a blanket," he yelled, then eyed the cuts more closely. "You need stitches. Has anyone called Mom?"

"We were waiting for you to get here before we made any further decisions," Ryal said.

"Call her. Tell her you're taking Meg to the E.R. in Mount Sterling."

"What are *you* going to do?" Ryal asked.

"I'm going hunting," Quinn said, and stood abruptly. "Don't worry, sister, we'll find the son of a bitch and make him sorry, okay?"

"Be careful," Meg said.

Beth came back with an old quilt and wrapped it around Meg's shoulders. The warmth of the quilt was secondary to the feeling of shelter that swept through her as she tucked it under her chin.

A look passed between the brothers as Quinn went out the back door, pausing to look at where the lock had been jimmied. Moments later he was gone.

The baby started to cry in the other room.

Meg felt like joining her, but it would solve nothing and only add to the confusion.

Beth gathered up the first-aid supplies and put them back in the box. "Ryal, you go on to Mount Sterling with Meg. Sarah and I will stay here to wait for Jake and Dolly. Quinn's already on the hunt, so we'll be fine. In the meantime, I'll finish cleaning up in here, and we'll have everything all shipshape by the time you two get back."

Ryal hesitated and then picked up Meg's empty rifle. "Where's the ammunition?" he asked.

"In the hall closet on the top shelf," she said.

"I'll be right back," Ryal said, and went to get the ammo and reload the rifle. He didn't like the idea of leaving his wife and child alone in a house that had just been vandalized, but Meg had been bleeding too long as it was, and Beth was right. Quinn was already after the perpetrator, so there was no chance of him coming back here. Still, he wasn't going to leave them defenseless.

He paused in the hall and hung the rifle on the gun rack, then went back to the kitchen.

"The rifle has been reloaded. If it wasn't for Sarah, I'd say leave it in a corner somewhere in here. It's hanging on the gun rack in the hall, okay?"

Beth nodded. "We'll be fine."

"You better be," he said softly, then picked Meg up and headed for the front door with Beth leading the way. They settled Meg in the front seat, then buckled her up.

Ryal turned to his wife and kissed her goodbye. "We'll be back as soon as possible. Be careful. Pay attention."

"I will. I'm going to go call your mother now. It won't take them long to get here. You two drive safe and hurry home."

Beth hurried back inside to console her baby, only to find out that she'd fallen asleep in the playpen. She covered her with a blanket and then picked up the phone to call Dolly.

Quinn found the tracks easily enough and saw that Meg had been right. They were on the small side for a grown man, which meant nothing in the grand scheme of tracking. It could even be a woman. Not everyone was the size of the Walker clan. Another thing he noticed was that the man made no attempt to hide his tracks, and from the length of the stride, he had been moving fast. Quinn smiled grimly. That would be because his sister had been emptying the rifle at his ass. Too damned bad she'd missed.

He lost the trail twice when he ran into a patch of rocky ground but picked it up again within minutes. The man was still moving uphill, but Quinn noticed from the length of his stride that he was also slowing down, and that was when he found the first sign of blood. Meg had gotten a piece of the bastard after all.

A mile up he came out into a clearing and realized he'd walked up on the old Fox homestead. There was nothing left of the house and outbuildings but a chimney and a pile of rotting lumber. He seemed to remember hearing that it had taken a bad hit one year during a storm after old man Fox's death, but he hadn't been on this land in years. Obviously the story had been true. The storm must have blown the roof off, and the ensuing years of weather had rotted what was left. The place was grown up with weeds and grass, so he began looking around, trying to pick up the trail again.

The first thing he saw that was out of place was an old rusty door in the side of the mountain. He guessed it was some kind of storm shelter and tried it, but it wouldn't open. It was either locked or rusted shut, and from the amount of undisturbed weeds and brush around it, the man couldn't be hiding in there.

After circling the area and finding what looked like tracks from a dirt bike, he had to accept that he'd lost the trail. The thought of going back to Meg without good news was frustrating, but there were still things they could do to ensure her safety. He made a quick call to his boss, filled him in on what was happening and then headed back down the mountain.

There was a hole in his coat. It and his shirt were soaked with blood when he finally pulled it off. The damn bitch had nicked him with her first shot. The pain had been a shock, but it had lent speed to his exit. The last thing he'd expected was for her to come out shooting. There was more fire to Meg Lewis than he'd expected, and he was regretting his decision to fool with her awhile before making his approach. He had a big question, and she had the answer. He should have just knocked on her door and found a way to trick her into telling him. The only reason he'd decided to tease her for a while was pure meanness on his part, and it was a mistake that had almost cost him his life. He wouldn't make that mistake again.

He grimaced as he shifted in front of the bathroom mirror to eye the wound. Thankfully it was just a graze and had almost stopped bleeding. He grabbed a bottle of alcohol from the medicine cabinet, dousing the wound liberally, cursing loud and long from the pain. With no gauze or tape to make a bandage, he ripped up an undershirt, folded it into a pad and stuck it down with a half-dozen Band-Aids.

As soon as he was satisfied that the makeshift dressing was going to hold, he got a long-sleeved shirt out of the closet. It wouldn't be wise for anyone to see the bandage or the wound and start asking questions. He moved quietly through the house, dodging sleeping dogs. Thankful that his brother was a heavy sleeper, he took some pain pills out of the cabinet and a cold beer from the fridge, and he dosed himself as he headed for the door.

It was almost ten in the morning and not a bite of food in the house to eat. It was time to go down to Boone's Gap, pick up some groceries and grab some food at Frankie's Eats.

Two

By the time Quinn got back to the house, not only were Jake and his mom there, but so was his wife, Mariah. He found Dolly scrubbing and sweeping the kitchen floor all over again, and Beth feeding Sarah a snack. Except for remembering all the blood and Meg's pale face, it would seem like old times in this house. But the moment he came in, they began bombarding him with questions.

"Give me a minute," he said, and hugged Mariah, who gave him a careful look. They were both veterans of the Iraq and Afghanistan wars, and each other's monitor on the PTSD that came and went in their lives. After he winked at her, she relaxed.

"I brought Moses. He's tied up on the front porch," Mariah said. With Jake's help, she was teaching their dog, Moses, to track. "Want me to put him on the trail?"

"Maybe," Quinn said. "We need to talk first."

His mother set the mop out on the back porch to dry and then came back in and joined the conversation.

"Talk to me, Quinn. Who did this?" she asked.

"I wish I knew," Quinn said. "I lost the trail up around

the old Fox place. He got away on a dirt bike, but I found blood. Meg got a piece of him when she fired."

"Damn shame it wasn't his head," Jake said.

Quinn silently agreed. "Has anyone heard from Ryal and Meg?"

"I did," Beth said. "He called about a half hour ago. They're on their way home. She has six stitches in her right foot and three in her left."

Quinn's eyes narrowed angrily. "I'm so upset with her for not telling us about what's been going on."

Dolly's face crumpled as a fresh set of tears slid down her cheeks. "It was because she was living on her own now and didn't want anyone to think she couldn't handle it."

Mariah frowned. "Meg is the most resourceful woman I've ever met. She'll always be fine on her own if the playing field is level."

"You're right, honey." Quinn nodded. "I called my boss and told him I'd be off all day. I'm going into Mount Sterling to get some motion-activated security lights and an alarm system. I also need to fix the lock on the back door. When that bastard walks up on this house again he won't have the convenience of hiding in the dark to jimmy a lock. I'm getting the loudest damn alarm I can find, and next time he tries breaking in, maybe he'll die of a heart attack and save me the trouble of killing him."

Mariah grinned. "My hero."

Beth laughed. "No one ever accused Quinn of being the family pacifist."

Quinn eyed his wife. "Mariah, if you intend to put Moses on the trail, don't take him into the woods by yourself."

Jake spoke up. "I'll go with her. I brought my rifle. We'll see what happens."

Beth tested the floor to see if it was dry and then put Sarah down to play. "Dolly and I will wait here for Ryal and Meg. You should meet them coming back on your way down."

"Okay," Quinn said. "Oh, did anyone call James? He'll be seriously pissed if he finds out what's happening from someone other than us."

Beth nodded. "I tried his cell a couple of times but only got voice mail, then just called his house and told Julie everything. She'll fill him in when he gets home."

"Okay, so call if you need me, but I won't be gone any longer than I have to," Quinn said. "I'll have this place wired like a prison before the sun goes down tonight."

"Jake and I are spending the night with her," Dolly said. "We've already decided. And I'm staying here with her until her stitches are out and she's able to get around again."

"I'll be right here with them every night," Jake said. "My boys can watch our place while we're here."

"Meg isn't going to be happy about that," Beth said. "She's going to think we don't believe she can take care of herself."

"She'll get over it," Dolly said shortly.

"So Mom's still in charge, huh?" Quinn said, and winked at his mother.

A few minutes later he was on his way down the mountain, while Mariah and Jake took Moses outside and set him on the intruder's trail.

As they left the hospital in Mount Sterling, Meg felt light-headed from the pain meds and realized it was because her stomach was empty. She would rectify that after she got home, but for now all that mattered was that her feet were blessedly numb. She glanced over at her brother, grateful for his presence but at the same time worried about how she was going to cope. She wasn't supposed to walk until the stitches came out, except when it was completely necessary, and she had chickens to feed, a cow to milk and a quilt to finish, although she could work on that sitting down.

Her head was spinning, trying to figure out how to make everything work, when Ryal glanced over at her and smiled.

"You doin' okay, sister?"

"As good as can be expected, but what a mess I've made of everything. If only I'd seen that glass on the floor."

He frowned. "You're not responsible for any of this. The sorry bastard who broke into your house is responsible for all of it, and speaking of sorry bastards…can you think of anyone who would do this to you?"

She shook her head. "No, but since he was on foot, I think it must be someone who lives fairly close. We know everybody on this side of the mountain, but I've never looked at my neighbors and thought of them as possible stalkers."

Ryal sighed. "It doesn't have to be someone within walking distance, honey. They could have a vehicle stashed somewhere nearby. I was wondering if anyone had been coming on to you at church, or maybe trying to hit on you down in Boone's Gap and you turned him down. Anything like that ring a bell?"

She snorted softly. "I haven't been asked out in so long I can't remember the last man who tried."

"I'm sorry," he said.

"I'm not. There's not a man, single or married, living on Rebel Ridge that I'd give a second look at, and that's the truth. My first boyfriend wound up going to prison for manslaughter, although to be fair, I never thought he did it. As for the man I married, he *did* kill someone, and I'm glad he went to prison for it. I've never had the guts to give it another try."

Ryal glanced at her, eyeing the closed expression on her face. "I had forgotten all about you and Lincoln Fox."

She shrugged, ignoring the pang of regret she always felt when she heard his name. "We were teenagers. It was a long time ago."

"Your ex wasn't a bad guy when you married him," he added.

Meg shrugged. "No, but he was a weak one. The first time someone waved money under his nose, he caved. He was making meth in the back pasture just like his granddaddy used to make moonshine up in the hills, and when he began cheating his customers, he wound up killing one who dared to complain. Lord. Even divorcing him after he went to prison wasn't enough to live that down."

"Damn it, Meg, that's on him, not you."

"Yes, well, Mrs. White probably had a different opinion, God rest her soul. It was her son Wendell who Bobby killed."

"Yeah, Wendell, the oldest of the three losers she gave birth to, and the druggie who spent his mama's social security check on meth before she even got a chance to buy groceries. This sounds a little harsh, but if you ask me, your ex did her a favor."

Meg knew she should be shocked, but the smirk on Ryal's face made her smile.

"I guess there's a case to be made there," she said.

He nodded. "However, I do remember their financial situation had turned around before Wendell was killed. One day they'd been bordering on losing everything, and then suddenly they were fine. By the time Mrs. White passed, the place was a little showpiece… flowers in the yard, a new barn and even a small tractor. Then the property passed to Prince and Fagan, and it's gone downhill ever since."

"You're good for my soul," she said.

"Well, I don't want to hear any more crap out of you about any shame falling on your shoulders. You did nothing wrong, so don't go and turn yourself into some damn martyr, do you hear me?"

"Loud and clear, brother."

"Good. And now you're home," he said, eyeing the number of cars in the yard. "Looks like the only ones who have yet to arrive are James and Julie."

Meg pointed. "Oh, Lord. Here comes Mom, and she's crying."

"If this had just happened to Sarah, I'd be crying, too, so get over it," Ryal said.

"Point taken," she said, and opened the door.

"Hang on. You're not getting out on your own, remember?"

She sighed. "Actually, I'd already forgotten."

"You won't forget when the pain meds wear out. Just hold your horses."

Moments later she was enveloped in her mother's teary hug before Ryal picked her up and carried her into the house. Dolly chastised her all the way inside for not telling them what had been happening. Before Meg could get in a word of explanation, Jake finished up the scolding by telling her that he and Dolly were staying there until she could walk on her own again, and they didn't want to hear a word about it.

"I hear you, and I thank you," Meg said, trying not to cry as Ryal put her down in the recliner and pulled out the footrest. As he did, the quilt that had been wrapped around her in the car slipped down to her waist.

Dolly took one look at the nightgown Meg was wearing and gasped.

"Oh, Lordy be, Margaret Ann, you actually went to the emergency room in your nightgown? What did people think?"

"Well, Mom, just be glad they didn't have to take the nightgown off to treat me, because I'm not wearing anything under it, either."

Dolly gasped as the rest of the family burst into laughter.

Quinn was back from Mount Sterling. He'd already fixed the lock on the back door and was outside hanging the first of the motion-sensitive security lights when Moses came bounding out of the woods with Mariah and Jake behind him. The dog saw Quinn on the ladder and began barking to signal their arrival. Quinn waved at the trackers, and then kept on working as the dog bounded up onto the porch and flopped down in the shade, his tongue hanging out of the side of his mouth, panting from the exertion.

Mariah and Jake stopped to talk.

"How did it go?" Quinn asked.

Mariah looked disappointed. "We lost the trail in the same place you did."

Jake took off his cap and combed his fingers through his thick gray curls. "I found bike tracks right where you said they'd be. I'm thinking he had it stashed there for a getaway."

"That's what I thought, too," Quinn said. "Regardless, I'm putting in some security here. If there's a next time, I'm making sure Meg has light to aim by."

"Are she and Ryal back?" Mariah asked.

"Yeah, she's inside."

"I'm going to go see her," she said, and tied Moses up before going inside.

"Need any help?" Jake asked.

"I'm good," Quinn said. "I helped set up communications in Iraq, so most of this is familiar territory."

He kept on working, and when he was finished with the first light he gave Moses some water before moving the ladder to the front of the house. He installed another light on the front porch, and just as he was finishing up, the last Walker brother arrived.

James was alone, which meant Julie had been able to contact him before he'd gone back home. He got out on the run, without the jovial smile he usually wore. He looked as deadly as Quinn felt.

"What the hell happened to Meg?" he asked.

Quinn frowned. "Someone's been stalking her. She'll fill you in on all the details. Everyone else is inside."

James bolted up the steps, letting the door slam behind him as he went inside, but not before Quinn got a whiff of chicken frying and corn bread baking in the oven. It was almost noon, and his mom was obviously on a mission. She couldn't fix what had happened, but she knew how to feed the people who could, and she was hard at it.

He finished with the last outside light and then proceeded to install the alarm system inside the house, putting sensors on both the doors, so that once the alarm was set it would go off if either door was opened. If he could, he would have dug a moat around the house and installed a drawbridge, but this was the best he could do for the location they were in.

As Quinn headed for the bathroom to wash up, he saw the local sheriff's car coming up the drive. Ryal, who was standing head to head with James, must have called him.

"Hey, Ryal, Sheriff Marlow just pulled up," he said, pointing toward the door, and then kept on walking.

Ryal handed his daughter to James and went outside to greet the sheriff.

Marlow promptly shook Ryal's hand as he came up the steps. "Good to see you, Ryal. Sorry it's under such circumstances. How's Meg?"

"She's okay, no thanks to the man who broke into the house."

"Is she up to giving a statement? I'll need to talk to her to file the report."

"Sure, come on in," Ryal said, and led the way to the living room. "Hey, everybody, why don't you go see if Mom needs any help? The sheriff needs to talk to Meg."

They left the room as the sheriff chose a chair beside the recliner where Meg was sitting.

"You'll have to ignore my clothing," Meg said. "Mom is already horrified that I went to the emergency room in my nightgown, so when it dawns on her that I'm giving my statement to the authorities in the same condition, she won't be happy with me."

Marlow chuckled. "You're just fine, Meg." But the smile ended when he got down to business and took out his notepad. "So, talk to me. Ryal mentioned when he called that you're being stalked, so start from the beginning."

She nodded, then once again repeated her story, from the missing feed bucket to the squeaky floorboard in the kitchen and chasing him out with the rifle. At that point, Quinn returned.

"I'll add a little note to the story," he said. "I think one of Meg's shots hit the target. I found blood on the trail, and I also think he had a dirt bike stashed up on the old Fox place for a getaway."

Meg looked startled. "Really? I hope the shot was in his ass."

Her brothers grinned.

The sheriff chuckled. "You're certainly a chip off the Walker block. Where is that glass vase he brought in with him?"

Ryal groaned. "Swept up and in the trash. Sorry."

"So what happens now?" she asked.

"Since you couldn't identify him and we don't have any witnesses, there's not a lot I can do, since the glass will be too compromised for prints. But the report will be filed, and that's the first step. What I *will* do is notify medical clinics and hospitals in the area to let me know about any gunshot victims. If any of the patients live on Rebel Ridge, they're gonna have some explaining to do."

"So you think it's someone local?" Ryal asked.

Marlow shrugged. "It makes sense that only a local would know Meg lives by herself now. Of course, that's not an accusation, but it's definitely a thought to consider."

At that point Dolly came in, her face pink from the heat of the kitchen, and saw the sheriff.

"Hello, Mel. It's good of you to come so quick."

"Part of the job, Dolly. How's new-married life treating you?"

She blushed. "Just fine, thank you. If you-all are through here, dinner is ready. Mel, you're welcome to stay and eat. There's plenty."

Marlow reluctantly rejected the invitation. "It all smells really good, and I appreciate the offer, but I'd better get back down to Boone's Gap and file this report." He glanced down at Meg as he stood. "If there's a next time, I expect you to call me first."

"I will," she said.

"I'll walk you out," Ryal said, and left the room with the sheriff.

Dolly eyed Meg's attire but said nothing. "Honey, do you need to go to the bathroom before we eat?"

"Actually, I do," Meg said. "And, Mama, if you'll get me something clean to put on, I'd appreciate it. I've had about all I can stand of this bloody nightgown."

Dolly headed to Meg's bedroom with a relieved smile on her face.

Quinn scooped Meg up out of the recliner and carried her toward the bathroom.

"We need to get you a wheelchair," he said.

Dolly heard him as she came back up the hall. "I think I know where we can borrow one. I'll make a call after we eat."

The day that had begun in such a traumatic fashion ended on a quiet note as Jake wheeled Meg to her bedroom in the borrowed wheelchair and then bade her good-night.

She thought about the nearly finished quilt on the frame but was too weary to seriously consider working on it. Instead she took out a couple of pain pills and reached for the glass of water on the bedside table. Her feet were hurting, but there was nothing to be done but get through this day by day.

She swallowed the pills, slid down beneath the covers and closed her eyes while listening to the murmur of voices beyond her door. She hated to admit it, but she would never have been able to relax without someone with her tonight. She fell asleep listening to crickets chirping outside her window and the sound of a coyote yipping somewhere on the ridge above the house.

His arm was infected and he was running a fever, but going to the doctor wasn't happening. They would know immediately that it was a gunshot wound and would be bound by law to report it. He needed some medicine, but he was going to have to lie to get it. Luckily he knew right where to go. Aunt Tildy Bennett was the resident herb woman on Rebel Ridge, and she had all manner of ointments for all manner of conditions. She wasn't really his aunt, but it was what everybody called her. He had a story all ready to explain away the injury and knew she would be none the wiser. When his brother left to work his marijuana patch, he got dressed and left the house.

A half hour later he pulled up in Tildy Bennett's drive. He grabbed his cap just before the wind took it and made a dash toward the house. The only good thing about the cold day was that the wind felt good on his feverish face.

He knocked, then waited for her to come to the door. As soon as it opened, he quickly yanked off his cap and put on his best manners.

"Aunt Tildy. I've gone and hurt my arm on a piece of broken sucker rod, and it got infected. I was wondering if you'd take a look at it."

The old woman's eyes narrowed as she eyed the man on her porch. He had a terrible reputation, but it wasn't in her nature to judge.

"Come inside out of the cold. I need to see it before I know what to do."

"Yes, ma'am." He stepped inside, then followed her to the kitchen.

"Just take off your coat and hang it there on the chair. You don't need to take off your shirt all the way, just take your bad arm out of the sleeve," she said.

He did as she asked and waited for her reaction.

Her eyes narrowed as she eyed the wound. "You say you hurt this on a piece of pipe?"

"Yes, ma'am. It was a thin piece of sucker rod.... The end of it was all broken and ragged, and, well...I admit...I was drunk as a skunk when it happened. I fell on it with all my weight. It gouged this big hunk outta my arm, and now I got myself into a fix, what with it getting infected and all."

Aunt Tildy's attention shifted to the wound. "You're right. It *is* infected, but not to the blood-poisoning stage. Have you had a tetanus shot recently? If that pipe was rusty, you'll likely get yourself a case of lockjaw. You can die from that."

He was getting worried and then remembered the lie. It hadn't really been a rusty pipe. It had been a hot bullet.

"Yes, ma'am, I'm good on that. Had one just last year when I got a fishhook cut out of my leg."

Tildy turned to a cupboard and began shifting bottles and tins aside until she found what she was looking for, then got a pan of hot water and some antiseptic soap.

"This is likely gonna hurt," she said, and began cleaning the wound with short rigorous swipes.

"Holy crap, excuse my language," he said as tears sprang to his eyes. "That hurts."

"I warned you," Tildy said, and kept working.

A half hour later he was on his way out with a tea to brew for fever and a tin of ointment to put on the wound three times a day. He was twenty dollars lighter in the pocket, but it was all worth it as he got back in his truck and drove away.

The week passed without incident. Meg finished the quilt on the frame, added the binding around the edges, and got it and the four others ready to ship. After Jake took them down to Boone's Gap to drop off with FedEx, she breathed a little easier. Without any pressing orders, she could take a little downtime.

Once word began to spread on Rebel Ridge about the attack on Meg Lewis, every widow woman in the area began sleeping with a loaded gun beside her bed. Despite the security system Quinn had installed at the house, Jake still worried about what might happen once they were gone. He solved the problem by giving her a dog.

Her name was Honey, a year-old hound with a light brown coat, who'd been born with a crippled paw. She had big brown eyes and long legs, but had yet to fill out to her adult weight. She would never be any use for tracking, but her bloodline was pure, and, as Jake claimed, she was as sweet as the name he'd given her.

For Meg and Honey, it was love at first sight. Meg thanked Jake profusely and immediately felt safer, knowing no one could sneak up on her again.

Having the motion-detector light go off every time a possum or a raccoon wandered through the yard was going to take some getting used to, but Honey would bark loud and long if a human approached, especially in the dark.

The real test would be when Jake and her mom finally left, but Meg was ready for her world to get back to normal, and once they took the stitches out tomorrow, she would be on her own.

It was just after dinner when they headed for the doctor's office in Mount Sterling. Meg had the backseat to herself as Jake and Dolly manned the front, talking quietly to each other. She couldn't help but notice the lilt in her mother's voice and the joy in her laugh. Dolly was happy. Meg was happy for her but ready for them to leave. The honeymoon phase they were still in kept reminding Meg of what was missing in her own life, but as her mother was fond of saying, "this, too, shall pass."

It felt good to be out of the house, and it was the time of year when the leaves were beginning to turn. The sun was shining, but there were days when there was a nip in the air, and today was one of them. When they reached Boone's Gap, Jake pulled in at the gas station.

"I need to gas up. You ladies need anything?"

"Nothing for me, thanks," Meg said.

"I think I'd like something cold to drink, but I'll get

it while you pump the gas," Dolly said, and got out of the car, leaving Meg inside on her own.

Meg watched her mother enter the minimart and then leaned back, absently watching traffic come and go while thinking about the Storm at Sea quilt blocks she'd had to put aside. She was itching to piece them together.

She watched a woman come out with a baby on her hip and two kids following behind her. When the woman saw her and waved, Meg quickly waved back, but it was just another reminder of how behind she was on living life. No husband. No kids. No prospects. God. How pathetic could she get?

A pickup truck pulled up on the other side of the pumps. She saw the driver get out. Heard him speak to Jake and tease him about starting on his second marriage when neither of Jake's sons had even begun a first. Jake laughed. Meg looked away.

All of a sudden someone knocked on the window behind her. She turned to see her ex-husband's younger brother, Claude, smiling at her. As she rolled down the window, he leaned partway in, casually giving her the once-over.

"Hey, Meg. Just wanted to say hi and tell you how sorry we all were to hear what happened to you. You doin' okay?"

Meg wasn't crazy about any of her ex in-laws, but they'd never done her any harm and didn't seem to hold a grudge against her for divorcing their kin.

"I'm fine, Claude. Tell your family I said thank-you for their concern."

"So that fella who broke into your house didn't hurt you none?"

"Nope. I did it all to myself when I ran through broken glass."

Claude Lewis frowned, making his narrow-set eyes almost disappear. "Well, I'm real sorry that happened, and I hope they catch the bastard soon."

At that point Dolly came back to the car just as Jake was putting the gas nozzle back in the pump. She gave Claude a cool look, which ended the conversation, but Meg knew everyone was talking about her, and once she was out and about again, this wouldn't be the last time she got grilled.

Claude thumped the window as a way of ending their conversation and gave her another big smile.

"I guess y'all are ready to go. Just wanted to pay my respects," he said again.

"Uh, sure…and thanks," Meg said as he walked away.

Dolly got back in the car with a cold bottle of Mountain Dew in her hand. "Well, that was unexpected," she said, and put the pop in the cup holder between the seats.

"Lots of things are weird these days," Meg said, and then Jake got in and they drove away.

She never gave Claude Lewis another thought until late that evening, when she was standing on the porch in her house shoes, watching Jake and her mom driving away, and then she chided herself for the thought. She could pretty much guarantee he wasn't a threat to anyone.

In the middle of her reverie Honey nosed the back of Meg's leg. She reached down and gave the dog a quick pat.

"So, it's just you and me now, girl. Are you up for all this? You think you can stand guard without chasing after the four-legged visitors?"

The young dog woofed.

Meg smiled. "That sounded like a yes to me. So let's go back in the house. I need to get off my feet, and you need some supper. What do you say?"

She went back in the house with Honey at her heels.

He hadn't been to the old Walker homestead since the night Meg shot him. He'd had some healing to do, but he knew all about her family coming to her rescue, and that Jake and Dolly were staying with her, so he was biding his time.

But today he'd gone to get gas down in Boone's Gap and heard Meg Lewis was getting the stitches out of her feet, and now he was banking on the Doolens leaving soon, if they weren't already gone.

He glanced at his watch. It had been dark for hours and was nearing ten o'clock. The urge to go back was so strong he got hard just thinking about it, but he'd been hasty before. This time he had to get it right, and he needed to make sure she was really alone. He intended to scare the holy shit out of her, maybe torture her a little until she gave up the location of what he was looking for. Then, once she did, he would show her what a man was all about before he cut her sweet throat. But not now. Maybe tomorrow or the next day, but not now.

Three

Meg woke to sunlight coming through a crack in the curtains. She rolled over and glanced at the clock— almost 8:00 a.m.

"Good grief, the chickens will think I've forgotten them," she said, and threw back the covers. Honey jumped up from her mat beside the bed and padded down the hall behind her. Meg let her out and went back to get dressed. She was trying to decide which shoes would be most comfortable to wear when the phone rang. She sat down on the side of the bed to answer.

"Hello?"

"Hey, it's me, Ryal. I just wanted you to know that I'm about to pull in your driveway. I didn't want to get shot on the way to feed your chickens. Oh, and just so you know, James is coming over tonight to milk the cow."

Meg sighed with relief. "You didn't have to come do that, but I'm grateful just the same."

"We all have orders from Mom. You're not to step foot in the barnyard until your feet are completely healed."

She laughed. "Will we ever be old enough for Mom to stop treating us like kids?"

"Probably not, but I want to do it, so that's that. And since I am now in your yard, you have my permission to make some coffee, if it's not already made. Turn off your security alarm and I'll be up to get a cup after I'm done."

Meg could hear Honey beginning to bark and made a U-turn back to the door to call off her dog. Walking barefoot was painful. Her feet were still tender, and putting weight on them made them feel like they were going to burst open. She was almost wishing her mom hadn't already returned the borrowed wheelchair.

She got to the front door and let Ryal in. He quickly made peace with Honey. "I thought it best to let me in first so when you let her out, she didn't take a hunk out of me on the way to the chicken house."

She smiled, but Ryal quickly keyed in on the pain in her eyes.

"You doing okay, sister? Did anything happen last night?"

"Not a thing."

"Were you uneasy?"

"No, although I thought I would be. Have you eaten?"

"Beth made pancakes this morning. They were so good I ate way too many, but I *will* take that cup of coffee when I'm done."

"After you feed the chickens, let me know how much feed is left so I'll know when to get more."

"Will do," Ryal said, and headed toward the kitchen with the dog at his heels as Meg followed at a slower pace.

Two weeks had come and gone with no repeat of the initial home invasion. The family finally backed off, leaving Meg to cope on her own. She had settled into the notion that because she'd wounded the stalker, he'd given up. The incident began to slide further and further away as she got back to her work. The Storm at Sea quilt top was finished and she was ready to add the batting and backing.

The day had been cold, and she'd spent part of the morning hauling cut firewood from the pasture up to the house. The house had always been heated with propane, but the old fireplace still added a toasty element to a long winter night. By the time she finished supper and cleaned up the kitchen she was exhausted, but in a good way. She passed up the television for a little downtime outside before settling in to watch some shows.

She took a jacket from the hall closet and the rifle down from the rack in the hall, checking to make sure it was loaded, then slipped outside and settled into the porch swing to watch night coming to the mountain. As long as she didn't set foot off the porch the motion light wouldn't come on, and with the rifle in her lap she felt safe sitting in the dark. It was the time of day when one part of the animal world ended and another came to life. Night birds called. Owls were in flight. A coyote tuned up on a ridge somewhere close by, and his pack mates echoed his song with yips and howls of their own. Crickets were still chirping, but as the nights grew even colder, that would soon end.

Honey got up from the corner of the porch and flopped down at Meg's feet. Meg leaned over to pet the dog, almost wishing she could talk back.

"Hi, Honey girl. You're such a good girl, aren't you? Yes, you are. You worked so hard today taking care of me and this place. You want a treat?"

Honey looked like she was grinning as she abruptly sat up, watching every movement of Meg's hands. When Meg reached into her pocket, Honey's tail began wagging back and forth, sweeping clear the little spot on which she was sitting.

Meg held out the doggie treat. Honey took it from her fingers, crunched once and swallowed it.

Meg laughed. "You ate that so fast you don't even know what it tasted like, do you?"

But Honey wasn't complaining. She lay down near the steps, her gaze fixed on a point out in the trees.

Meg settled back into the swing and looked out toward the clearing, and then the woods beyond. She was a little nervous but determined to live her life without fear, and so she stayed, almost in defiance of what had already happened.

The nights were cold now, and they'd already had the first frost. But she loved the crispness of pine-scented air and the sounds that came after the sun went down. She pushed off in the porch swing, letting the motion lull her into a sense of complete relaxation.

Hounds were baying farther up on the mountain. Hunters were out running their dogs. The occasional hoot from the owl in the tree by the gate was as familiar to her as the sight of her own face. Still, she couldn't help but search the shadows, wondering if the stalker was hidden somewhere in those trees, watching her.

After a time she began to feel the cold and thought about going back inside. She'd started to get up when she realized she could hear a big vehicle coming up the mountain, and, from the sound of the engine, it was pulling a load. It made her curious, but living a quarter of a mile from the road with a forest of trees between, her curiosity would have to remain just that. A few minutes later the phone began to ring and she forgot about the car as she ran to answer, bringing Honey in with her and locking the door as she went.

He'd waited as long as he could and decided tonight was the night he got serious with Meg Lewis. She'd shot at him last time. He was going back armed, and he wasn't leaving until he got the information he needed. He was walking just inside the tree line bordering the main road when he saw headlights coming up over the hill and darted back into the woods. He didn't recognize the vehicle but gave the fancy fifth-wheel travel trailer behind it the once-over and envied the man who owned it. Once the truck was out of sight he resumed his walk. The closer he got to her house, the more excited he became.

When he finally saw it, he put on his night-vision goggles and began scanning the area. He quickly spotted her sitting in the dark on the porch swing, then frowned when he saw the rifle in her lap and the dog at her feet. The dog was an unexpected problem, and he shifted locations so that he was safely downwind.

He could, of course, just shoot the dog, but that would give her time to shoot back, and he had no doubt of her ability or willingness to kill. Pistol or not, he had no desire to face her and that rifle again.

When she bent down to pet the dog he saw her breasts shift beneath her jacket. He got hard all over again, thinking about what she would look like stripped naked beneath him.

His frustration was at an all-time high, but he held his ground and maintained surveillance. Several minutes passed, then all of a sudden she was on her feet and rushing into the house, taking the dog with her.

His pulse kicked up a notch. This was his chance! The dog couldn't stop him from getting to the porch if it was inside with her. Once he got that close, he could take the dog down with a shot through the window and then take her down when she came charging out again. He bolted out of the trees and across the yard in an all-out sprint, the pistol in his hand.

The sound of his own heartbeat was loud in his ears when, all of a sudden, the front yard was bathed in a light so bright it blinded him. Startled, he stumbled and fell. The pistol went off, and before he could get up, the dog had already begun an insane barking fit inside the house. In a panic, he scrambled to his feet and was in a frantic dash toward the trees when the ungodly screech of a security alarm sounded off behind him.

Son of a bitch! Not only did she have motion-detector lights, but there was a security alarm on the door! When he realized the frenzied barking was getting louder, he knew she'd set the dog on him, too.

He could hear her screaming over the noise, yelling for the dog to attack, and then she took her first shot. The bullet whizzed so close to his head that he heard the sound of it passing. When he finally ran into the cover of the trees, the dog was only seconds behind him.

Her next shot hit a tree right beside his head. He veered sharply, knowing she wouldn't realize he'd changed direction. When the third shot missed him by several yards, he knew his ruse had been wise, and it gave him time to fire off a shot at the dog. Even though he missed, the maneuver worked. He heard her call off the dog, which gave him just enough time to get away.

* * *

Meg dragged Honey back inside the house and reset the alarm, wavering between shock and anger. She'd let herself be lulled into a false sense of security. If it hadn't been for Honey and the safeguards Quinn had installed, it would have happened again, and with more disastrous results. She dropped down on her knees in front of Honey and began patting her and praising her.

"You are such a brave girl," Meg said, suffering the constant licks to her face. "Yes, I know you wanted to chase him down, but he changed the rules on us. He had a gun, too, and I didn't want anything to happen to you, okay? Am I forgiven?"

Honey whined and licked her again.

"I'll take that as a yes," Meg said, then got to her feet. "Come with me, little girl. I need to make a phone call."

It had taken Lincoln Fox eighteen years to come home to Rebel Ridge, and when he finally did, it was under cover of darkness.

He'd been betrayed by the people he thought had loved him, and blamed for killing his father during a fight, then setting fire to his home to hide the deed. After being convicted of manslaughter, he'd spent the next four years in a juvenile detention center, until he turned twenty-one. Once they released him, he struck out on his own and never looked back.

Bitter with what had happened to him and hating the people who'd let him down, he'd spent his first years on his own in self-imposed exile. Because of his size and strength, construction had been a perfect fit. He'd started out in Dallas, Texas, hauling lumber and driving nails, and ended up fourteen years later owning a construction company with two full crews under his direction. He worked hard and lived a simple life, but he'd never found a woman who compared to the girl he'd left behind, and now he lived his life without regrets.

Then, a month before Easter, everything had changed. While on a routine inspection on one of his job sites, he'd been electrocuted in a freak accident. He'd been clinically dead and resuscitated on-site by EMS, then frantically rushed to a hospital. During the time he was healing, his father kept coming to him in his dreams, telling him to go home. He didn't know whether the dream was a message or just a side effect of what had happened to him. But coming that close to eternity had certainly changed his attitude. It was time to stop running.

It was a given that someone had set the fire that killed his father, and he owed it to both of them to find out who it was. If he could clear his own name and get justice for his father's death in the process, the rest of his life just might be worth living.

As the sole heir to his grandfather's property back on Rebel Ridge, he knew he had a place to stay, but he had no idea what shape it would be in. But once the decision was made to go home, it didn't take him long to pack. He put what he wanted in his gooseneck travel trailer, hooked it to the back of his four-wheel-drive pickup truck and headed east, leaving the busy streets of Dallas behind him.

He was prepared to see change where he'd grown up. It had been a long damn time since he'd been there, but as he drove the narrow two-lane road up the mountain, he was surprised that it still felt familiar. Although it was dark, he could see lights on in the houses that he passed, and he wondered what their reactions were going to be once they found out he was back in their midst.

Still lost in thought and weary from the long trip, he almost missed his turn. If it hadn't been for catching a glimpse of the old metal gate with the letter *F* welded into the center of it, he would have driven right past.

He got out, dug a pair of bolt cutters from the tool-box in the back of his truck and cut the chain holding the gate shut. It toppled like the little pig's house made of straw. He dragged it out of the road and headed up the overgrown trail onto the place where five genera-tions of his people had lived and died.

When his headlights swept across the homesite, he hit the brakes, staring in disbelief. He didn't know what he'd been expecting, but this wasn't it. There was nothing left of the house but the chimney and a few rotten boards. Weeds had grown up through the rubble where the roof had fallen in. He had no one to blame but himself, he realized. His grandfather had been dead all these many years, and he'd let the house fall into ruin by his absence.

But he wasn't going to let that stop him. Houses could be rebuilt. The land was still here, and it was his. He'd made it home, but now he was hesitant to get out of his Jeep. Once he took this step, there was no going back. His presence was going to stir up old trouble—even hurt feelings and resentment—and there was no way to prevent it.

Back then, someone had used his grief and youth against him to cover up their crime. It was a different story now. Lincoln Fox was thirty-five years old, and just shy of six feet eight inches tall. There would be no railroading an innocent again, and this time if anyone cried, *he* would be the one putting on the hurt.

Since staying in the house was now out of the question, he started to look for a good place to set up his trailer and then remembered the old bomb shelter his great-grandpa Fox had built in the side of the mountain during the fifties. He'd played in there as a child, and they'd used it for a storm shelter and extra storage. It was something to consider. The least he could do was check it out. Without knowing what kind of debris could be hidden in the high weeds, he backed up carefully, then circled the old house site and drove toward the shelter a short distance away.

At first he couldn't see the entrance for the brush that had grown up in front of it; then the headlights swept across a rusting iron door, and he braked. He remembered it as one large long room, but if it was still dry and sound, it would beat the trailer once winter set in. He was a skilled carpenter. He would make it work well enough to live in until he could rebuild. Still, the hair rose on the back of his neck as he reached for his flashlight and got out.

The air was bone cold but, within moments, the familiar scent of pine drifted up his nose. He swung the flashlight back into the brush and caught sight of a possum scurrying out of sight, then aimed the light into the underbrush, checking to make sure there were no more surprises. At that moment the silence was broken by a single gunshot, then the rapid and familiar screech of a security alarm somewhere nearby. In Dallas he wouldn't have thought a thing about it, but up here on the mountain, it was the last thing he would have expected to hear. He spun toward the sound, only to be further startled by a series of gunshots.

"What the hell?"

He caught movement from the corner of his eye and saw a falling star streaking across the sky. He watched as it burned out behind the treetops, just as he'd fallen from grace so many years ago. It was weird, hearing that alarm and the gunshots, then seeing that shooting star. If it was an omen, was it good luck or bad? Then he frowned at the absurdity of the thought. He didn't believe in luck. He turned on his heel, swung the beam of light toward the door and went to see what the years had done to the place.

He kicked aside scrub brush to gain access, only to find out that the door wouldn't open. He finally managed to get the knob to turn, so at least he knew the door wasn't locked, but it was obviously rusted shut. Using nothing but brute strength, he drew back and kicked, planting his size-fourteen boots squarely below the knob. The door rattled on its hinges. This time when he tried to open it, it gave way with a loud metallic screech, but when he aimed the flashlight inside he was beyond discouraged by what he saw. The room was full of debris, like the things a hoarder would have kept.

His first thought was, no way in hell could he ever make the place habitable, but the longer he stood there, the more he began to see the possibilities. One good bonfire, followed by a power spray to disinfect the walls and floor, might change his opinion. But it wasn't happening tonight.

He shut the door and headed back to the truck, then decided to pull the trailer a little farther into the trees. It wouldn't be entirely hidden, but, after hearing those shots, he felt the need to err on the side of safety. After he parked, he got his phone and wallet out of the truck and went into the trailer, then opted not to start up the generator and call attention to himself.

Without power to hook up to, he lit a couple of candles, and then made a sandwich and dug out some chips. He was about to sit down to eat when he heard sounds outside. Remembering the earlier gunshots, he quickly blew out the candles and grabbed a hunting rifle out of the closet before moving to a window. Once his eyes adjusted to the dark, there was enough moonlight to show him a small herd of deer a short distance away. They were milling around as if settling in for the night. That must have been what he'd heard.

Just as he was about to turn away the deer suddenly bolted. He tightened his grip on the rifle and began checking the perimeter, expecting to see a cougar, or maybe a bear hunting for a little more food before winter hibernation, but not the man who came running out of the trees.

The man was of average height, wearing what looked like a leather biker jacket. His head was bare, because Linc could see the bounce and sway of his hair in the moonlight, but he was too far away for Linc to see his face. He watched as the man ran all the way across the clearing before disappearing into the forest.

At that point Linc moved to the door. Just as he stepped out, he heard what sounded like a dirt bike start up and then speed off.

The first thing that crossed his mind was that the man had something to do with the shots and the security alarm he'd heard. The timing was just about right. Frowning, he made a mental note to clear up the grass and brush as quickly as possible and let people know someone had taken residence here. Whatever was going on, he wanted no part of it. Rebel Ridge had always been a place for keeping secrets. It appeared that was still true.

He went back inside, locked the door and felt his way through the trailer, undressing in the dark. He put the rifle on the floor beside the bed, then crawled between the covers. It had been a long day and a grueling drive. It didn't take long to fall asleep, but sleep brought memories that turned into a horror from his past.

He'd been seventeen, and he and his grandpa Fox had been fishing at his grandpa's pond all afternoon. It was almost dark before Grandpa began gathering up his pole and the stringer with the fish that they'd caught.

"I think we're done for the day, boy. It's gonna get dark before we get all these fish cleaned."

Linc grinned. "You mean before I get all those fish cleaned. You haven't cleaned a fish in years. For sure not since you taught me how."

Wayne Fox smiled. "Why do you think I taught you to do it?"

They laughed and headed for the house.

Linc cleaned all the fish and packed them up, saving back a few to leave with his grandpa, and headed home. He was about a quarter of a mile from home and thinking that since his stepmother, Lucy, was away, he would fry up the fish for himself and his dad. Lucy didn't like the smell of fish in the house, but what she didn't know wouldn't hurt her.

Meg Walker popped into his head then, as she often did when he was quiet. She was the love of his life, and he let his thoughts wander to where they might be this time next year after they were both out of school. He was dreaming about their future when he looked up and saw an orange glow over the treetops. It wasn't until he'd turned up the driveway leading to his house that he realized it was a fire. He stomped the accelerator and tried not to panic. But the closer he got, the more frightened he became. By the time he arrived he had already figured out the house was on fire. Flames were coming out of the windows and burning through a hole in the roof. He expected to see his dad somewhere outside trying to fight the fire on his own, but he was nowhere in sight. The horror of what that might mean shot through him as he skidded to a sliding stop and jumped out of the old pickup, screaming for his father as he ran.

He was only yards from the house when it suddenly exploded, throwing him back beyond his truck and knocking him unconscious. He woke up to someone saying his name and pouring water on his face. When he sat up, he could see people everywhere, silhouetted against the blaze. They'd formed a bucket brigade but had been too late to save the house, and now they were making a valiant effort to keep the fire from spreading into the nearby forest.

Linc struggled in his sleep, kicking the covers, and despite the cold air, he was bathed in sweat as the dream sucked him further into the past.

The ambulance ride to the hospital in Mount Sterling was a blur. Still suffering from shock and concussion, and so stricken with grief that he couldn't do anything but cry, he barely noticed his grandpa and Aunt Tildy in his room. Grandpa was leaning over him, and Aunt

Tildy was standing at the foot of the bed with a sad expression on her face.

Later, getting the news that there wasn't much left of his father's body to bury was one thing, but learning Marcus Fox had been dead before the fire ever started left the family in shock.

Linc was at his grandpa's house, still recuperating, when the sheriff drove up and began an interrogation that left him reeling. The panic he was feeling came out in his speech—the short, jerky sentences between deep, painful breaths.

"We didn't fight. Dad and me...we didn't have problems...Grandpa's house...fishing all afternoon."

The fact that his grandfather corroborated the claim hadn't seemed to matter later, when everything went to hell.

Linc's stepmother, Lucy, who had been on the other side of the state at a family funeral, was the next member of the Fox family to be interrogated, although she had an alibi nobody questioned.

But it was Wesley Duggan, Marcus's best friend and a man Linc considered a member of the family, who sealed his fate. When Wesley was interviewed, all of a sudden Linc's status went from grieving son to prime suspect, despite his insistence that he would never hurt his father—that he loved him. His words fell on deaf ears. When they went to trial, the M.E.'s autopsy report finished Linc's plea of innocence. The back of Marcus Fox's skull had been crushed inward in a distinct pattern, not unlike being hit in the back of the head with a baseball bat.

Linc had been a member of the high school baseball team, one of the star players. Strike one.

Wesley claimed that Linc and his father had been fighting like crazy. Strike two.

Lucy wept on the stand, claiming she would never have left them alone if she'd known their fussing would lead to something like this.

Strike three.

Linc was tried as a juvenile, and when the jury found him guilty of manslaughter, he couldn't believe it was happening. The last thing he remembered were the looks of shock and disgust on the faces of the people he'd grown up with, and the tears on Meg Walker's face. Whatever future they might have had was over.

Three strikes and he was out   and on his way to prison.

Then, as dreams had a way of doing, this one segued from Linc in prison to Linc making love to Meg in the back of his old pickup truck while a country music station drifted out from the rolled-down windows of the cab. Despite the beauty and passion of the interlude, he slept fitfully, locked within the memories of his past.

Four

Meg was watching the driveway for the sheriff's car, but Honey heard it coming first and growled as she walked to the door.

"No, Honey. This time it's the good guys."

The security light came on as he pulled up to the house. She opened the door as he came up the steps.

"Are you all right?" Marlow asked.

"Yes, thanks to Quinn's security system and my dog."

She shut the door behind him and then followed him to the sofa.

"Now, tell me again exactly what happened," the sheriff said as he took out his pad and pen.

"Honey and I were out in the porch swing when the phone rang. We came inside, but whoever it was had already hung up. I had just set the alarm and was headed to the kitchen when I heard a gunshot. Of course Honey started barking, and that's when I realized the outside security light was on. When I looked out the window, I saw a man on his belly in the yard. It looked like he'd fallen…I guess startled by the light. I think his pistol went off when he hit the ground."

"Did you get a look at his face?"

"Not really. He was bareheaded, and his hair…it was kind of long and brown…and it had fallen forward, hiding most of his features. He wasn't very tall…maybe five feet ten inches or so. He was wearing jeans and a black leather jacket, like the kind a biker would wear. Oh, wait! I just remembered…it had a patch on the sleeve. I saw it when I saw the pistol he was holding."

"Do you remember what the patch looked like?" Marlow asked.

She closed her eyes, trying to picture it in her mind. "The Confederate flag. It was the Confederate flag."

He added that to the info he already had down. "Unfortunately, that's not as unique in this part of the country as I would like. Do you think you'd know him again if you saw him?"

"I doubt it…maybe…I don't know."

"That's okay. So…back to what you were saying. You saw him through the window, then what?"

"The rifle was by the door, because I'd had it outside with me, so I opened the door and sicced Honey after him. She flew out, barking like crazy. The alarm was shrieking, and I shot at him…twice, maybe three times, before he disappeared in the trees. Honey was still running after him when I heard him fire off another shot. I panicked and called her back. She has a crippled paw and can't run as fast as another dog might."

Marlow frowned as he continued to make notes. "So he came armed this time."

Her shoulders slumped as she nodded. "Why is this happening to me?"

"Meg, I need you to think. Off the top of your head,

who do you know who would be capable of doing something like this?"

"I've done nothing *but* think ever since this started happening, but no one comes to mind."

"Excuse me for being personal, but have you been dating anyone?"

"Ryal was thinking along the same lines, but absolutely no. Like I told him, I can't remember the last time someone asked me out."

"Have you had harsh words with anyone recently?"

"No."

"Okay, let's think of this from another angle. Is there someone you can think of who has a grudge against any member of your family?"

Her eyes widened. "I have no idea. I'll have to talk to them and find out."

He nodded. "You get back to me on this, okay, because right now, I've got nothing to go on and this is getting serious. You know that, right?"

"Yes."

"You're not going to like this, but I think you should consider moving in with your family until we figure out who's doing this."

Anger swept through her so fast it made her voice shake. "Not only no, but hell, no. I'm not taking this danger to them. Ryal and James have wives and children, and the last damn thing Quinn and Mariah need is for me to bring a war to their door. They're still struggling to forget the last one they were in."

Marlow frowned. He hadn't thought about it like that. "So what about staying with Jake and Dolly?"

"You mean the newlyweds? I'm thirty-five years old and nearly six feet tall. I'm younger and stronger than both of them, but don't tell them I said so, and I'm a damn good shot. Between me, the security system and my dog, I'm here to stay."

"Are you going to tell them that this happened again?"

"Eventually."

He sighed. "You are one hardheaded woman."

"I'd rather consider myself self-sufficient."

He chuckled. "Yes, ma'am, I'd say that's about right. So, if you'll show me the general direction that your intruder took when he hightailed it out of here, I'll leave you to try and get some rest."

Meg followed him out and into the yard to show him where the intruder had fallen and which direction he'd run. The security light had flooded the yard and the frosty grass, but Marlow got a flashlight from his cruiser for a more thorough look.

"You say this is about where he fell?" he asked as he swept the beam along the ground.

Her house shoes were getting damp as she paced off the distance from the porch to where she'd seen the man lying.

"Right about here," she said, pointing a few feet off to the right.

Something glinted in the grass as Marlow swung the light in that direction.

"Wait. What's that?" she said.

Marlow bent over and picked it up. "It's a toy car, a little black race car with a number on it. No...wait...I don't think it's a toy. I think it's something you'd see on the end of a key ring. Oh, hey, I know what this is. It's a replica of Dale Earnhardt's crash car. Is it yours, or something one of your brothers had?"

The skin crawled on the back of her neck. "I've never seen it before."

Marlow pulled a little baggie out of his pocket, dropped the charm inside and zipped it up.

"The weird thing is, I *have* seen it before, but I can't remember where. However, I'm thinking we just found our first lead."

"This is good, right?"

He grinned. "Yes, ma'am, this is good. You say he went uphill and to the right?"

"Yes."

"Okay. It's cold out here. You go on back inside. I don't expect to see much of anything, but I'm going to drive up the road and take a look around."

"Thank you so much for coming out so quickly."

"It's what I do, Meg, and don't hesitate to call again if the need arises."

"Yes, and I'll let you know what my brothers have to say after I talk to them, too."

He waved goodbye, waited until she and the dog were back inside the house, then got in his car and headed back to the road. He drove slowly with his floodlight on, scanning the roadside and into the trees. He flushed a deer and a raccoon, and sent an owl into flight, but there were no humans around that he could see. He'd started to turn and head back to town when he noticed the gate at the old Fox place was down. He hit the brakes, then radioed headquarters to tell them where he was going. After fingering the pistol in his holster, he aimed the floodlight straight ahead and took the turn up the overgrown drive.

Something hit the top of Linc's travel trailer with a thud. He'd been back in high school, dancing on the creek bank with Meg, when the sound woke him. He was still trying to figure out what it was when he heard something running on the roof. A squirrel. It must have jumped out of the trees and used his trailer for a short-cut to somewhere else.

He rolled over, then sat up on the side of the bunk with a groan. Now that he was awake, he got up to go to the bathroom, then, from there, went into the kitchen to get a drink.

He was just about to put the empty glass in the sink when a bright light came through the window and swept across the opposite wall. Headlights! He made a run for the bedroom and grabbed the rifle before moving to a window to look out. When the vehicle suddenly stopped and an array of red-and-blue lights started flashing on top of the car, followed by a couple of bursts from the siren, he couldn't believe it. Either rural law enforcement had improved greatly since last time he was here or that shooting star he'd seen had been an omen of bad luck after all. He dropped his head in frustration.

"Son of a bitch! So much for quiet arrivals," he said, then leaned the rifle against the wall and opened the door.

Marlow was more than surprised to see the pickup truck and travel trailer parked behind the wreckage of the old house. He didn't recognize the vehicle or the trailer, and wondered if he could be this lucky and find the stalker in residence.

He flashed the spotlight on the door of the trailer, and then hit the lights and gave the siren a couple of short bursts to get the occupant's attention. Lights came on inside the trailer, but the moment the door opened and the man's body filled the space, he knew this was not his stalker. The man he was looking for was less than six feet tall, with small feet and shaggy brown hair.

This man was so tall he had to bend over to look out. His hair was short and black, and considering his feet and chest were bare, Marlow could safely say he had the biggest hands and feet he'd ever seen. And he had no idea who the hell this guy was.

He killed the floodlight but left his headlights on as he got out, then moved toward the trailer with his hand on his pistol, just in case.

"You're trespassing, mister. State your name."

"No, sir, I am not trespassing, but I might ask you why you're on *my* property?"

Marlow froze. When Wayne Fox died, except for his sister, Tildy, he was the last of the family on Rebel Ridge. Then it hit him—there was another Fox, but the last time he'd been seen, he was on his way to prison.

"Lincoln Fox…is that you?"

"Sorry, Sheriff, but you have me at a disadvantage. I don't believe I caught your name."

"Sheriff Marlow, Mel Marlow. I'm investigating a break-in that happened earlier at a house down the road."

Linc's attitude shifted. "Oh…I heard a security alarm go off just after I pulled in here for the night. I was out looking at the old bomb shelter when I heard a gunshot, then the alarm, then more gunshots. Is everyone all right?"

"Mrs. Lewis is all right, but I was hoping to find me a stalker lying bleeding somewhere up here."

Linc remembered a Lewis family, but they'd lived much farther up the mountain and deeper into the woods. However, he wasn't going to ask for details.

"It's a little cold to be visiting out here. You're welcome to come inside."

Marlow took his hand off his pistol and headed for the trailer. Even though Linc stepped aside to let him in, Marlow was dwarfed by the man.

"Have a seat," Linc said as he closed the door.

Marlow moved toward the small sitting area, then took off his hat and set it on the sofa beside him as Linc lit a candle, pulled a chair from the dinette set and faced him. That was when he saw the burn scars on Fox's chest.

"What happened there?"

Linc ran a hand over the scars. "On-the-job accident."

Marlow nodded. So Fox wasn't interested in sharing. Fine. "I have to say, I'm surprised to see you. What brings you back?"

Linc fingered the scars again. "Let's just say I had a life-altering experience and decided to come home."

"Why now?"

Linc's eyes narrowed as a muscle jerked along his jawline. "Cops always want the details. Fine. I work in construction. Earlier this year I was electrocuted on the job, which is where the scars came from, and when they brought me back to life, I came with a message from my daddy."

Marlow frowned. Lincoln Fox had been convicted of killing his father.

"What kind of message?"

"To go home and find out who killed him. Now you know why I'm here, and I have something to tell you that might help you."

"Like what?"

"After I heard that alarm go off down the mountain,

I pulled a little farther into the trees here for the night. A herd of deer had just come up to bed down, and I was watching them from inside the trailer when something spooked them and they ran. I thought it would be an animal, but it was a man, and he was running at a good clip heading west, up the slope."

Marlow's heart skipped. Could he actually have another witness? "What did he look like?"

"He was too far away for me to see his face, but there was enough moonlight to see that he was about average height, maybe five-ten or so, and his hair was kind of shaggy. He was wearing a dark leather jacket. The kind bikers wear. I don't think he saw my rig, because he kept running through the clearing and up into the trees. A few moments afterward I heard a bike start up and then he rode away. It sounded more like a dirt bike than a motorcycle. Then I went to bed, thinking that was my last visitor for the night. I had no idea the official Rebel Ridge greeting committee would show up so soon."

Marlow was taking notes as fast as he could write. "Is there anything else?" he asked.

Linc stood up. "Yes. I'd appreciate it if you didn't tell the world why I'm here. The fact that I'm back is going to be trouble enough without everyone taking sides all over again. Although to be honest, I don't think there was a damned one of you who was on my side to begin with except Grandpa and Aunt Tildy. Grandpa's gone, and I haven't seen Aunt Tildy in years. Don't even know if she's still alive."

"I wasn't working for the law when all that went down, but for your information, your aunt is still hale and hearty and dispensing her herbs and salves to all who ask." After that Marlow stood up, too intimidated by Linc's size to stay seated. "I'll be going now. Thank you for your information. If you happen to see or hear anything more, give me a call. This is my card. Got my home and office numbers. Use either. My job is twenty-four/seven. If I have any more questions…"

"Then you know where to find me," Linc said softly, and opened the door.

Marlow walked down the steps, then turned around to say good-night, but Linc had already closed the door behind him.

He stood for a few moments, watching as the candle was snuffed. It was as good a signal as any that his presence was not appreciated. He didn't know what to think about Lincoln Fox's reason for returning, but he began to wonder if finding Meg Lewis's stalker would become the least of his troubles. He got back in his cruiser and drove away.

Linc stood in the dark, waiting until the sheriff was gone, then opened the door and stepped out. He was shaking with anger and had to get past it. He couldn't react like this to everyone he came in contact with or he would fail in his quest before it began.

The blast of cold air on his face chased away the last of the rage as he gazed out at the wreckage of the old house. He felt sorry that it had come to such ruin, but sometimes it was better to start fresh than to try to patch up something that was beyond redemption. He didn't know whether he was thinking about himself or the property, but either way he was here to stay.

There was a frost on the grass. In the moonlight, it looked silver. The deer he'd seen earlier had not come back. It was quiet. Unlike Dallas, the quiet in this place was almost holy. No streetlights, no sirens, no traffic noise from a freeway like the one near his apartment. He looked up at the sky, slightly stunned by the vast array of stars. One thing he'd forgotten was that up this high on Rebel Ridge, it was that much closer to heaven. He took a deep, shuddering breath, a little shocked by the fact that he felt like crying.

Meg slept fitfully, half-afraid the man would come back. By morning she was in a mood, and tended to the chickens and feeding Daisy without the usual bounce in her step. Even Honey stayed back, sensing her turmoil.

As luck would have it, before she had a chance to tell her family what had happened, Quinn stopped by on his way to work.

She heard Honey barking in the front yard and, when she went to look, saw her brother getting out of the car. She hurried to the door.

When Quinn saw the expression on her face, the smile he was wearing disappeared.

"What's wrong? Did your stalker come back again?"

She nodded.

"Damn it, Meg! When were you going to tell us?"

"Eventually."

He followed her in, checking the sensor on the door as he went.

Then she began to explain what had happened.

"He didn't make it to the door, thanks to the security light in the yard, which startled him. When he fell, the pistol he was carrying discharged, which sent Honey into a fit. When I looked out and saw him getting up, I set Honey on him, then followed with a couple of shots, which unfortunately missed again."

Quinn shoved a hand through his hair in frustration. "He was armed. Why didn't you call?"

"I did. I called the law. It's their job to take care of this stuff, not you."

"But—"

"No buts, Quinn."

His eyes narrowed, but he didn't argue. "So you saw him. Did you recognize him?"

"No. I saw an average-size man with shaggy brown hair, wearing a black leather biker jacket. It had a Confederate flag patch on the sleeve, and Sheriff Marlow found a toy in the grass. It was a little black car with a number 3 on the side...like something that would hang on a key ring."

"That's Dale Earnhardt's crash car," Quinn muttered, more to himself than to her. "What else?"

"When Honey gave chase and disappeared into the trees, he shot at her."

She watched Quinn's face pale. "Son of a bitch."

"There's more. Sheriff Marlow asked me if there was anyone who might have a grudge against a member of the family, who would try to get back at one of you by hurting me."

Quinn's eyes widened.

"I told him I'd ask," she said.

"I'd have to think about it," he said. "I'll talk to the others and get back to you."

"Just call Sheriff Marlow and talk to him if you come up with a name. It will save me the trouble."

Quinn had been watching the muscle jerking at the side of her right eye. "Come stay with Mariah and me."

Her chin came up. "No."

Growing up with Meg, Quinn had seen that look a thousand times and knew the discussion was now over.

He hugged her. "I'm so sorry this is happening."

She rested her cheek briefly against the soft fabric of his goose-down jacket and then hugged him back.

"Thanks for that. You're a good brother. I'm sorry, too, but we'll find out who it is and then it will be over."

"So what are you going to do?" Quinn asked.

"Wait and see what happens next. And, Quinn, don't tell Mom. I do not want her and Jake moving back in. Please."

He shrugged. "It's your call. Is there anything you need?"

She rolled her eyes. "Oh…I don't know…if you happen to run across a great big hero-type guy on the loose up in the park, I might be interested in making his acquaintance."

He laughed. "I'll keep that in mind."

She pushed him toward the door. "Go to work. I'm fine. It's all good."

She watched him walk out, shaking his head and muttering beneath his breath about hardheaded women, but her mood had changed. Just telling him what had happened had shared the burden. She would remember that for future reference.

He woke up in Boone's Gap in a hooker's bed with vague memories of getting drunk off his ass after last night's debacle, then took one look at the woman in the bed beside him and frowned. She didn't look so hot in the light of day. He reached for his boots.

The mattress shifted as he rolled out of bed, waking the woman.

"Hey, sugar, don't you want a little quickie before you leave? I'll do it for free?"

He frowned. "No. I got places to be."

She rolled over on her back and parted her legs, then cupped her breasts, rolling the nipples between her fingers in what was supposed to pass for a come-on.

He grabbed his coat and walked out without comment. She was cursing as he shut the door.

"Same to you, bitch," he muttered, then got in his truck. Just as he started to put the key in the ignition, he noticed the Dale Earnhardt token was missing from the key ring.

"Well, hell."

He thrust his hand back into his pocket, expecting it to be there, but it wasn't. He searched between the seats and the floorboard, but to no avail, and had to face the fact that it was gone. It was just a little doodad and didn't amount to anything, but he liked it. Maybe he could find another one next time he went to the races. His belly growled, reminding him of where he'd been going, and he started the truck and drove to the other end of town to Frankie's Eats. One thing was for certain; he was going to have to rethink his plan for Meg Lewis.

Linc was up at daybreak. He cleared the brush from in front of the shelter door and began dragging debris from inside, anxious to see what he had to work with. The first thing he would need was power. He couldn't do the work he needed on just his generator. The utility poles were still in place where the old house once stood. All he had to do was have the power company add a pole here by the shelter, string new lines and install a meter. He went inside, pulled out his cell and found the number for the local power company. Within the hour he had a work order in place for a pole to be set and line to be run.

Over the next few days he burned rubbish and dug trenches to lay pipe from the old existing water well, and then he replaced the pump. Every time he drove down the mountain he thought about the Lewis woman and wondered if she was okay. It was weird, this odd connection of having seen her assailant without knowing who she was, but he wasn't ready for the world to know he was back.

The few times he stopped in Boone's Gap to get gas or pick up a few groceries, he made sure to wear a cap and sunglasses. It wasn't all that much of a disguise, but he was counting on the change in his size and appearance as backup to make sure no one recognized him. For the time being his focus was getting a winter shelter set up.

He had a new propane tank installed, and ran pipe inside the shelter for future heating and cooking use. He rented a tractor and brush hog down in Mount Sterling and cut down the weeds and brush in the clearing. When the power company arrived they set a new power pole, strung the wire, set a new meter and just like that he had power and water. Once he got the interior walls and floor clean, he could start construction on the house.

He went to bed that night satisfied with his progress, and he was sound asleep when he was suddenly awakened by the sound of an approaching dirt bike. He immediately thought of the prowler and bailed out of bed, grabbing his pants, coat and boots as he ran. Within moments he was out of the trailer carrying his rifle. If the little bastard thought he was going to take a shortcut through this place again, he had another think coming.

The night was dark. The new moon cast few shadows between trees and ground as he darted across the clearing. Within moments he heard someone coming toward him at a jog, making no attempt to hide his presence. If this was the stalker, the last time he'd come through here he'd been armed. Linc didn't want to get into a gunfight with the man, but he wasn't going to have him using his land as a freeway, either. He waited until he could see him coming, wanting to get a look at his face, and then, when he finally saw him, he was stunned to realize that he knew him. Taking care to stay concealed behind a trio of pines, he fired the rifle into the air, taking quiet pleasure in the shock on Prince White's face.

"This is private property!" Linc yelled. "The next time you set foot on it without an invitation, the shot I fire won't be a warning,"

He watched Prince grab his pocket as he scanned the trees and knew that pistol he'd been carrying before was probably in the leather jacket. Then he watched Prince rethink the notion and put both hands up in the air as he called out, "Whoever you are, I didn't mean nothin'. This place has been vacant for so long I didn't know that it sold. I'm right sorry. Okay? I mean you no harm. I was just—"

"Just what? Going to mess with that Lewis woman again? If that was what was on your mind, then I advise you to change it, understand?"

All of a sudden the man spun on his heel and started running back through the trees the way he'd come. That was when Linc knew for sure he was the same man. Just to mess with him, he fired the rifle again, then waited until he heard Prince start up the bike and speed away.

"Sorry little bastard," Linc muttered as he made his way back to the trailer. He started to go back to bed, but the thought of a woman alone in her house somewhere down the road, afraid to close her eyes for fear that her stalker would return, was too strong to ignore. He picked up his cell phone and, after digging up the card Marlow had given him, made a quick call.

"Sheriff's department," the dispatcher said.

"I need to speak to Marlow," Linc said.

"He's working a fender-bender down by the bar. Is this an emergency?"

"No, just passing on some information he needed."

"Oh. Well, if it's confidential info, then call his cell phone. I'll give you the number."

"I have it," Linc said, then disconnected and called the other number on the card.

Marlow sounded preoccupied when he finally answered.

"Sheriff, this Lincoln Fox. I know who your stalker is."

Marlow froze. "And how do you know that?"

"I heard him ride up on his bike again tonight, and I went out and confronted him. Told him he was trespassing on private property and not to do it again. Even though I recognized him, I wasn't sure he was the one who'd been threatening the Lewis woman until I threw out a warning. I told him if his intent on crossing my property was to go mess with her again, then I advised him against it. The moment I said that he turned tail and ran. I fired a shot up in the air just to punctuate the suggestion and waited until I heard him ride away."

"Well, I'll be damned," Marlow said. "Who was it?"

"Prince White."

"Prince White. I'll be a... Uh, wait, that's your step-mother's younger brother, isn't it?"

"Lucy is no longer my stepmother, and so what?"

"So are you sure it was him? You know if I arrest him you'll have to identify him, which is going to reveal your presence. You also know that there will be some who'll say you just named him because of your history with the family."

"What the hell are you talking about? I don't have a past with the Whites."

"They *are* your stepmother's brothers, and she testified against you at the trial."

Linc was getting angry. "Well hell, Sheriff, everyone who got on the stand testified against me at the trial, despite my grandpa Fox's claim that I couldn't have set the fire because I was at his house all afternoon, and I didn't accuse any of them of stalking Mrs. Lewis."

"Well, a body could understand Wayne Fox's need to alibi you," Marlow said. "You were his grandson."

"And my father was his son," Linc snapped. "Are you actually implying that Grandpa lied to protect his own son's killer?"

"Well, I—"

Linc was furious. "So you're saying that no matter what I saw, you're going to ignore the fact and let that Lewis woman continue to live in fear for her life?"

"Hell no, I wasn't saying that, I was just—"

The line went dead in Marlow's ear.

"Son of a bitch," he muttered, and then glared at Bo and Pete, the two drunks who'd caused the wreck he was working, and hauled both of them to jail.

Once he got the men booked and back in his office, he began making notes regarding the phone call from Fox. Of course he would follow up on the accusation, but he had to be careful how he did it. If Fox was right, then Meg Lewis could be in serious trouble. He didn't know two more worthless men on Rebel Ridge than Prince and Fagan White.

The thing was, Marlow knew he'd handled that call from Lincoln Fox all wrong. He could have kept his doubts to himself without confronting the man like that, at least until he'd talked to Prince White, but he hadn't, and it was too late to take it back.

What he *could* do was call Meg and feel her out about the White family, see if there was any bad blood between them, or if she'd had a run-in with Prince that could have been the start to all of this. But not tonight.

Tonight *was,* however, the optimal time to interview a suspect. As soon as the sun rose, he was going up Rebel Ridge to talk to Prince. Maybe Lincoln Fox was on the up-and-up. If he was, it would be interesting to hear what Prince had to say once Marlow told him he had a witness.

Prince White was in a panic. He didn't know who'd caught him trespassing on the old Fox place, but the man now knew too damn much about him. He needed to get the hell off the mountain or he would wind up in jail. It took nearly half an hour to get back home, and by the time he arrived, he'd already made himself a plan.

Fagan's truck was parked behind the house, and he was obviously still up, because all the lights were on. Prince rode the bike into the barn, parked it beside his own truck and jumped off on the run. When he went in the back door and found his brother asleep in the living room in front of the TV, a half-eaten bowl of popcorn in his lap, he yelled, "Fagan!"

Fagan jumped, sending the popcorn flying.

"What the hell's wrong with you?" he mumbled as he set the bowl aside and looked down at the mess on the floor.

"I'm going to Mount Sterling for a while. How much cash you got on you?"

Fagan frowned. "What have you done?"

"Nothing."

"Let me ask that another way. What are you going to be charged with?"

"For starters, probably breaking and entering, and stalking Meg Lewis."

Fagan's eyes bugged. "What the fuck? You're the one who broke into her house and got her hurt?"

"I didn't touch her. She's the one who ran through broken glass."

Fagan groaned. "Why? Why would you do such a dumbass thing? There's plenty of women around here who'll spread their legs for a twenty-dollar bill. You didn't have to go messin' with a decent woman, especially one who's got three mean-ass brothers."

Prince's chin jutted, and his eyes narrowed angrily. He wasn't about to share his info with Fagan and wind up giving him half the money he was looking for.

"It's none of your damned business," he said.

Fagan stared at his brother as if he'd just lost his mind. "You are truly as crazy as Wendell was."

Prince glared. "You don't talk about the dead like that. Besides, you're not my boss, and you're not my conscience. So answer my damn question. How much cash you got on you?"

Fagan sighed. "Less than two hundred dollars."

"I need it," Prince said, and held out his hand.

Fagan dug his wallet out of his pocket and gave him the cash. "What do you expect me to do when the law comes callin'?"

"Tell them I left without a word and you don't know where I went."

"Great. Just great," Fagan muttered. "We haven't been in trouble like this in years. I'm too old for all this crap. So go find yourself a hole to crawl into, because I don't want her brothers pissed off at me. There's three of them and only one of me."

Prince sneered. "They don't scare me," he said.

"Yeah, right. You're not scared, you're just running away from Rebel Ridge with your tail tucked between your legs because you like how it rubs against your balls."

"Shut the hell up," Prince said, and stuffed the money into his pocket and headed down the hall to pack.

Linc was too pissed to sleep and wished for the distraction of a TV. Now that he had electricity, he didn't have to run the camper on generator power, but he needed a satellite dish to hook up his flat-screen or he wouldn't have any reception. Instead, he dug in the refrigerator for a cold beer, then grabbed a handful of cookies and a notepad and began making a list of things he needed to do to begin his investigation. He wanted a copy of the police report from the night of the fire, a copy of the transcript of the trial and copies of the affidavits from the people who'd pointed fingers at him and gotten him arrested. They were the first ones he was going to find and talk to once he moved into the shelter.

By the time he was through with the beer and cookies, his mood had shifted. He kicked off his shoes, but when he lay down on the bed he didn't take off his clothes. The way shit was going down around here, he would probably need them again before morning.

But he was wrong. The sun was already up before the next knock came on his door. He groaned as he rolled out of bed, rubbing the sleep from his eyes. He headed for the door, glad that he'd slept in his clothes.

As he passed a window he noticed that whoever was here had come on foot, which brought Prince White to mind. Unwilling to go to the door unarmed, he returned to the bedroom and picked up his rifle.

Before he could get back, his visitor knocked again and yelled, "Hey! You in this here trailer! Open the door!"

It sounded like a woman, which meant it wasn't Prince White. He leaned the rifle against the wall and decided to take his chances.

He opened the door to find an old woman standing just beyond his doorstep with a rifle cradled across her arms. Her brown wool coat was patched in half a dozen places, and the knees were out in her overalls. A long gray braid hung down her shoulder, while most of her features were hidden under a well-worn felt hat she wore low on her forehead.

"Mister, you're trespassing, and I reckon you need to pack up your stuff and get on off here before I call the sheriff."

"Hi, Aunt Tildy…it's me. Lincoln. I'm not trespassing, I just finally came home."

Her frown shifted to shock as Linc stepped out of the trailer. He wasn't sure what kind of a reception she would give him, but he opened his arms, just the same.

"Do you think I might get a hug?"

Tildy Bennett stared at him as if he was a ghost. "Lincoln, is that really you?"

"Yes, ma'am."

The rifle she was holding slid out of her arms as she walked into his embrace.

"Oh Lord, Lord, I thought I was gonna die without ever seeing you again."

"I'm sorry I waited so long," he said, and hugged her close. "Come inside. You're half-frozen. What are you doing this far away from home on foot?"

"It's not so far as the crow flies, and anyway, I was checking my sang patches. Have to keep an eye on them or people will help themselves."

Linc hadn't heard the mountain term for *ginseng* in years, but he knew immediately what she meant. It was a good money crop, especially if it was growing wild.

Lincoln was helping her up the step when she stopped. "I gotta get my rifle."

"I'll get it," he said as he suited the action to the words, then followed her into the trailer.

As soon as he got her settled on the sofa he started the coffee and then sat down beside her.

"I don't know how you do it, Aunt Tildy, but you haven't changed a bit."

Tildy Bennett couldn't quit staring at him. "Well, *you* have. I wouldn't have known you if I'd passed you on the street. Lordy be, but you made a big man."

His shirt was unbuttoned, revealing just enough of his scars to make her ask, "What happened to you there?"

"It's a long story, Aunt Tildy, but it's what brought me home."

"Are you gonna stay?"

"Yes, ma'am."

"What have you been doing all this time?"

"I've worked construction for most of my life. I own a construction company now in Dallas."

"There's no work like that around here," she said.

"It doesn't matter. I didn't come home to build houses. I came home to find out who killed Dad."

She gasped. "But it's been so long. I don't see how you can do that."

"I don't know how it's going to turn out, but it's why I'm here, and I don't intend to quit until I've cleared my name."

The aroma of freshly brewing coffee filled the trailer as she took off her hat.

"I'll help you in any way I can, boy. I know pretty near ever'thing there is to know about the people living on Rebel Ridge. You just ask me, and if I don't know, I know how to find out."

Linc grinned. "Want some coffee?"

Her eyes crinkled up at the sides as she smiled. "I don't mind if I do, and I take mine black."

"So do I," Linc said. He filled two cups and carried them back to the sofa.

She took her cup carefully, warming her hands on the thick crockery. "Smells good."

He lifted his mug. "To us…and to justice."

"I'll drink to that," she said, and took the first sip, then set it aside to cool. "So you're here, now what's your plan?"

"Rebuild on the homesite, but it'll take time, so I'm

remodeling the old bomb shelter to live in during the winter. It'll be warmer than this travel trailer."

"You could come stay with me," she said.

"Thank you for the offer, but no. I'm not going to be a popular guy once word gets out what I'm doing. I've already made my first enemy."

She frowned. "How so?"

"The night I got here I became an accidental witness in a stalking case. A guy's been bothering a lady down the road. The sheriff says her name is Mrs. Lewis. The only Lewis family I remember lived a good distance farther up. Anyway, I happened to see the man who's bothering her."

Tildy shook her head. "Oh, you know her, honey. It's Meg Walker. She married Bobby Lewis right out of high school and then divorced him a couple years later, after he went to prison. She lives in her granddaddy Walker's old house, which is about a mile from here, as the crow flies. He gave it to her right before he died, and up until a year ago her mother, Dolly, was living with her. Then she remarried and moved out."

The hair stood up on the back of Linc's neck. He'd blanked out on everything his aunt was saying after he heard her say Meg's name.

"Meg Walker is the woman who's being stalked?"

"Yes, it's the talk of Rebel Ridge. Got every single woman on the mountain antsy and sleeping with a gun beside her bed. You say you saw who it was? Reckon I'd like to know that. I wouldn't be spreading it around or anything."

"Prince White," Linc said.

Tildy gasped. "Well, if that don't beat all."

"What?"

"He was at my house a few weeks back with a suspicious wound I went and doctored. I thought it looked like a bullet wound, but he swore different."

"What's the deal with him? Why would he be chasing after Meg? Did they date or something?"

Tildy rolled her eyes. "Lord, no. No one wants Prince or his brother Fagan. They're worthless as tits on a boar hog. Besides, Meg don't have a thing to do with men of any sort. Years back her ex went to prison for killing Prince's older brother, Wendell. That was a very long time ago, though. I can't imagine him trying some kind of payback at this late date, especially since Meg and Bobby have been divorced for so long."

There was a knot in Linc's belly, just thinking of his pretty Meg going through so much heartache. First him, then the man she married. No wonder she was done with men. The only ones she'd given her heart to had let her down.

Linc listened absently as Tildy rattled on, but he was picturing Meg Walker as he'd seen her last, at the courthouse after the trial, crying as they took him into custody. She'd been his first love—the first girl he'd kissed, the first girl he'd made love to —and Prince White was causing her grief. If Sheriff Marlow didn't do something about things, he might have to pay a visit to White himself.

They visited a little longer, and when she was ready to leave he loaded her up in his truck and drove her home. He came back with a dried apricot pie and half a fried chicken, stored both in the trailer for later and got to work. All he needed now was to figure out a way to get both a bathroom and a washer/dryer hookup into that old shelter and he would be ready for winter.

By the end of the day he'd come to the conclusion that building a small room in front of the existing doorway was the only possible answer. The shelter was small enough as it was, without taking up space with a bathroom or a washer and dryer. It would be simple to build and plumb the small structure and install ventilation. Once the propane was hooked up, he would have to vent that, too, and it would be easy to do through the new structure.

He set to work on the new plans at a steady pace, but his thoughts were never far from Meg. Knowing she was so close was maddening. But he had too much to do to set himself up for what was bound to be heartbreak or rejection—or both.

Either way, living this close to her meant nothing, because they were still a thousand miles away in his heart.

Five

Roger Eddy had been Marlow's deputy for more than ten years, and from day one Marlow couldn't take a simple ride anywhere with the man without Eddy keeping up a running commentary, which was making the ride to Prince and Fagan White's home seem endless. Marlow was relieved when they finally reached the property.

"Man, what a dump," Roger said as the sheriff parked beside a large rock at the edge of the yard, eyeing the single-story dwelling and the sagging porch. "All it needs are a few scrawny chickens pecking around."

Before they could get out, the front door opened. Fagan White came out, followed by a couple of hounds who promptly flopped down at his feet. He was a younger version of Prince—medium height and skinny, but his hair was blond and thin. The jeans and shirt he was wearing were stained, and he didn't appear bothered by the fact.

Roger eyed the man and the state of his clothing, and he frowned. "Are we going in?"

"Not if I can help it," Marlow muttered. He took the

little black car charm out of his pocket and palmed it. "I'm ready. Let's go."

"Morning, Sheriff! What brings you up this way?" Fagan asked.

Marlow nodded his hello and got right to the point. "We need to talk to Prince."

Fagan shrugged. "He didn't come home last night. I don't rightly know where he is. What do you want to talk to him about?"

Marlow's eyes narrowed. "So you're saying he's not hiding out somewhere inside?"

Fagan threw up his arms. "Look for yourself, damn it. His truck's not here, and neither is he."

Marlow rolled the little car charm around in his hand, making sure that Fagan got a good look. And the man bit, just like a hungry fish after a dragonfly.

"Hey, where'd you get that?" Fagan said, pointing to the charm. "That was on Prince's key ring. Did you find it lying out here in the yard?"

Bingo, Marlow thought. "No, it's evidence from a crime. Do you have any problem with my deputy checking your house?"

"Do I have a choice?" Fagan muttered, but he stepped aside.

Roger Eddy looked at his boss in dismay. When Marlow gave him a nod, he gritted his teeth and moved toward the doorway. One of the dogs stood up and growled as he walked past.

"Dog! Shut the hell up!" Fagan yelled.

The dog tucked his tail between his legs and slunk off the porch.

"Sorry about that," Fagan said, then eyed the sheriff. "You sure you won't come in?"

"Mind if I look around first?" Marlow asked.

"Feel free," Fagan said, and closed the door.

Marlow began to circle the house. Except for weeds and the occasional pile of rusting iron, the yard was vacant. He headed toward the barn, but it, too, was empty. No hay, no signs that a horse or a milk cow had been in there in ages, and the upkeep on the building was a joke. They'd been patching up holes in the roof and walls with odds and ends— pieces of tin, half a sheet of plywood, even an old Wisconsin license tag. He saw the numbers and knew no one from this mountain would ever drive a car with 666 on the tag. That was the mark of the devil.

He could see tire tracks going in and out of the structure, but no truck. Then he saw the dirt bike leaning against the far wall and stopped.

"I'll be damned."

He went back to the front door and knocked, then poked his head in the house.

"Hey, Fagan, whose bike is that in the barn?"

"Well, it's mine, but I don't ride it anymore. Broke my leg in two places on that thing about a year ago. Kinda took the fun out of it for me, if you know what I mean. Prince rides it some. Why?"

"What do you know about the attacks on Meg Lewis?"

Fagan blinked. He hadn't expected the sheriff to come right out and ask that.

"Well, I heard about 'em, for sure. I guess everybody has. Why?"

"Do you own any guns?"

Fagan laughed. "Well hell, Sheriff, don't everyone?"

"Do you mind showing them to me?"

"Not a bit. Come on in. Shut the door behind you when you do. It's hard to keep heat in the house."

Marlow sighed. There was no getting around it. He was going to have to go inside, and, as he'd feared, the place was as big a dump inside as out, and smelled twice as bad. His deputy walked back into the living room as Fagan went to get the guns, and Eddy glared at his boss for making him search through the filth.

Marlow grinned. Giving orders was the only perk of his job. "I take it Prince is not on the premises?"

Roger shook his head. "No one here but Fagan and some more dogs."

Marlow nodded, curiously eyeing the mounted hunting trophies and a pair of women's bikini panties hanging from the rack of a twelve-point buck's head. Then he spotted a picture hanging on the wall and moved closer. It was a picture of Prince holding up a big tom turkey that he'd killed, but it wasn't the grin on Prince's face that Marlow was interested in. It was the black leather biker's jacket he was wearing and the Confederate flag patch on the sleeve.

First the car charm.

Then the bike.

Now the jacket.

Things were adding up fast against Prince White.

Fagan came back carrying three guns, all rifles.

"You don't have any handguns?" Marlow asked.

"I don't care much for 'em," Fagan said.

"What about your brother? Does he have any weapons?"

Fagan thought about lying, but the way he figured it, the more honest he was, the less trouble Prince could get him into.

"Yeah, he's got a couple rifles and a pistol."

"Can I see them?" Marlow asked.

Fagan shrugged. "The rifles are on that rack behind you. He usually carries the pistol in his truck."

"Does he have a license to carry?"

Fagan was getting pissed at this line of questioning, as if the White brothers were the only gun-toting people on Rebel Ridge.

"Dang it, Sheriff, everybody up here carries weapons in their vehicles, and I doubt a single one of them has any license to carry. Why do you keep harpin' on us?"

Marlow took that as a slur against his leadership as an officer of the law, but he could hardly contest it. It was pretty much the truth.

"So where do you think Prince went?"

Fagan frowned. "I can't say. He does his thing, I do mine. What's this all about, anyway?"

"We have a witness willing to testify to the identity of the man stalking Meg Lewis."

Fagan's belly rolled. "Oh, yeah? Well, that's good, right? She's a nice lady. Seems a shame she's been put through all that."

"Look, Fagan, let's quit talking around the obvious," Marlow snapped. "Your brother has been identified as the stalker. I'm going to file charges against him, which means there's going to be a warrant out for his arrest. So if you talk to him anytime soon, tell him it will go better for him if he just comes and turns himself in before this all gets real ugly and something happens that can't be taken back."

Fagan wanted to retaliate but was too afraid he'd be drawn into the arrest, so he opted for surprise.

"I had no idea, and I'm shocked and sorry to hear that. I can't imagine why he would do something like that, and I'll find it hard to believe until I hear it from his own lips."

Marlow glared. "Believe this," he said. "If I find out you're hiding him, then I'll arrest you, too, for harboring a criminal. So if you want to stay on the outside of a jail cell, then I expect your cooperation in letting me know if he shows up back here."

Fagan glared back. "You're asking me to turn my own brother in?"

"No. I'm *telling* you—unless you want your name added to the arrest warrant. At the moment Mrs. Lewis is an unhappy woman, and she has three very big brothers who are going to be mighty damn upset when they find out who's been terrorizing their sister. Even though I will warn them to let the law handle things, I can't control what they might be tempted to do if the danger to their sister is not removed."

Fagan felt the blood drain from his face. This was exactly what he didn't want to happen.

"If I hear from Prince, I will call you, and if he calls, I will try to talk him into turning himself in. Is that enough to keep you off my ass?"

"I make no promises other than if I find out you've been lying to me, you're going down, too. Deputy Eddy, we're done here," he said, and went out the door with Roger right behind him.

"How do you think that went?" Eddy asked as they headed back to Boone's Gap.

"I'd bet money he's on the phone with his brother as we speak, which is fine, because I'm filing charges and issuing a warrant for Prince's arrest as soon as we get back to the office. However, I want to stop at Meg Lewis's house on the way down and reassure her that we're well on the way to getting her situation under control."

Meg had been in her sewing room for the better part of the morning, bonding the layers of her Storm at Sea quilt together with tiny, perfect stitches. The task was mindless and calming, with the radio playing softly in the background. When she had to stop to rethread the needle she noticed it was almost noon. She had planned on driving up to her mom and Jake's this afternoon, so now was as good a time as any to quit. She stuck the needle into her pincushion and stood up, stretching to get out the kinks from sitting so long.

The house felt chilly as she moved down the hall, and with good reason. The thermometer registered sixty-eight degrees. She shivered, thinking it must be getting colder outside, because it had been comfortable in the house earlier on. She turned up the fire on the propane heater in the living room and turned on the TV so she could listen to the noon news and weather forecast, and she lit the stove in the kitchen, as well.

With an eye on the clock she reheated soup, dug a box of crackers out of the pantry and sat down to eat. As she suspected, the weatherman was forecasting a drastic change. An early Arctic cold front was coming down from the north, increasing the possibility of snow at the higher elevations.

She ate without worry, confident her store of cut wood outside and a nearly full tank of propane would keep her warm. While she was cleaning up the kitchen she heard Honey barking and made a run for the window to make sure her stalker wasn't back. When she saw the sheriff and his deputy getting out, she opened the door and called Honey down so they could pass. As she did, a strong gust of cold wind whipped through the door and around her legs.

"Sorry to come unannounced, but I have some news," Marlow said. "Is it all right if we come inside?"

"Absolutely. It sure is getting cold," she said. "Take a seat. Can I get you some coffee?"

"I'd love one, and I take it black," Deputy Eddy said.

"If it's no trouble, and I'll take black, as well," Marlow added.

"I just made it fresh. I'll be right back."

She returned a couple of minutes later with the coffee and a plate of cookies and set everything on the coffee table in front of them.

"Help yourselves," she said, and then sat and waited for them to get settled.

"I came with good news," Marlow said as he chased his first cookie with a sip of coffee. "We've identified your stalker."

Meg's stomach knotted; she dreaded the revelation that it would be someone she'd thought she could trust.

"Who is it?"

"Prince White."

She was dumbfounded. "Prince White? Why on earth would..." And then it hit her. She stopped, pressed a finger to her mouth, as if to stifle a gasp, and then let her hand fall to her lap. "Oh, my God."

"What?" Marlow asked.

Just saying the words aloud gave them a power she didn't want to face. "My ex-husband killed his oldest brother, Wendell."

Marlow frowned. Could that actually be the last piece to this puzzle? "That must have been a long time ago.

Why wait 'til now to do something about it? Maybe he's just got a thing for you," he said.

"Feuds have started for less reason and lasted for generations in these hills, and you know it," she said. "And I can't see any other reason for this to happen. I've been here for years without him so much as looking my way. Something must have happened to trigger this. What did he say when you arrested him?"

Marlow frowned. "He's not exactly under arrest yet. And he's disappeared. But I'm filing charges and issuing an arrest warrant. I wanted you to know, so in case you ran into him somewhere you'd be forewarned." He took another bite of cookie and glanced up at her again. "Do you ever have any contact with your ex, Bobby Lewis?"

She frowned. "No. The day my divorce was legal, I set that part of my life aside, and I try not to revisit it any more than I have to."

"Is he still in the same prison here in Kentucky?"

"As far as I know."

"Hmm, I wonder…"

"Wonder what?" she asked.

Marlow pointed at his deputy. "Roger, go out to the cruiser. Bring me the black notebook out of the console."

The deputy grabbed another cookie from the plate as he ran for the door.

"What are you thinking?" Meg asked.

"I don't know…just playing a hunch. What's Lewis's full name?"

"Bobby Ray Lewis," she said.

Marlow made a mental note as the deputy came back, bringing a gust of cold air with him. He handed the sheriff the notebook and helped himself to another cookie.

Marlow scanned a list of names and numbers he had

on file, then took out his cell phone and began making calls.

Meg couldn't help but be anxious. All these years she'd tried to live down the shame Bobby Lewis had brought to her life, but if the sheriff thought there was a tie to the attacks…

After being put on hold twice, Marlow finally located the prison and was connected with the warden.

"Warden Bristol. This is Sheriff Mel Marlow. I'm out of Boone's Gap, just north of Mount Sterling. I'm calling to inquire about the status of a prisoner incarcerated in your facility. His name is Bobby Ray Lewis. He's a lifer.…Yes, thanks. I'll hold."

He glanced up at Meg. "He's checking."

The warden came back on the line. Meg watched Marlow's face, and when his eyebrows rose suddenly, she unconsciously clenched her hands into fists.

"One more question," Marlow said, still talking to the warden. "Has he had any visitors in the past few months?" A few more seconds passed, and then his eyes narrowed sharply. "I see. Yes, thank you for your help," he said, and disconnected.

"What?" Meg asked.

"Bobby Lewis is dying of lung cancer. When they notified the family a couple of months ago, one of his brothers, Claude, went to visit, and then a few days afterward Lewis had another visitor. Prince White."

Meg was shocked. "Why on earth would Bobby want to talk to Prince? And after all these years?"

"I don't know," Marlow said. "Maybe Bobby wants forgiveness for his sins. He's dying, and people have done stranger things for less reason. I'll check with

Claude and see if Bobby told him anything that would help us figure this out."

Meg was struggling to take everything in. "I don't understand how you knew it was Prince. We had next to no clues...just that little car charm off a key ring, a vague physical description and a description of his coat. How did you figure it out?"

Marlow hesitated. Fox had asked him not to advertise his presence, but he didn't have to tell her the name.

"We had a witness come forward. I don't know if you're aware of it or not, but someone has moved into the old Fox place."

Meg frowned. "How do we know he wasn't the stalker?"

"He only just arrived the night your mom and Jake went home. And he's too damn big to be your man. Remember when you said the stalker fired his pistol, then your security alarm went off when you opened the door and you two exchanged gunfire? Well, your neighbor heard all that, and a short time later he saw a man running across his place in the dark. And then he heard a dirt bike start up and leave. So when I went up to investigate after leaving your place, I saw the gate was down at the road and went in to check it out. I found him setting up camp in a travel trailer. I knew the minute I saw him he wasn't your stalker, because like I said, he's a big man. When I questioned him, he told me what he'd seen, and I explained about your break-in. So the deal is, last night, he heard that bike coming back and went out and confronted the man."

Meg hadn't known anyone was living there and was impressed that a total stranger had acted on her behalf.

"What happened then?" she asked.

"He actually recognized the man as Prince White, then scared him off. As soon as the guy accused Prince of harassing you, Prince freaked out, went running back to his bike and rode away. After that the guy called me. Roger and I went up to White's place this morning, talked to his brother Fagan. Prince is gone. Fagan swears he doesn't know where he is, but I warned him that if he concealed his whereabouts, I'd include him in the arrest warrant, too."

Meg shook her head. "All that was happening, and here I was sleeping peacefully without a clue."

"I'd say it's about time you got some peace back in your life," Marlow said, then frowned at Roger, who had just taken the last cookie off the plate.

Roger caught the look and grinned. He considered it his due for having been sent in to search for Prince in that pigsty of a house.

"About the man who bought the Fox property, is he planning to live there?" Meg asked.

"I believe he is," Marlow said, and then stood up before she could ask him anything more. "We need to get back. Thank you for the coffee and cookies. You take care, and I'll give you a call when we run White down."

Meg walked them to the door. "Thank you, Sheriff, and you, too, Roger. You don't know what a relief it is to at least know my enemy's face."

Marlow grinned, pleased to have given her some good news.

As soon as they were gone she ran to change into some warmer clothes. She was horrified by all she'd learned and anxious to talk to her mother, but not on the phone. And, if the weather was going to change, she needed to get over there before she got snowed in.

She called Honey inside. If it was going to get that cold, she didn't want the dog stranded outside until she got back. She put out food and water for her in the kitchen and gave her a quick scratch behind her ears.

"You take care of the place while I'm gone, okay?"

Honey licked Meg's fingers, then flopped down close to the heating stove and closed her eyes.

Meg was still smiling as she got in her TrailBlazer and drove away. When she passed the road that led up to the Fox land, she thought of her new neighbor and all of a sudden remembered Marlow saying the man had recognized Prince White. That meant he wasn't a stranger to the mountain. But who was he? She wished she'd thought to ask.

Dolly was thrilled by Meg's unexpected arrival and ushered her into the kitchen, where she was making pies for supper. Her two stepsons, Cyrus and Avery, had been unloading firewood in the backyard when Meg arrived, and they came in to greet her. They were big men, like their father. Both were redheaded like Jake had been, although his hair had long since turned white.

Cyrus gave Meg a quick hug. "Good to see you," he said.

Avery followed suit with a wink and a grin. "I see your feet healed up okay."

"Yes, thank goodness. Where's Jake?" Meg asked.

"I'm right here," Jake said as he walked up behind her. "It's good to see you back on your feet, girl."

"I have news," she said.

Dolly slid the last pie in the oven to bake, then wiped her hands and moved toward the kitchen table, where Meg had taken a seat.

"What happened?" Dolly asked.

"Sheriff Marlow identified my stalker. It's Prince White."

Dolly gasped. "No!"

Jake realized Dolly's reaction was more than just surprise. "What am I missing?" he asked.

"You may not remember, but Meg's ex went to prison for killing Prince and Fagan White's oldest brother, Wendell," Dolly said.

Everyone began talking at once.

"Wait," Meg said. "There's more. Sheriff Marlow called the prison. Bobby is dying of cancer. When the prison notified the family, his brother went to visit him, and then just a few days afterward, Prince showed up, too. I don't know what all that has to do with me, but Prince isn't around to ask. Sheriff Marlow went up to interrogate him and he'd skipped out."

Dolly groaned. "I don't understand. How on earth did Mel figure all this out?"

Meg related what Marlow had told her about the man who'd taken up residence on the Fox place.

Jake frowned. "You say the man recognized Prince?"

Meg nodded. "That's what the sheriff said."

"Then whoever bought the Fox place isn't a stranger, or he wouldn't have known Prince White."

"I thought of that, too," Meg said. "But not before Marlow was gone, so I didn't get a chance to ask his name."

"No matter," Cyrus said. "You'll find out soon enough. For now, it's good to know that sorry-ass White is on the run."

"I'd rather he was behind bars, but you're right," Meg said.

Dolly gave Meg's hand a quick squeeze as she stood. "This is good news, and I'm going to take it."

Meg smiled. "I knew this would make your day."

"It's call for a celebration, for sure," Dolly said. "I've got a chicken stewing. I'm making dumplings for supper. If I get it all ready a little early, will you stay and eat with us?"

"Absolutely. I've been missing your cooking and can't think of anything better."

Jake left the women to visit, saying he needed to take care of some things before the snow hit. He penned up his tracking dogs and put fresh straw in their houses while his sons continued to haul up more wood. By the time they were finished, the food was done. They sat down to an early supper, laughing and talking about family and making plans for Thanksgiving, which was only a few weeks away.

Dolly was cutting one of the pies for dessert when Avery glanced out the window.

"Hey, look! It's snowing!"

Meg frowned. She'd planned to get home before the storm arrived. She looked out at the small flakes swirling in the wind gusts. It was nearly dark, which meant it would have taken at least an hour to drive home anyway, but the snow would add time to the trip. She tried not to let her anxiety show, but Dolly read it in her face.

"Honey, I don't like the idea of you driving down in the dark in this weather. Why don't you just stay the night? There's plenty of room, and you can borrow a nightgown from me."

"I'll be fine," Meg said. "It's barely snowing and it may not get any worse than this. Anyway, I left Honey in the house alone. I need to tend to her, and I can't be snowed in up here with my chickens to feed and the cow to milk, although Daisy is showing signs of drying up and I'm tempted to let her. Milking all winter does not appeal to me."

Dolly was still worried. "We'd get you home in plenty of time tomorrow. Jake could—"

"No. Thank you, but I can take care of myself, and I'll be home long before the roads have time to get bad. And by the way, I'm not going anywhere until I get my pie."

Cyrus laughed. "I'd be happy to eat it for you."

"Not a chance," Meg said.

She ate with an eye to the weather and, just as soon as it was polite, excused herself from the table.

"I'm going to leave now, Mom. I'll let Cyrus and Avery take my place helping clean up the kitchen."

Avery snorted. "Oh, thanks a lot."

Meg grinned as she began gathering up her things, but Dolly was uneasy.

"As soon as you get home, promise me that you'll call to let us know. I won't rest easy until I hear from you."

"I will, Mom, I promise," Meg said.

After another five minutes of hugs and goodbyes she was in the car and heading back down the mountain. Her windshield wipers were working overtime as the headlights sliced through a frantic swirl of falling sleet and snow.

It was close to ten miles from their house to hers, and mountain roads were narrow and winding, which made travel even more treacherous in the dark. Night came early in winter, and the snow was heavier than she'd realized.

About four miles down she ran into trouble. The roads were now snow packed and treacherous. The frantically swiping windshield wipers were unable to keep up with the blizzard, leaving her with nothing but a blurry view of the road. Her fingers were numb from holding so tightly to the steering wheel, and if it hadn't been for the dark border of trees on either side of the road, she would have been unable to tell where to drive.

All of a sudden her car fishtailed and started sliding sideways. She had a moment of panic before she steered into the slide and then slowly eased the car back into the middle of the road. As she did, she caught a glimpse of herself in the rearview mirror and saw the fear on her face. She knew if she had it to do over again, she would never have left.

A quick glance at the clock on the dashboard shocked her. She'd been on the road almost two hours. With no visible landmarks to judge the distance, she had no idea how far she'd come. All she could see was the continuing swirl of flakes illuminated by the beams from her headlights. She could have already driven past her turnoff.

Suddenly a gust of wind blew a blinding swirl of snow straight into the windshield. When it cleared she had a momentary glimpse of a big buck standing in the middle of the road and only moments to react to keep from hitting him.

She yanked the wheel hard to the left.

The deer leaped one way as her car went airborne the other way, sailing over the ditch and into the trees.

Meg screamed and then…

Impact.

There was a sound of crunching metal, a spew of steam from under the hood, the continuous honking of the horn, and a blinding pain over her right eye. The windshield wipers were still going, and she could smell smoke and the scent of burning rubber. She thought the car was on fire.

Dazed and in a panic, she began fumbling for the door latch, trying to get out, but her seat belt was still fastened. Then she realized the car was in gear and the wheels were spinning in place. She managed to shift into Neutral and was trying to turn off the engine when something crashed on top of the car.

After that, everything went black.

Six

Linc had just washed up his supper dishes, and was thinking about taking a shower and getting into bed early. He'd spent the afternoon cutting wood, and had hauled two full loads to Aunt Tildy's house before going back to haul the rest up to his place. He was bone tired, but it was a satisfied kind of tired. Having his aunt accept him back into her life without question had been an unexpected joy. They were the last two surviving members of the Fox family, and now that he'd come home, he'd been faced with her advancing age and how close he'd come to losing that connection.

It began to snow as he was loading up the last of the wood. By the time he got home, it was coming down thick and fast. The cold was numbing, but the silent swirl of falling snow left him with an odd feeling of peace. The quiet was so profound that even the sound of his breath seemed out of place.

He was heading for the trailer when he heard the loud sound of crunching metal, followed by the sudden continuous honking of a car horn and the sharp crack of a falling tree. Someone had just had a wreck!

He wasn't ready to get mixed up in other people's business, but they could be hurt, and that was something he couldn't ignore.

He was already wearing his heavy fur-lined parka and gloves, but he ran to the trailer to get his cell phone and a flashlight, then jumped in his truck and took off. His pickup had four-wheel drive and a well-stocked toolbox, and there was a log chain in the truck bed. He was hoping he wouldn't need anything more.

By the time he got to the main road he had to reorient himself. Had the wreck happened above or below him? There were no visible tracks in the snow, and it seemed that the sound was coming from up the mountain, so he turned to the right and headed up, although it was nearly impossible to see anything beyond the snow swirling in his headlights. Finally he thought to roll down the window to listen for the horn. As he drove, the sound was getting louder.

He saw headlights as he rounded a bend, and as he drew closer, he could see that a red SUV had crashed into a stand of trees. A very large limb had fallen on top of the car, blocking the doors and most of the windows. He pulled as close to the wreck as he dared, and left the lights on and the engine running as he got out. The bitter cold was a slap in the face, and he quickly pulled the fur-lined hood up over his head, grabbed his flashlight and a crowbar, then jumped the ditch and ran.

The entire front end of the car was crushed and wedged tightly into the trees. The hood had popped up during the crash, and then something—presumably the branch that had fallen afterward—had knocked it sideways, giving him easy access so he could disable the horn.

The sudden silence made the rapid thump of his heartbeat seem even louder as he circled to the driver's side. He shoved aside the smaller limbs to try to get to the door, only to find it wouldn't open. Even though the windshield wipers were still on, ice was beginning to form on the glass, making it difficult to tell how many people were inside, and the large limb on top of the car was impeding rescue. He pulled at the limb from both sides of the car, but he couldn't get it to budge. Finally he climbed up on top of the car and shoved the branch off. By the time he got back to the driver's side, snow had completely blanketed the window. He swiped it away and aimed the flashlight inside.

It was the sudden silence after the horn stopped honking that brought Meg back to a semiconscious state. She felt groggy, as if she'd had too much to drink, and couldn't figure out where she was. Her head was hurting, and when she felt her forehead, her fingers came away covered in blood. She tried to focus on the headlights, but her vision was severely hampered by the growing curtain of ice on the windshield. All she knew was that she'd driven off the road and into the trees.

"Get help...gotta get help," she mumbled, and was looking for her cell phone when she caught a glimpse of something huge and furry walking between the trees and the headlights. She blinked, trying to clear her vision, and thought she saw a large furry head on an equally massive chest and shoulders.

What the hell did I just see? Was that Bigfoot?

In something of a panic, she froze, not wanting to call attention to herself as the creature began moving around outside the car. Then all of a sudden she heard something jump on top of her car. When the roof popped from the added weight, her last thought as she passed out was that Bigfoot was real.

Linc quickly deduced the only person in the car was the driver—a woman with long dark hair. What he could see of her face was covered in blood, which amped his anxiety. He tried again to open the door, only to see that it was locked, on top of being crumpled by the crash. He began banging on the glass and shouting.

"Hello! Hello! Lady, can you hear me? Wake up! You need to unlock the door!"

When she didn't respond, his heart sank. *Please, God, don't let her be dead.*

Then all of a sudden her head dropped forward, her chin bouncing against her chest. The motion seemed to wake her up. He watched as she pushed the hair away from her eyes and got his first clear view of her face.

Shock swept through him, leaving him momentarily speechless. He hadn't seen her in eighteen years, but there was still enough left of the girl he'd known to recognize that it was Meg. He doubled up his fist and began pounding on the window.

"Meg! Meg! Unlock the door!"

He saw her eyelids flutter, but when her head slid sideways toward her shoulder, he knew she'd passed out again.

Without hesitation he swung the crowbar at the window, shattering the glass, then jammed his arm through the opening and unlocked the door. He grabbed the door handle, took a tight grip and yanked. When the door succumbed to his greater strength, he quickly leaned inside, feeling her neck for a pulse.

"Meg! Meg Lewis! Can you hear me?"

She moaned but didn't respond further.

Her pulse was rapid, and it was obvious a gash on her head was the source of all the blood. Although she was still wearing a seat belt, it didn't mean she didn't have internal injuries.

He grabbed his cell phone to call the sheriff's office. It rang twice, and then he lost the signal. Although he tried several more times, he quickly realized it was hopeless trying to get through in this storm. He hated to move her, but leaving her here was even more dangerous. He saw a folded blanket and a flashlight in the backseat of her car. He grabbed the blanket, shook out the broken glass and wrapped it around her as carefully as he could before lifting her out and carrying her to his truck.

She moaned again as he crossed the ditch, and she began trying to push the blanket off her face. When he got to the truck he slid her onto the seat, reclined it as far back as it would go and buckled her in.

His hands were shaking from the rush of adrenaline as he got behind the wheel. He wasted no time turning the truck around and heading down the mountain. His mind was racing through possible scenarios as to what his best move would be. He could take her to the sheriff's office in Boone's Gap, which wasn't that much farther from the wreck, but they would have to call an ambulance from Mount Sterling, which would only waste time. So he kept on driving, deciding to head for Mount Sterling himself, checking on her every few minutes to make sure she was still breathing and praying to God that she would come to.

Not knowing where she was hurt made everything worse. If she had broken ribs, moving her could have punctured a lung. If she had a spinal injury, he could be the reason she never walked again. If her concussion was serious, she could have a brain bleed and die before they ever reached a hospital. By the time he reached the highway—which was wider and provided some relief—and headed toward Mount Sterling, he was sick to his stomach.

Once she sighed and then moaned, but it was the only sound she made.

Being this close to her again brought back memories of every moment they'd shared, from their first kiss under the bleachers at a high school football game to the first time they made love. Remembering the look on her face when they'd taken him to jail had been his undoing. It was part of why he hadn't come back once his jail term was over. Without her, he no longer had a reason to come home. He didn't know how this was going to play out, but finding her had definitely marked the end of his exile. Once this got out, everyone would know he was back.

He glanced at the clock. Nearly forty-five minutes since he'd pulled her out of the wreck. He had to be close. Traffic had kept the snow from piling up on the highway, and travel was no longer an issue.

And just like that, his headlights caught on a sign by the road.

Mount Sterling. One mile.

He breathed a quiet sigh of relief and drove her straight to the hospital, following the signs all the way to the E.R.

Linc hadn't moved ten feet from Meg's side since they wheeled her into an examination bay. His brief

explanation about finding her in the wreck up on Rebel
Ridge and then being unable to get a phone signal had
been accepted without question. When they asked for
personal information, he knew her name and very little
else, until a nurse thought she recognized Meg's name
from a prior visit. A quick check of their records and
then a look at the bottoms of her feet to see the newly
healing scars verified her identity. After that they had
all the medical history they needed to proceed.

Linc was shocked by the healing cuts on her feet.
They were visible proof of what she'd already gone
through on Prince White's account. He sat with a lump
in his throat as she was x-rayed from head to toe, and
watched mutely as they cleaned and stitched the wound
in her scalp to stop the bleeding.

They left her in the examining room with him on one
side of her bed and a nurse on the other, continuing to
monitor her vitals.

"Has anyone notified her family?" Linc asked.

"I believe the contact information she gave on her
earlier visit was for a brother. He has been notified."

He didn't want to be here when Meg woke up. He
didn't think he could bear to see the shock and disgust
on her face when she recognized him, but he couldn't
bring himself to leave. She'd gone through too much
crap alone already, and so he sat, waiting for the next
shoe to fall.

When two and a half hours passed and Meg still
hadn't called or answered her phone, Dolly was convinced she was stranded in a ditch on the side of the
road. Within minutes she had Jake and the boys up and
they were all on the way down the mountain to res-

cue her. It had stopped snowing, but the roads were a mess. The old four-wheel-drive Suburban was plenty big enough to hold them all, plus rope and chain to pull her out of the ditch.

Given the conditions, they made good time, but the farther they drove without finding a sign of Meg, the more frantic Dolly became.

Then they came upon the wreck and Dolly panicked.

"Oh no, oh, Meg… Stop the car, Jake! Stop the car!"

Jake braked as they quickly took in the sight. The front of Meg's car was smashed into a stand of trees with the lights still on and the driver-side door wide-open. But Meg was nowhere in sight.

"I don't see her!" Dolly said, and fumbled for the door latch.

Jake and his sons were out of the car and running, all of them afraid she'd gotten out of the wreck on her own and stumbled off into the woods, only to pass out somewhere in the snow.

Dolly was so scared that when she stepped out, her legs wouldn't hold her and she fell to her knees. She was shaking so hard she could barely breathe as she dragged herself up and quickly followed.

"Is she there? Can you see her?" she cried.

"No, no, she's not here. She's not here," Jake said.

"Maybe she wandered off into the woods," Cyrus said.

"I don't see tracks. There should be tracks," Dolly cried, running from one side of the car to the other, but the snow was pristine. If there *had* been tracks, they were covered with snow now.

Avery was the one who voiced what no one wanted

to say. "What if it was Prince White? What if he ran her off the road and took her?"

Before they could pursue that theory, they heard a Johnny Cash song coming from their car.

"Dolly, that's your phone," Jake said.

"Oh, my God, it is!" she said, and started running.

She was gasping as she answered. "Hello? Meggie, is that you, baby?"

It was Ryal.

"Mama, it's me. I just got a phone call from the hospital in Mount Sterling. Meg is in the E.R. She had a wreck. Someone found her and brought her in."

"Oh, Jesus...oh, sweet Lord," Dolly said, and then sat down on the running board and started to cry.

Jake took the phone out of her hands. "Hello? Who's this?"

"Hey, Jake, it's me, Ryal. Is Mama okay?"

"She's crying. What did you tell her?"

"Meg had a wreck. Someone found her and took her to the E.R. in Mount Sterling. I don't know how bad she's hurt or anything other than that she's there. I'm getting dressed and heading there myself. I called your house, but when you didn't answer, I tried Mom's cell. Julie is sick with the flu, and James can't leave her alone with the kids. Quinn and Mariah are even farther up the mountain than the rest of you, which means their roads will be worse. I say there's no need calling anyone else until we know what to tell them."

"Agreed," Jake said. "We were already out looking for her. We just found her car, but no Meg. We were afraid she was somewhere in the woods buried under all this snow. That's why your mama is crying. It's relief."

"Oh, my God, I had no idea."

"We're already halfway down the mountain. We'll meet you at the hospital," Jake said, and hung up, then yelled at Avery and Cyrus, who were still searching the woods.

"Boys! Someone already found her and took her to the hospital. Let's go," he said, then leaned down and hugged Dolly close. "Honey, you need to climb into the car now. We're gonna go see Meg, and you need to have faith that she's going to be all right."

It was the calmness in Jake's voice that brought Dolly out of the mind-numbing panic. She got back in the car, swiping tears as Jake kissed her cheek and then closed the door.

Even though Meg's car appeared to be a total loss, Cyrus had the sense to take the keys out of the ignition, turn off the lights and push the door as closed as it would go. Then he jumped the ditch and followed his brother to the Suburban. When Jake put the car into gear, the tires spun on the snow before they caught traction.

Cyrus leaned forward from the backseat as Jake headed down the mountain.

"Dad, remember Meg said she left Honey in the house? I took her car keys. If her house key is on it, when you get to her driveway let me and Avery out, and we'll stay there and tend to Honey and her stuff until you and Dolly get back."

"Let me see it," Dolly said, and when he handed her the ring, she quickly pointed out the door key. "It's this one," she said, and gave it back.

"That's a good idea, son," Jake said, then gave Dolly's arm a quick pat. "Help me watch for the turnoff, Dolly. It's hard to tell where I'm at."

"Look for the big black mailbox," she said.

Less than a mile later they saw it. Jake paused long enough to let his sons out of the car. They waved with their flashlights as they crossed in front of the car and trudged off into the darkness.

Dolly shook her head. "She was so close to being home when this happened." Then she began crying all over again as Jake stepped on the gas.

"I know, sugar, I know. I'm just sick all of this is happening to our girl, but we need to trust in the good Lord that she's gonna be all right."

Dolly wiped her eyes and blew her nose. "You're right, Jake. I don't know what I'd be doing now without you."

Linc went with them when they moved Meg from the E.R. to a bed in the hospital. She had an IV in one arm and a blood pressure cuff on the other that automatically tightened every fifteen minutes to take a reading. The nurse who came in to get Meg settled eyed him curiously as he stood watch but didn't question him. She left, telling him to call the nurses' station if Meg woke up.

Linc almost panicked, knowing that they'd just given Meg's care over to technology, and then guessed the same thing had most likely happened to him when he was electrocuted. It was daunting to realize how fast a life could cease to exist.

A small light was on overhead, but it might as well have been a spotlight, because she was all he saw. He pulled a chair next to her bed, then proceeded to map the changes the years had put on her face. Despite the bruises and swelling, it was obvious she'd grown into a beautiful woman. Since the only knowledge he had of her was from their past, he couldn't help but wonder, what made her laugh now, and what music made her cry? What did she do with her days, and how did she pass her nights? Aunt Tildy said she'd given up on men, and it hurt his heart to think he'd had a part in turning this woman into a loner.

So he sat, waiting for her to wake up, with a thousand questions running through his head. When she woke, would she know him, and if she did, would she reject him?

Something was beeping nearby. It must be the alarm. Time to get up. But when Meg opened her eyes and tried to get up, a pain shot through her body so fast that she gasped. Then she saw the IV needle in her arm and realized she was in a hospital. Flashes of blowing snow and a large buck frozen in the oncoming headlights of her car slid through her mind—and just like that, she remembered the wreck. But how had she gotten here?

Her head was throbbing as she looked toward the window. It pounded even harder when she saw the stranger standing there, looking out. The massive span of his shoulders, and the fact he was so tall his head was higher than the window, reminded her of the furry giant she'd seen at the wreck. She realized it must have been him.

"You're not Bigfoot."

Linc was startled by her voice. He'd wondered what her first words to him might be, but this definitely wasn't what he'd expected. He took his hands out of his pockets and turned around.

"Not in the critter sense. How do you feel?"

"My head hurts. My chest hurts. Did I break anything?"

"You have a few stitches in your head, a concussion and a couple of bruised ribs. The only thing that broke is your car."

She frowned. "The snow…there was a deer. I swerved to keep from hitting it."

He'd wondered what had caused her to run off the road.

"Did you pull me out of the car?" she asked.

"Yes."

"Thank you. You probably saved my life."

"You're welcome."

Her frown deepened. That voice was tugging at her memory.

"Do I know you?" she asked.

Linc sighed. *Here it comes.* He'd never dreaded an introduction more.

"You used to," he said softly, and walked out of the shadows and into the light.

Meg blinked.

"Have I changed that much?" he asked.

Her heart stopped, then picked up an irregular beat so fast it left her breathless.

"Lincoln?"

"Yes."

She reached for his hand, clasping it fiercely, and as she did, she felt the strength and the calluses.

"You're the one who moved onto your grandpa's place. It was you who told Sheriff Marlow about Prince White, wasn't it?"

He shrugged. "It seems like I came home just at the right time."

She was almost afraid to ask. "Are you here to stay?"

She watched an odd expression move across his face before he nodded.

"Yeah, I'm staying."

There wasn't time to think about why that felt like good news. There were other crowding questions.

"Why did you come home *now,* after all these years?"

He sat down in the chair beside her bed.

"I got tired of running from something I didn't do. I came home to find out who killed my dad and clear my name."

"But how are you going to do that? It's been so long."

"I'll figure it out as I go."

She couldn't quit staring. It was surreal to be talking to him like this when she'd thought she would never see him again.

"Why didn't you let anyone know you were back?"

"I intended to, sooner or later. I'm trying to remodel the old bomb shelter on Grandpa's place to winter in until I can rebuild the house. I plan to start my investigation after I get the place finished."

Meg's head was beginning to throb. She felt herself losing focus, but she didn't want to pass out with so many unanswered questions hanging between them.

"What was happening to me messed that up, didn't it?"

"Things change, sometimes for the better," he said.

"Just for the record, I never thought you did it."

It was more than he'd hoped for, yet the best thing she could have said, and he still felt the need to apologize.

"Aunt Tildy told me some about what's gone on with you. I'm so sorry the men you cared for let you down."

Tears slipped from the corners of her eyes. It was surely from the pain and the shock of the wreck, but it was the first time anyone had ever acknowledged how the actions of others had impacted her life. Twice, at a very young age, she'd been ostracized by her friends because of an association with someone else. Feeling emotional over a man she hadn't seen in eighteen years was not only ridiculous but totally unlike her. And yet she was crying and couldn't stop.

Linc saw the tears. "Oh, Meg, don't cry. I'm so sorry."

She closed her eyes, unwilling for him to see how vulnerable he made her feel. She'd known a boy, but she didn't know this man, and even though he'd saved her life, trusting him wasn't wise.

He started talking fast, hoping to calm her down. "I know me being here is the last thing you needed. I would have already left, but I didn't want you to wake up alone. The hospital called your brother Ryal. I'm sure your family is on the way."

She squeezed his hand, because she understood, but she couldn't talk.

His fingers curled around her wrist. "Don't cry, Meg. Damn it, don't cry."

The pain in his voice hurt her heart, but before she could say anything more, the nurse came back.

"Oh good, you're awake. Your family is on the way up. Is there anything I can get for you?" she asked.

Meg wouldn't turn loose of his hand. "Would it be possible to have something for pain?

"I'll check and be right back," the nurse said.

Linc looked around for his coat. "I'd better be leaving."

Meg held on even tighter. "But they'll want to thank you."

He gently pulled out of her grasp, then brushed a

tear off her cheek. "No, they won't, Meggie. Trust me. No, they won't."

She choked on a sob.

He started to say more, then shook his head and slipped out of the room. Unwilling to meet her family coming out of the elevator, he ducked into the stairwell and headed down.

Seven

Just like that, Linc was gone again. Meg didn't want her family to see her crying and have to explain what was wrong, so she wiped away her tears and made herself calm. It was none too soon. Within moments her mother opened the door and quietly slipped inside, followed by Jake and her brother Ryal.

She took a slow, shaky breath and then made herself smile. It was as halfhearted as the tone of her voice.

"Hi, Mom."

"Oh, honey, what have you done to yourself?" Dolly said as she hurried to the bedside.

"A few more stitches, a couple of bruised ribs. Nothing is broken."

Ryal stopped at the foot of the bed and gently patted the covers over her foot.

"Hey, sister…what happened?"

"There was a deer in the road. I didn't see it until I was almost on it. I swerved and wound up in the trees."

Jake shook his head. "I can't tell you how many times that's nearly happened to me. One of the hazards of living in the mountains, for sure. Really glad to see you awake and talking."

"We thought…" Dolly stopped, shook her head and blew her nose, unable to voice her fears.

"Who found you and brought you here?" Ryal asked.

Meg surprised herself by hedging. "I came to at the wreck long enough to see a huge furry shape moving in front of the headlights. I thought it was Bigfoot and then passed out again. I don't remember the drive here, only waking up in this room."

It wasn't a lie, she'd just omitted a few things—like the fact that the Bigfoot had been in her room when she opened her eyes.

Jake chuckled. "Bigfoot, you say? That's a good one."

Dolly cupped Meg's cheek and then brushed a lock of hair away from her forehead.

"I'm grateful, whoever it was," she said.

"Me, too," Meg said, and then looked away.

Ryal frowned. He knew his sister, and for whatever reason, she'd just told a lie. Something was going on.

Meg saw Ryal's expression. Damn. She'd never been able to fool her brothers about anything. Okay, he was suspicious. Big deal. He was going to have to stay that way. Twice now Linc had intervened on her behalf. The least she could do was not give him away. A change of subject was in order.

"I have a favor to ask. I think they'll let me out tomorrow once they're sure my concussion isn't an issue, but I left Honey in the house. Someone needs to go let her out," she said.

Jake touched her shoulder. "We're way ahead of you, girl. Cyrus and Avery are already there. They're taking care of everything. You don't worry yourself, okay?"

Meg sighed with relief. "Tell them I really appreciate it."

"You can tell them yourself when you go home," Dolly said, then looked at the time. "You need to rest. Ryal isn't going to stay, but Jake and I will be just down the hall in the visitors' waiting room."

"I'm sorry. It seems like I've been nothing but trouble lately."

"And none of it your fault," Ryal said. "Do you need anything?"

"No. I hurt, but as Granny Foster used to say, 'this, too, shall pass.'"

Dolly leaned over and kissed Meg on the cheek. "I'm so grateful you're okay. Try to sleep. I love you."

"I love you guys, too," Meg said, and then closed her eyes.

She heard footsteps leaving, the door closing, and then she opened her eyes. Ryal was still standing at the foot of the bed.

"What's the secret?"

Meg frowned, then winced from the pain. "I don't know what you're talking about."

"Whatever," he said. "But just so you know, I don't believe you."

"Just so *you* know, I don't care," Meg muttered.

The nurse came in with a syringe of pain meds, shot it into Meg's IV and gave Ryal a look, which he interpreted as *take yourself out of the room now,* which he did. He knew Beth would be worried about Meg's condition and planned to call her before starting home.

It wasn't until the door closed behind him that Meg breathed easy. The hall outside her room was quiet. Her anxiety was slowly dissipating as the pain meds kicked in. The last thing she thought about was the look on Linc's face when he'd stepped out of the shadows. It wasn't unlike the look she'd seen on that deer's face right before she swerved—both of them afraid of what was about to happen.

While Meg slept and his mother and stepfather stood watch, Ryal did some snooping. He went down to E.R. to ask the admitting nurse the name of the person who'd brought his sister to the hospital and got a name he hadn't expected.

So Lincoln Fox was back. They should have figured it out when they heard that someone had moved onto the old Fox property. He wanted to be pissed that Meg was protecting the man, but until he knew all the facts, he would reserve judgment. For now, it was enough that Fox had been the person who'd given a name to her stalker and rescued her from the wreck.

The doctors released Meg to her family before noon the next day. Her ribs were sore, her head hurt and, with her car a shambles, she was going to be afoot. But for now her mom and Jake were taking care of things. After they left the hospital they stopped at a supermarket in Mount Sterling to stock up on groceries, leaving Meg alone in the car.

The snowfall had not been as heavy here and was already beginning to melt, turning the streets to slush. She watched kids throwing snowballs and cars spinning out on the slick spots. A police cruiser went by with flashing lights, followed shortly by an ambulance and the fire department. Without knowing what was going on, she still said a quick prayer. But for the presence of Lincoln Fox last night, she would have been in similar need.

She'd done nothing but think about him after he'd slipped out of her room. Her heart ached, but from old memories. Seeing him again had resurrected all the old pain—of how much she'd loved him, and how desperate she'd been when they'd taken him away. She'd never understood how their friends had written him off as bad news, believing the worst of a boy who'd never done anything wrong. Having him for such a close neighbor could be a recipe for more heartache, but one thing was for certain: she would be talking to him again.

Last week's early snowfall had melted away, leaving the earth soft and wet, which made digging the footing for the last of Linc's construction a lot easier. Every day was a rush to get as much done as possible while there was still daylight. The satellite dish had been installed, and at night he caught up with his construction crews back in Dallas by phone or by Skype, and dealt with the hitches as competently as if he'd been right there on-site. When he slept, he wrestled with the old demons that slipped into his dreams, leaving him an emotional wreck by morning. It didn't help knowing Meg was his nearest neighbor, but his thoughts of her were on constant rewind—remembering the day he'd first seen her as someone other than just the tallest girl in class.

Boone's Gap High School was competing in the state high school track meet in Louisville, and Linc was on his way to the concession stand when he heard them announce the next race—the girls' fifty-yard dash. He was hungry, but the race wouldn't last long, so he stopped to watch.

The starter's pistol went off, and the runners flew off their marks. They were running pretty much neck and neck until they passed the halfway point. All of a sudden one tall, long-legged girl separated herself from the pack as if she'd just shifted into high gear. Of course he knew her, but for some reason he'd never really looked at her before. He caught himself holding his breath as she passed him, running yards ahead of the others. He was stunned by the power in her stride. When she crossed the finish line her arms were over her head in a gesture of jubilation, and when she turned around and waved to her cheering teammates, the beauty of her smile stopped his heart.

He asked her out within a week and never looked back. For the next two years Meg Walker was his girl and everyone knew it. The first time they'd made love had been in the back of his daddy's pickup truck under the stars on Rebel Ridge. After that they'd made love whenever they got the chance, and when their senior year rolled around they were making plans for what came after high school with all the innocence of youth. When Lincoln's world burned down around him, it burned all their dreams, as well.

As days passed, being back where his world had crashed was resurrecting far too many bad memories for Linc. He struggled daily to control his emotions. He was hammering a nail with more force than necessary when his focus was suddenly shifted by a phone call. When he saw caller ID, he dropped the hammer to answer.

"Hey, Aunt Tildy."

"Hello, Lincoln. How are you doing?"

"I'm fine. Are you staying warm? Do you need any more wood hauled up to the house?"

"I'm fine, Lincoln, but since you asked, there's something you could do for someone else, if you were of a mind to."

He frowned. "Like what?"

"I have a friend named Beulah Justice who lives up the road from me a piece. Her only kin is a grandson, but he's in the army. She was over this morning asking for some salve for her arthritis, and while we were visiting, she told me that her back door has come off its hinges and she's been suffering something fierce because of the cold. If you were willing to fix that door for her, I'd take it as a favor to me. I'd go with you, of course, to put her mind at rest about letting a stranger in her house, but she needs help in the worst way. No one pays her any mind, so word's not likely to get out that she's in need, and she's not the kind to ask for help."

Linc was horrified, thinking of how cold it had been during the recent snow and how poorly she must have fared without being able to shut out the wind.

"Give me fifteen minutes to gather up some tools and I'm on my way."

"The Lord will bless you for this," Tildy said.

"See you soon," Linc said.

He began loading up the tools he thought he might need, then threw some new two-by-four lumber into the truck bed, as well. He dug through his supplies for the extra set of hinges he'd bought, just in case, and then added some caulking and a couple of big rolls of weather stripping, hoping the door itself wasn't too rotten to rehang. After locking up, he drove off, stopping long enough to pick up Tildy. At her direction, he headed for the house where Beulah Justice lived.

"I really appreciate this," Tildy said.

"You're a good neighbor to a lot of people, Aunt Tildy."

"I try to live by the Good Book. Do unto others and all that. So tell me what you've been doing?"

He sighed. "Getting mixed up in other people's business."

She caught the regret in his voice. "Like how?"

"Oh, it's a long story, but it's probably going to spread the word about my presence a little faster than I had planned."

She frowned. "Maybe that's not all bad. Sometimes our plans aren't what God means for them to be. If it was me, I'd just go with the flow and see where it took me."

He smiled. "That sounds like good advice. I'll be remembering that."

She pointed up the road. "You'll need to take the first left just past the curve. You can't miss it. Her house is right on the road."

Linc's heart sank when he saw the tiny gray weathered shack and the thin spiral of smoke coming from the chimney.

"Does she know we're coming?" he asked as he pulled up into the yard and killed the engine.

"No. Let me talk us in," she said, then got out and marched up to the door as if she was going to war.

Watching Tildy in her take-charge manner reminded him of his father and his grandpa. Attitude ran strong in the Fox family. Too bad it had taken him so long to get his own into gear.

He saw the door open slightly and then saw Tildy begin talking. She pointed back at the truck, and he knew they were in when Tildy came running.

"Pull around to the back of the house. It'll save you some walking," she said, then hurried back to the house and went inside.

As Linc circled around, he saw a very small pile of dead tree limbs and a hatchet on the ground beside it, and he realized that was her woodpile. He was already frowning as he pulled to a stop near the sagging back porch. The lady of the house and a skinny gray cat came out together through the canvas-covered opening where the door should have hung. He got out to shake her hand, dwarfing her tiny five-foot stature by well over a foot.

"Mrs. Justice, I'm pleased to meet you," he said.

The little old lady tilted her head back to look up. "You're just about the biggest man I reckon I ever met up with." Then she smiled, turning her face into a wreath of wrinkles and revealing a set of very white false teeth. "I sure do appreciate you coming to hang up my door. I been dreadin' winter comin' on because of it."

"Happy to help," Linc said as he walked up to check out the doorframe, as well as the fallen door leaning up against the outer wall. "I'll need to take down your canvas."

"Son, you take down anything you want. I don't mind as long as I get my door back in its rightful place."

Tildy was standing in the kitchen. "Beulah, why don't you come on back into the living room with me? We'll sit by the fire while my nephew fixes up your door, okay?"

Beulah gave Linc another look, as if assuring herself he was capable of doing what was needed, then let herself be led away.

Linc eyed the tiny kitchen curiously. She cooked on a stove fueled by propane, as did nearly everyone on Rebel Ridge. Her refrigerator was old and yellow from age, not paint. He was guessing the appliance had been new about twenty years ago. The linoleum on the floor had lost most of its color from years of wear and scrubbing, but despite the lack of a door, the room was cleaner than he would have imagined she could keep it.

He pulled down the canvas, which let more light into the room, and quickly spotted the problem. The facing on which the door had been hanging had rotted away. Having wood on hand had just saved him a trip into Mount Sterling. He grabbed his tools and began prying off the strips of rotten wood, then set up his sawhorses and began measuring and cutting new pieces.

The sound of his power tools startled the gray cat. It hissed, ran up a porch post onto the sloping roof and disappeared. He grinned, thinking to himself that if he'd been that agile, he would have made a better roofer.

After he finished framing up the new opening, he cut and planed wood for the missing threshold and then went to inspect the door itself.

The wood was good enough, but the hinges weren't. They were both rusted, and one was broken. He got out the new hinges and set to working, ever conscious of the cold wind blowing down his neck. He worked fast, sighting and attaching the hinges. Then he quickly hung the door, tapping the long bolts through the hinges before testing it out. It swung freely back and forth, and when he shut it to make sure it latched, the bolt slid right into place and the lock easily turned. Success.

The kitchen was freezing, though just being able to shut out the wind made a world of difference. But now that the door was closed, he could hear other evidence of the wind and began checking out the windows.

The glass panes were loose, and he could feel cold air coming in around the bottoms. He went back to the truck, returning with the caulking gun and the rolls of weather stripping, caulked up the window panes, then tacked up some weather stripping around both windows.

As soon as he finished in the kitchen, he headed to the living room and again was struck by the effort Beulah made to keep up her house. Except for a fine layer of dust, which was easily attributed to the lack of a back door, everything was old but neat. Her sofa was worn and threadbare, but the throw pillows at either end were little round puffs of blue. There was a crocheted doily beneath a table lamp, and another one on a little coffee table beneath a Bible. The pictures on the wall were old, like Beulah herself.

He eyed his aunt sitting close to Beulah by the fireplace and realized that the two women were very much alike—the last of their line, except for two men who were absent in their lives. He was grateful all over again for the accident that had made him come back.

"Mrs. Justice, if you don't mind, I have some extra caulk and weather stripping. I'd be happy to seal up the drafts around the rest of your windows."

Beulah Justice beamed. "That would be wonderful," she said, and then patted Tildy's hand. "You sure are lucky to have such a handy nephew."

Linc began going through the tiny house, sealing up cracks and gaps as best he could. As soon as he was finished, he went back to the living room and found Tildy adding a stick of wood to the fireplace, and he made a mental note to bring up a load of wood. Then he noticed there was a gas heating stove at the other end of the room that wasn't lit.

"All done," he said. "It'll take time to heat your house back up, but once it does, it should hold the heat way better than it did before." Then he pointed to the stove. "Do you want me to light the fire in your stove?"

"Won't do no good, son. Propane tank is empty. I'll do fine with my fireplace, but I thank you just the same."

He was stunned. That explained the teakettle and the cast iron stew kettle sitting near the fireplace. Her cook stove ran on propane. She hadn't been able to shut out the cold *or* cook a decent meal. *God in heaven, how long has she been living like this?*

Beulah got up to thank him, struggling not to cry as she clasped her hands against her little belly. "I am more grateful than you will ever know."

Linc had been building houses from the ground up for years, but he couldn't remember ever being as satisfied with a finished job as he was right now.

"It's been my pleasure," he said, then glanced at his aunt. "If you're ready to go, I'm finished, Aunt Tildy."

Tildy stood. "Then we'll be off," she said, and took a small jar from her jacket pocket and handed it to Beulah. "Use this during the day and the other salve at night. It'll fix your aches right up."

"I sure thank you, Tildy."

"You're welcome, Beulah, and when you write to your grandson again, give him my best. Tell him we're all praying for him to come home."

"I will do that," Beulah said, and led the way through the little house to the kitchen, where she inspected the door and windows with delight. "My, my, this is fine work. I'll be snug as a bug this winter now, for sure."

Linc loaded up his tools as Tildy got back in the truck. As they circled the house to get back to the road, Beulah was visible through the windows, admiring his work.

"I am grateful," Tildy said.

"You know what, Aunt Tildy? So am I," he said.

She smiled. "It feels good to help out, doesn't it?"

He nodded. "Yes, ma'am, it does."

When they got back to her place, he parked, and before she got out, he took her hand.

"Is there anything I can do for you?"

She smiled. "Not today, Linc, but I thank you for the offer."

He nodded but didn't turn her loose.

Tildy saw the look on his face and calmly waited for whatever else was on his mind.

"Aunt Tildy, I've been wondering something."

"Like what?"

"Like, when was the last time someone took you out for Sunday dinner?"

Her eyes widened; she was clearly surprised by the question.

"Why, I reckon it's been so long that I don't think I can actually remember."

"Would you let me take you to dinner? Frankie's Eats isn't very fancy, but I noticed on their sign that they have chicken and dumplings on Sundays."

"People will see you. Some might recognize you."

"I know."

She squeezed his hand. "Then I'd be honored. I haven't eaten any cooking but my own in so long, I just might make a pig of myself."

"Do you go to church?"

"Not anymore. The Good Lord and me understand each other just fine without being in a church. I do my best communicating with Him when I'm on the mountain gathering up my herbs."

"Then I'll pick you up about eleven, if that's all right?"

She grinned. "Now I've got to go see if my dresses still fit. I don't reckon I've worn one since the day I buried my man, and that was some years back."

"There's a lot gone on around here that we've both missed out on," he said, and then he leaned across the seat and kissed her cheek. "Thanks, Aunt Tildy. You're the best."

She fussed to keep from crying as she got out, but there was a bounce to her step as she headed for the house.

Linc waited until she was inside before he drove away. In a way, he was relieved that he'd finally made the decision to step out of his exile, and, after helping Beulah, the anger in his heart had miraculously disappeared.

He could almost hear his grandpa's voice. *Do unto others.*

"I will remember that better, Grandpa, but thanks for the reminder."

As soon as he got home, he called his propane company and gave them an order to fill Beulah Justice's tank, make sure her heating and cooking stoves lit before they left, and send him the bill. Then he went back outside, loaded up a cord of firewood he'd planned to use for himself and started back up the mountain.

When he pulled into Beulah's place and began unloading the wood, she came out crying with her apron over her face.

"I'm not too proud to take this," she said, wiping tears with the hem of her apron. "But I'm gonna say big prayers for you, son, when I lay my head down tonight."

Linc paused. "And I'll thank you," he said, then carried in an armful of wood, added some to her fire and put the rest by her fireplace. "This should hold you for a week or so. Just don't worry about staying warm or try to save it to make it last. You use what you need and I'll keep you in wood."

"God bless you," she said, still crying as he drove away.

Even after he'd gone to bed that night, sleeping snug and warm in his trailer, he couldn't stop thinking about little Beulah and wondering how many other lone women on Rebel Ridge were in the same leaky boat.

Fagan had been trying to call Prince ever since the sheriff drove away from the house, but his calls weren't being answered. He didn't know whether Prince was drunk off his ass and whoring around, or if he'd gone and broken his phone. But he knew that two hundred dollars he'd given Prince had to be gone. If Prince had tried to pull a heist he could even be in jail, although Fagan was pretty sure he would have found out if Marlow had his brother in custody. So when Prince finally called him, he was shocked.

Fagan glanced at the caller ID as his cell phone rang and then rolled his eyes.

"It's about damn time you finally return a call," he said as he answered.

"And a hello to you, too, brother dear," Prince said. "What's going on?"

"The sheriff was here the morning you left. There's a warrant out for your arrest."

"Shit," Prince muttered. "I was hoping she didn't get a good look at me," he said.

"Oh, it wasn't her. There was a witness who named you."

Prince's heart suddenly started pounding. "That bastard on the old Fox place. The one who called me out."

"I didn't know about anyone moving onto that place or I might have made it my business to find out who it was," Fagan said.

"Well, if he saw me and knew me, it can't be a stranger," Prince muttered. "But who could... Oh, shit."

"What?" Fagan asked.

"Who would be living on the Fox place now who knew who I was?"

Fagan snorted. "Anyone on Rebel Ridge, that's who."

"Not on the Fox place. As long as Tildy Bennett still lives, it won't ever be for sale."

"But there's no one else who—"

All of a sudden, Fagan's mind went right where Prince's had gone. "Do you think...?"

"I don't know, but who else could it be?"

"But why come back now, after all these years?"

"I don't know, but it doesn't give me any peace of mind to consider the reasons why," Prince said.

"I'll find out for sure, and when I call you back again, answer the damn phone," Fagan said.

"Yeah, yeah. Meanwhile, I'm broke."

"Well, so am I. The cops are breathing down my neck

because of you, and I can't take a chance on selling any weed until this situation is resolved."

"So what am I gonna do for money?" Prince asked.

"You figure it out," Fagan said. "You're the one who pulled the dumb stunt. And by the way…what the hell made you do it to begin with?"

Prince sighed. He needed money, and if Fagan could pull off what he had messed up, then they would be set for a good long while.

"One day a few weeks past Claude Lewis came to see me. He said his brother, Bobby, wanted to talk to me. I told him to tell Bobby Lewis to go to hell, but then he said Bobby was dying of lung cancer and there was something important he needed to tell me before he died. Something that would set us up fine. So I went down to the state prison to see him."

Fagan frowned. "Why am I just now hearing about this?"

"Well, I thought I'd—"

"Don't lie," Fagan snapped. "I know exactly why you didn't tell me. If you could get away with it, you were gonna keep whatever it was all to yourself."

"Now, brother, that's not so," Prince said.

"Whatever. So what does Meg Lewis have to do with it?"

"Bobby said when he killed Wendell, that Wendell had over twenty thousand dollars on him. Bobby said he buried it where he buried his hunting dog, Ike, and that the only person who would know that particular location was his ex-wife, Meg."

"But why didn't he just tell you outright? And why didn't you just go ask her—in a roundabout way, of course—for that very information?"

Prince picked at a sore on the back of his hand, knowing this was going to piss his brother off, but such was life.

"I don't know what Bobby's reasoning was, but I know mine. I wanted to fuck with her first, that's why. She thinks she's so high-and-mighty, and she's no better than the rest of us."

"Why would you say that?"

"Well, she's been a single woman for all these years, but she has nothing to do with men, like she's too good for them to mess with her."

Fagan sighed. "I'd say that's because the first two she picked were losers and she was too damned fed up with men in general to try again, but that's just me."

Prince frowned. "It don't matter. I'm gonna fuck her, and then I'm gonna slit her damn throat…but that's after you find out where the money is hid."

"Me? After what you did, do you think her or any of her family is gonna let me close to her? No. You messed this up. You figure it out."

"Damn it! You go find out where that money's buried!" Prince screamed. "I'm near to broke. I would already be there, but I rolled a drunk I found passed out the other night."

"No," Fagan said. "You figure something else out." He wasn't good at telling his brother no, so he hung up before Prince could push any more.

The days passed quickly as Linc worked from daylight to dark, and the closer it got to Sunday, the more anxious he became. In one single meal he was going to set wheels in motion, but he had no way of knowing where they would take him. He wanted his life back, and with Meg in it. Knowing she was so damn close made him antsy—made the need to clear his name more vital than ever.

By the time Friday rolled around he was putting the finishing touches on his new living quarters.

Instead of letting it take up space in the shelter, he had removed the old iron door and built a ten-by-ten room in front of it. He added a shower stall and toilet, along with a washer and dryer, then put a door on the west side of the new room and used it for the entrance to his place. He had just hammered the last nail in the lone kitchen shelf, stopping to make sure it was level. As long as his meager assortment of dishes didn't slide off, it would suffice.

He had brought in a small refrigerator a few hours ago, and had an apartment-size cookstove that ran on propane, as well as a small wood-burning stove he'd set just inside the old entrance and vented through the new addition. He'd bought a couple of small cabinets from a used-furniture store in Mount Sterling to use for kitchen storage, and a long narrow table instead of countertops to serve dual purpose. In a short space of time he'd transformed the dark, dirty shelter into a warm, cozy place to winter.

He'd built his own bed frame at the far end of the room, and laid two regular-size mattresses end to end to accommodate his size and height. He had an old dresser and a portable rack for his clothes, and a recliner and a floor lamp for the seating area, with a red-and-brown braided rug on the floor between the recliner and his flat-screen TV.

Even if it was a snug fit for a man his size, the good feeling he got from knowing he was now living on the land that had been in his family for five generations lifted his spirit.

His stomach growled, reminding him that he hadn't eaten since early morning. There was food in his travel trailer, and as soon as his refrigerator cooled off overnight he would move it all inside. But tonight he was sleeping and eating in here, and he couldn't wait.

The fire burning in the woodstove by the door was heating the place just fine. He washed his hands at the kitchen sink, satisfied with how quickly the water drained, and was on his way out to get food when he saw a car driving up.

Meg had gone home the day after the wreck. Once her family got past the fact that she'd come out of a scary situation with very few injuries they'd backed off and let her recuperate on her own. Ryal had been noticeably silent. Although it was unlike him, it was a relief. However, she knew the day was coming when they would all find out who her rescuer had been.

She'd been at the mercy of family for food and errands as she waited for her insurance to settle up. When the money came through, Dolly took her to Mount Sterling to look at cars. Meg knew what she needed, and she knew how much she had to spend, which made the decision fairly simple. Once she found what she wanted and the dealership began the paperwork, Dolly left. A short while later, Meg drove home on her own.

Once she returned, she began counting up how many finished quilts she had and thinking about the annual quilt show she participated in every year. It opened the day after Thanksgiving and provided a large part of her yearly income.

When she went to bed that night, with Honey on a rug beside her bed, it didn't take her long to fall asleep. Between the security Quinn had added to the place and knowing Linc was but a short distance away, she felt safe.

She woke up the next morning with one thought in mind: to see Lincoln Fox. Considering what he'd done for her, it was the neighborly thing to do.

But knowing she *could* go didn't mean she had the guts to do it. It took another day before she got up the nerve and, even then, she went bearing gifts.

Meg was sick to her stomach with nerves as she drove up to where the old house used to stand. When she saw Linc walk out from what looked like a new shed, her heart skipped a beat.

She'd seen him in the dark with a fur-lined parka over his head, and she'd seen him in the shadows of her room, but this was the first time she was seeing him in the bright light of day, and there was no way to describe him without a hitch in her breath.

The tall, gangly boy she'd known had grown into a giant, and a good-looking one at that. Strong arms, long legs, shoulders wide enough for two men, and only a hint of silver in his thick, dark hair. The thought went through her mind that it was a good thing he was big and strong, because he'd come home with a heavy burden to shed.

She took a deep breath, killed the engine and got out.

"See you got yourself a new car," he said, eyeing the shiny chrome on the silver SUV.

She nodded. "It's a 2007, but new to me, and it runs well, which is all that matters."

He eyed the healing cut at the edge of her hairline. "How's your head?"

She shifted nervously from one foot to the other and then stuck her hands in her coat pockets to keep them warm. "It's good. I hope you don't mind that I just dropped in like this."

His eyes narrowed thoughtfully as he noticed a muscle tick at the corner of her eye. Damn it to hell, she was scared. He didn't know whether to be hurt or mad, but either way, he couldn't let it show.

"I don't mind at all, and you're way prettier than the sheriff."

Meg smiled, a little embarrassed by the compliment, and then she remembered why she'd come, moved back to the car and got a big garbage bag out of the backseat.

"This is for you," she said, handing it over. "It's part thank-you for saving me and part housewarming gift."

Linc smiled. "I can't remember the last time someone gave me a present. Come inside where's it warm while I open this. I want to show you what I've been doing."

When she hesitated, he remembered the fear on her face and thought she was uneasy about going inside with him.

"I'm sorry. I didn't mean to—"

"Don't apologize," she said. "I'm the one being stupid. Truth is, I don't know how to do this."

"Do what?" he asked.

"Pretend I'm not attracted to you. Pretend you're not attracted to me."

Pain for what they'd lost rolled through him in a long, continuous wave, then it passed, leaving him weak and wanting.

"Hey...I never was any good at pretending, either,

so why don't we just admit it's there and let it grow or die at its own pace?"

Relieved, she nodded.

"So come and see," he said, and led the way inside.

Eight

Meg was surprised, and then entranced by Linc's ingenuity. What she'd thought was just a shed was actually a well-insulated utility room and entryway leading into the shelter. She followed him inside. The woodstove was just to her right, putting out heat, and she held her hands to it, briefly warming them as she eyed the rest of the room.

"Linc! This is amazing! You're really good at this."

He shrugged. "It's what I do for a living."

"Construction? There's definitely a need for remodeling and new housing here, but no money to build it. You won't get much business."

"It doesn't have to be here to be viable," he said. "I have a construction company in Dallas. It's not hard to run a business like that long-distance when you have a good people working for you."

She eyed him curiously. "You have all that and yet you still came back. Why now, Linc?"

There was only one way to explain, but she would have to see to believe. He set down the package, took off his coat and started unbuttoning his shirt.

"Wait!" Meg said. "I didn't—"

"It's not what you think," Linc said as he undid the last button and dropped the shirt on the table.

Meg gasped. The scars on his chest were indescribable.

"There are more on the bottoms of my feet where it exited my body."

"Lincoln! Oh, my God! What happened to you?"

"I was electrocuted. It was a freak on-the-job accident. I was dead for four minutes before they resuscitated me. I have no memory of anything except waking up in the hospital, burned."

Her eyes welled. "When did this happen?"

"About six months ago. During the time I was healing, I kept having the same dream of my dad telling me to go home. I finally accepted it was the reason I'd come back from the dead. I was supposed to find out who really killed him and clear my name. It took a while to get well, and then a little longer to get everything lined up with my crews, but once it was done, I headed for Kentucky...and...well...here I am."

Meg kept staring at the scarring, imagining the pain he'd gone through. "I don't know what to say."

He picked up his shirt. "I'd take a simple 'welcome home' and be grateful."

She took a deep shaky breath. "Welcome home, Lincoln."

"Thanks," he said, then eyed the package. "Okay if I open this now?"

She nodded.

He untied the knot in the bag and then pushed the edges aside, revealing the blue-and-white quilt within. He carefully pulled it out, then ran his hand over the surface, tracing the tiny stitches on one of the blocks with the tip of his finger.

"Meg! Oh, wow! This is beautiful."

"Thanks. I just finished it a few days ago."

Surprise was evident in his voice. "You made this?"

"You build houses. I make quilts."

"To sell?"

She shrugged. "It's not much, but I don't need much. It's how I support myself."

"This is absolutely stunning. I know this was meant to keep me warm, but it's also going to become my new bedspread. It's too pretty to cover up. I didn't have a bedspread, but I do now."

He took it to the back of the room, and spread it over the sheets and blankets, but he didn't get the full effect of the pattern until it was completely unfolded.

"Meg! This is amazing! It looks like it's in motion."

She smiled, pleased that he appreciated her skill.

"I found the pattern in my grandma Foster's old trunk. It's the first time I've made one like this. It's called Storm at Sea."

Linc looked back at the quilt, seeing the waves and motion built into the fabric with color and print. "Yes, I see it." The corner of his mouth tilted wryly. "And it's an apt choice, considering what's ahead of me."

She frowned. "I didn't think of it like that. If you'd rather have—"

He stopped her with a touch. "Don't even think it. This is perfect, and—amazingly—long enough for my oversize bed."

Meg looked back at the bed, marveling at the size. "It's a good thing I always make my quilts extralong. How did you find a bed that big?"

He grinned. "Oh, they don't sell beds like that. I made the frame, then put two mattresses end to end."

"Good Lord! And Mama thought she had it bad raising all of us long-legged Walkers. No telling how big your children will—"

She realized what she was saying too late to take it back and looked down at the floor. She was too close to him, and the bed was too close to them both, and she didn't know what she wanted more, to strip or run.

Linc wanted her in his arms. Instead, he held his ground. Saying anything at this point would make everything worse.

"I think it's time for me to go. I've already outstayed my welcome," she said, and headed for the door.

"Meg!"

She stopped, but wouldn't look at him.

"You're wrong," Linc said. "You'll never outstay your welcome with me."

The urge to turn around was so strong that she was shaking, but she kept walking. By the time she got outside, she was running. She jumped in her car and drove away—knowing no matter how fast she drove, or how far she went, she would never get far enough to make the longing go away.

Prince had been lying low in first one no-tell motel and then another, never staying in one place too long for fear the cops would find him, but he'd run into an inevitable hitch. He was down to his last thirty dollars, and since Fagan had balked at helping him, short of pulling a heist—which wasn't a good idea, considering he'd pawned his pistol for the money in his pocket—he was about to hit up another sibling for dough.

It was just after daybreak when he left his motel room. The sky was overcast and gray, the day already cold and, from the looks of the weather, bound to get colder. He just hoped it didn't snow again. It took several tries before his truck would start. When the engine finally turned over, he breathed a sigh of relief. He couldn't be broke *and* afoot. The cops would find him for sure.

Even though he knew his sister's address he'd never been to her house, but he intended to pay her a visit as soon as he got himself some food.

He stopped at a quick stop, picked up a couple of sausage-egg biscuits from the deli counter and a large coffee, then went back to his truck to eat. He kept one eye on the clock and another on the people going in and out of the store, and was down to his last few bites when a police cruiser drove up. Just seeing the black-and-white turned his stomach. He washed down the food in his mouth with a big gulp of coffee and drove away.

It took him nearly fifteen minutes to find the gated community in which Lucy lived, then another five before he located her house. He parked a few houses down to wait until her husband, Wes, left for work. As he sat, he thought about the buried money and how he could get to Meg to make her talk.

His first mistake had been in fucking with her—moving her stuff around, letting the cow out, then those damned flowers he had intended to leave on her kitchen table just to freak her out a little more before he made his move. Who knew something as simple as a squeaking floorboard could have given him away, or that she was as good a shot as her brothers? Looking back, he should have just gone to her house with some made-up story about Bobby Lewis telling her he was sorry for all he'd done to cause her trouble, then struck up a conversation with her and found out what he needed to know without all the other drama.

But the truth was, he had wanted to get in her pants. His daddy used to tell him his dick was going to get him in trouble one day, only Daddy had meant that Prince would most likely wind up running from some girl's pissed-off father, not running from the law.

He upped the fan power on the heater, wishing he had more coffee to warm his belly, too, when he realized Lucy's garage door was going up. Wes was finally leaving for work. Prince's eyes narrowed, watching as a shiny black Lincoln came backing out of the garage and down the driveway into the street. Wesley Duggan owned a car dealership in Mount Sterling and drove nothing but the best. Lucy should be good for several thousand, for sure. Prince slumped a little farther down in the seat as Wes drove past, and as soon as the car was no longer in sight, Prince pulled up into her driveway. He rang the doorbell several times and then began knocking loudly until he got results.

When his sister finally came to the door, the shock on her face was worth the wait. He grinned. Lucy was still in her robe and nightgown, and her hair was all flat on one side, like she'd just gotten out of bed. She looked like she was going to faint.

"Hello, sister. What's the matter? Aren't you gonna ask me in?"

Lucy pulled her robe tighter beneath her neck against the cold.

"What are you doing here?"

"Why, I was just in the neighborhood and stopped to pay my respects."

She gave a quick look up and down the street, then grabbed his arm and yanked him inside, out of sight.

"I smell coffee. How about you pour me a cup while we talk?" he said.

"Yeah, well, I smell shit. How about you clean your shoes next time before you step into my house?"

He glared. "Damn it, Lucy White! You come out of the same woman's belly as I did, so don't pull this high-and-mighty attitude with me. You don't want to be neighborly? Fine. You want me gone? It'll cost you five thousand."

She gasped. "Dollars?"

Prince rubbed his thumb and forefinger together under her nose in a "pay up" gesture. When Lucy slapped it away, he laughed.

"That don't change a damn thing. I need some money, sister dear, and I need it fast."

Her eyes narrowed. "What have you done?"

"That ain't none of your business."

She drew back her hand and slapped him. Hard. Within seconds she was in his face and pushing him backward toward the door.

"Just because I live in a nice house with a good, decent man doesn't mean I forgot how to fight back. You don't come into my house and threaten me. You don't come into my house and expect to blackmail me just to get you off my back. If I want you gone bad enough, I'll shoot you dead where you stand and tell the cops you were breaking into my house, that I didn't know it was you before I shot. And if you're wanting money that bad, then I'm guessing the cops are already after you and will thank me for ridding them of your sorry ass."

Prince's belly rolled. This was the Lucy he remembered, and he knew she was fully capable of what she'd threatened. He decided it was time to try another tack.

"Oh hell, Lucy, calm down. I need some money to lie low and I thought you'd be good for some. Don't worry. I'll just find a liquor store and pull a heist, and hope I don't get caught. Course, if I do, people might find out that your worthless brother robbed a liquor store, and then where would you be?"

Lucy wanted to scream, but he'd found her weakness. She'd spent her whole life trying to live down where she'd come from, and with one visit Prince could bring it all down around her head.

"I'll give you what cash I have and you'll have to be happy with that," she muttered.

"Depending on how much it is, it's a deal. But if you're short on cash, then I'm gonna be short on cash, and that heist becomes a viable possibility."

"I'll get my purse," she said, and when he went to follow her, she turned and pointed. "Stay there and don't touch anything! You hear?"

He grinned. "Yes, I hear just fine."

She ran out of the room and came back seconds later carrying a large brown purse.

Prince saw it and frowned. "That's one of them Coach purses. I know for a fact they cost a pretty penny, so you better have some cash money in it or you and me will be making a trip to your bank."

Lucy took out her wallet, grabbed all the paper money in it and flung it in his face.

"There," she screamed. "It's over six hundred dollars.

If you can't make do on that, I'll call the cops on you myself and the consequences be damned."

He frowned again. He'd pushed her too far. He got down on his knees and picked up all the cash, stuffed it in his pocket and headed for the door.

"And don't come back!" she screamed.

He slammed the door shut behind him and kept moving.

Inside, Lucy Duggan fell to her knees, then threw back her head and screamed. She'd tried hard—so hard—to keep her name above reproach, but as long as one member of her family still lived, it seemed that goal would forever be in jeopardy.

As she started to get up, she noticed a single dollar had fallen under the edge of the sofa. She crawled over on her knees and picked it up, then got up and put it back in her wallet. At least the son of a bitch didn't get it all. She started to go to the kitchen to get a cup of coffee, then turned around and went to the wet bar, poured herself a whiskey, neat, and downed it in one gulp. It burned good all the way down, so to be on the safe side she poured herself another one and knocked it back as quick as the first.

Linc woke abruptly just as his daddy was about to whisper the name of his killer in his ear. He sat up with a groan, his daddy nowhere in sight. He grabbed the TV remote and turned on the flat-screen, then lay back and flipped through channels until he found a weather report in progress. According to the forecaster, there was another storm front coming through the area, but this time without snow. He was thankful he'd finished construction and already moved in. Wintering in the travel trailer would have been a cold, miserable prospect. He started to throw back the covers, then stopped and ran his hand over the surface of the quilt Meg had given him. Knowing he'd slept beneath something she'd made gave him hope that one day he would be sleeping with her, as well.

He aimed the remote at the TV and hit Mute, then got up to check email. There were a couple of things he needed to confirm with the crew back in Dallas, and he wanted to catch the foreman before he left home.

Although the two rooms had held the heat well throughout the night, he needed to stoke up the coals and get a new fire going. He'd slept in sweatpants, but he grabbed a sweatshirt and pulled it over his head as he hurried across the floor to the stove and the wood stacked beside it.

After the fire was going he started coffee and popped a couple of slices of bread into the toaster. He got out the peanut butter and jelly, then turned on his laptop as he waited for the toast to pop up. He had an agenda today that was bound to open a floodgate of trouble, and he didn't want to be sidetracked.

The toast popped up. He made himself a sandwich, washing it down with two cups of coffee as he ran through the email, then made a call to one of his two foremen, a man named Toby Sheffield. Toby was a forty-something man with two ex-wives and four kids. He was as faithful with his child support payments as he was to the job he held with Fox Construction.

"Hey, Toby, it's me, Linc."

"Hey, boss. How goes it?"

"Finally got moved in but we're expecting some bad weather. So fill me in on the project."

"It's good. I fired Ortiz."

Linc frowned. "Why?"

"Stealing."

"Shit. Make sure he doesn't come back and try it a second time out of spite."

"Already on it," Toby said. "We poured concrete all day yesterday. As soon as it cures up another day or so, we'll start framing."

"Have you talked to Gerald about the other job site?"

"Yeah, last night. He said to tell you that the geological report on the subsoil came back. We're in the clear, and the city inspector who was raising hell is now off our back."

"Good. That's what I like to hear. I'm going to be out and about today, but you have my cell number. Call if you need me."

"Yeah, sure," Toby said, and then added, "Hey, boss. Are you really gonna stay there?"

"I'm for sure staying until I finish what I came to do, but the road to Dallas runs both ways. I'll be there off and on. Have no fear."

"Okay...so, take care and good luck."

"Thanks. Talk to you later."

He hung up, made himself another sandwich and ate quickly, anxious to get down to Boone's Gap before he changed his mind. Just before he left he sat down on the sofa and made a call to Aunt Tildy. She answered on the first ring.

"Hello?"

Linc grinned. "Hey, Aunt Tildy, it's me, Linc. You must have been sitting on that phone."

"I was just walking down the hall with a load of clean

towels. I'll admit it startled me some when it went to ringing."

He chuckled. "Sorry about that. I won't keep you, but I was wondering if you'd talked to your friend Beulah since we were up there. Has the propane been delivered?"

"Yes, I went up yesterday to check on her. Her aches are better, and her house was just as warm as could be. She had a fire going in the fireplace, stew cooking on her stove, and her heating stove burning, as well. She said she felt like a plutocrat, with all that luxury."

"Good. I couldn't help but worry about her. She's sure a little bitty thing, isn't she?"

Tildy laughed. "Honey, compared to you, we're all little bitty."

Linc laughed again. "I guess you're right about that. Oh…one other thing, but I wanted you to know. I'm going down to Sheriff Marlow's office this morning to get copies of the file they have on me. I barely remember anything after the house exploded."

He heard Tildy sigh.

"So you're ready to stir the pot, are you?"

"Yes, I'm ready."

"I'm behind you all the way, boy. If you need anything, all you have to do is ask. Marcus was my brother. I loved him dearly, and I'd like to see his killers pay."

Linc frowned. "Killers? I never thought of the guilty party as plural. Why do you?"

"You're a big man, Lincoln, and so was Marcus. It would take more than one man to put him down."

Linc's stomach turned. "I wish the law had talked to you before they decided to arrest me."

"Oh, the sheriff heard everything I had to say, just

like he stood and listened to what your granddaddy was saying about you being at his place all afternoon. He said it wouldn't make any never-mind to the jury, because we were your kin and would say anything to get you off, even though we kept saying we would never lie to protect Marcus's killer, no matter who it was."

Linc frowned. He'd been railroaded, but why?

"Wow. Between him and my public defender, they already had me guilty as charged before the trial ever started."

"There's stuff to be told, for sure," Tildy said. "Don't forget, once you open this can of worms, you'll need to start watching your back. If the killers still live here, they won't want this rehashed."

"Yes, ma'am. I will. So let me know if you need anything, will you?"

"And you the same," Tildy said.

He hung up, dropped his phone in his pocket, then grabbed his coat and headed out the door, taking care to lock it behind him.

Meg felt aimless. She had two more quilts in different stages of progress. One had the batting and backing attached and was already on the quilt frame, so that if she got tired of cutting and sewing blocks she could sit and quilt for a while. But she had gotten up this morning feeling her life was in a loop, running over and over doing the same daily things: feeding chickens, sewing, feeding Honey, then going to bed and getting up the next day to repeat the tasks.

Just the effort it took to cook something decent to eat was beyond her. Ever since her mother had moved out, she'd gotten in the habit of eating on the run, and never at regular times. Sometimes she wouldn't eat breakfast until nearly noon, then wouldn't eat dinner at all and instead snack on whatever was easiest to make for supper. She needed some order in her life. She needed to get out of her rut and knew the only way to make something happen was to change what she'd been doing. After a quick check of the pantry it became obvious that if she was going to cook, she needed more than cans of soup and packets of tuna.

Honey followed her through the house, her head down, her eyes sad and droopy. Meg realized the dog was picking up on her attitude, and that made her feel even guiltier than ever. She sat down on the side of the bed, and Honey immediately sat down on her feet.

Meg laughed and quickly patted the dog's head, then gave her ear a quick scratch.

"You look as mopey as I feel," she said.

Honey looked up with her big brown eyes and then licked Meg's fingers.

"Well, thank you," Meg said. "I needed that good-morning kiss. *And* I need to go get groceries. Wanna go for a ride?"

Honey stood abruptly, wagging her tail and looking toward the hall.

"Give me a couple of minutes to brush my hair and put on some warmer shoes."

While Meg began to change, Honey sat in the doorway, making sure she didn't get left behind.

Meg put on a red sweater and jeans and then slipped into her brown fur-lined boots. She started to tie her hair back and then decided to leave it down. It would be warmer that way. She eyed herself in the dresser mirror, then finished the look with a swipe of lipstick called

Ripe Tomato, picked up her shoulder bag and headed for the living room with Honey at her heels. She paused in the hall to get her coat and stopped at the door to set the security alarm, and then they were on their way.

The cold air was a slap-in-the-face reminder of the winter that was almost upon them. She walked the length of the porch to the attached carport, and then took the steps down two at a time and opened the back door of her car.

"Get in, Honey," she said, and laughed when Honey barked. "You're right. We've been hibernating alone too long when we get excited about a simple trip to the grocery store."

As soon as the dog was inside Meg got into the driver's seat and buckled up. Just the act of driving away from the house made her feel she was stepping out of a shadow.

When she reached the main road her thoughts went to Linc. She wondered what he was doing, if he'd started his investigation, and wondered if she would fit into the world he'd made for himself, or if she should stay back and consider him a part of her past.

About two miles from her house she met her brother James going up the mountain on his mail route. She honked and waved. He waved back and made a goofy face at her, which was typical. It set the mood for the rest of the trip. With Honey's hot breath on the back of her neck and the idea that she was about to shift her attitude and focus, she was feeling good by the time she reached Boone's Gap.

The small town was unusually busy, which she attributed to people stocking up in case weather and bad roads changed their options. She parked at Barney's Groceries and gave Honey a command.

"Stay, Honey."

The dog immediately dropped into the backseat and laid her head on her paws. By the time Meg got out and locked her door, the dog's eyes were closed. Meg headed for the store with a bounce in her step that set her long hair swinging. To the eye, she was a tall, pretty woman on the go. Only she knew the turmoil in her heart.

She walked inside, waving at Louise, the checkout clerk.

"Meg! Good to see you out and about. Did you get healed up okay?"

"Yes, I did, Louise, and thank you for asking."

"They catch that good-for-nothing Prince White yet?"

"No, not yet."

"You be careful," Louise said. "People like him are wild cards. You never know how they're going to behave."

"That's for sure," Meg said. "It still doesn't make sense why he'd fixate on me after all these years."

Louise shrugged. "Probably got drunk one night and let old wounds get the best of him. But no matter. He's history. You go on and do your shopping, and pay attention in the produce aisle. We got bananas on sale. To my mind they're a little too ripe for eating, but they're just right for banana bread or banana pudding."

"Thanks," Meg said, and walked away smiling. Bigger grocery stores had large banners hanging from the ceilings and big Sale signs sticking up on all their displays. Barney's had Louise.

She hadn't made a list, so she began going down each aisle slowly, checking out what was on the shelves and adding items to her cart when the mood arose. She'd been there almost thirty minutes and was think-

ing about Honey waiting for her in the car when she
heard someone whisper her name.

Sheriff Marlow was finishing up the paperwork to
release Bo and Pete, the local drunks he'd arrested after
a crash. They'd both bonded out, and were now sober
and penitent, sorry as they could be with their decision
to break into the Church of the Firstborn to bathe in
the baptismal font so that when they went home, their
wives wouldn't know they'd been drinking. He signed
his name, handed a copy of the paperwork to the bonds-
man and then told the jailer to let them go. A few moments later they came out, still apologizing to anyone
who would listen.

Thinking he would finally get a chance to finish the
breakfast he'd been trying to eat for the past two hours,
Marlow picked up his ham-and-egg sandwich and sat
down with a thump. Just as he was about to take a big
bite, the door opened. He saw the man walking in and
wrapped the sandwich back up.

"Didn't expect to see you in town," he said, eyeing the
fine-looking gray Stetson and sheepskin coat Lincoln
Fox was wearing and wishing he had an outfit like it.

Linc didn't bother answering. He had an agenda, and
that was all that mattered.

"What do I need to do to get a copy of everything
in my case file?"

Marlow wasn't surprised by the question, considering why Fox had come back, but he eyed his food re-
gretfully. This was definitely going to take longer than
he would have liked.

"That was eighteen years ago," he said.

"I didn't ask how long ago it happened. I asked for a copy of the report," Linc said.

Marlow blinked. So the man was still pissed because he'd doubted his word about Prince White being the stalker.

"It's in storage somewhere in the back room."

"I'll wait," Linc said as he took off his coat and hat and sat down in a chair near the door.

Marlow sighed. "We don't have a secretary around here. I'll have to get it myself."

Linc's eyes narrowed.

Marlow sighed. "It'll take a while to find. You can come back later, if you'd like."

"I'll wait," Linc said again.

Marlow glared, picked up his sandwich and took a big bite as he walked out of the room.

Linc glared at his retreating back. He didn't care how pissed off the sheriff got.

He could hear voices coming from the back, then a lot of doors banging and the sounds of furniture or boxes being moved. He eyed a Wanted poster tacked up on a corkboard behind Marlow's desk and then folded his arms across his chest and leaned back in his chair.

Fifteen minutes passed.

Two people came inside looking for the sheriff, eyed Linc curiously and then muttered something about coming back later.

Five more minutes came and went before Marlow returned, the front of his shirt and pants smeared with dust and a file clutched in his fist.

"Gotta make copies," he said, and headed for the copier.

Linc watched without comment.

Finally the duplicate was ready. Marlow slid a form across his desk and held out a pen.

"You need to sign this. It says I gave you a copy of the file."

Linc stood, put on his hat and coat, and then headed for the desk. He signed, picked up the stack of papers and slid them into the file folder the sheriff offered. "Where do I go to get a transcript of the trial?"

Marlow's eyes widened. Fox wasn't messing around.

"The courthouse in Mount Sterling. If it was me, I'd call ahead so they'd have time to find it and all. Eighteen years is a—"

"Long damn time, especially if you were living in my shoes," Linc said softly, and walked out the door, letting the wind slam it behind him.

Marlow flinched and then sighed. This was going to cause trouble. He could feel it.

Nine

Resisting the urge to read through it right now, Linc slid the file onto the seat beside him and drove to a Quik Stop to get gas. The wind was sharp as he got out of the truck. He settled his Stetson and tilted his head into the wind as he reached for the nozzle. A couple of men eyed him curiously as they parked on the other side of the pumps. He knew he looked more cowboy than local. So much the better. One man even caught his eye and nodded cordially. It was obvious no one recognized him—yet. When he went inside to pay, he handed the clerk even change and walked out without making eye contact, then drove down the street to Barney's. He only needed a few items. Surely he could get in and out without raising too many eyebrows, although it was damn hard to be insignificant when you stood six foot eight.

The grocery was small, the merchandise limited, but Linc wasn't hard to please. Bread, milk, eggs, cheese, lunch meat and cookies. The rest he could get in Mount Sterling next time he went. He hit the meat and dairy aisle first, and quickly cleared four items off his list. He was heading for the bread aisle when he saw her.

"Hey, Meg," he said softly.

She looked up, saw the hat and then the face beneath it, towering head and shoulders above the endcap. She grinned.

"What are we having for supper?" he asked in a teasing manner.

And just like that, she felt the world open up before her. This was it. This was the answer to what she'd been feeling. All she had to do was go for it. So she did.

She arched an eyebrow. "What do you want to eat?"

Linc's heart skipped a beat. Was she flirting? "Uh... pork chops?"

"I can do that," she said. "When are you free?"

He couldn't believe this was happening. Not after the way she'd left the other day.

"Uh...tonight?"

She nodded. "Sure. Why not?"

Now he was past curious. "Are you serious?"

"I am if you want me to be."

He grinned. "Six o'clock good for you?"

She nodded again.

"Want me to bring anything?"

"Your appetite?"

"Then we're set, because I don't go anywhere without it."

And just like that, he had a date.

All of a sudden he realized Meg was wheeling her basket around.

"Hey, where are you going?"

"To get pork chops."

"Oh. Right. So I'll see you later?"

The last sight he had of her face, she was smiling.

He grabbed a loaf of bread, moved to the end of the

aisle and threw a couple of packages of Oreos into the cart, and headed for the checkout with a bounce in his step. Not even that file full of riddles riding shotgun beside him could ruin the good mood he was in.

Meg's hands were shaking by the time she got to the checkout. She was still in shock at the brazen way she'd just conducted herself. She'd heard of women picking up guys in a bar, but not in the bread aisle at Barney's, and she was hoping the little interlude had not been overheard. She would never hear the end of it, if it had.

"Hey, Meg, how's it going?" Louise said as she began scanning the items from Meg's cart.

"Just staying busy making quilts. You know how it goes."

Louise nodded as she picked up the first package of pork chops and scanned it. When she picked up the second package, she paused.

"Reckon this will be enough? That's a real big fellow you're about to feed."

Meg sighed. So much for not being overheard. "Yes, I'm sure."

"He's a looker, that one," Louise said as she continued scanning.

"Uh, yes, I guess he is," Meg said. "Oh, wait. I have a coupon for that." She pointed to a big can of pineapple rings. She dug the coupon out of her purse and gave it to Louise.

"Gonna make pineapple upside-down cake for dessert?" Louise asked. "My man likes his sweets after a meal, too. Oh, by the way, I didn't hear you call his name."

Meg was writing a check and pretended not to hear.

By the time Louise handed her the receipt, she was ready to bolt.

"Hey, Meg. Wait up," Louise called as Meg headed for the door.

"Gotta hurry or this ice cream will melt," Meg said, and kept on moving.

She quickly transferred the sacks to the hatch of her new SUV, gave Honey a pat and praise for being such a good girl and then headed home. It wasn't until she was driving out of town that she began to smile. Her life was taking a turn for the better, and all she could think was that it was about damn time.

Most days Wesley Duggan considered himself a fortunate man. He had himself a pretty wife and a business that was making good money. He'd gone from hiring on as a car salesman at the Ford dealership in Mount Sterling to owning it ten years later.

He'd tried to call his wife off and on all morning, but without any luck. He'd assumed she was simply out shopping and hadn't heard her cell ring, but when lunch came and went and she hadn't called back, he decided to go home to eat and make sure she was all right. She'd been in bed asleep when he left, and she might be sick.

He wheeled into their driveway, tapped the garage-door opener and drove inside. He was thinking about making a sandwich with some of that baked ham left over from Wednesday night's dinner when he entered the kitchen, but the moment he walked in, he knew something was wrong. There was an empty liquor bottle on the kitchen island and a bowl of melting ice cubes on the counter.

"What the hell?"

He strode through the house, yelling, "Lucy! Lucy! Where are you?"

She stepped out of their bedroom into the hall in her bare feet. Her hair was awry and she was still in her nightgown, but the glass in her hand was full of ice and whiskey. He could smell it from where he was standing.

"What the hell's wrong with you?"

She swung her glass up in the air as if she was about to make a toast and then began to laugh. The hollow sound was anything but funny. He grabbed her by the arms and gave her a little shake, and when he did, part of the whiskey splashed onto his pant leg and then his shoe.

"Damn it, Lucy! I thought you'd put this kind of drinking behind you."

"I can't put anything behind me," she said, and then started to bawl. "No matter how good I try to be, or how hard I try to make everything pretty and nice, it all turns to shit."

Wes frowned, then took the glass out of her hands, set it aside and pulled her into his arms.

"Talk to me, honey. Tell me what's wrong and I'll make it all go away."

She buried her face against the front of his suit coat. "You can't. I'm cursed by the blood running through my veins, and there's nothing you can do to fix it or me."

The mention of the blood in her veins was all it took. "Who was here? Prince or Fagan?"

"It was Prince!" she cried, and then let out a wail. "He's running from the law about something, and he coerced me into giving him all my money or else he was going to rob some store. He said if he got caught then everyone would know he was my kin."

Wes's eyes narrowed angrily. "The sorry little bastard. Did he say where he was staying? I'll teach him to threaten you!"

"No. I don't know anything except that I gave him about six hundred dollars and told him if he came back I'd kill him and tell the cops it was self-defense."

Wes rocked her where she stood, feeling sorry for her misery and at the same time so damned pissed off at his worthless brother-in-law that he couldn't think.

"There, there," he said, patting her on the back and smoothing the wild hair away from her face. "Let's get you out of that gown and into some nice warm sweats. I'll go make us some sandwiches and coffee while you clean up a bit. It's gonna be okay, Lucy Bee. You'll see. He won't come back, but if he does, I'll tend to him then."

It was the pet name he used that touched her heart. Even when she'd been married to her first husband, Marcus, she'd been Wesley's Lucy Bee.

"Yes, give me a few minutes to clean up," she muttered, shoving her hair out of her eyes and smoothing her hands down the front of her gown.

Wes kissed her cheek and left, taking the half-finished glass of whiskey with him and downing it on the way to the kitchen. By the time Lucy got there he had sandwiches made and hot coffee in the pot, and was thawing a half of a coconut cake that he'd found in the freezer.

She paused in the doorway, eyeing the spread, and then sniffled to remind him she was still upset.

"My sweet Wesley...you are such a good man," she said.

He turned and gave her the once-over. She didn't even look like the same woman from a few minutes ago. Her sweats were a robin's-egg blue, and her long blond hair was pulled back in a neat ponytail and fastened at the nape of her neck. She had on just enough makeup to take away the pale tinge in her skin, but when she blinked, he could still see tears.

"Come sit with me," he said, and held out his hand.

She offered her cheek for a kiss, which he dutifully gave, and then she sat in the chair he'd pulled out for her. She was a lifetime away from the way she'd been raised and wasn't ever going back, no matter what it took.

"Would you rather have ham or turkey, Lucy Bee? I made some of both," he said as he handed her the platter of sandwiches.

"I think turkey," she said as she took a half sandwich from the platter and put it on her plate. "I don't want to ruin my girlish figure."

He winked. "Your figure is perfect—just like you."

Perfect? Lucy blinked as a memory slid through her mind so fast she could almost have imagined it never happened. She took a bite of her sandwich, chewing and swallowing before she spoke.

"How was your morning? Everything going okay at the dealership?"

"Yes, everything is fine," he said. "Want some chips?"

"A few," she said, and slid her plate toward the sack of chips he was holding and then took a quick sip of her coffee.

Wes watched her closely, making sure her meltdown had safely passed. He didn't want to go back to work and think she would fall back in the bottle. He had known Lucy all his life. He'd been in love with her since the age of fourteen, and when she'd married his best friend,

Marcus, a few years later, he'd nearly died. When Marcus and Lucy began having troubles, he'd shamelessly stepped in as the shoulder she needed to cry on, and when Marcus was murdered, he'd felt joy that she was free instead of grief that his friend was dead.

He downed half a sandwich and reached for another, as well as a few more chips.

"Do you think you're going to be all right if I go back to work?"

She nodded. "Yes, and I promise I won't drive anywhere. I've had too much to drink to get behind the wheel. Thank you for worrying about me, but I'll be okay. It was just the shock of seeing Prince and then being threatened like that."

She shuddered, which pissed Wes off all over again.

"If he comes back, don't let him in," he said.

"Oh, don't worry. I won't. But I doubt he'll be back. I made it pretty clear that I'd call the cops on him myself if he did."

"I wonder what he did," he said.

"I don't want to know," she said, and got up to refill her coffee, then tested the cake he'd set out. "Do you want some cake? It's thawed enough to slice."

"Yes, please."

She cut two pieces and carried them back to the table, then watched him take the first bite.

"Is it still good?"

He rolled his eyes. "No, Lucy Bee, it's not good, it's *amazing.*"

Lucy smiled. It was good to be appreciated.

Linc set his groceries on the table, dropped the file on the sofa as he walked past, then took off his coat and hat and left them on the bed. The quilt reminded him of Meg and the fact that he was going to eat supper at her house tonight. He was still a bit surprised that she'd invited him and hoped he wasn't reading too much into the offer.

He started a pot of coffee, then put away the groceries, except for the cookies. He grabbed a handful and headed for the sofa. He popped a cookie in his mouth and began chewing as he reached for the file. It was weird that he had no idea what was in these reports, and yet they were part of what had put him in prison. It didn't take long to get caught up in the cut-and-dried sentences, although they were shockingly sparse. How could such a traumatic event be captured in such emotionless words?

Call to suspicious fire at the residence of Marcus Fox.

Empty gas can found behind a shed.

Body of a male believed to be M. Fox found just inside the back door.

Teenage son, Lincoln Fox, found on his back beside his truck, unconscious, with blast burns on exposed skin.

Linc stopped, too shaky to keep reading, and got up to pour himself a cup of coffee. He walked outside to get some air, relishing the slap of cold against his skin, and watched a hawk circling in the sky overhead. The quiet here was still something remarkable to him. Coming back was good for more than clearing his name. It was refilling his soul. He stood until his coffee was cool enough to drink before he went inside.

It had been a very long time since he'd let himself "go there," but reading the reports brought back every moment of the nightmare and made it difficult to stay objective. He took a drink, popped another cookie in his mouth and kept reading.

Arrived on scene at 8:37 p.m. Neighbors in the act of fighting the fire. See attached list for names and numbers.

He flipped through the pages until he found the list and quickly scanned it. He knew the people but didn't remember a one of them being there. All he could remember was someone shouting his name as he lay there looking up into a night sky blanketed with stars, and then the silhouette of some man blocking his view. He felt the heat before he saw the fire, and when he tried to get up he passed out again. That was all he remembered before waking up in a hospital bed with his grandpa holding his hand and Aunt Tildy standing at the foot of his bed crying. She was the one who'd told him his dad was dead.

A couple of names caught his eye, and then he leaned forward, a little surprised to see them bunched together. Dolly Walker. Margaret Walker. Ryal Walker. Prince White. Wendell White. It took him a few minutes to realize they were listed in alphabetical order.

He stared at Meg's name. He'd had no idea she was there.

He went back to reading and found a note penned in the margin near the bottom, almost as an afterthought.

Wayne Fox and grandson Lincoln Fox fishing all afternoon. Lincoln Fox at grandfather's house until approx 7:30 p.m.

He scanned the report, trying to find when they'd gotten the call about the fire and found a note where the call had come into the sheriff's office at 8:15 p.m. Then he searched for a report from the fire department as to when the fire had started, but there was nothing else.

It figured. This was Rebel Ridge, not Dallas. There was no fire marshal to run an arson test. Just the word of bystanders who found an empty gas can. Then another bit of info surprised him. Fagan White was the one who'd called in the fire to the sheriff's office. He went back and read the names on the list of witnesses at the fire. How did the one brother who wasn't there become the one to call in the fire? This deserved some investigation for sure.

Granted, his stepmother, Lucy, was their sister, and they'd been at the house a time or two before. But he knew for a fact that Lucy didn't like them coming over, and she had left early that morning for a family funeral on the other side of Lexington. Her brothers would have known that she was gone. Why hadn't they gone, too? They wouldn't have been dropping by to visit, knowing full well she wasn't there. Still, he guessed if they'd been driving by, they could have seen the fire. The house wasn't that far off the road, and Linc remembered that he'd seen the glow of the flames before he got there, too.

He closed the file, then laid it aside. He would read more later, but right now he needed to do something to take his mind off the past, and there were several hours to kill until his supper date with Meg. He changed into his work clothes and headed for the door. He had a rick of wood to haul to Aunt Tildy's, and he wanted to talk to her about what he'd read. He glanced up at the sky as he got in the truck. It looked like that storm was coming for sure. He just hoped whatever came out of those clouds stayed liquid.

A short while later he pulled up to his aunt's house

and hit the brakes. There were three pickup trucks in the front yard. Unless she was having an impromptu party, he was guessing there were some sick or injured people in her house. Rather than block anyone's exit, he drove around to the back to park, then went in the back door and found her and three men standing around the kitchen table.

"Aunt Tildy?"

She looked up and when she stepped aside Linc saw the trembling man stretched out on an old oilcloth on top of her kitchen table, caught up in coils of barbed wire.

"Come in, son. George here got himself in something of a fix. Do you happen to have some wire cutters in your truck? We could use another pair."

"Yes, ma'am," he said, and hurried back outside.

He came back on the run, shed his coat, put on a pair of leather gloves and slipped into place around the table where the others were methodically cutting away the rusting barbs from George's clothes and skin.

The others gave him a quick look and nodded, but they were too caught up in helping their friend to pay him much attention.

The pain on George's face was as obvious as the tears on his cheeks.

Tildy pointed at the coils still wrapped around the man's head and shoulders.

"We've figured ourselves out something of a system here. If you make a cut down close to the wire beneath him and then hang on to the wire that comes loose it will work better. Then cut off what you're holding on to as far down as you can without making it worse. Lay what you cut away on that pile on the floor."

He got what she meant and glanced down at the man. "I'm real sorry," he said. "I'll try not to hurt you."

"You can't do much worse than what I already done to myself," George said. "It's the last time I'll ride a four-wheeler, I can tell you that for sure."

Tildy paused to stretch a kink out of her neck, adding even more to the explanation.

"George was out hunting. Thought he was just riding through a brushy patch and didn't know it was an old fencerow. The posts had rotted away, but the wire was still caught up in the underbrush. I'm guessing from the amount of wire we been cuttin' off that it was a four-wire fence. He's lucky it didn't blind him or cut a major artery, and even more lucky that his son was following a short distance behind in the truck. His family tried to get it off, but there was some wrapped too tight against that big vein in his neck, so they brought him to me."

"I know some about accidents," Linc said softly as he made the first cut. George was shaking so hard it was difficult to separate the wires, and Linc knew it was from a mixture of shock and of pain. He kept talking, hoping it would help distract the man. "I work construction myself. Had an on-the-job accident about six months ago. Got myself electrocuted. I'm here to tell you that dying isn't so bad."

George's eyes widened. "You sure nuff died?"

"Yes, I did," Linc said as he snipped another length of barbed wire loose and dropped it into the pile near the wall. "The bolt of electricity knocked me down, and went straight through my body and out my boots. They said I was flatlined for more than four minutes. I woke up in the E.R. with some big time burns and no memory of how I got there."

The man standing beside Tildy paused. "Did you see the light? You know…the one they say everybody sees when they have one of them near-death experiences?"

Linc made another cut, then held the wire firmly until he had snipped it away.

"No. I didn't see the light. But I saw my daddy."

"Is your daddy dead?" George asked.

Linc nodded. "Since I was seventeen."

Now everyone was caught up in the story, and Tildy caught Linc's eye and nodded her approval as she quickly went to work cutting away the wire wrapped around George's crotch while he was distracted.

One of the other men spoke up. "What did your daddy say?"

Linc paused. "He told me to go home, so I did. That's why I'm here."

"So you're from here?" George asked.

Linc nodded but didn't add anything further.

Silence followed as they all kept cutting, but the story had bonded the man on the table with the stranger in their midst. It was nearly an hour later before they finished.

"That's the last of it," Tildy said as she dropped the bit she'd pulled off onto the pile.

"I'll get this out of your house, Aunt Tildy," one of the men said, and wrapped it up in a bundle with a roll of masking tape and carried it out to his truck.

George was still trembling from pain and shock, but he wasn't spewing blood from any important veins, and that was what mattered.

Tildy handed him a tin of salve.

"You go straight home, take a hot shower and make sure you wash all these punctures and cuts up real good.

Have your wife put some of this ointment on every place the skin was opened, and then get yourself down to the doctor for a tetanus shot. All of this misery will have been for nothing if you go and die on us."

George shuddered as he stood up. "Yes, ma'am." He pulled out his wallet and handed Tildy a ten-dollar bill. "I know it ain't much, but it's what I got. You're a life-saver, Aunt Tildy, and that's a fact."

Tildy took the money and put it in her pocket. "I'm happy to help."

George started to take a step, and then his legs went out from under him. Linc caught him before he fell.

"Well, hell, that was embarrassing," George said.

"Adrenaline crashing," Linc said, and slid an arm around his waist. "I'll walk you out to your ride, okay?"

George was shamefaced that he was wobbling like a drunk, but he took Linc up on the offer.

"I thank you," he said as, with Linc's help, he followed his friends out to their vehicles.

"That's my boy's truck," he said, pointing to a dusty black Dodge with a dented fender. "If you can help me to it, I'd be obliged."

"Sure thing," Linc said, making sure to keep a tight grip to keep him from falling.

As soon as George was settled in the seat, Linc stepped back to close the door, but the man grabbed him by the arm.

"I never did get your name," he said.

Linc took a deep breath. Now was as good a time as any.

"My name is Lincoln Fox. But my friends call me Linc."

The man's eyes widened as he took in Linc's height and breadth.

"I'm grateful for your help, Linc," he said, and offered his hand.

A little shocked, Linc shook it, then stepped back and closed the door, and waited for them to drive away.

But George wasn't through with his questions and rolled down the window.

"About when you died…"

"What about it?" Linc asked.

"Do you reckon you know why your daddy wanted you to come home?"

"Oh, I know why. He wants justice. Someone got away with murder up here, and he sent me home to find them."

Then he turned around and walked into the house, knowing he'd just lit the match to a wildfire of gossip that would soon be springing to life. And the oddest part of it all? After all the dread and waiting for just the right time, it had come out in a moment of impulse. What was even more surprising was how light the load felt once the words had left his mouth.

Tildy was inside cleaning up the mess they'd made in her kitchen. She already had the oilcloth in the washing machine, and was scrubbing down the table and floor with a strong Lysol cleanser.

"Need some help?" Linc asked.

"No. I'm fine, Linc. This is a pretty common occurrence."

He picked up his gloves and coat. "Then I'll go on out back and unload the rick of wood I brought."

She looked up briefly and smiled. "You are a good man, Lincoln. I am so grateful that you came home."

Linc nodded. "Me, too, Aunt Tildy. It won't take long to unload. I don't suppose I could talk you into a cup of coffee when I come back?'

"Coffee and some pie," she said.

"I'll be quick," he said, and headed outside.

The air felt damp against his skin, as if it was gearing up for a downpour. He worked quickly, wanting to finish and get home before the weather changed.

When he came back inside the kitchen smelled clean, the room was warm, and coffee was dripping from the coffeemaker into the carafe below. There was a big cherry pie out on the counter, and a knife and two plates beside it. He took off his coat and was washing up at the sink when Tildy came back in the room.

"I had to get out of those clothes," she said. "They were covered in blood and rust. My, my, but that was quite a mess George got himself into, wasn't it?"

"Yes, ma'am, it was." He stepped back to watch as she cut pie and poured coffee.

"You carry the cups. I'll take the pie," she said, and headed for the table she'd covered with a fresh red-and-white gingham tablecloth.

Linc slid into a seat, remembering all the times he'd watched her do these simple tasks and taken them for granted. Life had taught him to never take anything for granted again.

When she pulled out a drawer in the sideboard for tableware, it squeaked.

"I need to rub that wood down with a bar of soap," she muttered.

"You keep a good house, Aunt Tildy."

She looked up with a smile. "Why, thank you, Lincoln! Don't wait on me. Dig into that pie, and there's more where that came from if you want it."

He took the first bite, savoring the flaky crust and sweet-tart cherries on his tongue.

"So good, but then I knew it would be," he said, and kept eating.

Tildy chattered about the day, and what she'd been drying in the herb shed and the ginseng she'd harvested earlier in the fall, and then finally she asked him what he'd been up to.

The pie was gone, and he was working on his second cup of coffee as he leaned back and began to explain.

"I went to the sheriff's office this morning and got copies of the file they had on me, then I saw Meg Lewis in the grocery store and talked myself into a supper invitation at her house tonight."

She smiled. "I'd say you've been busy. I remember you two used to be real sweet on each other when you were young. How do you feel about her now?"

He sighed. "It's hard to say. All the old feelings for her are still there, but we're different now, you know? The boy loved the girl, but I don't know if the man and woman are going to find their way back to that, or if they even should. Maybe it's about starting over. I don't know, but I'm sure interested in finding out."

Tildy reached across the table and patted his hand. "That's about as wise an answer as I could have hoped for. Take your time, I say. Know what's in front of you before you take the next step."

"Speaking of steps," Linc said. "I'm curious about some things I was reading in the file."

"Ask away. If I know the answer, I'll sure tell you."

He leaned forward, his elbows resting on the table. "You and Grandpa were at the fire."

"Before it was over, nearly everybody on this side of the mountain was at that fire."

He nodded. "I guessed that."

"You don't remember?"

"I don't remember much of anything except driving up and seeing the house engulfed. I remember running toward the house and then something exploding. I came to on the ground by my truck, flat on my back and looking up at the stars. Someone was yelling at me."

"That was your grandpa."

"Did you know that it was Fagan White who called in the fire?"

Tildy gasped. "No. I did not."

He tapped the table as he thought back through what he'd read.

"Fagan called it in, but Wendell and Prince were the only ones who came to the scene. Their names were on a witness list. And so were some of the Walkers...Dolly, Ryal and Meg."

"Oh yes, my goodness. I'd forgotten all about that. When the Walkers drove up, the house was just about gone. Meg got out, running and screaming your name. The ambulance crew was already there, loading you onto one of them stretchers. She begged and cried for them to let her go with you, but they wouldn't. And then her brother pulled her back out of the way and the ambulance left."

The hair crawled on the back of Linc's neck, thinking of how panicked she must have been. If the story had been reversed, he would have gone crazy, thinking he might lose her. As it turned out, he *had* lost her—along with everything and everyone else he held dear.

"I was thinking it was strange that the Whites would have even been in the area. I mean…they knew Dad didn't like them. They knew Lucy was gone overnight to that family funeral over by Louisville."

Tildy frowned. "There's no way to explain away what makes them men tick. Their mother was a good woman, but she married a reckless man. After he died, they fell on hard times. That was a couple of years after Marcus and Lucy married. I remember, because he used to talk to me about how worried Lucy was for her mama. Everyone knew the bank was about to foreclose on their property. Marcus had already told Lucy her mama could come live with them, but that her brothers were on their own. Then all of a sudden the bank was paid off, and Mrs. White was painting her house and building a fence around the yard to keep the chickens out of her flowers. They put up a good barn and were farming a patch of tobacco right up to the day she died. Whatever windfall they come into was a godsend for sure. Course, those worthless sons of hers let the place go to hell, especially after Wendell was killed. He was the only one with a lick of sense, and even he turned his smarts to no good."

Linc realized that he'd known nothing about all of Lucy's turmoil. She'd just been the stepmother who'd tolerated him as he had tolerated her. He filed the info away for future reference.

Tildy leaned forward. "I will tell you one other thing that I know about the Whites. There was gossip before your daddy was killed about Lucy cheatin' on him with someone local, but no one could put a name to him."

Linc frowned. "I never knew that."

"Not surprised. Your daddy wouldn't have said a word to you about it."

"You mean you think he knew about the gossip?"

"I know he did," she said.

"Do you have any idea where Lucy is now?" he asked.

Her eyes widened. "Why, I guess I thought you already knew."

"Knew what?"

"She and Wes Duggan got married about four months after your daddy was laid in his grave."

"Uncle Wesley? Married Lucy?"

Tildy shrugged. "Yes. They all grew up together. I suppose it wasn't that big a deal, but we all were guessing when it happened that it might have been him she was seeing. However, that was years ago, and time changes people."

Linc kept remembering Wes Duggan testifying on the stand about Linc and his daddy being at odds with each other. It had been the biggest shock of all in the whole chaotic trial. Wes wasn't his blood uncle, but he'd loved him like family. He hadn't understood then why Wes would lie, and he still didn't. Maybe it was time to pay Wes and Lucy a visit. Shake the tree and see how many snakes fell out of it, so to speak.

"Do you know if they're still married?" he asked.

"Oh, yes. Wes is doing well for himself. He owns the Ford dealership down in Mount Sterling, and he and Lucy live in a big fancy house in one of those gated communities."

"Thank you, Aunt Tildy. For the pie and coffee, for the information and for sticking by me."

She reached across the table and gave his hand a squeeze.

"We're family, and family sticks together." Then she winked. "And speaking of family, you tell that pretty Meg Lewis that Aunt Tildy says hello."

"Yes, ma'am. I will do that. And speaking of Meg, I better get going. There are a few other things I need to do before our supper date."

He stood up and carried their plates and cups to the sink before giving his aunt a quick hug.

"If you know of any more widow ladies or single women with houses in need of a little repair, let me know. I still have some leftover lumber and don't mind the work."

She beamed. "I'll be thinking on it some. If anyone comes to mind, I'll let you know. You have a good time tonight." Then her expression shifted to a frown. "You know, those men who were here are gonna tell everyone who you are."

"Yes. I know."

"You watch your back."

"I will. Don't worry about me. You take care of yourself, and I'll be up at eleven o'clock on Sunday morning to pick you up for dinner, remember?"

"I haven't thought of much else," she said. "See you soon, and thank you for the wood."

"You're welcome, Aunt Tildy. Take care."

He grabbed his coat and gloves on the way out, then headed home with a lot more to think about than when he'd come, like Wes and Lucy's quickie marriage, and Fagan White calling in the fire and his brothers being on the scene soon after. It was all a puzzle yet to settle into place.

Ten

Meg had a pineapple upside down cake cooling on the counter, potatoes baking in the oven and a skillet full of pork chops about ready to come out. She was trimming the fat off the last of the chops still left to fry when her phone began to ring. She grabbed a paper towel to clean her hands and propped the receiver against her ear.

"Hello?"

"Hi, Meg, it's me."

"Hi, Mom. What's up?"

"What do you mean, what's up? Can't a mother call her only daughter without having a reason?"

Meg frowned. That sounded defensive, which was weird. Why on earth would—

Oh, crap.

Dolly kept talking. "I just called to say hi. So, how's that pretty Storm at Sea quilt coming? I can't wait to see it."

Double crap.

"I finished it," Meg said. "I'm working on some other stuff. Got a new order from Louisville day before yesterday."

"Oh, that's nice."

Meg frowned. "Mom. You're about as obvious as that wart on Mrs. Peevy's nose. Just ask."

"You have a date, and you never said a word about seeing anyone. I know you're a woman grown and I don't need to know your business, but I just wanted you to know I—"

"Mom. Stop. It's obvious the mountain grapevine grows fast around here, but the reason you don't know anything is because there isn't anything to know…yet. I am not seeing anyone. I have yet to have a date. However, tonight I *am* making supper for the man who pulled me out of the wreck."

"Oh. Well. A thank-you dinner. I guess everyone just misunderstood and—"

This was about to get out of hand, and Meg knew how lies could ruin a life.

"Look, I need to tell you something, and I don't want advice—I'm just informing you of a fact."

There was a moment of silence, and then she heard a soft sigh. "If you're about to tell me that Lincoln Fox moved back to his granddaddy's home place, we already know. And if you're *finally* going to tell us that he is also the one who saved you the night of the wreck, we know that, too."

Now Meg was the one who was speechless. "But how—"

"Seriously, Margaret Ann. Give us some credit. Your brother James carries the mail—with people's names on the letters—and puts it in the mailboxes, thereby knowing where they live. And your brother Ryal made it his business to go to the E.R. and find the name of the man who saved you from the wreck, and before you get all in a huff, he did it because you said you didn't know who it was, and we wanted to thank him—which we have yet to do, by the way, because his presence seems to be a big secret."

"It wasn't my information to tell," Meg said.

"I don't understand."

"I know. I don't understand much, either, but I do know why Lincoln came home."

"What do you mean? I thought—"

"He came back to clear his name."

Total silence.

Meg held her breath. This was something they'd been through eighteen years ago, and she didn't want to hear her mother spout some "I forbid you to have any contact" crap again. To her surprise, her mother's voice was fairly calm.

"Well, it certainly took him long enough," Dolly said.

Meg sighed. "That's sort of what I said."

"So, why now?"

Meg hesitated. The more she said, the more she felt she was revealing things he might not want told, but this was her family, and they needed to understand why she was even considering the possibility of reigniting the relationship.

"Six months ago he was electrocuted in an on-the-job accident. After they resuscitated him and while he was still in the hospital, he said he began dreaming about his dad, and in every dream his father kept telling him to go home. He came back for justice, Mom. Someone on Rebel Ridge got away with murder, and he's going to open a big can of worms when he begins digging into the past. People took sides before, and they'll do it again.

But he's not a kid anymore, and I have no doubt that he's not going to stop until he gets the answers he came for."

"This could become dangerous," Dolly said.

"He knows that."

"I don't want to think about you getting hurt in—"

"Mom. Seriously? I've already been hurt by a man who has nothing to do with Lincoln Fox. If it hadn't been for Linc showing up when he did, there's no telling what would have happened to me. He stopped Prince White and set the law on his trail. I am safer right now because of him, so don't go down that road, okay? A few years back we weathered Ryal protecting Beth from the mob, for God's sake. We all went through hell with Quinn and Mariah. Can the Walker clan just please back off and let me see where this goes without trying to tell me what to do? He was my first love. I wouldn't mind it if he became my last."

Dolly sighed. "You're right. Be happy, Meg. Be safe. And bring him to Thanksgiving dinner. I've already cleared it with everyone else that we're having it on Wednesday evening instead of Thursday noon, so you can make your quilt show."

"Okay."

"If he gives you any trouble about it, remind him that because it's Thanksgiving, we want to thank the man who continues to be your knight in shining armor."

Meg's vision blurred. "Thank you, Mom."

"You're welcome. And don't cook those pork chops too early. They're best right out of the skillet."

Meg laughed through tears. The gossips had even reported what she'd bought to feed him. Lord.

"Yes, Mom, I know, and thanks." She hung up, then

dropped her head and closed her eyes. "God, please don't let this be a mistake."

She took the pork chops out of the skillet and put in the last two to cook. After a sprinkle of salt and pepper, she checked the heat, then tested the potatoes in the oven. When the last pork chops were done, the potatoes would be, too. Coleslaw was chilling in the refrigerator, and coffee was made. All she needed was a man to eat with.

Honey started barking.

A little shot of panic came and went as she glanced up at the clock. It was fifteen to six.

"Showtime."

She took off her apron, checked her blue sweater and jeans for any stray bits of flour, then started for the door, pausing at the hall mirror to check her appearance. Her eyes were still shiny from the unshed tears. Maybe he wouldn't notice.

Honey kept barking.

Meg lengthened her stride. It wouldn't be good if her dog sent him running before she got him in the door. As it turned out, her fears were groundless. When she opened the door Linc was on the porch with the dog at his feet.

"I see you've met my vicious guard dog."

Linc could hardly think what to say except what was on his mind.

"You look beautiful," he said softly, then glanced down at Honey. "Don't be upset with her. She just knows the good guys from the bad, that's all."

"Thank you," she said, and tried not to hyperventilate as he walked past her, dwarfing her by nearly a foot. "Let me take your coat and hat."

Linc took off the coat and Stetson. "Are they okay here on this chair?"

She nodded.

"Then I've got this," he said.

It took her a few seconds to focus on something besides the ripple of muscles beneath his shirt, and the width of his shoulders.

"Something smells good. Is there anything I can do to help?" he asked.

And just like that, the awkwardness was gone. "I need to turn the pork chops. You can set the table."

"Yes, ma'am. Lead the way."

His steps on the hardwood floor were sure and long as he followed her into the kitchen—as if he knew where he was going and it wasn't going to take him long to get there. Then he saw dessert and groaned.

"Oh, Lord. Pineapple upside-down cake. I haven't had that in ages."

Meg hid a smile as she pointed. "Plates are in the cabinet above the sideboard. Tableware is in the top drawer."

"Got it," he said, and began setting down their plates with an easy motion. "Oh…I want to tell you how much I appreciate that beautiful quilt. You're the last thing I think of when I pull it over me at night and the first thing I think of when I throw back the covers every morning."

Meg's heart stuttered. She felt heat rising from her neck up to her cheeks, and there wasn't a damn thing she could do to stop it. Less than two minutes in the house and he'd already made her blush.

"I'm glad it's keeping you warm."

"And then some," he said. "Are we having coffee?"

She nodded.

"Which cups do you want me to use?"

"Use the white mugs. They'll keep it warm longer."

He took down a couple and set them in the proper places, then had begun to add the knives, forks and spoons when he paused to study the design.

"I remember these," he said softly.

Meg sighed. It was inevitable that their past would resurrect itself in an infinite number of ways, but she hadn't expected him to remember her grandmother's flatware.

"It was Grandma Foster's service."

Linc paused and looked over at her, remembering a picnic dinner up at their place one Fourth of July. "Are they both gone?"

"Yes, and the old house, too."

She wasn't going to get into the fact that it had been blown up by the mob who'd been after Beth for witnessing a murder. If he stuck around, he would find all that out in good time.

"Just like my grandpa Fox and his place," he said, and finished setting the table.

Meg took up the last of the pork chops and carried the platter to the table, then went back to get the baked potatoes out of the oven.

"What next?" Linc asked.

"We'll need butter for the baked potatoes, and there's also a bowl of coleslaw in the refrigerator. If you can get both of those things, then we're good to go."

She had baked three potatoes and brought them to the table in a wide, shallow bowl, then poured coffee in the mugs while Linc added the other items to the table.

"Please tell me we're ready to eat, because I'm starving," he said.

She chuckled. "We're ready."

"Praise be," he said, and then once again surprised her by seating her first. As soon as he sat down, he reached for her hand. "I assume you still say grace?"

"Uh…yes," she said, and closed her eyes as Linc blessed the food, but she couldn't remember a thing he said for thinking of how it felt to be holding his hand. It wasn't until he said "amen" that she realized he was through.

The meal that had begun with a blessing continued with an ease she hadn't expected. By the time they got to dessert she knew all about Beulah Justice's door falling off, and that he was taking Tildy to Sunday dinner down at Frankie's Eats. He'd talked about the two crews of men who worked for him in Dallas, how many houses they'd already built this year, the name of his favorite Mexican restaurant in Dallas, and the old stray tomcat they called Chili who lived in the warehouse where Linc's equipment was stored.

She was struck by the differences in their lifestyles, and yet he'd come back to this isolated world without bemoaning the lack of amenities he'd taken for granted. She had not asked him what it had been like to be in prison until he'd turned twenty-one, and he had not mentioned a word regarding her failed marriage to a killer. It seemed they were on the same page about moving forward. It was the only option they had if this was going to work.

When he got up to carry plates to the counter, she cut the cake and refilled their cups.

"I'm assuming it's fair to ask for seconds," he asked as he took the first bite of cake. Then he rolled his eyes as he chewed. "Oh, man…make that thirds."

Meg laughed. Success was a heady thing. "You can have all you want," she said.

He paused, his fork halfway through the cake, and looked up. "Of cake."

"Is that a question or a verification?" she asked.

He grinned. "I figured it wouldn't hurt to ask."

"One thing at a time," she said.

"Right," he said, and kept eating, but the proverbial hat had just been tossed into the ring. At least he'd given her something to think about. God knows, he'd been thinking about it—a lot.

Linc was finishing his second piece of cake when they both realized the wind was rising.

Meg pushed her coffee aside and got up to look out. "That storm front is finally here."

"As long as it's liquid," Linc said, repeating what he'd been thinking earlier.

She turned around and then stopped, caught by the sight of him sitting at her table. This still didn't feel real.

He looked up and caught her staring.

"What? Got cake on my face?"

"No. I was just thinking how surreal this moment feels."

He stood and walked toward her.

She watched him coming and felt as if she'd been waiting for this moment all her life.

He cupped her cheeks, brushing a thumb across her lips.

"One of my biggest regrets was that I never got to tell you goodbye. But I'm close enough now to tell you hello."

He lowered his head slowly, giving her plenty of time to back off. Instead, she lifted her face and closed her eyes. The beginning of the kiss was a tentative foray, but it exploded into lust so fast they both stopped and pulled apart simultaneously.

Linc took a deep breath.

Meg was trembling with a need she hadn't felt in years.

"So…hello, Margaret Ann."

She sighed. "Hello, Lincoln Wade."

The wind blew rain beneath the porch roof, splattering the droplets against the glass like little bullets, but they didn't hear.

"So now what?" he asked.

She took a deep breath. "I will be honest. I would seriously like to go to bed with you."

His heartbeat slammed against his rib cage, then skittered back into rhythm.

"Why do I feel like there's a 'but' coming?"

"Do I really have to say it?" she asked.

With great reluctance, he shook his head. "No, you do not. The fact that you want to is good enough."

All the tension she'd been feeling was gone. "Thank you. Oh…I almost forgot. You're officially invited to Thanksgiving dinner at Mom and Jake's. They already knew you were back. And coming here." She rolled her eyes. "My brother James carries the mail. My brother Ryal went to the E.R. after you left and asked who brought me in. The fact that they never said a word and waited for me to tell them is still surprising. Also, we're having Thanksgiving Wednesday evening instead of Thursday noon, because I leave to go to Lexington on Thursday for a craft-and-quilt show. I'm sorry they—"

He shrugged. "It's no big deal, honey. I already let the cat out of the bag myself. If I had to guess, I'd say pretty much everybody on Rebel Ridge knows I'm back by now, and why I came."

"That's good, right?"

"Yeah, that's good. And you can tell your mother thank-you and I'll be happy to come." Then he pointed at the dirty dishes. "Now...you wash and I'll dry."

"Oh, I'll clean up after—"

"No. You cooked. I'll help clean. And while we work, can I pick your brain a little? I have copies of all the paperwork about the fire and my arrest, and a lot of questions without answers."

"I'll do anything I can to help," she said.

At that point Honey began barking. Meg jumped. Visitors were rare for her at night, and they never came without calling ahead.

Linc frowned. "Are you expecting anyone?"

"No."

"I'll go look," he said, and strode out of the kitchen, with Meg right behind him.

The security light was already on outside, and Honey was on the front porch, still barking. Even through the rain, Meg recognized the man standing beside the truck and grabbed Linc's arm.

"That's Fagan White. What in the world?"

Linc frowned. "Let him in and we'll soon find out, only don't tell him I'm here."

"He can see your truck."

"But he won't know who it belongs to. Talk to him. I won't be far. We might be able to figure out what Prince was up to."

She turned on the living room light and opened the door to a blast of cold and rain. As soon as she stepped out she grabbed Honey's collar.

"Good girl, Honey," she said. "That's enough." Then she waved Fagan up to the porch.

He came running. Once he got out of the rain, she stopped him.

"That's far enough."

Raindrops were running off Fagan's poncho onto the legs of his pants and his boots. He shifted from one foot to the other as he looked down at the dog and then at the porch ceiling above her head—anywhere but her face.

"I'm real sorry to just show up like this, and I didn't want to scare you none, especially after what my idiot brother has done."

Meg stayed in the doorway, still holding on to Honey. "What are you doing here?"

"I've been gone all day and I'm just on my way home. I intended to come by before now and tell you how sorry I am about how Prince treated you, but the time got away from me, and then the storm hit. I was about to lose my nerve and just keep driving, but I decided I couldn't sleep another night with that guilt on my soul. I had to apologize for my brother's actions."

"Okay, so you're sorry. Thank you for coming by," she said, and started to back up into the house.

Then Fagan called out, "Uh, wait up, Meg. There's another matter I wanted to speak to you about."

"And what would that be?"

"I don't know if you heard about Bobby Lewis's health, considerin' how long you two have been divorced."

"I know he's dying," she said.

Fagan nodded. "Right. So here's the deal. I've been trying to buy a piece of land for some years now that Bobby owns. I've mentioned it now and then to Claude, but he never said much, then Claude went to visit Bobby a few weeks back, and it seems Bobby has finally decided to give a bit of it up. He sent word by Claude to tell me to come see him, but I wasn't home, so Claude told Prince instead. I just found all this out after Prince lit out for parts unknown, so I went to visit Bobby myself today, but he's too sick for visitors. So I don't know exactly which piece of his land he was willing to sell… just that he's only selling enough to pay for his buryin'."

Meg listened to the rambling explanation and knew every word coming out of Fagan's mouth was a lie. She knew because Fagan had yet to look at her. He had talked to the dog. He had talked to the porch light and her left shoulder. He had done everything but meet her gaze.

"And what does this have to do with me?" she asked.

"All I know is that the piece he's willing to sell is five acres near where he supposedly buried Ike, who I was told was his favorite hunting dog. I don't suppose you would remember where that was? I'd like to take a look at it myself before I give him any kind of a bid. It might not be to my likin'."

Meg stifled a gasp. She knew exactly where that land was—right behind the old barn on the homestead. And it was proof Fagan was lying, because Bobby didn't own that land by himself. It belonged to him, Claude and their sister, Jane.

"I'm sorry, but I don't have the faintest idea. That must have happened after we were divorced."

Fagan frowned. Either she was lying to him or Prince had lied. He took a step forward.

"Are you sure? I mean—"

"She's sure," Linc said.

Fagan stopped in his tracks. The man who'd just appeared behind Meg was so big he blocked the light. *Who the hell is that?*

He began to mumble. "Uh...I didn't know you... I mean, I was just..."

Linc put his hands on Meg's shoulders and moved her gently aside, then walked right up to where Fagan was standing.

"It looks like you and your brother don't know when to stop."

"Well, here now...I didn't mean nothin' by... Uh, wait a minute! That's not true! I didn't come to hurt her. I just thought she could save me another trip back to the prison before it was too late."

"But obviously she can't. And it's time you said good-night."

Fagan shaded his eyes against the porch light as he continued to stare at Linc's face.

"You look familiar, but I can't seem to place—"

"Lincoln Fox. Tell the lady good-night."

Fagan took a quick step backward and then stumbled on the top step. He would have fallen out into the rain if Lincoln hadn't grabbed him by the arm. He didn't know whether the firm grip Lincoln had on his arm was because he'd saved him from a fall or because he wanted to break his neck.

He quickly pulled free, his heart hammering inside his chest.

"Well, it's been a long time since we seen you here. You just visiting, or you planning to stay?"

"I came home for a reason. It remains to be seen whether I stay or not afterward."

"I hope your aunt Tildy's not ailing. I don't know what we'd do up here without her tending to our ills."

"She's fine. I came back to clear my name. And while I'm thinking about it, how did you come to be the person who called in the fire at my daddy's house?"

Fagan stared. He knew he should say something, but for the life of him he couldn't think for wanting to puke. Meg's dog growled, reminding him of where he was.

"That was a long time ago. I'm not sure as how I exactly remember."

"You saw a house burning down and can't remember calling it in?"

Fagan's mind was in free fall. *What the hell was happening here?*

"Well, I didn't actually see it. I was just passing on what Wendell and Prince saw when they went to visit Lucy."

"Oh, so now you're remembering how you found out about the fire? Well, you should also know that's a piss-poor alibi. Lucy wasn't there, because of a family funeral, which you-all would have known about. Do you remember now?"

Fagan felt himself losing ground. He'd come to grill Meg Lewis, not the other way around. It was time he made himself scarce.

"I don't need no alibi. I didn't need one then. I don't need one now. I reckon I will just get on home. Real sorry to have bothered you, Meg. Y'all have a good night." And then he bolted for his truck, thankful the rain gave him the excuse to run.

Meg and Linc stood on the porch watching until the taillights disappeared. Meg took Honey inside when they closed the door. They walked back to the kitchen and began clearing the dishes.

He paused, watching as she wrapped up the leftover pork chops in foil and set them on the counter.

"Why do I feel like everything that came out of his mouth was a lie?" Linc asked.

"Because it was. Honestly, he looked like he'd seen a ghost when you gave your name. And was he really the one who called in the fire?"

Linc shrugged. "Yes, according to the police report. As for seeing a ghost, I'll probably get a lot of that in the weeks to come. I'm trying to figure out what's so important about a piece of land where a dead dog is buried."

Meg frowned. "I have no idea, but that's how I knew he was lying. I know exactly where that dog is buried, and I also know for a fact Bobby wouldn't be selling the land, because it doesn't belong to him. It's the family home place. Yes, we were living there at the time, but it belongs to all the Lewis kids—Claude, Bobby and their sister, Jane. He can't sell it."

Linc was watching her face, trying to judge her state of mind at the unexpected arrival of yet another White brother.

"I don't think he'll be back, but I don't mind staying the night—on the sofa, of course—if his visit made you nervous," he said.

"You couldn't fit on the sofa, and I'll be fine," she said as she ran the sink full of hot water, then added some soap.

He watched the running water making bubbles while contemplating the idea of reminding her that he would fit just fine if she gave him her bed. He could tell she was thinking the same thing by the quick look she gave him before thrusting her hands in the water.

She washed. He rinsed and dried. When they got down to the pans, he offered another option.

"I can live with leaving you on your own tonight, but we're going to exchange numbers. All you have to do is call if you need me. I'm the closest help you would have."

"Yes, I think that's a good idea," she said.

"Hang on a minute," he said, then took out his cell phone and entered the number she gave him into his contacts. "This is my number," he said, and quickly wrote it down on a pad by the phone.

After that they finished cleaning up, flirting, touching hands even when it wasn't necessary. The tension between them was palpable. All the while they were working, he could still hear the rain on the roof.

Meg packed up the leftover pork chops and a good third of the cake when they had finished.

"This is for you," she said.

"I won't say no," Linc said. "But there is one thing I wanted to ask you before I left."

"What's that?" she asked.

"Back before the fire, did you ever hear any gossip about Lucy cheating on my dad?"

Meg frowned. "I don't know…maybe. That sounds familiar, but it's been so long… And I wouldn't have paid much attention to anyone else's love life, because I was so wrapped up in mine."

The words tore into him like knives, poking at his conscience, reminding him of what they'd lost.

"Yeah…same here."

Suddenly she was uneasy all over again. If he kissed her now like he had before, her resistance would be nil.

"Don't look so worried," Linc said, and then opened his arms.

She walked into them without hesitation as he held her close.

"This will work itself out the way it's supposed to," he said.

She felt like crying. "I loved you so much."

His vision blurred. "I loved you, too. I'm sorry…I'm so sorry."

She leaned back in his arms so she could see his face. "We're not kids anymore."

He nodded. "We lost eighteen years. You don't know me now the way you knew me then, and I feel the same. I want to know everything there is to know about you. What makes you laugh…the music you like to listen to. I want your cold feet on my legs in the middle of the night and for you to know that when you cry, I will be there to hold you. I want you to trust me. I want you to look at me and *know* that I am an honorable man."

His words swept through Meg in a wash of emotion. It was a revelation to hear this. He had turned into a man worth keeping.

"You know I always believed you were innocent."

He put a finger across her lips, then touched his forehead to hers. Her breath was soft against his neck. He could have held her that way forever.

"The world needs to see me the way you do. You've already been tainted by other people's actions. You don't deserve to suffer that again, and I won't ask anything of you that you aren't willing to give, okay?"

She sighed. "Can we both agree that tonight was the first of more good times to come?"

"Absolutely."

She slid her arms around his waist and laid her cheek against his chest. The steady thump of his heartbeat against her ear was as reassuring as his strength

"I think it's time I said good-night," he said gruffly.

"I'm so glad you came."

"Ah, Meggie...so am I, honey. So am I."

She carried his sack of leftovers as he put on his coat and hat. When he pulled out his car keys, she followed him to the door.

Honey eyed them from her spot beside the stove, then let out a big sigh and laid her head back down.

"Drive safely going home," Meg said.

Linc centered a hard, swift kiss on her lips.

"Lock up. Set your alarms. Call me if you need me," he said, and took the sack she handed him.

Then, just like that, he was gone. She watched until his taillights disappeared, then set the alarm and moved about the house, securing it for the night. It wasn't late, but she was suddenly exhausted.

"I'm going to bed, Honey girl."

The dog looked up when she heard her name, then followed Meg down the hall and curled up on a rug beside the bed.

When Meg crawled between the covers she took comfort in Honey's soft snore. As she closed her eyes, the image of Lincoln's face slid through her mind. She sighed, wishing it was him snoring beside her and not her dog.

Eleven

Fagan drove home in something of a panic. The windshield wipers swiped aimlessly at the downpour as he took the curves on two wheels, coming dangerously close more than once to running off the road. He was frustrated with himself for paying any heed to Prince and going to Meg Lewis's house. He'd known it would be a disaster, and yet he'd done it anyway. Why, he wondered, was he made like that? Growing up, he'd been a shill for whatever Wendell and Prince wanted done. It had always been a case of tell Fagan, send Fagan, make Fagan do it. And he had yet to even contemplate what could unravel with Lincoln Fox's return. What he knew was that the Whites were sitting on a powder keg and Fox had just struck the match.

By the time he got home he was bordering on tears. In the dark and the downpour, the place looked like a Hollywood version of a haunted house. No matter how dark it got, there was no hiding how dilapidated it had become. It had been nice when Mama was still alive, but she was long gone, and the place was falling down around their ears.

The hounds barked when he drove up and parked, and were still barking as he jumped out on the run, slogging through the mud and puddles to get to the porch.

"Shut the hell up!" he yelled.

They slunk off into the dark as he unlocked the door. He turned on the lights as he went through the rooms, turned up the flame on the heat stove, then stood shivering before it as he began shedding his wet clothes. His skinny shanks were a pale, pasty white as he bolted down the hall, knowing a hot shower and something warm in his belly would fix his immediate needs.

A short while later he came out in dry, somewhat-clean clothes and a pair of mismatched house shoes— one blue plaid and one a solid brown—because his dogs had chewed up the mates. He turned on the television and upped the volume so that he could hear it from the kitchen as he worked.

As he dug through the pantry, it was apparent he should have shopped for groceries instead of hanging out at the bar all day trying to drink up enough courage to face Meg Lewis. The shelves were pitifully low on food.

Once he had coffee brewing and a can of chili heating on the stove, he made a call to Prince, needing to inform his brother of the latest development on Rebel Ridge, but, like always, Prince didn't answer and the call went to voice mail.

"Call me, damn it! There's trouble afoot."

Long after Meg had gone to bed, she lay sleepless and staring up at the ceiling, going over and over the conversation she'd had with Fagan White. Why would he lie about something so trivial? How did a dead dog matter to the Whites, or the location of where it was buried? And did Prince's behavior have anything to do with what Fagan wanted to know?

She finally fell asleep, dreaming about Lincoln and cake and crying in the rain as he drove away, begging him to come back. When she woke it was already daylight and the rainstorm had passed. She threw back the covers and began to get dressed.

The day after Thanksgiving was the beginning of Christmas shopping, which also meant it was the first day of the annual Christmas craft-and-quilt show in Lexington.

Today was Saturday. She needed to be packed and ready to leave on Thursday morning. She would have to be at the fairgrounds on Friday before daylight to set up her booth, but it was part of the fun, seeing other quilters and crafters, and getting in a quick visit before the doors opened to the public.

She got dressed, turned up the fires to warm the house back up and headed to the kitchen to make coffee so that it would be done when she came back from feeding the animals. As she was filling the carafe with water, she noticed the notepad with Linc's phone number written on it and smiled, thinking of their days to come.

Linc went to bed with Meg on his mind, reliving every bit of conversation they'd had and, for the first time in years, feeling hopeful about his future. He'd nearly given up on ever having a wife and family, and was so elated from the evening he'd spent with her that he could hardly close his eyes. But he had a big day planned tomorrow and knew it wouldn't be easy. Now that he'd seen the reports on the fire from the police point of view, he wanted to go back to the scene of the crime—to the place where his father had died. He thought he wouldn't sleep, but once he closed his eyes he slept like the dead for the first time in months.

It was the frantic sound of a dog barking madly that woke him up the next morning. It took a couple of seconds to remember he didn't have a dog, and then he ran to the utility room to look out the window.

The ground was white with frost, and three deer were grazing in the clearing where the old house once stood. He had been dreaming after all. The deer wouldn't still be here if a dog had been barking that close to the house, although the sound had seemed so real.

But now that he was up he shifted into mental gear. After a quick trip to the bathroom he built a new fire and started the coffee. He was having pineapple upside-down cake for breakfast, and at least a quart of coffee as a chaser to buck him up for the day ahead.

Less than an hour later he was on the road and heading up the mountain. The sun had yet to top the trees, deepening the shadows in the underbrush. Lingering mist that had been low to the ground was head-high and rising, giving the trip a ghostly feel. Spindly strands of gray smoke spiraled upward from the chimneys of the houses as he passed. He thought of the families just waking up and breakfasts being put on tables. It was Saturday, so no school. He remembered watching cartoons on Saturday mornings and his mother telling him to come eat before it got cold. She'd died right after his ninth birthday, and he didn't think of her often. Sometimes she didn't even seem real. It had always been him and his dad, the man who was his safe place to fall. That people could ever have believed he would kill the father he worshipped was just as inconceivable now as it had been then.

He passed Aunt Tildy's house, saw smoke coming out of her chimney and knew she was probably making biscuits and ham. He could almost taste them. She did have a way with bread. As he drove on farther he passed the house where Beulah Justice lived. There wasn't any smoke coming out of her chimney. Maybe Beulah was the kind who liked to sleep in.

When he finally reached the turnoff leading up to where his parents' house once stood he tapped the brakes, then accelerated into the turn. It was immediately obvious that no one traveled this way anymore. Weeds and grass had grown up in the middle of the old ruts, and the trees that had once been saplings on either side of the road were so huge that their leafless branches had come together, turning the road into a wood-roofed tunnel. He hadn't been back here since the night they'd taken him away in the ambulance, and his heart was racing. He caught a glimpse of something darting out of the brush behind him and glanced up in the rearview mirror just as a big deer disappeared into the woods. Then he caught sight of himself and quickly looked away. He wasn't ready to see what he was feeling and knew it would be all over his face.

All of a sudden he was out of the tunnel and coming up on the site where the house had been. There was no longer a yard, just knee-high brush and grass. The blackened timbers were nearly gone, long rotted away by time and weather. But the natural rock fireplace that had once been the entire north wall of the living room still stood, a sad monument to the family who'd lived and died there.

He drove as close to the house site as he dared and then got out, minding his step as he walked through the damp, frosty grass all the way to the chimney. He stopped and then turned around, looking east out across the overgrown meadow into the sun just topping the trees, and that flash of light in his eyes brought back that night and the fire in a painful rush.

Fire! Oh, my God, our house is on fire! Dad! Dad! Please, God, don't let him be inside.

With adrenaline pumping, he got out on the run, charging toward the house. There was a dog — a hound—barking somewhere nearby, barking crazy loud like they do when they're threatened.

We don't have a dog.

He heard someone yell, "Shut the hell up!" and then the world exploded.

Linc stumbled and caught himself on the chimney before he fell. Now the weird dream he'd had this morning made sense. Knowing he was coming here had released a memory from the past that he'd forgotten. He'd been so concussed by the explosion and then in such complete shock at his ensuing arrest that he'd completely forgotten he'd ever heard it.

But he was getting the picture now.

People on Rebel Ridge didn't let their hunting dogs run free. They considered them valuable property that could be in danger of being stolen or sold. They usually kept them in the house, in a pen or tied up—unless, of course, they were hunting.

Back then, their closest neighbor had lived five miles away, but someone had been here that night—someone with a hound—watching the evidence of their crime go up in flames. Even if it wasn't the killer, he could have seen who did it. But if he was innocent, then why hadn't he ever come forward?

"Son of a bitch."

Linc was so stunned he was shaking. Another puzzle piece thrown onto the table, but where did it fit? So many questions. So many lies. And one man's lies had sent him straight to prison. *He* was the one Linc wanted to talk to next.

He walked to the truck with his head down and drove away—all the way down the mountain, straight into Mount Sterling. He stopped at a convenience store to get the location of the Ford dealership and then kept on going. When he pulled into the lot and up to the office, he killed the engine, then couldn't move. He sat with his fingers curled around the steering wheel so tight that the knuckles were white, trying to get to a place in his head where he could trust himself to talk.

Cars were coming and going around him, salesmen walking in and out with prospective buyers. The lot was full of bright, shiny cars and lots of colorful flags hanging from nearby poles. It appeared as if Wesley Duggan had done well for himself.

When Linc could breathe without wanting to hit someone, he went inside and began scanning the little offices at the back of the room, looking for the man who'd betrayed him. When he finally spotted him in the last cubicle to his right, he took a step forward, only to be cut off by a smiling salesman with an outstretched hand.

"Hey there, how's it going? I'm Kevin Collins. What's

your pleasure today? Souped-up truck? SUV? Sports car? You want it, we've got it."

"I want to talk to Wes Duggan."

The lack of a smile and the curt tone of Lincoln's voice told the salesman this man was pissed about something.

"Uh, yeah, right. Let me see if he's got a minute, okay? Just have a seat over there and I'll—"

"I'll wait here."

Collins wasn't going to argue with someone who made two of him. He turned on his heel and headed for the boss's office.

Linc watched the salesman knock and then step inside. He saw him gesturing, saw Duggan look up, then through the glass at him. It wasn't surprising that Duggan didn't recognize him. He was as far removed from that scared seventeen-year-old boy as a man could be. So much the better. Shock value was priceless.

Linc didn't wait for permission. He just started walking. When he got to the office he opened the door, then caught the salesman's eye.

"Get out."

All of a sudden Duggan was on his feet. "I don't know who you are, but you can't come in here and talk to my employee like that."

Linc smiled, but it never reached his eyes. "Why, what's the matter, Uncle Wesley? Don't you recognize me?"

Wes Duggan gasped. His legs went out from under him as he sat down in the chair with a thump. Still trying to maintain control, he cleared his throat and then waved the salesman away.

"It's okay, Kevin. You can go."

Collins was still uneasy. "Are you sure? Do you want me to call the police?"

Linc's eyes narrowed warningly. "Yeah, how about that, Uncle Wes? Do you want him to call the police?"

All the color washed out of Wes's face. "No, no, that won't be necessary."

Linc shut the door as Collins slipped out, then turned to face the pasty-faced man on the other side of the desk and waited for him to make the first move.

Wes was still trying to get a grip as he started a conversation.

"I will say, I would never have recognized you, Lincoln. You've grown into quite a large man."

"Bigger than Dad," Linc said softly.

Wes nodded. "Have a seat," he said, gesturing toward a chair.

"No, thanks. I won't be here long."

Wes's heart was pounding. "I had no idea you were back. Are you here for a visit, or—"

"I moved back to the homestead. Come spring, I'll rebuild."

Sweat was popping out on Wes's forehead even though it was almost chilly in the large building.

"That's great news. What finally brought you back? I hope Aunt Tildy's all right? I've pretty much lost touch with everyone on Rebel Ridge since—"

"Since you tucked my ass so neatly into prison and walked away with Dad's wife?"

Wes shivered. "It's not like you think."

"You don't know what I think," Linc said.

"You're right, I don't. But I hope you don't hold a grudge against me for—"

"Lying on the stand? Actually, I do. As a matter of

fact, it's a real big grudge, and part of why I came back. I came back to clear my name. I am doing my own investigation into Dad's murder. And since you were one of the prime reasons I was convicted, and we both know it was because you lied, you can consider this meeting your first interrogation."

Wes reached for the cup of coffee sitting near the phone, but his hand was shaking too hard to hold it, so he gave up and dropped his hand back in his lap.

"I didn't lie."

Linc braced both hands on the desk as he leaned down, and as he did, he caught a glimpse of the Duggans' home address on a bill lying on the desk.

"Yes, you did," he said. "You said my dad and I didn't get along, which was the biggest damned lie I ever heard. I worshipped the ground he walked on, and you knew it. What I want to know is, why did you lie? Who were you protecting?"

Wes gasped. "No, no, that's not... I mean...I knew you and your dad had disagreed about your relationship with that Walker girl and—"

"That's another damn lie. My relationship with 'that Walker girl' had been going on for three years. Dad loved her. If he'd been going to object to our going out, he would have done it when we were way younger, not when we were about to graduate."

Sweat was emerging from Wes's sparse hairline and running down his forehead. He mopped his face with a handkerchief, then got up and began to pace.

"No, Linc, that's not true. You were fighting. He told me—"

"No. Dad didn't tell you anything, because there was

nothing to tell. That's how I *know* you lied. Again, who the hell were you protecting?"

Wes shook his head, too rattled to think.

"Since you can't find the balls to tell me the truth about that, I'm guessing you won't have the balls to tell me the truth about my last question, either, but I came all this way, so I have to ask. Were you sleeping with your best friend's wife before he was murdered?"

Wes's face turned red, then white, then red again. Linc was wondering if the man was about to drop dead in front of him when Wes finally got his wits about him and pointed to the door.

"Get out," Wes said, wincing noticeably because his voice was more squeak than censure.

Linc's eyes narrowed angrily. "That's answer enough for me. And know you've been forewarned. I was convicted on the lies you and Lucy told. Damn the both of you to hell and back. You killed the boy I was and destroyed the future I could have had. I will find out who really killed Dad, and if you're mixed up in it, I will do the same to yours."

He turned away. Behind him, Wes Duggan reeled as if he'd been sucker punched, watching as Linc strode out of the office, letting the door slam as he went.

A few minutes later Linc merged back into traffic with one more stop on his mind. Now that he'd seen the address where Wes lived, it would be downright rude not to pay his respects to his ex-stepmother—just to see what happened.

Lucy Duggan unplugged her curling iron, then leaned toward the mirror and smiled widely, checking to make sure there was no lipstick on her teeth. They gleamed as pure a white as money could buy. She patted her hair, making sure every curl was in place, and eyed the lilac-colored sweater and cream-colored slacks she was wearing to make sure there were no snags or lint that didn't belong. Then she smiled. As Wes would say, she had her war paint on and looked good enough to eat.

She glanced at her watch. Quarter to eleven. She was on her way to meet her girlfriends for lunch. They'd recently discovered this charming little Asian fusion place on the other side of town, and now everyone was talking about it. Being a trend starter was what she lived for. She stepped into lilac-colored Louboutins and began digging through her handbag for the car keys.

She was getting her coat out of the closet when the doorbell rang. She glanced at her watch again and frowned. Just enough time to get rid of whoever it was and make her date.

The doorbell rang again. The click-click sound of her four-inch heels marked the length of her stride.

"I'm coming, damn it."

When she opened the door to find one seriously huge but good-looking hunk on her doorstep, her aggravation shifted as she flashed him a quick smile.

"Yes? How may I help you?"

"You could ask me to come in. It's cold out here," Linc said.

A little taken aback by the familiarity, her mood shifted to caution. "I'm sorry I—"

"Come on now, Lucy. Surely you haven't forgotten the stepson you used to tuck into bed at night?"

"Oh, my God!"

She gasped and staggered backward, hung the toe

of her right shoe behind the heel of her left and fell flat on her butt.

Linc followed her inside, shut the door and grabbed her by the arm.

"Upsy-daisy," he said as he yanked her upright.

Lucy was shaking so hard she couldn't think. She wanted to tell him to get out, but he'd just helped her up, and she was still struggling between manners and shock.

"I...uh..."

"I would have appreciated a simple 'I'm sorry.' You didn't have to fall at my feet," Linc drawled.

Lucy's eyes narrowed as she took in the size of the man in front of her and tried to see the boy she'd known. It was impossible. He looked a little like Marcus, but better—and bigger, much bigger.

She lifted her chin. "I have nothing to apologize for, and I'd like for you to leave."

"Actually, yes, you do, Lucy. You lied, and your lie got me sent to prison. I thought it only fair to warn you and your husband that I've come back to find out who killed Dad."

Breath caught in the back of her throat. "That's ridiculous. You were convicted, sentenced and did the time."

"But I didn't do the crime," he said softly. "Someone on Rebel Ridge got away with murder, and I came back to clear my name." He took a step forward. "Why did you lie about me?"

"I did not—"

"Shut up, Lucy. I'm not a scared seventeen-year-old kid this time around. You *did* lie. What I want to know is, why? Who were you protecting?"

"I wasn't—"

"Hmm, I can see we're getting nowhere with this

question. So I have another. How long had you and Uncle Wes been screwing around before Dad was murdered?"

It felt as if he'd just punched her in the stomach. It took a few seconds for her to realize they'd only been words. Then it took her another few moments to regain her senses.

"Get out!" She doubled up her fist and screamed, "How dare you come back here and accuse me of—"

Linc took another step forward.

She choked in the middle of the word. She wanted to defy him. She couldn't let him walk out of here thinking he'd had the last word, but all she could think was how fast a carefully structured world could fall.

He pointed a finger in her face. "When you close your eyes at night, think of what you did. With every waking hour of your existence, think of me digging up the secrets you thought you'd buried for good...turning over the rocks of respectability you and Wes have been hiding under. The law on Rebel Ridge already knows I'm back and why...and soon so will everyone who lives there."

Her voice was shaking, but from a blind fury she couldn't express.

"I want you to leave."

Linc stared her down. "No problem. I've said all I came to say."

He turned his back on her and left as abruptly as he'd come in, leaving the door wide-open behind him, inviting the cold air to enter at will.

The air was so cold, Lucy thought. All she had to do was take six steps and close the door, but her feet wouldn't move. As he was getting in his truck and driving away, the heat went out and the cold came in. She was afraid to move, to lose sight of him for fear he would sneak up on her again when she wasn't looking. She watched the truck grow smaller the farther he drove, and the farther he drove, the colder the room became. When he finally turned the corner and disappeared, she jerked as if she'd been slapped, then leaped forward and slammed the door.

Her chest felt tight, her breath coming in short, painful gasps as if she'd been running, and then she slowly turned around, gazing at every piece of fine art on their walls and the high-end furniture the interior decorator had placed so carefully to show the rooms to their best advantage. She looked down at her clothing, running her palms against the cashmere sweater and then down further to the lilac Louboutins she'd chosen with such pride. They cost more than her father had ever made in a single year. She'd spent too many years climbing out of that hell they called poverty to go back without a fight.

Lunch was off. She had a war to plan and soldiers to recruit. She picked her purse up off the floor where she'd dropped it, then headed for her room at a fast clip, with those same high heels still marking the cadence. She traded the heels for a pair of flats, then turned to her first order of business: canceling lunch.

She thought about calling Wes, but this wasn't something she could discuss over the phone. That left her with only one more call to make. It was time to phone home. But first she needed a drink.

Twelve

Fagan watched his last customer driving away and smiled as he pocketed the money. Nearly a kilo of weed, and it was good stuff. He knew the guy would cut it and make a bigger profit, but Fagan was comfortable where he was at. It was far less dangerous to be a marijuana grower and sell to the dealers who peddled it than to be on the streets dodging cops and getting screwed over by potheads trying to score with no dough. With this sale and the other two he'd made in the past week, he had a little over three thousand dollars in the house. The rub was that the White brothers didn't do banks, and having money in the house and a brother who would have no qualms in taking it posed a problem. He needed to hide the bigger part of it, but where?

He walked through the house a couple of times, looking for a place that would be off Prince's radar. And then it hit him. Prince never cooked.

Fagan headed for the kitchen, dug an empty coffee can out of the trash, counted out all but three hundred dollars into the can, then started pulling out pots and pans beneath the counter. When he came to an old enamel pan his mother had used to cook down her collard greens, he poked the can inside, stacked a couple of pans on top of it and shoved it as far back as it would go.

He pocketed what was left of the money and went to get his car keys. Like it or not, he needed some food in the house. If he got snowed in again before he made a trip to the grocery store he would be out in the woods trying to hunt down something to eat, and he was a lousy shot.

He picked up his phone, checking to see if Prince had returned his call, but he had not. He was so disgusted. How the hell did Prince expect to learn what was going on if he chose to drop off the face of the earth every time it suited him? Just as he pocketed the phone, it rang.

"About time," he muttered as he pulled it back out and answered. "Hello."

"Hello. Fagan, is that you? It's me, Lucy."

Fagan was dumbstruck. His sister hadn't called home since their mama died, which had been a good many years ago.

"Yes, it's me, and you would have known it if you'd ever called here before. What do you want?"

"Where is Prince?"

"No idea. I tried to call him last night, but he didn't return the call, why? What's wrong?"

She laughed, and the hair stood up on the back of his neck. She was pissed about something for sure.

"What's wrong? I'll tell you what's wrong. Lincoln Fox was just at my house, threatening me. He said he came back to Rebel Ridge to clear his name. He's about to start digging into things that need to stay buried, if you know what I mean."

"I know exactly what you mean, but don't expect me to get involved," he snapped.

"You're involved by blood, you idiot, so don't go playing all innocent with me. Here's what I want you to…"

Fagan felt sick to his stomach. Why did he have to be born into such a crazy-ass family? Lucy was still talking when he hung up. He didn't want to hear another word. He just grabbed his car keys and headed out the door.

Lucy was in the kitchen screaming into the phone as the dial tone buzzed in her ear, calling her brother every filthy word she'd ever heard. She didn't know her husband had just walked in the door.

Wes was already in a panic about Lincoln's reappearance and what he had said. He had come home to reassure himself that he had not been duped by the woman he loved, but when he heard her tirade, he stopped, listening to the filth spilling out of her mouth. His shoulders slumped as he closed his eyes. No matter how much money they had and how fancy their clothes, they were never going to live down their upbringing. It was the sound of breaking glass that got his attention. He headed for the kitchen.

"What the hell's going on in here?" he shouted.

Lucy spun to face him. Her hair was awry, her eyes swollen from crying. And she was drunk. Again.

He already felt defeated. "We need to talk."

Her head went back and her chin came up. "I don't like your tone."

"And I don't like to come home and find my wife throwing dishes and screaming like a madwoman. Who the fuck were you yelling at?"

She threw her hands up in the air. "It doesn't matter. Nothing matters," she muttered, and headed for the whiskey bottle on the counter.

He cut her off. "No more booze."

She spun and slapped him, then gasped. She knew the moment she'd done it that it was a mistake.

"I'm sorry, Wes. I didn't—"

He jammed his finger against her breast, punctuating every word with a jab.

"I had a visitor at work today, and from the way you're behaving, I'd say you had the same one."

She was shaking. "Lincoln Fox pushed his way into my house and threatened me."

"He was at the dealership, as well. What I want to know is, who were you screaming at when I came in?"

She blinked. "What does that matter? I'm telling you that Lincoln—"

"He thinks I lied on the stand."

"I need a drink," she mumbled.

Wes grabbed her by the shoulders. "Why would he say I lied? He and Marcus were fighting, right?"

"Let me go. How dare you treat me like this?"

The knot in Wes's gut grew tighter. "You answer me, damn it! He and Marcus were fighting. Right?"

Lucy wouldn't look at him. "Yes, of course. I said it, didn't I?"

He shook her. "Look at me!"

"You're hurting me!" she screamed, and slapped him again.

He picked her up, dragged her kicking and screaming into the living room, and slammed her down on the sofa so hard her shoes came off. The silence that ensued was frightening for both of them.

Lucy was losing control, and Wes was losing his wife, and they both knew it was happening.

"Did you lie to me?" he asked.

Lucy covered her face and started to weep.

"Son of a holy bitch," he whispered, and walked out of the room.

She was sobbing, but when he walked out, she screamed, "Come back! Damn you, Wesley! You don't walk away from me!"

When he didn't return, she shrieked, and then kept on shrieking, until it felt as if her throat was on fire. She started to get up and go after him, but she only staggered drunkenly, fell onto the floor and passed out.

Wes was in their bedroom throwing clothes and toilet articles into a bag. He didn't know what was going to happen, but he couldn't be in the house with this woman when it did. She was passed out when he left, but he didn't care. There was a motel across the street from the dealership. That was as good a place as any to figure out what to do next. His heart was so heavy he could hardly breathe and walk at the same time. He felt dirty all the way to his soul. He could just hear his mama's voice.

You reap what you sow, Wesley. You reap what you sow.

He'd coveted his friend's wife and taken her to bed. He'd been so blind with love—or had it just been lust?— that he'd believed everything she said. He'd even been happy Marcus had done them all a favor and died, but after finding out his friend had been murdered, his guilty conscience had shifted to a need for swift justice. That was how he would atone for his transgressions. He would make sure the killer was punished. But instead he'd crucified a boy on account of a lie. What had he done? What the hell had he done?

Prince was on the run. In a card game, he'd lost every penny Lucy had given him, then robbed a gas station for a tank of gas and a few quick bucks. He lit out of Mount Sterling and headed back to the hills. It was where he felt safest, and he knew a thousand places to hide where the law would never find him. All he needed was for Fagan to keep him in food until he figured a way out of the mess he was in.

It was just after midnight when he pulled into the driveway. Fagan's truck was parked out front, but the house lights were out. The dogs started barking. If Fagan wasn't drunk, the noise was bound to wake him up. Prince tapped the brakes, checking out the premises as he circled the house, then drove all the way into the barn and parked out of sight. All four dogs came running, sounding like they were ready to eat him alive. Already pissed, he walked out of the barn, shouting.

"Shut the fuck up!" he screamed, and threw a rock at the redbone hound in the lead.

They recognized his voice—and the threat—and slunk off into the woods.

Prince kept walking. The back door wasn't even locked, which meant Fagan was most likely passed out, either from the weed he'd smoked or the booze he'd drunk. He hadn't even put the dogs up for the night. Prince turned on lights as he went through the house, calling his brother's name.

Fagan came stumbling out of his bedroom wearing nothing but a pair of long johns and carrying a rifle.

"What the hell?" he mumbled, blinking rapidly against the sudden onset of light.

"Put the fuckin' gun away," Prince said. "We need to talk."

Fagan came to himself enough to be pissed. "Oh, so now you show up and think you can start ordering me around? Why didn't you return any of my calls? You have no idea what a damn mess we're in."

Prince stopped short. "What are you talking about?"

"Lincoln Fox is back. He's after blood. Claims he came back to get justice for his daddy's murder. He already done challenged me, wanting to know how I came to be the one who called in the fire at his house that night. He's been to the law. They know what he's doing, I guess, and are letting it happen."

"Son of a bitch," Prince said, and started pacing.

"That ain't the half of it," Fagan said. "He showed up at Lucy's house today and freaked her out to the point that she called here, trying to tell us what we were gonna do to stop him."

"What did you tell her?" Prince asked.

"I didn't tell her a dang thing. I hung up on her ass. She's too damned high-and-mighty to even claim us as brothers until she wants dirty work done, and then she comes begging. I'm done with all that. I grow and sell weed. I don't want trouble with anyone, especially the law."

Prince stared. "Are you crazy?"

Fagan glared back. "What I am is fed up. The law is after you for assaulting and stalking Meg Lewis, and I don't want to think about what else. Lucy is a bitch. I don't want anything to do with her. You can take yourself on out of here for all I care, because I'm not covering up for either one of you."

Prince was stunned. "You'd turn your back on your own brother?"

Fagan shifted the rifle to his other hand. "You didn't seem to have any problem getting into trouble and then leaving me here to catch all the flak."

This was not the welcome Prince had expected. "Look. We started out all wrong. What we need to do is—"

Fagan shook his head. "There's no more *we*. There's Lucy, and there's you. I am not part of the equation. I never was, and I don't intend to be now."

Prince was getting desperate, but he wasn't stupid. Fagan was the one holding the weapon.

"You still knew everything and didn't tell. You said Fox challenged you about calling in that fire?"

"And I told him my two older brothers are the ones who told me it was burning."

Prince lost it. He began stomping back and forth in the hall and waving his arms, screaming to the point that spit was coming out of his mouth as fast as the words he was spewing.

"You're a Judas goat! By God, you would turn on your own and side with the law! I never thought I'd see the day this would happen!"

"I didn't ask to be born into this fucking family," Fagan said. "You can take yourself back on out of this house, and if I never see you again, it'll be too soon!"

Prince leaped, ready to take a swing.

Fagan hit him on the jaw with the butt of the rifle, knocking him to the floor.

Prince rolled to his knees, blood dripping from his chin and lip, then staggered as he got to his feet.

Fagan shouted again. "You get the hell out and don't come back. I mean it, Prince! So help me God, if I see you again I'll call the cops and tell them exactly where you're at."

Prince couldn't think straight. The blow had knocked out a tooth and what was left of his good sense. He wanted to curse his brother, but when he opened his mouth he found himself sobbing.

"Don't do this, brother. Please. I don't have any money, and I've got nowhere to go."

Fagan was unmoved. For the first time in his life he could see daylight in being rid of his brother's constant troubles. He stepped back into his bedroom, grabbed his wallet and came back into the hall. Prince hadn't moved a muscle.

He took out what was left of the three hundred dollars he'd taken to buy groceries and threw it at Prince's feet.

"Go find Lucy. She called here wanting to know where you were. She asked for help. I can guarantee she'll welcome you back with open arms."

Prince grabbed the money and stuffed it in his pocket.

"I'm tired and I'm hungry, Fagan."

"You drove up here like that. You can leave the same way."

Prince swiped at the blood running down his chin and then pointed his finger at Fagan's chest.

"You'll pay for this."

Fagan pointed the rifle at his brother's feet. "I've been paying for all the bad my family's done my whole life. I'm done. Get the fuck out."

Prince turned too quickly and staggered into the wall,

leaving bloody handprints as he caught himself from falling.

Fagan followed him all the way through the house and then outside into the cold, and he watched until Prince and his pickup came out of the barn and drove away. Then he went back inside, locked both doors, turned out the lights and sat up in the dark with the rifle in his lap and tears running down his face.

It had taken Linc an entire afternoon of chopping wood to get past the rage he'd brought home. The day had been cold but clear. The sound of his chainsaw and the thump of his hammer against the splitting wedge had echoed on the mountain as the pile of lumber continued to grow.

Life and experience had made him a good judge of other men's character, and the longer he thought about it, the more convinced he became that Wes Duggan's testimony had been what someone else told him to say, not something he knew for a fact.

According to Aunt Tildy, Dad already believed Lucy was cheating, which explained the distance he'd felt between them in the months prior to his father's murder. Even if Wes and Lucy had been screwing around, it wouldn't have been worth a fight to the death for his father. And there was the irrefutable fact that Lucy's alibi was rock solid, so she definitely wasn't the murderer.

Her brothers wouldn't have cared who she fucked. He was missing something. He just couldn't figure out what.

He quit just before dark, hauled what he'd cut to the house and stacked it up near the door, then carried a couple of logs inside. It didn't take long to stir up the coals and add some more wood to feed the fire. His belly was growling as he washed up, a reminder that he hadn't eaten since breakfast. He took out the pork chops and the extra baked potato Meg had given him, and put them in the microwave to heat.

The thought of Meg made him lonely. It was too late to go calling, but he could at least hear her voice. He sat down in his recliner and kicked back to make the call. The wood he'd just put in the stove was beginning to catch fire, popping like popcorn inside the iron belly as the flames took hold.

The aroma of the heating pork chops and the warmth gave the place a homey feel. He waited as Meg's phone began to ring, and just when he thought it was going to go to voice mail she answered, sounding slightly out of breath and laughing. He stifled a groan, remembering all the times they'd spent together laughing and playing at being grown-ups.

"Hello?"

"Hey, Meg, it's me. Are you okay?"

"Lincoln! Hi! Yes, I'm fine. I was in the shower. When I sat down on the side of the bed to answer the phone, Honey licked my toes. It made me laugh."

The thought of her wet and naked did nothing for his peace of mind. "I remember that you were ticklish, but I am not going to ask you what you're wearing."

She laughed as she pulled the towel a little closer around her body.

"I've been busy today, packing up quilts and digging out my price tags and decorations for the show in Lexington."

"You mentioned something about it the other day. Is it a big one?"

"Yes. I've participated every year for the past ten years."

"When do you leave?"

"Thursday morning. I already have a reservation in a motel near the show, and I need to head to the fairgrounds before daylight on Friday to set up. The show opens at nine in the morning and runs through 'til three o'clock on Sunday afternoon. I normally make at least half my yearly income at that show."

He liked hearing about this aspect of her life and realized that she must have quite a presence in her field to be so successful.

"That sounds like quite a big deal," he said.

"It is for me. So what have you been doing today?"

He sighed. "Stepping in shit."

"What?"

"Sorry, but that's what it felt like."

She could hear the dejection in his voice. "What's wrong?"

"I saw Wes Duggan today. I went to the dealership and confronted him about lying at the trial."

Suddenly Meg felt anxious. He'd thrown down the gauntlet in a very public way.

"Oh, Linc, that's a little scary. Now it's all out in the open. What did he say?"

"It's weird. I expected him to deny it, but the strange thing is that I think he actually believes he told the truth."

"What do you mean?"

Linc shoved a hand through his hair. The microwave dinged, but he ignored it.

"I got the impression that he had just repeated something he'd been told to say and passed it off as his own observation. When it's gossip, you can always choose to ignore it, you know? But testimony is supposed to be a true fact, and he swore on a Bible that it was."

"I do remember people saying at the time that they were all surprised by his claim, because none of them had ever witnessed any disagreements between you and your dad. But Wesley Duggan and your dad were best friends, so that's why they took it to heart…thinking he would know the truth if anyone would."

"Exactly, but it's also what crucified me—and it was a lie," Linc said. "However, I did hit a nerve—a big nerve when I accused him of betraying his best friend by sleeping with his wife. I thought he was going to have a stroke. That's when he ordered me out of the office. But I said what I went to say. When I left, I went by their house to ask Lucy the same set of questions."

Meg groaned. The Whites were not a family to piss off, and the thought that he'd done that scared her. She already knew what Prince was capable of, and Fagan wasn't much better. She'd heard all about how Wes and Lucy had moved up in the world when they'd moved away from Rebel Ridge. Threatening Lucy to the point of making her think she might lose all that was like teasing a mean dog. Lord only knew what kind of havoc she could bring.

"You did not! Oh, Linc, there's no telling what she's capable of doing. What did she say?"

"Had herself a screaming fit and told me to get out of her house, but that was after I asked her why she lied about me and who was she protecting when she did it. That's when she lost *her* cool."

"I'm so sorry," Meg said.

"Yeah, and I'd guess right about now so are they."

She frowned. "If she did have anything to do with it, you do know that you've just painted a very big target on your back?"

"Yes, I know, but I'm a very big man. I can take the flak, as long as I get the answers I need."

"Are you okay?"

He sighed. "Yes, I'm okay. It takes a lot more than cursing and shouting to rattle me. So what are you doing tomorrow?"

"I'm skipping church. I have too many things to finish up before the trade show, and I need to do some baking later in the week to take to Mom and Jake's on Wednesday. Don't forget, you're with me that day."

"It sounds to me like you'll need to be more than half-packed for your quilt show by then. How about if I pick you up and we go in my truck instead?"

"That would be great!"

Just listening to the happiness in her voice made *him* happy, and thinking about spending the day with her was even better. Even if her family got weird about him being there, he wasn't going to let it bother him.

"Ah, Meg…you are good for my soul. Thanks for talking me down from my bad mood."

She shivered and closed her eyes as his soft, husky voice wrapped around her, and wished it was his arms instead.

"I'm glad you called," she said. "Have a good dinner with Aunt Tildy tomorrow, and tell her I said hello."

"I will. I was wondering, would you mind if I stopped by tomorrow afternoon? I have a hankering to look at your sweet face."

"I would not mind at all," she said.

"Great. See you then."

Meg heard the click as he disconnected and reluctantly hung up the phone. She was still smiling as she bent down and gave Honey's ear a quick scratch.

"Hey, sweet baby…that was Lincoln. Talking to him makes me happy. You make me happy. Right now I'm just a happy fool. I'll bet you wanna go out."

Honey licked Meg's fingers.

"Then let me get my robe. You take a run around the yard while I tend to my sudden urge for something hot and sweet. Since Lincoln is out of reach, I'll have to settle for hot chocolate."

When Linc stepped out of the house on Sunday morning to get some more wood, he paused, struck by the clear beauty of the day. The air was Popsicle cold, the early sun so bright it turned the look of the frosty grass into shards of white ice. The far-off screech of a hawk circling overhead broke the pristine silence and sent the rabbit hiding behind his woodpile into a panicked dash to safety. Linc inhaled deeply and, as he exhaled, the warmth of his breath formed a cloud in front of his face. It was moments like this that reminded him why it was a gift to have been born on this mountain.

After a pause for silent adulation of the glorious morning, he picked up an armful of firewood and went back inside, kicking the door shut behind him. The aroma of fresh coffee brewing mingled with the scent of burning cedar as he popped a couple more sticks into the stove.

Today was the day he took Tildy to Sunday dinner at Frankie's Eats. He was looking forward to treating her, and at the same time he was afraid the whole experience might be a disaster. It actually depended on the diners' reactions to his appearance as to whether it would be a memorable meal or a hot mess. But no matter what happened, he had no doubt Tildy Bennett could handle the situation.

Since he was counting on a big dinner, he went small with breakfast and only made himself one peanut butter and jelly sandwich. He ate as he logged on to his laptop, checking emails for updates from his crews back in Dallas. For a change there were no pressing problems to be solved. Quite the opposite. He read with pleasure an email from Gerald informing him that they were going to come in under deadline by about two weeks and get the twenty-five-thousand-dollar bonus that had been built into the contract.

He sent back a "way to go" message with a couple of exclamation points for good measure, then got up to pour himself a cup of coffee and was doing a mental rundown of what to do next in his investigation when he remembered Tildy telling him about the Whites coming into extra money before the fire.

She had mentioned that they'd been about to lose their place when the bank loan was miraculously paid off, ending the foreclosure proceedings. As a teenager, he wouldn't have paid any attention to that news, but looking back now, he had to wonder how they'd come into that kind of money. Unless they had a rich relative who had died and left them an inheritance, it was a sure bet that it wasn't obtained by legal means. He made a mental note to ask her if she knew any more details. He couldn't imagine how it might have anything to do with his father's murder, but he had to consider everything connected to the people who'd been connected to him and his dad—even by marriage.

He sat down at the laptop and sent a message to Toby, the foreman on the other crew, then kept working, but with an eye on the clock so he would be on time to pick up his aunt. He ran a quick check of his bank accounts, personal and business, before logging off. All was in order, which gave him the freedom to continue his pursuit of justice.

As the time to leave drew near he went to shave, then got out a good shirt, his bolo tie and his favorite Western suit, cleaned his good boots so they would be shiny and began to get dressed. The knot in his gut was still there. In a way he felt he was getting dressed for a funeral rather than a Sunday outing, and he knew it was because of the uncertainty of his reception. By the time he was ready to go he was tense and defensive. He settled the Stetson on his head and locked up.

He started up the road with the heater going full blast so it would be warm in the cab by the time he picked up his aunt. The farther he drove, the easier he became. As he came around a curve in the road he braked suddenly to keep from hitting a coyote that had darted out in front of him, running with a chicken in its mouth. The coyote leaped into the trees on the other side of the road and disappeared.

Linc shook his head at the unexpected sight. It wasn't common to see that in broad daylight. Someone was now minus a good laying hen.

He reached Tildy's house without further delay, noting as he pulled up to her house that it was straight up eleven o'clock. Perfect timing.

As he walked through the gate, he saw the curtain move at the window. He smiled. She'd been watching for him. And when he got to the porch, she opened the door before he could knock.

The woman standing in the doorway was nothing like the one who walked the mountain in old overalls and work boots, gathering herbs and ginseng with no care for appearance. She had taken the braid out of her hair and wound the length on the top of her head like a silver crown. The dress she was wearing was a long-sleeved blue shirtwaist, with a round collar trimmed in white tatting.

"Aunt Tildy! You look beautiful!" Linc said.

"Oh, this old thing," she said, and tried to pretend it didn't matter, but he saw her smile.

"Are you ready to go?"

"Yes. I need to get my coat and bag, and then I'm ready."

Linc got her coat from the back of the sofa and helped her put it on, then leaned down and kissed her cheek. She smelled of flowers and ladies' face powder. Another revelation about a woman who lived and breathed the healing herbs that she gathered.

"You even smell good," he said.

She patted his cheek. "Thank you. I haven't heard that in a while."

He waited as she locked her door, offered her his arm as they went to the truck, then helped her up into the seat.

"Nice and warm in here," she said as he got in behind the wheel.

"Yes, ma'am. Can't have you freezing your little feet in those pretty shoes you're wearing."

Tildy beamed. "I haven't put on a pair of dress shoes

in so long I nearly forgot how to walk in them, but I must say, I have been looking forward to this day."

"Me, too, Aunt Tildy. I'm just a little anxious about our reception. I don't want the cold shoulder I might get to ruin your meal."

"I don't care what other people think. I got my own mind about what's right and what's not."

"Then we're good to go," he said.

Thirteen

"I thought I'd let you know what's happened since I talked to you last," Linc said. "I confronted Wes and Lucy yesterday. It was pretty ugly, but at least now they know I'm here and why."

"Good. I hope it gave both of them nightmares last night," Tildy said.

He chuckled. "Yeah, me, too. But it also set me to thinking about something you said a while back. About the White family home being in foreclosure and then it suddenly getting paid off."

She nodded. "Yes, that did happen."

"I don't suppose anyone knew what happened?"

"I never heard anything beyond what Mrs. White said, that they came into some money."

"And that's all she said?"

"It's all I heard."

"I don't suppose you know what kind of money we're talking about?"

Tildy frowned. "Well, I can't say how much they got, but I do know how much they owed, because Mrs. White used to cry when she'd come get my salve for her rheumatism. She kept saying they were no more likely to ever come by four hundred dollars all at once, let alone the forty thousand they owed."

"Forty thousand! That's a lot of money to owe on any land here on Rebel Ridge. I wonder how they came to owe so much on land that had been in their family for generations."

"Her husband was a poor manager and hated to work worse than anyone I ever knew. I think what happened is that he mortgaged it a piece at a time until they found themselves without a single acre of land that was free and clear."

Linc listened as he drove, letting Tildy talk and nodding when it was necessary, but he was convinced his next step was to find out where that money had come from. But not today. Today was about chicken and dumplings and putting another smile on Aunt Tildy's face.

"Here's hoping this goes well," he said as he parked at Frankie's Eats. "Looks like we got here at a good time. Only three other cars."

"Church isn't out yet," she said. "It'll be packed later."

He put on his Stetson and then helped Tildy out of the truck, shielding her from the cold wind with his body. She slipped her hand in the crook of his arm, and walked into the restaurant with her chin up and a satisfied smile on her face.

Sue Ellen was heading toward a table when she saw Tildy Bennett come into the restaurant all dressed up. Then she saw the big good-looking cowboy on the old woman's arm and stopped. She knew who it was because she'd heard the gossip, but she wouldn't have recognized him as the cute boy her cousin Meg used to date. Lord, but he had filled out just fine.

"Hey, Aunt Tildy! My, you look pretty!" Sue Ellen said, and smiled at Linc. "Y'all sit anywhere. I'll be right there to take your orders."

He recognized Sue Ellen, remembered she was one of Meg's cousins and was pleasantly surprised by the smile. He led Tildy to a booth along the wall and then helped her off with her coat.

"This okay, Aunt Tildy?"

"It's fine."

He saw the others watching, but when they realized he'd caught them, they quickly looked away. He sighed as he took off his hat and put it on the seat beside him.

Sue Ellen showed up still wearing the smile. "I swear, Lincoln Fox, I would never have recognized you. You sure did turn into a big, good-looking man."

He grinned. "And you're still a flirt, Sue Ellen. I hope you married a generous-hearted man who can handle it."

She giggled. "All I can say is that my Jesse likes me just the way I am. Now y'all know that Sunday dinner is just the chicken and dumplings with two sides, right? We don't cook anything else today."

"That's why we're here," Linc said. "We'll take two dinners, with whatever is for dessert."

"That would be coconut-cream pie. And what would you like to drink? Coffee or iced tea?"

"I'd like coffee," Tildy said. "It's right cold out today."

"Make that two," Linc said.

The diner began to fill up as their meal progressed. Everyone knew Tildy and identified her dining partner by process of elimination, Lincoln Fox being the only stranger in town who happened to be Tildy Bennett's kin.

He'd expected the curiosity and suspected there was

a good deal of judgment with it. A couple of men made a point of staring straight at him and didn't bother looking away. No secret as to what they were feeling.

As Linc and Tildy were finishing their meal, the door opened again with another couple coming in to eat, and Linc recognized George, the man who'd run through the barbed-wire fence. When he saw Linc and Aunt Tildy, he headed straight for them.

"Good to see you again," George said, and quickly introduced his wife. "This is my wife, Loretta. Loretta, this here is Lincoln Fox, Aunt Tildy's nephew. He helped cut off that wire. Lincoln, Loretta's kin to the Duroys, on the other side of the mountain."

Lincoln stood up as the introduction was made, which did not go unnoticed by the other women in the room.

"I don't believe I know your people, but it's nice to meet you, ma'am."

Loretta shook hands vigorously. "I sure appreciate what you did for my George."

"I was happy to help." He glanced at George. "I trust you're about healed up?"

"Pretty much. It's good to see you again. If you're ever up our way, stop in and say hello. I make a real good peach wine you might like to try."

"I will," Linc said.

"We better seat ourselves or Sue Ellen will give our table away," George said, and led his wife over to the last empty table in the room.

Linc sat back down, aware that the mood in the room had shifted slightly in his favor.

Sue Ellen came sailing by with a trayful of desserts, took off two servings of coconut pie and put them on their table, winked and left.

"She's a caution," Tildy said, and took a bite of the pie. "It's good pie, but I think it's shy a bit of vanilla flavoring."

Linc hid a grin. "You're right, it is good pie, but not as good as yours."

She smiled. "Why, thank you."

"You're most welcome, Aunt Tildy."

They finished their pie while talking about little memories from the past. Linc was getting out his billfold to pay when an elderly couple walked in.

The woman saw Tildy and headed straight for their table, much like George had done, and once again Lincoln was on his feet as the old woman began to talk.

"Hello, Tildy. My sakes, don't you look nice. Is this here your nephew, Lincoln…the one who hung Beulah Justice's door, and set her up in wood and propane?"

Tildy gave Linc an apologetic look. "Lincoln, these are my nearest neighbors, Elvis and Jewel Thurgood."

"Ma'am…Mr. Thurgood. Pleased to meet you," Linc said.

Jewel squinted as she looked up. "Lordy be, but you're a big one, aren't you?"

"Yes, ma'am," he said.

Jewel took a deep breath and then started talking again. "Tildy, you know how I am…. I believe in signs and fate…and since Elvis and I are in desperate need of help, I consider this meeting fated to be. Elvis can't remember which is up and which is down these days, so I don't trust him with the tools anymore. He's not much, but he's mine, and I take good care of what's mine."

Linc stifled a smile. Poor Elvis didn't look as discombobulated as Jewel claimed, but then again, it was hard to tell, because he was following Sue Ellen to an empty table, leaving Jewel on her own to do the talking.

"What do you need?" Tildy asked.

"It's my back stoop. It's falling in, and I'm afraid to walk out on it anymore, even though Elvis keeps going out when I tell him not to. I'm afraid he's going to break a leg and then I'd have to put him down."

Linc blinked. "You don't mean you'd shoot him?"

Tildy hid a grin. The expression on Linc's face was priceless.

Jewel frowned. "Well, Lordy be, no. That's illegal. However, I would have to put him down in the old-folks home in Mount Sterling, and Elvis isn't good with strangers. I am appealing to your Christian duty to help thy neighbor as they would help you."

Tildy frowned. "That's not exactly how that goes."

Jewel glared at Tildy, then shifted her gaze back to Linc.

"So will you fix up my back porch like you fixed Beulah's door?"

"Yes, ma'am, it would be my pleasure," he said. "I'll have Aunt Tildy show me where you live and I'll be there first thing in the morning to see what supplies I'll need to fix it, if that's all right with you."

Jewel threw up her hands. "Praise the Lord!" Then she realized her husband was gone. "Where's Elvis?"

Linc pointed to the table across the room, where Elvis had taken a seat and was visiting with Sue Ellen.

Jewel gasped. "That old flirt. I'll give him a piece of my mind."

She sped across the diner and took a seat with her husband.

"I'm so sorry," Tildy said. "I didn't know this was going to happen."

Linc chuckled. "It's all right. But you have to come with me."

Tildy grinned. "Surely you're not scared of one little old lady?"

"I plead the fifth, and I see another car pulling up out in the parking lot. We'd better get out of here so they can clean up this table for someone else."

"I'm ready when you are," she said as he helped her on with her coat.

He threw down a handful of bills that included a generous tip and settled the Stetson back on his head as they started toward the door. As he passed a tableful of men, one of them stated loudly what had been on the minds of many in the room.

"'Bout time he left. I wasn't in no mood to eat a meal with a killer."

Tildy stumbled and would have fallen if Linc hadn't been holding her arm. But before she could speak on Linc's behalf, another man on the opposite side of the room spoke up.

"You need to keep your mouth shut, Bill Staley. Wayne Fox swore his grandson was innocent. I believed it then, and I believe it now. He wouldn't have covered up a damn thing for the person who killed his own son, and you're a fool if you think otherwise."

And that was all it took. Like throwing a match into a pile of dry leaves, the shouting began. Before it could become an all-out fight, Linc raised his voice.

"Stop! All of you. This isn't your war, it's mine, and there are no sides to take. Someone on Rebel Ridge got away with murder. I came back to clear my name and get justice for my daddy."

"What took you so long?" someone muttered.

That was when Tildy jumped into the fray. "That's enough!" she said loudly. "I know more about every family on Rebel Ridge than they know about themselves, and I can state with some assurance that there's not a one among you who's pure enough to cast the first stone. If there's one thing I hate its gossip and innuendo. This man here—the one you're pointing fingers at and thinking you know all there is to know about—has been through something few of us will know on this side of heaven. Earlier this year my nephew died and was brought back to life by nothing short of a miracle. He came back to Rebel Ridge because his daddy came to him in spirit and told him to go home. There has been no justice for my brother's murder, and his daddy's spirit is not at rest. Do you hear what I'm saying? The next time one of you comes knocking on my door wanting some healing, you better hope I haven't heard that you were saying bad things about Lincoln, because I'll send you packing, no matter what your misery."

Lincoln put his arm around his aunt. She was so mad she was trembling.

"Are you all right, Aunt Tildy?"

"Of course I'm all right. My belly's full of good food and I'm ready to go home."

"Yes, ma'am," he said softly.

The diner was as quiet as the local bar on a Sunday morning as they walked out, leaving the discord behind them. They drove from the parking lot and headed home.

"I'm so sorry," Lincoln said.

Tildy snorted beneath her breath. "I'm not. I had a

wonderful dinner with you, and that little bit of huff and puff did not ruin a bit of it. But I am full as a tick and ready for a nap."

He smiled. "If you nod off in the truck, I'll wake you when we get home."

She sighed. "Pinch me if I snore."

He laughed. "I know a wildcat when I see one. My daddy raised me smarter than that."

She laughed, and the sound filled the cab all the way to Linc's heart.

It was midafternoon, and the sun was hidden by the cloud cover blowing in by the time Linc drove up to Meg's house and parked. Honey was on the porch barking as he got out.

"Hey, girl, you know it's just me," he said, and the long-legged pup came hobbling toward him with her tail between her legs. He squatted down and cupped her muzzle as he scratched at a spot behind her ear. "Hi, baby…hi, pretty girl. What's Meg doing? Huh?"

Meg guessed it was Linc when she heard Honey bark, and she came out to welcome him. But when she saw him on his knees in the yard playing with the dog, her heart melted. In her eyes, he was so beautiful. She ached at the thought of loving and being loved by this man for the rest of her life.

A gust of cold air suddenly shifted her focus and she called out, "Hey, you two!"

Linc looked up. Meg was standing in the doorway smiling. The blue jeans she was wearing accentuated her long, lean body, and when he stood up and headed for the house he had the strongest urge to take them off her.

"Afternoon, Meg," he said as he stepped up onto the porch.

"Hi, you," she said, and shut the door behind him.

As Linc began taking off his coat and Stetson, he noticed her sweater was the same green color as her eyes. He hung the hat on the back of a rocking chair and dumped his coat on the seat. His voice deepened as he wrapped his arms around her, intending to just give her a quick hug.

"You are a beautiful woman, Meg Lewis." Moments later he buried his face against the curve of her neck. "Oh man, you smell good. What are you wearing?"

The feeling of déjà vu was bittersweet. Being held in Lincoln's arms made her ache. The only thing going through her mind was, what was she waiting for? Then she realized he was talking to her, and she stuttered some kind of response that she hoped made sense.

"Huh? Wearing…uh, no perfume. It's probably just vanilla. I made cookies."

He pulled back long enough to get a good look at her face. Her eyes said yes and her lips were parted. He didn't wait for her to change her mind.

He centered his mouth on her lips and then groaned as the kiss deepened. She tasted as good as she smelled.

"Cookies," he whispered as he lifted his head. Then he kissed her again—softer, longer—before lifting his head again. "Chocolate chip?"

Meg's sanity was teetering. Did he want to make love or eat?

"Yes…with pecans."

"Have mercy," he whispered, and kissed her again. "Are you going to let me have some?"

Her knees went weak. She was completely lost as to where this conversation was going.

"Have what?"

"Whatever you're willing to part with."

"Lord have mercy, Linc. Cookies are in the kitchen. My bedroom is the last door on the left at the end of the hall. Take your choice."

He held out his hand. "Can I have both?"

Her heart was pounding, and there was a slight roaring in her ears, making it difficult for her to hear what he was saying, but she could tell from the look on his face that he wanted it all. She sighed.

"I have no shame. I want to make love with you."

He grunted softly as he scooped her up in his arms and carried her down the hall to her bedroom. The door was ajar as they went inside. He toed it shut and laid her down on the bed.

Meg's hands were trembling so hard she couldn't unfasten her jeans.

Linc's shirt was already off when he saw her struggling and pushed her hands aside.

"Let me, baby."

The snap popped, the rasp of the zipper was loud in the silence, and then magically the jeans were on the back of a chair. She was thinking that his skills in this department had definitely improved when her sweater was suddenly over her head. Seconds later he kicked off his boots and stripped out of his jeans.

The burn scar spanning his body enhanced the play of muscles in his chest and arms as he stretched out beside her on the bed. She rolled toward him, arching her back as he unfastened her bra. When he hooked his thumbs in the elastic of her panties and began pushing them slowly downward, she wanted to scream. Even though it had been a very long time since she'd made love to a man, there were no awkward moments between them. He'd taught her how to make love, and she had been an exceedingly good student. She'd known everything there was to know about the boy he'd been, but this man was a stunning enigma, and she was shaking with the need to be with him.

Their gazes caught, the passion and lust they were feeling mirrored in each other's eyes. He cupped the back of her head and slid his mouth across her lips, then straddled her body, pinning her between the soft mattress at her back and the rock-hard muscles of his body. It was but a hint of what was to come.

Blood was roaring in Meg's ears. Every muscle in her body felt as if it was strung too tight to move, and yet she reached for him, curling her fingers around his forearms as he put his hands on her breasts.

Then he rolled her nipples between his fingers, and before she could catch her breath she climaxed. Too many years of doing without—then one man's touch and she came undone. The moan that came up her throat was an echo of every night she'd spent alone.

The moment she began to come Linc rose up and slid inside her, taking her hard and fast. His erection was throbbing, and the wet heat of her body was like gasoline to a flame. He needed to make love to make it better, to put his stamp on the woman the same way he'd marked the girl. So he did, rocking thrust after thrust—remembering how it had been and at the same time making memories. He didn't slow down and he didn't let go until he felt her coming again. After that he lost his mind.

He heard her crying, felt her arms around his neck as he collapsed on top of her, and couldn't think—couldn't move. Eighteen years of rejection had just been cured by making love to the girl he'd left behind.

He felt blessed.

He felt healed.

And too soon or not, he felt love.

It wasn't his fault it hadn't died, and there was nothing he could do to slow down the emotions rushing through him. He cupped her cheek, wiping away the tears on her face, then ran his hand down her neck, across her breast and stopped, splaying his fingers on the flat of her belly.

"You are so beautiful, Margaret Ann."

A fresh set of tears suddenly blurred her vision. It was the same thing he'd said to her the first time they'd made love. Her voice cracked.

"Ah, Linc, it makes me sad to think of all the years we lost."

"No regrets, Meg. No regrets. We have now, and that's all that matters."

She traced the ridge of scar tissue beneath her fingers. "I used to tell you right about now how much I loved you."

Linc took her hand and held it against his heart. "I remember."

A soft sigh slid from between her lips. "I don't know what you're thinking, but I have to be honest because it's how I am. For me…what just happened here didn't happen for old time's sake."

"Not for me, either. I've only loved but one woman in my life, and that was you. The love didn't die. I never dreamed that when I came back I'd find you free. I'm hoping you'll give me another chance to make this right…although I won't make a commitment to anything or anyone until the people who killed Dad are brought to justice."

She gasped. "People? As in more than one?"

He nodded. "It's something Aunt Tildy said about Dad being too big to be taken down by one person. She said she always believed there had to be more than one killer, and it makes sense to me, too."

Meg's voice was shaking. "Then that just adds to the danger you're in."

"I know, but I will be careful."

She heard him, but it didn't make her feel any better.

Linc rolled off and then pulled her toward him, until they were lying face-to-face with nothing between them but the truth. He slid a hand beneath her hair, searching her expression for regret that they'd gotten here so fast.

There was none.

"Meggie…sweetheart…losing you was always the single biggest regret of my life. There are no words to express what I'm feeling right now except that I am so damned grateful for a second chance. I don't take this lightly, and I will do everything in my power to stay safe. What does concern me is someone using you to get to me."

She cupped his cheek. "We'll figure this out. I'll do anything I can to help you."

"I don't want you involved in this in any way."

"But—"

He put a finger on her lips. "No buts. I'm serious."

She sighed. "I get it, and okay."

"Thank you. Now…about those cookies…"

She grinned. "They're cooling on a rack in the kitchen."

He leaned over and gave her a quick kiss. "I'll make coffee."

"Already made."

"Then what are we waiting for?" he said, and rolled out of bed, gathered up the clothes they'd shed and tossed them back up on the mattress.

Meg sorted through the stack for her clothes and headed for the bathroom, leaving Linc on his own. By the time she got to the kitchen he was swallowing his first cookie and had another in his hand.

"I poured coffee," he said, eyeing her long stride with appreciation as she sauntered into the room. He handed her a cookie and winked.

"Thank you," she said, and then sat down at the table and pulled the hot mug toward her. "Tell me about your dinner with Aunt Tildy. How did it go? Was anyone mean?"

He picked up his coffee and sat down. "Oh, there was a little dustup just as we were about to leave. I had my say, and then Aunt Tildy lit into the middle of all of them, pretty much told them my daddy's ghost sent me back for justice, threw out a verse from the Bible about no one there being clean enough to cast the first stone, then threatened to cut off her healing treatments to anyone bad-mouthing me. It was a pretty staggering vote of confidence."

She laughed. "Oh, my Lord, I would have liked to hear that! Most everyone on Rebel Ridge is superstitious. Throwing out the ghost business and then threatening to cut off the healing will definitely shut them up."

A clap of thunder abruptly ended the conversation as Honey began to bark.

Meg frowned. "I can't believe it's going to rain again. Poor baby. She doesn't like storms. I need to go let her in."

She darted out of the room.

Moments later Linc heard the dog whining and her toenails clicking on the hardwood floors as she followed Meg back into the kitchen. Meg gave her a treat and then settled her on a rug by the stove.

Linc was standing at the window, looking up at the sky as she came up behind him, then ducked under his arm and leaned against him.

"Here it comes," he said as he slid an arm around her shoulders and pulled her close. And just like that, the sky opened and the rain came down in sheets. "Do you have evening chores?"

"I already fed the chickens and shut them up because I knew the weather was changing. I was milking at night, but the cow finally dried up. I already fed her, too, but I'm glad not to have to milk her this winter."

He was quiet for a few more moments, watching the rain coming down. All of a sudden he turned her loose, shoved his hands in his pockets and turned to face her.

"You said you wanted to help."

"Yes!"

"There *is* something you could do, and no one would know you're doing it. Do you have a laptop?"

"I do now. Quinn fixed it for me so that it uses the same signal I use for my cell phone…at least I think that's how it works. I use it to contact my customers. What can I do?"

"Something is bothering me about the White brothers being so 'on the spot' the night of the fire. Their presence may have nothing to do with it but, either way, I need to eliminate them as suspects. There's one weird thing I've learned that may or may not have anything to do with the murder. They owed forty thousand dollars on their home place and it was in foreclosure. Two weeks before Dad was killed it was abruptly paid off, with enough left over for renovations. I'm almost positive the money was obtained illegally."

"I'd believe that," Meg said. "But how do we go about finding out?"

"It'll take some time and research on your part, and if you don't have time now because of your quilt show, then wait until it's over."

"I'll make time. Tell me what to do."

"Find out how many unsolved thefts occurred in Kentucky in the month Dad was killed. Thefts involving large sums of money."

"You've really been thinking about this, haven't you?"

He nodded. "I don't know how Dad might have played into this, but if it happened and he found out... he would have turned them in. I know it. That could be grounds for murder and the motive that has been missing all these years."

She was excited to be able to help him. "I'll make a list of anything I think might fit the criteria, and you can go from there."

Another clap of thunder rattled the windows. The pup jumped up from the rug in front of the fire and loped out of the room. Meg shivered. "It's getting colder. I need to turn up the heat."

Linc slid a hand beneath her hair and pulled her close.

"Or we could go back to bed."

"Or we could go back to bed," she echoed.

"You have the best ideas," he whispered, and lowered his head.

Fourteen

After Fagan ordered him out of the house at gunpoint, Prince had bawled for about a mile and then started working on his next step. The plan he came up with was a good one. The quickest way to get people off his back was to die. It would mean giving up his only means of transportation, but that would be fine if it worked.

The next step was how to off himself and make it believable that there would be no body to be found. The solution came to him just before daylight as he was crossing a long bridge over the Kentucky River. He began looking for another access and found a smaller bridge over another arm of the river, and that night he went back, wedged a beer can against the gas pedal to rev the engine, put the truck in gear and aimed it at the gap between the bridge railing and the highway. The truck hit the bridge as it rolled toward the river, raking paint off on the driver's side door before going airborne.

Prince watched as it hit the water nose first and then began to sink. He'd left the windows down, his wallet in the console and a suitcase full of clothes on the floor, hoping that when the truck was found the authorities would think he'd drowned and been washed downstream.

"Rest in peace," he said, and then laughed at his own joke as he started walking the highway in the opposite direction of Mount Sterling. It was miserably cold, and he was wishing he'd had the sense to keep his hat and gloves.

Just before daybreak he stole a car from a trailer park and finally headed back to the only person he knew who might still take him in: his sister, Lucy. Once he got to Mount Sterling he found another motel and hid out in the lot. Then, when no one was looking, he traded license plates with a traveler who'd stopped at the motel for the night. He watched as the man left the next morning, unaware of the switch.

Prince knew it could be days, if not weeks, before the man ever discovered the theft, which gave him plenty of time to work his next con. He drove by Lucy's house the next morning, then lost his nerve and spent the next two days holed up in a motel by day and driving by her house at night, trying to work up the courage to go to the door.

What surprised him during his surveillance was Wes's absence. He finally found Wes's car parked at the motel across the street from the dealership. Whatever was going on with Lucy wasn't good, and Prince was happy to get the gist of how desperate she just might be.

The next night, as he was watching the late news, eating take-out burritos and downing beer, he realized the story they were doing was about him.

The law had finally found his pickup.

There was his brother Fagan standing on the riverbank beside the sheriff and the truck that had been winched out of the river, and damned if the bastard wasn't crying. Prince sloshed beer down the front of his shirt as he reached for the remote to turn up the volume.

"I'll be a son of a gun," he said, and then chortled with glee.

The camera panned to a close-up of the sheriff as someone shoved a microphone in front of him.

"So, Sheriff Marlow, have you found the body yet?"

"No. It's been raining a lot lately, and the current is strong. Of course we have searchers already at work, but there's no way to know how long the vehicle has been in the water."

"Has the family made a statement of any—" the newsman asked.

Marlow nodded curtly. "That's all. If you'll excuse me…"

The camera swung toward Fagan again.

Prince grinned. The little bastard was bawling big-time.

Good. It's what he gets for running me off like that.

And if they thought he was dead, the warrant for his arrest would slide right off Marlow's list of things to be done.

Prince swung his feet from the bed and began getting dressed. If Lucy thought he was dead and he showed up suddenly resurrected, she might be more likely to forgive and forget. A few minutes later he was in his car, taking alleys and back roads to get to her house.

The liquor cabinet was empty. The two bottles of champagne that she and Wes had been saving in the fridge for New Year's Eve had long since been popped and emptied, as well. Lucy was more sober now than she'd been in days, and it was only because everything alcoholic was gone and she was too hungover to drive. She had called a liquor store that they frequented to see if they would deliver, only to have her credit cards—all of them—rejected when she'd tried to pay.

At first she'd been shocked, then confused. It didn't occur to her that Wes had anything to do with it until she called the bank and found out the bank accounts had been emptied, as well. For all intents and purposes she was broke and about as close to being homeless as she'd ever been. She was scared, and she was desperate.

When she got a phone call from Fagan telling her that they thought Prince was dead and the law was pulling his truck out of the river, she didn't have any emotion left to spare on anyone else.

"Fagan...will you help me? I'm desperate!"

"Help you how? Our brother is dead, and all you can think about is yourself?"

"Wes cut off my money. The next thing coming will probably be divorce papers, and I can't let that happen. I can't lose everything I've worked so hard to get."

It was the silence on the other end of the phone that made her panic, thinking he'd hung up on her again.

"Fagan? Fagan! Are you still there?"

"Yes, I'm here. What do you expect me to do about your marital problems? Whatever is going on between you two is not my business."

She hesitated, then blurted it out. "I need to stop Wes before he can get to a lawyer. For all I know, he may already have done it. But until I'm served with papers, technically I would know nothing about it."

"So?"

"So...make me a widow. If something happened to

him before he had time to file, then everything would be mine."

This time there was no mistaking what she'd asked, and there was no mistaking the click in her ear when he hung up.

This latest setback was yet another nail in her coffin.

She sat, staring blankly at a painting over the mantel, going back over the past few days and trying to figure out what she could have done differently that would have kept her out of this mess.

She still had one hand to play. If she could just find a way to appeal to Wes's sympathies, she could handle the rest. She took a deep breath and dialed Wes's number, praying he would answer.

Wes was staring at an odd mark above the television, wondering how the outline of a man's shoeprint had wound up that high on the wall, while his life flashed before his eyes. He was reliving every mistake he'd ever made, beginning with the day he'd stolen a candy bar out of Barney's Groceries down in Boone's Gap when he was ten.

You reap what you sow, Wesley. You reap what you sow.

He groaned. For the past few days he'd been unable to get that out of his head. Mother had always been right. It was just a damn shame it had taken him the better part of his life to admit it. When he realized the people in the news clip on the television were people he knew, he upped the volume. He was stunned that he knew them, and even more so when he recognized one of his brothers-in-law.

"What the hell?"

A few moments later he figured out they were look-ing for Prince's body. The way he felt about the family, he couldn't see how Prince's death could be a bad thing. He heard the sheriff say the family had been notified, which meant Lucy knew, too.

Lord. He couldn't wrap his head around ever talk-ing to her again, and yet he knew it would happen. No sooner had the thought gone through his head than his cell phone rang.

He saw caller ID and sighed. *Think of the devil and he—or she—turns up unannounced.*

Lucy.

The thought of hearing her voice begging him to come home was going to kill him, and he knew she was going to beg, because he'd taken away the single one thing she valued most. Money.

He let the phone ring a couple more times just to make her wait, then answered gruffly, needing the an-tagonism to help him keep his edge.

"What?"

Lucy heard the anger in his voice and wanted to scream at him, but this was not the time to be confron-tational. She needed to play on his sympathy and started to weep, but quietly, not shrieking in anger.

"Oh, Wesley, something terrible has happened. Prince is dead," she said, and then started to sob more loudly.

"I already heard."

"What am I going to do? I'm so sad I can't bear it. I want you to come home. Please, Wes, come home to me. I need you. I can't lose *you,* too."

"No."

She choked on a sob. "What do you mean, no?"

"No, I'm not coming home."

She took a deep breath and turned off the tears. "Ever?"

"Ever. I don't know who you are anymore. I'm not even sure I ever knew you."

"Why did you cancel my credit cards and take the money out of our account? I didn't think you could be this cruel. Wesley, please…what do you expect me to do?"

"You've been using me for years, Lucy. I don't intend to be used like that again. I have reparation to make, and I don't know what's going to happen to me after it's done. For all I know we'll both wind up in prison for what we did to Lincoln Fox."

Horror swept through her so fast she forgot she meant to stay calm.

"No! You fool! You crazy fool! You don't mean it! Wes, please…don't. If you ever loved me, don't do this."

"We committed an unforgivable sin, Lucy. We lied about an innocent boy, and the lie sent him to prison for a crime he did not commit."

"That's not true."

"Even now you're lying, Lucy. When will it stop?"

"Are you going to divorce me?"

"What do you think?"

She was so mad she was shaking. "What do I *think*? I think you're weak. I think you're a quitter. *That's* what I think!" Lucy screamed. "I don't deserve to be abandoned like this."

"Why? It's what we did to Lincoln."

Lincoln. He kept harping on Lincoln. Too bad *he* hadn't died in the fire, too. "I'll get the best lawyer in the state. I'll take you to court for all the alimony I can get," she screeched.

Wes sighed. "You still don't get it, Lucy. The law is not going to ignore what we've done. We committed perjury, and they'll reopen the murder case. When they do, it will be interesting to see who crawls out from under the rocks on Rebel Ridge."

She was still screaming when he disconnected. He laid the phone on the bedside table, and then turned off the television and closed his eyes. He'd already contacted his lawyer and made a full statement about his part in the lie and how it had come about. They'd sent the notarized confession to the sheriff's office in Boone's Gap and another notarized copy to the district attorney. Lucy's anger was the least of his worries. It was only a matter of time before the proverbial shit hit the fan.

Prince pulled up in the alley behind Lucy's house and parked. The air was so cold it stung his face as he got out. He turned his coat collar up around his neck, thankful for the gloves he'd found in the stolen car, and slipped through the gate leading into her backyard, confident that the eight-foot privacy fence would conceal his presence from the neighbors.

Lights were on in the kitchen. When he looked through the window he expected to see her, but the room was empty. What he did see, however, was shocking. Dirty dishes were piled all over the counters and in the sink, while dozens of empty liquor bottles were scattered about. Lucy always *had* been a hard drinker. He didn't know what was going on with her and Wes, but whatever it was, she was drowning her sorrows.

He knocked on the back door, then waited, hoping she wasn't passed out somewhere. A couple of minutes passed and he knocked again, louder and longer. Finally he heard footsteps, saw a curtain shift slightly at the window, and then the door opened and Lucy was standing in the doorway in her pajamas.

"Hey, Lucy…"

"Oh, my God," she moaned. Her eyes widened, then rolled back in her head, and she fainted at his feet.

Prince sighed. At least she hadn't shut the door in his face. He slipped inside, dragged her out of the way and shut the door.

"Lucy! Hey, Lucy!"

She didn't move. He put his boot on her shoulder and gave her a shake.

She moaned, then slowly opened her eyes. When she saw her brother standing over her, she screamed and covered her face.

"Lucy, what the hell's wrong with you?" he asked.

"They said you were dead. I thought you were a ghost come to take me to hell."

He frowned. "Well, that's stupid. I never heard of a ghost being able to take a living person anywhere. What the fuck have you been drinking? Oh, wait. From the looks of this place, I should have asked, what *haven't* you been drinking?"

She moaned again and held up her hand. "Help me up."

Prince pulled her to her feet, then got her to one of the chairs at the kitchen table.

"I'm here because Fagan said you wanted to talk to me. What's going on? This place is a mess, I saw Wes's car at a motel, and you've got the mother of all hangovers."

"Lincoln Fox convinced Wes that he was innocent. Wes confronted me. It got ugly after that. He's taken away all my money, canceled my credit cards. I'm about to be homeless because he's filing for divorce."

Prince frowned. This wasn't what he'd bargained for. He'd come to her for help, not to fix her damn mess.

"Why did you call me? I can't fix your marriage."

She slapped her hand on the table, making the dirty glasses stacked up near her elbow rattle.

"Why did I call you? What's the matter with you? You truly are as dumb as you look. Think about it, brother. Lincoln is digging into everything, and Wes is going to tell the cops we lied. They'll start looking for someone else to blame. Guess who'll be the prime suspects?"

"Well, hell."

"Yes. 'Well, hell' is right."

"So what's the plan?"

"For starters, stop Wes before he divorces me and spills his guts to the cops."

"How do you propose we do that?"

She eyed him carefully. This was where Fagan had balked. Would Prince do the same?

"You could kill him," she said.

Prince didn't blink. "We've been down this road before."

"And?"

"Whatever...I don't have a gun anymore. I pawned it, and I ain't burning down an entire motel of people just to get rid of your problem."

"I have a gun."

"Oh, yeah, right. We use your gun to kill your husband? Seriously, Lucy, don't you watch TV? They got ballistic tests and all that shit. You got a way to explain how your gun killed your husband and not go down for it?"

Her eyes narrowed. "Maybe."

"I'm all ears," he said.

"I'm about to become the victim of a crime. Someone is going to kick in my back door, ransack my house looking for my husband, beat me up, make me tell him where my husband is, knock me out and steal shit, including my gun. While you're taking Wes out, I will have the police at my house making a crime report. All I'll know is that it was a man wanting Wesley Duggan. And nobody will be looking for you because you're already dead."

Prince sat there a minute, thinking. Lucy thought he was going to tell her no, and then he stood up.

"Well, if you're gonna convince the cops about all that, you need to take a bath, wash your damn hair and brush your teeth, then get rid of all these liquor bottles. Right now this place looks worse than mine and Fagan's."

Lucy's eyes widened. "Good thinking. There are trash bags under the sink. Help me." Then she stopped and looked back at her brother. "Put your gloves back on. If I'm about to be robbed, they'll fingerprint this place from top to bottom."

It took nearly an hour for Prince and Lucy to put the house back to rights; then, while she went to shower, he took the garbage bags out into the alley and distributed them among several of her neighbors' garbage bins. When he came back inside she was in a clean pair of pajamas and her hair was still wet. She handed him a bag with her jewelry in it, along with some of their silver and a laptop. The handgun was on top, loaded with a fresh clip.

"We just cleaned up the house, now we need to mess

it up again," he said. "Make it look like you fought. Where do you want to start?"

"I've already messed up my room some, tore stuff out of the drawers, and then I hit Wes's office. I'll say I'd been getting ready for bed when I heard you kick in the door. I came running with my gun to see what was happening, and you surprised me in the living room. We need to shove some chairs around, turn some stuff over."

"You're gonna need some bruises and wounds to match—including on your head—or they won't buy it. Especially since Wes and you are on the outs."

She frowned. "Then do it. Start hitting me. Shove me into the furniture. I'll fight back so that my hands will look bad, too."

Prince frowned. "Just don't scratch me. They can get DNA out from under your nails." Then he rolled his eyes. "Shit. We're going to a lot of trouble here."

"If we can't stop this from unwinding, we're in even bigger trouble," Lucy said.

"Fine," Prince said, and hit her on the side of her jaw with his fist. Her head snapped back as she fell against the sofa and end table, and just like that, the lamp went flying.

Her lip was bleeding when she got up. She came at him with her hands curled into claws, aiming for his arm, and broke two nails when she grabbed at his shirt.

He hit her again, and she staggered backward into Wes's leather chair. It scooted across the floor all the way to the fireplace, leaving scratch marks on her precious hardwood floor.

Back and forth they went, until Lucy could only see from one eye, and blood was pouring from her nose and mouth. There was a deep cut in her forehead, and large bruises were already forming on her face and arms. She couldn't imagine what her body must look like under the pajamas, but it had to be bad, because she couldn't quit sobbing from the pain.

"That's enough. Any more of this and I'll be breaking bones," Prince said, and picked up the bag with the loot. "Where's your cell phone?"

Lucy was light-headed and weaving on her feet, but this was good. It added credence to what had happened.

"It's in the kitchen on the table."

Prince went to get it, laid it facedown beneath the edge of the sofa and then glanced at the clock. "Lie down right there with the side of your face on the floor, like you were unconscious. Give me fifteen minutes, then crawl to the phone on your hands and knees. Make sure you're crying and your voice is shaking when you call 911."

"That won't be a problem," she said as she flattened out on the floor. "Oh, my God, I hurt. I think you broke my jaw."

"I'm going to the kitchen now. I'm gonna turn the lock on the door, then kick it in. The door will be open and you're gonna freeze your damn ass, but it will only add to the truth of your statement. Your description of me is going to be vague, because you only got a glimpse before I hit you in the face. After that, you were trying so hard to get away you didn't see much. Tell them I was a white man. Don't go the 'black man did it' route. Tell them you thought I was about forty, and that I had a salt-and-pepper mullet. And make me heavyset. I always wanted to be bigger."

"Forties, heavyset, salt-and-pepper mullet."

"I'm gone," Prince said. "Once Wes is dead, what are you going to do?"

She frowned. "I hate to say it, but I think that as a woman who was just robbed and assaulted in her home, I would be afraid to stay here. I'll figure something out. Do you have a cell phone?"

"I can get a throwaway."

"Call me. The next person who needs to go is Lincoln Fox, and then we're home free."

"I'll be in touch," he said.

"Prince."

"Yeah?"

"Thank you."

"We're not out of the woods yet," he muttered, and left the room.

She heard the door shut, then what sounded like three sharp blows to the wood before she heard it slam against the kitchen wall. She smiled. The bases here were covered. Now all Prince had to do was get Wes.

Wes couldn't sleep, and he couldn't get Lincoln's voice out of his head. There was a knot in his gut that kept getting bigger and bigger. What he'd done to Lincoln was horrifying. He'd prayed to God and was counting on that *ask and ye shall receive* verse being on the up-and-up, because he'd prayed hard for forgiveness. He didn't expect Lincoln to forgive him, but he wanted him to know that he was making amends. Trouble was, he didn't have Lincoln's phone number, so calling him was out of the question.

The couple next door was fighting, which didn't help solve his lack of sleep. He thought they were drunk or high. These days it was hard to tell which. He got up to go to the bathroom, wincing at the feel of grit on the floor and thinking of his beautiful home and the years he'd worked to make a nice life for himself and Lucy. Now she had turned into a lying drunk and he was holed up in this half-assed motel.

The room felt chilly as he crawled back into bed, but he didn't like to sleep in a hot room, so he pulled the covers up tight around his shoulders instead. He was drifting toward sleep when he heard a soft knock at the door and then a high-pitched voice. He couldn't tell what they were saying, but he figured someone had just knocked on the wrong door and ignored it.

The knock sounded again, followed the same muffled voice.

He threw back the covers and stomped to the door. "Damn it to hell, go away!" he shouted, and then yanked the door open. He got a glimpse of someone standing in the shadows with something pointed at his chest. He saw a flash of fire, then everything went black.

Meg and Lincoln were still in bed, and the rain was still coming down. The second time they'd made love it had been without the desperation that had overtaken them before. Maturity had changed the contours of their bodies, and age had given them perspective on how blessed they were to have found their way back to each other. Love was still a tentative word, but it was present in every look, every touch. Linc had professed his intentions. It was enough. All Meg had to do was hope for the best and pray that he could protect himself from the trouble he was stirring up.

When he dozed off beside her with his arm thrown

across her belly, she lay without moving, taking the time to study the man he had become.

His face was what her grandma Foster would have called noble. Even features, dark eyes below a strong brow, a square jaw and seriously sensuous lips. Just thinking what he could do with them made her shudder. But all the looking only enforced what she already knew: that she would never get enough of the man beside her.

Fifteen

It was still raining and nearing nightfall by the time Linc went home. Resurrecting his relationship with Meg had spurred the need to clear his name.

After the warm, homey place he'd just left, coming back to the dark, cavelike room was jarring. He began turning on lights, then carrying out the ashes from his woodstove, thankful for the rain that kept the embers from starting a fire outside. As soon as the stove was clean he built a new fire, then showered while the flames licking at the wood were taking hold. By the time he got out, the place was snug and warm. He dug in the fridge for a snack and settled for a beer and some cheese and crackers, then headed for the recliner to watch some TV.

He was channel surfing as he ate when he caught a news clip that made him up the volume on the remote. He recognized Sheriff Marlow as the man standing on a riverbank. Beyond him was a winch truck pulling a partially submerged pickup out of the water. When he saw Fagan White crying in the background, it only took a couple of minutes before he realized they were talking about searching for Prince White's body.

He grabbed his cell phone and called Meg.

"Hello?"

"Turn on your TV now!"

She threw back the covers and grabbed the remote. "Which channel?"

"Twenty-two."

"Okay...I'm there and...wait. It's over. Was that Sheriff Marlow?"

"Yes. That pickup they were pulling out of the Kentucky River belonged to Prince White. Fagan was in the background all the time Marlow was talking, and he was crying. They're looking for Prince's body."

"Oh, my God! I can't believe this! I wanted this to be over, but I didn't think it would end this way."

"Yeah, me, either. Were you asleep?"

"Barely. I'm glad you called. I will definitely sleep easier tonight."

"Good. And on a different subject, I want you to know that today was the best day I've had since we were in high school."

Meg leaned back against the pillows and closed her eyes. "Me, too, Linc. I've spent a long time waiting to feel like this again. Regardless of why you're here, I'm so glad you came home."

"So am I, honey. Sleep well. I'll call you tomorrow after I finish working on the Thurgoods' porch."

She giggled. "Watch out for Jewel. She'll be looking over your shoulder through the whole event."

"Oh, great. Thanks for the warning."

"It's what you get for being such a good guy."

"Love you, Meggie."

"Love you, too."

* * *

It was nearly eleven in the morning before Linc finished repairing the back stoop at Elvis and Jewel Thurgood's home. The entire morning had been something of a trial, measuring and cutting the lumber while, true to Meg's warning, Jewel Thurgood butted in on a regular basis, making sure Linc was doing it to suit her. Aunt Tildy finally coerced Jewel back into the house under the pretense that it was too cold for her to be outside. The quiet afterward was broken only by the sound of hammer and saw. Now it was just him and Elvis.

The old fellow was leaning against the house out of the wind, quietly watching Linc work, but Linc could see the intelligence in his thoughtful gaze. He was of the opinion that Elvis Thurgood wasn't as diddly as he pretended to be.

Finally Linc drove in the last nail, then stepped back to eye the job.

"What do you think, Mr. Thurgood? Look okay to you?"

"Yes. You did a right fine job," the old man said. "We sure appreciate it."

"I'm happy to help," Linc said.

Elvis Thurgood paused, then put his hands in his pockets and cleared his throat.

"I knew your daddy. He was a right nice guy. All he ever did was brag about you. I never did think you were guilty."

Linc was touched by the simple statement. "Thank you. At the time, it felt like everybody on Rebel Ridge believed I was the devil."

Elvis shook his head. "Not those of us who knew Marcus Fox. Good luck to you. Watch your back."

"That I will," Linc said. The two men shook hands, and the conversation ended.

Linc dropped Tildy at her house and headed home with one of her apple pies for his trouble, but he wasn't thinking about the past. He was thinking about Meg and what he hoped would be their future.

As he came around a curve he saw the mail carrier pulled over at a trio of mailboxes and remembered Meg telling him her brother James carried the mail. To his surprise, James saw him and waved.

Linc smiled and waved back. He was still smiling when he stopped at his own mailbox. He pulled out a large padded mailer, saw the return address on the package and realized the transcript from the trial had finally arrived.

He'd been in such deep mourning for his father that his memories of the entire event were pretty vague. The only clear recollection he had was of the jury foreman reading the verdict that had brought an immediate end to his youth.

A few icy snowflakes fell on his windshield as he pulled up to his place and parked. It was the perfect day to spend some time indoors.

He had the fire going and was making fresh coffee when his cell phone rang. A quick glance at the caller ID made him frown. It was the sheriff. So far, most of his calls had been grudging. He wondered what the hell was wrong now.

"Hello?"

"Lincoln, this is Marlow. I need to fill you in on something."

"I'm listening."

"I just got a document from a lawyer in Lexington.

It's a notarized confession from Wesley Duggan stating that he lied about you during your trial, and that everything he testified to was not something he had witnessed, but that it was something he'd been told to say by the woman with whom he'd been having an affair. He also said that he would testify in court that he lied and take the consequences for perjury."

Linc was stunned. "I can't believe it."

"That's not all. The lawyer wrote an accompanying letter stating that when Duggan confronted the woman, who is now his wife, she didn't deny it."

Linc's heart was pounding so hard he could barely think. "Legally, what does this mean?"

"I'm not a lawyer, but I'd say you're well on your way to having a reason to reopen the case."

"Son of a—"

Marlow sighed. "Yeah. Look. I just want you to know that I'm willing to do my part. I'm going to go through all the reports that are on file and see if I can find any loose ends that would point to someone else."

"I have a starting place for you," Linc said.

"Like what?"

"This won't mean anything to you, because you didn't know the family dynamic at the time. However, Fagan White was the one who called in the fire, and according to one of the reports I got from you, his brothers, Wendell and Prince, were two of the first people on the scene."

"What's unusual about that? Their sister lived there."

"Yes, but she wasn't there. She had gone to a family funeral overnight, and they knew it. See, Dad didn't like Lucy's brothers, and they didn't like him, so there is no reason they should have even been there. And there's something else, something I remembered after I went back to my old home the other day."

"What was that?"

"That evening, when I drove up at the house and saw it burning, I was so freaked out and thinking about my dad that I didn't have time to process this. Then, after the explosion knocked me out, I guess I forgot about it. But the bottom line is that when I got out of my truck that night, I heard a dog barking all crazy in the woods right behind me. It was barking like a dog might bark when it's tied up and then sees something that freaks it out, you know? Our closest neighbor was over five miles away. Hunters up here don't let their dogs run free, and we didn't have any dogs."

"Yeah, so?"

"So right after I heard the dog, I heard some man yelling at it to 'shut the hell up,' and then the house exploded."

"Are you sure that's not something you just imagined?" Marlow asked.

"As sure as I am that I didn't kill my father."

"Well, Wendell is dead, and now it appears Prince is, too, so talking to them about it is out of the question."

"I saw that on the news last night. Have they found the body yet?"

"No, not yet. And you know that river. The body could wash miles downstream before it's found, if ever. We don't even know for sure when the truck went in the water, just when Fagan last saw his brother."

"At least you still have Fagan to talk to. I don't know if she told you or not, but he showed up at Meg's the other night while I was there."

Marlow frowned. "I didn't know anything about that. What did he want?"

"It was weird. He started out by apologizing for what Prince did to her, and then he gave Meg some story about wanting to buy land from her ex, Bobby Lewis, for years and said Lewis finally sent word that he'd sell a part of it, but Fagan didn't get the message, Prince did. He says Prince stepped in and went to see Lewis in prison. Supposedly he was to ask Meg about a parcel of land, but Fagan doesn't know why he tormented her instead. Fagan claims that when he found out about the message from Lewis, he went to see him, but the warden wouldn't let him in because Lewis was too sick."

"But why bother Meg about this?" Marlow asked.

"It seems that the land Bobby is willing to sell is where he buried his favorite hunting dog, and Fagan wanted Meg to tell him where that was so he could see it before he made an offer."

"Did she tell him?"

"No. She told him she didn't know anything about that, and that it must have happened after they were divorced. When he tried to push her about it, I made my appearance. He disappeared pretty fast after that."

"So Meg didn't know?"

"Meg knows, but she didn't tell him because she said Fagan was lying about Bobby wanting to sell. She said Bobby couldn't sell that land, because it doesn't belong to just him. It belongs to all the Lewis kids, so Claude and Jane would have to agree to it, too."

Marlow sighed. "Son of a bitch. Those people just don't go away, do they? I'm gonna have to find out what's going on with them and that land. It doesn't even make sense that Lewis would have anything to do with them, unless he's making amends or something. He killed their brother, for God's sake. Meg's been through enough with all of them, Bobby and the White boys both."

"What are you going to do?" Linc asked.

"I think I'll be paying Bobby Lewis a visit myself, just to see what he has to say about all that. As for this letter, the lawyer says a certified copy was sent to the district attorney, but you need one, too. I'll make a copy for you and drop it in the mail.

"Thank you."

"Don't thank me. Thank Wesley Duggan. He's the one who spilled the beans."

"Yeah, I guess I should," Linc said. "Thanks for letting me know."

After Marlow disconnected, Linc looked up the number of the Ford dealership. The phone rang a couple of times, and then a young woman answered.

"Duggan Ford Lincoln Mercury. How may I direct your call?"

"I need to speak to Wes Duggan."

"I'm sorry, sir. Mr. Duggan is in the hospital. Can someone else help you?"

Linc frowned. "In the hospital? What happened? Did he have a heart attack?"

"No, sir. He was shot last night by an assailant. He's in intensive care."

"At the hospital in Mount Sterling?"

"No, sir. They life-flighted him to Lexington."

"Do they know who shot him?"

"I don't think so."

"What about his wife? Was she injured, too?" Linc asked.

"Mr. Duggan was staying in the motel across the street when he was shot. We were told this morning that his wife was assaulted in her home earlier in the evening. I think you need to speak to the police for further information."

Linc hung up, too shocked to think. He wanted to know the details of what had happened to Lucy, but he knew the cops wouldn't tell him anything. And then he thought of Marlow and called him right back.

The sheriff answered on the third ring.

"This is Marlow."

"I just called Mount Sterling to talk to Wes Duggan and was told he was shot last night at the motel where he'd been staying and taken to Lexington on a life-flight. He's in intensive care. Lucy was supposedly assaulted at about the same time in her home. It's pretty suspicious to me that he spills his guts about her and then he gets shot. I'm curious as to the severity of her assault. Can you find out details and share?"

"I'll make some calls and let you know."

Linc disconnected. Talk about going from high to low in record time. He didn't know how this would impact Wes's confession, or if it would even stand up in court now without him physically present. He felt a moment of defeat, then shook it off. He was far from done with this or with Lucy. Whether he could prove it or not, he knew she was behind his conviction and maybe the attack on Wes, too.

Meg felt somewhat guilty to be happy a man was dead, but if ever a person had been wasting air, it was Prince White. At least she could be thankful that he wouldn't be bothering her anymore. She'd called her mother and broken the news, then talked for almost an hour before they'd finally hung up.

She'd been going through the items she was planning to take to the craft show in Lexington, making sure she had everything she would need laid out. The last thing to do would be drawing cash out of her account so she could make change at her booth. And then her phone rang.

"Hello."

"It's me. Are you busy?"

She frowned at the tone of Linc's voice. "Nothing I can't stop. What's wrong?"

"Can I come over?"

"Of course."

"I'll be right there."

"You're scaring me, Linc."

"No. It's not that. I'll tell you when I get there."

When the line went dead in her ear, she headed for the living room and stood at the window, watching for his truck. Within a few minutes Honey was on her feet, looking down the road, and Meg knew he must be coming up the drive. When he pulled up in the yard Honey barked, but her tail was wagging as she went out to meet him. Meg watched him stop to pet the dog and then head toward the house. Even when he got close enough that she could see his face, she couldn't read his expression.

She went outside, met Linc on the top step and kissed him soundly. His cheeks were cold, but his lips were warm. And he was still in one piece, which was a plus.

"Two warm welcomes. A man couldn't ask for more," he said gruffly.

They walked into the house together; then he shed his coat and hat and turned to face her.

"Sorry for being so mysterious, but I can't decide whether to laugh or cry."

"Sit with me," she said as she made her way to the sofa.

Linc sat down beside her. "The good news first. Got a phone call from Marlow. Wesley Duggan confessed to his lawyer to lying on the stand. Admitted it was Lucy who told him what to say. His lawyer sent Marlow a notarized confession, along with the statement from Duggan that if this went back to court, he was willing to testify and take the consequences for perjury."

Meg gasped. "Linc! That's wonderful!"

He shrugged. "The bad news is that he was shot last night at the motel where he's been staying. Apparently he and Lucy have been living apart, probably since I paid them that little visit. Remember I told you I had the impression that he'd believed what he'd testified to? I guess he went back and confronted her, and it hit the fan. Anyway, they life-flighted him to Lexington. He's in intensive care, and I don't know anything about his condition."

She was stunned. "Dear Lord...what does that do to his confession? Did they arrest Lucy?"

"Hardly. My impression is she's trying to cover her ass by claiming she was assaulted in her home. Supposedly the cops were at her house taking the report when Wes was gunned down."

Meg stood abruptly, then began to pace. "That's pretty convenient. Do you have any idea how severe her injuries were? Did she give any description of the man who did it?"

"I don't know anything about that. Marlow is following up."

"Hang on a minute," she said, and strode out of the room. She came back carrying a notepad and sat back down beside him. "I hope you don't mind, but I roped Quinn into helping with that list you wanted. I kept running into walls online, and without going through all the newspapers in the state for that time period, which would probably take me months, this was the quickest route. With Quinn's job as a ranger, he has access to databases that a civilian wouldn't. And I want you to know he was happy to help, and he said he won't mention a thing about where you're going with the information."

Once again Linc was taken off guard by her family. "No, I don't mind. I'm just surprised he was willing to help."

She smiled. "My family loves me, therefore whoever I love is fine with them."

He wrapped his arms around her. "Thank you for believing, Meg."

She gave him a quick kiss.

"You're welcome," she said, and handed him the pad. "I knew you. It was easy. So this is what's listed on the police books as unsolved thefts with large amounts of money still missing."

Linc glanced at the list and smiled. "Woman…you amaze me. You are still my best backup."

She smiled. "This is a little more serious than the tests we studied for together."

"It's all relative. At the time, those were just as important," he said, starting to go through the list. "I think we can mark this one off. Over a half-million dollars still missing from a Brinks armored truck robbery in Louisville. If they'd stolen *that* kind of money, they wouldn't have had the sense to hide it."

"I thought the same thing, but you wanted all the big ones. This is one I thought looked promising." She pointed.

Linc eyed the info she'd indicated. "A hundred-and-thirty-two thousand still missing from a bank heist in Louisville. Considering Wendell was alive then, I think they could have pulled off something like that and gotten away with it."

"But how would it play into your dad's murder?"

He shrugged. "I'm not sure, but them coming into big money only a couple of weeks before he was killed seems too coincidental to ignore."

"What are you going to do with this information?"

"Ask Marlow for more help. If he can get details of the robberies, something might show up that I'm not seeing."

He set the list aside, smiled and pulled her into his lap.

She put her arms around his neck and kissed the side of his cheek, then his ear, then his lips.

"It's almost noon. I have a casserole in the oven. Do you have time to stay and eat?"

"Yes, gratefully, and after I eat, I'm going to take this list down to Marlow. The sooner he gets on this, the better. And he might have some info for me on Lucy, too."

"Why don't you use my laptop and see what you can find out from the Louisville papers? Do a Google search for the bank, theft and Louisville, and see what pops up? We can take that info to Marlow, too."

"We?"

Meg nodded. "I'm in this with you, Linc. You don't need to stand alone anymore."

He couldn't speak. He just wrapped her in his arms and held her.

The silence was as telling to Meg as their lovemaking had been. She had never felt more loved.

Lucy tried to roll over in her hospital bed and then groaned from the pain. She had four stitches in her head, two cracked ribs, a fractured jaw, and she was bruised over half her body. One eye was swollen shut, her lips were twice their normal size, and one nostril still continued to seep blood.

The bruising on her face was turning a darker purple with every hour, and it even hurt to blink. She was miserable, but at the same time happier than she'd been in days. The only thing that would have made it perfect was if Wes would hurry up and die.

The cop who had broken the news to her about the shooting hadn't given her much hope that he would pull through. She'd wailed loud and long, and he'd been apologetic that he'd had to be the one to give her the bad news. What he didn't understand was that she was crying because that bastard wasn't already dead.

On the plus side, the police had been at her house taking their report when Wes was shot. Without a ballistic test for proof of the specific gun, they did know that he'd been shot with the same kind of weapon she was claiming had been taken during her assault. It was the perfect alibi. She had told them that she and Wes had been arguing, and that he'd moved out of the house after a fight. And she'd already explained that the intruder had taken her gun from her, but that she didn't know what else was taken because she'd been unconscious when the intruder left. The fact that she'd just received the news of the recent death of her brother gave an even bigger boost to her claims of grief. The only thing that she'd changed from what she and Prince had decided was the description of her assailant. When they had asked her what he looked like, she had opened her mouth to say a middle-aged, heavyset man with a salt-and-pepper mullet, but what came out was a small, fortysomething man with brown hair and a thin face. That description, except for the hair color, would have fit either one of her brothers. Even now she didn't know why she'd done it, but it was her belief that the closer you stayed to the truth when you were being deceptive, the easier it was to make people believe you.

The police guessed from the condition of her bed-room and the office that things must have been stolen but were waiting for her to give them a complete list of the stolen goods. It didn't appear that the man had come to rob her, because there were bigger things in the house he could have taken. It appeared that he had turned robber on the spur of the moment, since his main target had been Wes.

As she was waiting for the pain to subside, she heard a knock on her door. Thinking it must be one of her friends, she was arranging herself as she watched it open. A middle-aged woman was standing in the door-way.

"I'm so sorry to disturb you, but are you Lucy Dug-gan? Wesley Duggan's wife?"

"Yes, yes, I am," Lucy said, and then tried to sit up as the woman came toward the bed.

"Please, don't get up," the woman said, and handed Lucy an envelope.

Lucy moaned as she took it. "What is this?"

"Divorce papers, Mrs. Duggan. You've just been served."

The woman pivoted quickly and left before Lucy could take a breath.

"No," Lucy muttered, and quickly opened the envelope and unfolded the contents.

She couldn't believe it. That sorry bastard had acted faster than she'd expected. Her hands were shaking as she scanned the pages, trying to read with only one eye. The words were blurry, but she saw enough to realize things weren't quite as simple as they'd been five minutes earlier. Then another couple of pages fell out from the stack, separate from the divorce proceedings. She unfolded them, saw they were from their lawyer and began to read.

Dear Mrs. Duggan,
Since I am representing your husband in these divorce proceedings, you will need to retain separate counsel. You understand that even though I have been counsel for both of you in the past, I cannot represent you now. Also, please be advised that your access to all moneys and property will be frozen until the terms of the settlement can be reached.

At my client's request, I am enclosing a copy of a notarized letter he has sent to the sheriff in the county where Marcus Fox was murdered. A copy has also gone to the district attorney in the district where the trial against his son, Lincoln

Fox, was held. Again, I urge you to retain counsel at your earliest opportunity. It appears you will
be needing it.
Sincerely,
Dwight B. Simpson, Esquire

Lucy read Wes's statement in growing disbelief.
When she got to the end, her heart slammed against her
chest with such a thud that for a moment she thought it
had stopped. She choked and then coughed as she struggled to catch her breath, her mind in an all-out panic.
He'd confessed to lying on the stand, and said that when
he'd confronted his wife to ask if she'd been telling him
the truth about Marcus and Lincoln Fox's relationship
she'd admitted to him it was a lie. She didn't know what
to think, what to do. After everything she'd just endured,
was she going to be too late to save herself?

Should she run or play dumb? She was a damn good
liar, but convincing a jury of her innocence, even though
she had not been present when her husband was murdered, wasn't going to be easy. Not when they found out
she'd been fucking her husband's best friend and he'd
just admitted he'd testified to her lie and pointed the
finger of guilt at an innocent boy.

She'd worked so hard to climb out of the poverty
into which she'd been born, and everything had been
perfect—as perfect as she could ever have wanted it to
be. Damn Lincoln Fox forever for coming back where
he didn't belong.

The phone at her bedside began to ring. She didn't
know whether to answer it or not. If it was more bad
news, she wasn't sure she could take it. But it continued
to ring until she finally picked it up. "Hello?"

"It's me."

A tear slid from the corner of her good eye and rolled down the curve of her cheek as she recognized Prince's voice. She began to whisper her news in frantic bursts of information.

"He's still alive, but he'd already confessed to his lawyer and filed for divorce. I was just served papers. They also a copy of his confession of perjury. It's already gone to the sheriff and the district attorney."

The silence on the other end of the line was unexpected.

"What are we going to do?" she asked, and then started to cry.

She was shocked when the line went dead in her ear. But the moment it did, the fear she'd been feeling increased a hundredfold. The only thing Wes had ever known about the crime was the story he told on the stand. He had no idea who she was protecting. She was the only person not involved in the actual murder of Marcus Fox who knew the guilty parties and the reason why it had happened. Would her brother get rid of whoever else he needed to in order to keep himself out of prison, even if it meant killing one of his kin?

In a heartbeat.

Lucy closed her eyes and eased down against her pillows, willing herself to a calm she didn't feel. There was still a way out of this. She just needed to figure it out.

A minute passed, and then another. She could hear trays banging and people talking out in the hall, going about their daily lives as if nothing was wrong. How could such mundanity still exist when her world was crashing down around her ears?

And then it hit her. It was so brilliant that if she hadn't been so sore, she would have patted herself on the back.

She looked toward the door and then began buzzing for the nurse. They needed to notify the police that she'd just received a threatening phone call from her assailant.

Within twenty minutes her room was crawling with cops. One was standing guard outside her door, and detectives Kennedy and Tate, who were working both Wes's shooting and her assault, were standing by her bed.

Lucy knew she looked worse than she had last night when she'd been admitted, which put the cops in her emotional corner. And she'd been crying nonstop since the threatening phone call, which only added to her pitiful state. A nurse was standing right there, monitoring her blood pressure as they began to interrogate her.

"Mrs. Duggan, just tell us what he said from start to finish."

She nodded, pulled a handful of tissues from the box and then dabbed at her eye. "It all began a few days ago with a visit from my brother Prince White. As you know, the police have been searching for his body ever since they pulled his pickup from the Kentucky River."

One of the detectives stopped her. "Yes, ma'am, but what does that have to do with your assault and the phone call today?"

"I'm getting to that," she said. "Anyway, as I was saying, Prince showed up at my house demanding money. He said the law was after him for stalking a woman named Margaret Lewis and he needed to get out of town. I told him to leave or I'd call the law on him myself. Then he told me if I didn't help him, he'd hurt Wesley. I panicked. I gave him all the cash I had, which was over six hundred dollars, and he left. Then the police called me to say he'd drowned, and I thought that was the end of it."

She'd cried so long her whole body was shaking, so she stopped to take a sip of water. The simple act made her lip begin to bleed again, which emphasized the damage she'd suffered during the attack. Everything was going according to her plan. She could tell by the looks on their faces that she had the detectives in the palms of her hands.

"I'm sorry," she mumbled as she dabbed at a dribble of blood on her chin. "Last night I was still so terrified by what had happened to me, and then, when I learned what had happened to Wesley, I panicked. I wasn't entirely truthful with you then, but now I'm telling you the rest of what I should have told you last night. I knew my attacker. It was my brother Prince. He isn't dead. He faked his death, then came by to get more money from me, and when he found out Wes had moved out and frozen our bank account, he went crazy. He asked me where Wesley was, and I wouldn't tell him. That's why he beat me. My brother is the man who shot Wesley, and he's the one who just called me and threatened my life. He's crazy. When he finds out that I told you, he'll kill me, too."

Lucy turned her tears into gut-wrenching, body-trembling sobs.

"Why is this happening? I've spent my life trying to live down the family into which I was born, but no matter how hard I try, they're always in the background, committing one ugly deed after another, and pulling me and my reputation down with them. I wish he'd killed me, too. I can't go through all this without Wesley."

"But, ma'am, your husband isn't dead. He's still in intensive care. I don't have an update on his condition, but while there's breath there's hope."

Lucy rolled over onto her side—groaning in genuine pain, though she would have faked it for effect if she'd had to—and covered her face.

"That's enough," the nurse said. "She's under too much stress. You'll have to leave."

One of the detectives paused. "There will be a guard on her room at all times until we apprehend the accused."

The nurse nodded. "I'll inform the head nurse and Mrs. Duggan's doctor."

Within moments the room was quiet, except for Lucy's sobs. The nurse came back and injected her IV with pain meds and a sedative. Lucy cried for a little while longer, just to make sure the guard out in the hall heard her, and then closed her eyes and gratefully let the meds take her away.

Sixteen

Lincoln was so focused on reading about the unsolved bank heist that he didn't realize Meg was setting the table around him until she put the hot casserole on a trivet and he smelled the aroma of melting cheese. He stopped and looked up.

"Oh man, that smells good."

Meg leaned over his shoulder. "What did you find?"

He pointed to the article he'd pulled up on her laptop. "There were two armed men wearing ski masks and camo-style clothes. One had a handgun, one had a rifle. No automatic weapons, which makes me think it was amateurs...although this *was* a little over eighteen years ago, before automatics became so commonplace. Also... see here...they had a good description of the getaway car and even a tag number. All that and they still never solved it. Hmm, it was a Wisconsin tag. Probably not what we're looking for, but we'll mark it just the same."

"Bookmark the site," Meg said. "We'll send it to the sheriff and let him read it. He can always get more details for us."

"Good idea," Linc said, and closed the laptop and

pushed it aside. He eyed the food she had put on the table and then grabbed her hand. "Is this a preview of what I can expect for the rest of my life?"

She kissed his ear and then gave him a hug. "It is if you want it to be."

He pulled her into his lap and kissed the hollow at the base of her throat.

"God, you are a stunning woman."

She rubbed her thumb along the curve of his lower lip. "Well, thank you very much," she said softly, then kissed the spot where her thumb had been.

There was a knot in Linc's throat that made it suddenly hard to speak. He coughed to clear his throat and said, "You asked me what I want. I want to be happy, and live to be an old man with a whole lot of kids and grandkids, and I want you standing right beside me until I've taken my last breath."

"Oh, Lincoln. You always took my breath away, and you just did it again." Tears welled as Meg buried her face against his neck.

The faucet at the sink was dripping into a bowl of standing water. The soft plink, plink, plink was like a metronome, marking off the timing in their lives. They'd lived, loved and lost once. Finding each other again and shooting for the same goal was scary as hell.

Honey barked once. It broke the tension of the moment as Linc looked up.

"What does one bark mean?"

Meg smiled. "Bird. Squirrel. Rabbit. Some critter too close to her territory."

He chuckled. "So now I'm forewarned that you will know my burk as well as you know your pup's."

She laughed. It broke the tension of the moment so

that they got to the food without any more tears. Linc was spooning the hamburger casserole onto his plate when Honey began barking in earnest.

"Not a bird," Meg said, and got up to see who was there. A quick glance out the window and she called back, "It's Quinn. Set another plate."

Lincoln's heart skipped a beat. He'd heard enough from Meg about Quinn's recent history to know that he would be the most suspicious member of the family. And yet he *had* helped Meg do that research. He sighed. First one-on-one with a family member and it *would* be the hard-ass.

When he heard a male voice in the living room, he turned around to see Meg coming back with Quinn at her side. She was smiling, but he could tell she was anxious on his behalf. There was no way to get over this other than to get through it. He went to meet Quinn with his hand outstretched.

"Quinn. It's been a long time," he said.

Quinn blinked, then grinned. "Damn, man. Talk about growing up. I hope you're through or your head is gonna go through the roof."

And just like that, the tension was over. "Yeah, I've been getting that a lot."

Quinn handed Linc a folder. "After I gave Meg that list, I thought you should have these, as well. They're printouts of the crime reports."

Linc's expression brightened. "Thank you! We were going to take the list to Marlow after we ate and get him to do this. You just saved him *and* us a lot of time."

"I should have thought of it before," Quinn said.

Meg poured another cup of coffee and set it on the table, then dished up some casserole for her brother.

"Linc. Tell Quinn your news."

"I hope it's good," Quinn said as they sat back down.

"It was for about three minutes, but now I'm not so sure."

Quinn frowned. "I don't follow."

Linc repeated what he'd told Meg about Wesley's confession, then explained that he'd been shot and was in intensive care, and that Lucy had been attacked in her home at around the same time.

"Holy…" Quinn shook his head. "I am stunned. All these years, they knew it was a lie and let you go down for it."

Linc shrugged. "I'm not sure Wesley knew until I confronted him the other day. And I'm sorry to say I don't believe for a minute that Lucy is innocent in what happened to Wes."

Quinn nodded. "Yeah, considering he just sold her down the river with his own confession, I can see why. At least this gives the authorities a new starting point. If you are no longer a suspect, they have to look elsewhere and…" All of a sudden his eyes widened. "Is this why you wanted these reports? But how does—"

"I'm not sure yet, but my gut tells me there's a connection. The White family's home was in foreclosure until two weeks before Dad's death. All of a sudden the place was paid off and they began fixing it up." Linc repeated the rest of the story, down to the fact that Fagan had called in the fire and the other two had been on the scene to help fight it.

Quinn chewed and swallowed. "But they were Lucy's family."

"But she wasn't there and they knew it." Linc explained the dynamic between his dad and the Whites.

"Okay. That changes things some."

Linc nodded and took a bite himself, then rolled his eyes.

"This is really good, Meg."

She smiled as she dug into her own supper.

"Don't brag on her too much," Quinn drawled. "She's already got a big head about her cooking."

She gave him a hard stare. "I so do not."

Linc laughed, remembering the sibling squabbles. "It's gratifying to know some things never change."

By the time they were down to dessert, Quinn was more than impressed with what Lincoln Fox had done with his life. The family would be thrilled to know about Wesley Duggan's confession, as well as the fact that Lincoln was solvent and a business owner.

Meg put the cookie jar on the table and refilled coffee cups. "Molasses cookies. Made them yesterday. Help yourselves."

Quinn took out a couple while covertly eyeing the byplay between his sister and Lincoln Fox.

"So, once you get all this mess cleared up, are you planning to stay or go back to Dallas?" Quinn asked.

"I plan to rebuild at Grandpa's place."

"You didn't exactly answer my question," Quinn said.

"Quinn, mind your own business," Meg muttered.

"I just wanted to know where my sister was likely to wind up. If you move, we might actually miss her."

Meg rolled her eyes. "Oh, my God! Quinn! Stop talking! Put a cookie in your mouth and chew."

Linc grinned. "Don't worry, the road between here and Dallas runs both ways. I can handle business from almost anywhere as long as I touch base now and then. I'll make sure she doesn't get homesick."

Quinn stuffed a whole cookie into his mouth and nodded. "Good to know," he mumbled.

Meg bopped the back of her brother's head. "Don't talk with your mouth full."

Linc grinned. Today just kept getting better.

Sheriff Marlow frowned as he hung up the phone. The one good idea he'd had in weeks, and he'd waited too long to act on it. He wouldn't be talking to Bobby Lewis about anything, because Bobby Lewis was dead. He'd succumbed to cancer last night, and the warden had already notified the family. Hell of a deal. Now he would have to wait until after the funeral to talk to Claude and Jane to see if they had any notion of why Bobby and Prince had talked.

He glanced at Lincoln Fox's file, picked up one of the reports and began making notes. A few minutes later the door opened. When he saw the couple who walked in, he closed the file and stood up, struggling as to how to break the news to Meg Lewis that her ex was dead.

"Have a seat, you two," Marlow said. "Meg, I'm glad you're here. I have something to tell you, and I'm not sure how you're gonna feel."

Linc glanced at Meg and then took her hand.

"What is it?" she asked.

"I just talked to the warden at the prison where Bobby was housed. I'm sorry to tell you that he passed away last night. I was hoping to be able to talk to him, but that can't happen now. I still want to talk to Claude and Jane, and see if they have any inkling of what was going on, but I won't do that until after they bury their brother. Once again, it's hurry up and wait."

Linc glanced nervously at Meg, unsure of how she was going to react.

She frowned. "I'm sorry he's dead, but I already knew that was inevitable. As for being sad that he's gone, I'm way past that stage."

Marlow was relieved, and so was Linc. Both men settled deeper into their seats.

"So how can I help you?" Marlow asked.

Linc handed him the file Quinn had brought and once again explained his theory about the Whites' windfall having something to do with his dad's murder.

Marlow listened politely but was frank about his opinion. "I think you're reaching here, but I'm happy to look these over and give your idea some thought."

Meg leaned over and pulled out the robbery they'd been focusing on. "Take a look at this one," she said. "The timing and the amount of money fit the scenario Linc was thinking about."

Marlow picked it up and scanned it, and then all of a sudden he looked up at Linc with shock on his face.

"Son of a bitch!" He glanced at Meg. "Sorry, but I think you two have stumbled onto something."

Linc leaned forward. "Why? What did you see?"

Marlow pointed at the spot where the tag number was mentioned. "I recently saw that very license tag."

Linc stood abruptly. "Where?"

Marlow spoke before he thought. "In the barn on the Whites' property…nailed onto the wall to cover up a hole."

Linc grabbed Meg's hand. "We're leaving now."

Marlow was on his feet. "Wait. Where are you going?"

"To get Fagan. To make him talk."

"You'll do no such thing!" Marlow said. "You leave this up to the law to handle."

Linc turned on him. "Like hell. The last time I left my life up to the law, I ended up in prison."

Marlow rolled his eyes. "Then wait, damn it. Let me get my deputy. I'll let you, and only you, accompany us, but that's it. Otherwise I'll lock you up right now. Understand?"

Linc strode back to where Marlow was standing, so furious he was struggling with the urge to punch the man. It was the same helpless, railroaded feeling he'd had when his grandfather had given him an ironclad alibi and the law had completely ignored it.

It was Meg who calmed him down when she took him by the hand. "Linc, you want this done properly so the court can't throw out anything Fagan might say because he claims he was coerced. Right?"

Linc took a deep breath. When he spoke to Marlow, the threat was still in his voice.

"If you don't ask the right questions, I will. This is my life the law screwed up, not yours. Do *you* understand *me?*"

"Fair enough. You can ride in the cruiser with Deputy Eddy and me. Meg, you drive his truck home. I'll drop him off at your place when we're done."

Meg gave Linc's hand a quick squeeze. "Yes, I will. Okay, Linc?"

He was still looking at Marlow as he dug out the car keys and handed them to her. "Drive careful." Then he turned around and took her by the shoulders. "I'm sorry. I swear to God, once this is over, I will never lose my temper again."

She cupped the side of his face. "Don't make promises you can't keep, Linc. I don't care how mad you get, as long as it's not at me."

Ignoring the fact that Marlow was watching, he kissed her.

"Like I said, drive careful."

"I will. See you soon."

She left the office, leaving Marlow and Linc alone.

"I need to radio Eddy and have him come in," the sheriff said.

"Where is he?"

"Gassing up the cruiser. Timely task, as it turns out, wouldn't you say?"

Linc shoved his hands in his pockets and started to pace, while Marlow had a conversation on the phone and then began digging through a file cabinet. Linc didn't pay any attention to what the sheriff was doing and was still pacing when the deputy came in the back door.

Marlow rolled a piece of paper out of his old type-writer and then stapled it to the others on the desk. "Let's go," he told the deputy. "I'll fill you in on the way."

When Linc followed them, Eddy stopped. "Where's he going?"

"With us, and I'm driving."

Eddy handed him the keys.

"We have to stop at Judge Early's office to get this search warrant signed," Marlow said.

They buttoned up their coats and headed out. The day was clear, but the wind was sharp. A good day for rabbit hunting, Marlow thought, but it would be even better if they were able to take down a criminal instead.

Fagan White was on a mission. He was turning his grief over his brother's untimely death into a motive for

change. For the past twenty-four hours he'd been hauling crap out of the house and burning it in a fire pit in
the bare ground out back. He'd cleaned out the old fireplace and had a fire going in it as he worked. Empty liquor bottles and beer cans were going into garbage bags
to recycle down in Mount Sterling. He'd swept cobwebs
down from ceilings that had been there so long they
were crumbling. He cleaned the trophy heads mounted
on the walls, then began sweeping dirt off the floors.
After he'd dusted the entire house, including window-
sills and blinds, the dogs were banned. As soon as he
made the last trip out to the fire pit, he got down the
mop and bucket and set to work.

He seemed to remember his mama putting something
in her mop water that made the house smell clean, but
there wasn't anything to hand but soap. It would have
to do. He sloshed the sponge mop around in the bucket,
squeezed out the excess water and got to work.

The water was brown almost instantly, but he kept
throwing it out and getting fresh as he mopped his way
through the house until the floors were shiny and the
rooms smelled like pine. That was when he realized it
wasn't anything Mama had put *in* the water to make it
smell good. It was the raw pine floors themselves. He
stood back, looking at the rooms with an air of satisfaction and eyeing the furniture. The cushions of the
couch were worn down to the foam rubber padding,
and the arms of the easy chair were coming apart. He
thought for a minute, then got down two old quilts from
the linen closet and draped one over the chair and the
other over the sofa. The room looked better, but even
more, Fagan *felt* better. When he got a little money he

might get himself a new couch and chair, but for now, this would suffice.

He started to sit down, then thought of the dogs he'd abandoned to the cold and sighed. It was hard being responsible. He grabbed his work coat and a pair of gloves, and headed out back to the dog run. He couldn't remember the last time they'd put new straw in the doghouses, but there were a few bales left in the barn.

A short while later he had all four doghouses filled with straw, and put bowls of food and fresh water inside the run. The dogs kept moving around him with their tails between their legs. It shamed him that he'd treated the dogs like Prince had treated him, but that wasn't happening anymore. After a quick pat on their heads, he closed the gate to the pen and hurried back inside.

The day had started out all sunny, but the sky was getting grayer. Only a couple of days before Thanksgiving and it felt like it was going to snow. If it did, it would be their second snow of the season, and it wasn't even winter yet, which didn't bode well for what lay ahead.

He hurried back inside, carrying an armload of new wood with him, and set it down in a small pile beside the fireplace. When he hung up his coat, the scent of his clothes and body were the only offensive smells in the house. He took himself to the laundry, stripped off everything he was wearing and dumped in into the washer, along with some of the clothes piled against the wall, and started up the machine. He took clean sheets and pillowcases out of the dryer, and walked naked through the house to remake his bed.

It felt weird to be taking a shower and washing his hair in the middle of the day, but he couldn't stop at just cleaning the house. He felt an overwhelming need to clean himself inside and out, as well. By the time he was dry and dressed in clean clothes, he was starving.

A quick glance out the window assured him that the fire in the fire pit was down to ashes. A thin wisp of smoke drifted up into the air and dissipated above the treetops. He turned on the television in the other room so he could hear it as he worked and began making himself a meal. After he started a pot of coffee, he opened a can of soup and put it on to heat, then cut some cheese off the block of cheddar to go with his crackers.

He carried his food to the table, then sat down to eat, crumbling some crackers in his soup without thought and popping a hunk of cheese into his mouth as he waited for his soup to cool.

As he sat, he thought about his brother's body, floating somewhere in the Kentucky River, and wanted to cry. They'd been close when they were little. It was only after they got older that Prince changed. He hung out more with Wendell and turned mean. Fagan never had understood how a person could change that radically and wondered if Prince had always been that way, and if he himself had been too little and timid to understand.

He worried some about how he would pay for the funeral when they finally found Prince and hoped Lucy would be willing to chip in. They didn't have to like each other, but when it came to dying, blood was blood and family had to do their part.

He was washing up his dishes when he heard the dogs begin to bark. He turned off the water and was drying his hands as he headed to the living room. When he peeked out the window he saw the sheriff's car and his heart dropped. They must have found Prince's body.

Oh Lord, he hoped they didn't make him identify it. He didn't want to remember Prince that way.

When he heard their footsteps on the porch he opened the door, then nearly slammed it in their faces. It took everything he had not to cut and run when he saw Lincoln Fox coming up behind the sheriff and his deputy.

"What's he doing here?" Fagan asked.

"Can we come in?" Marlow asked.

Fagan stepped aside, keeping a watchful eye on Fox as the men came into the house.

Marlow and Eddy had been in this house not too long ago and were stunned at the change. They glanced at each other and rolled their eyes, but didn't comment.

"I reckon y'all can take a seat," Fagan said, but Lincoln Fox didn't sit down when the others did. He was standing between the sofa and the door, like he was blocking the exit. It made Fagan nervous all over again. He glanced up at Fox and then quickly looked away.

"We need to talk," Marlow said.

Tears began to roll down Fagan's face. "Did you find Prince? Did you find his body?"

Marlow frowned. "No, no, I'm sorry. I didn't intend to lead you on about that. As far as I know they're still looking."

Fagan covered his face, ashamed to be crying in front of them, but he couldn't stop.

"Last time I saw him, we had a fight. I made him leave the house 'cause he's nothing but trouble."

Lincoln kept moving from one window to the other, then back again, wanting to take control of the conversation and get it over with.

Marlow could hear him pacing the floor and knew it

was just a matter of time until he lost it. He pulled the search warrant out of his pocket and handed it to Fagan.

"Fagan, this here is a search warrant. It gives us the right to search the premises, including all the outbuildings."

Linc was watching Fagan's face. The man didn't look perturbed in any way. Maybe he thought too many years had passed for him to worry, and maybe he'd been nothing more than a bystander to other people's crimes. Still, he must have known, and he had chosen to say nothing. In Lincoln's book, whether you did the killing or watched it being done, it didn't change the guilt factor.

"Okay," Fagan said. "I don't mind. If you tell me what you're lookin' for, I might be able to help you find it sooner. I been cleaning up a bit around here, and I sure would hate to have it messed up all over again."

"We noticed," Deputy Eddy said. "It's nice."

Fagan smiled. "Like Mama used to keep it."

Marlow took advantage of the fortuitous opportunity. "Speaking of your mama, God rest her soul…remember back to the time when the bank was gonna take your place? When the foreclosure notice had already been served?"

Fagan nodded. "Lord, yes. Mama cried for days. We were all just sick about it. We didn't know what to do."

Marlow leaned forward. "So how did you come by all the money to pay off the bank so suddenly?"

Fagan never blinked. "Wendell and Prince. They left one day and came back the next with it. Told Mama they'd gone to Louisiana and won it gambling."

"Like hell," Linc said.

That made Fagan nervous. He stood abruptly, fairly certain that if he confronted Fox the sheriff wouldn't let anything happen. "Damn it, Fox, either sit down or be still. You're getting on my nerves."

And just like that, Lincoln was in his face. "How did Wendell and Prince come by that money? And don't give us any bullshit about gambling. Marlow didn't ask what lie they told your mama. He asked where they got it."

Fagan blinked. He looked to Marlow, and it appeared he wasn't buying the story, either, so he sat back down and tried another one.

"I know they stole it. But I don't know where from."

Marlow frowned at Lincoln, but he wasn't backing down, so the sheriff sighed and motioned to his deputy. "Roger…go out back, get the evidence. Take pictures before you remove it. Bag everything else that looks interesting, too, and bring it all back inside."

"Yes, sir," Eddy said, and left the house.

Fagan stood up. "Where's he going?"

"To the barn to get the evidence nailed to the wall that proves your brothers robbed a Lexington bank over eighteen years ago."

Fagan frowned. "What evidence?"

"The license tag nailed on the barn wall matches the tag number of the car the thieves were driving when they made their getaway."

Fagan sat down with a flop. All of a sudden he was wondering if he'd begun these changes in his life a little too late to make a difference.

"I didn't know that," he muttered, and combed his hands through his hair in frustration.

"It's hell being the only one alive to take the blame, isn't it?" Linc said.

Fagan gasped. "But I didn't do it!"

"Yeah, neither did I, but it didn't stop a jury from sending me to prison," Linc snapped.

Fagan moaned.

"You'll need an alibi," Marlow said. "Where were you on April twelfth that year?"

"Well, hell! I don't remember!" Fagan cried. "Everyone's gone now except me and Lucy, and she's pissed off at me and wouldn't tell the truth if it kept me from hanging."

Lincoln frowned. "Why is Lucy mad at you?"

Fagan glared. "You started it by going to her house and threatening her," he said.

Linc smiled, and it made Fagan more nervous than the man's anger had done.

"I didn't threaten her. Is that what she called it? I just told her why I'd come back and asked her if she'd been fucking Uncle Wes while she was still married to Dad."

Breath caught in the back of Fagan's throat. He'd opened up a conversation he didn't want to have by mentioning his sister's name. Now how did he get out of it?

"I don't know anything about her love life," he muttered.

"But you knew your brothers stole the money that paid off your place," Marlow said.

Fagan shrugged.

"Who else knew about the theft?" Lincoln asked.

Fagan's heart stopped. Oh, shit. Now he knew why the man was here. Suddenly it made sense.

"I don't know what you mean," he muttered.

Lincoln lost the last of his patience.

"Damn it, Sheriff. I've had just about all of this pussyfooting around the truth I can take. The little bastard knew the money that paid off this place was stolen."

Fagan panicked. "So what if I did? It doesn't make me guilty of theft."

"Technically, you can be charged with abetting," Marlow said.

Fagan stood up again, but before he could move, Fox was in his face.

"You're not going anywhere," Linc said. "And we're not leaving until you tell Marlow how my dad found out, and which one of you killed him to shut him up."

Fagan took a step backward and fell over the coffee table onto the floor.

"I can't take any more of this!" Fagan shouted. "I'm grieving for my brother, and you-all can't come in here and accuse me of something him and Wendell did just because we shared the same blood."

At that point the deputy came back inside with the license tag neatly bagged for evidence.

"I got it," he said. "And there's an old wreck out behind the barn that fits the description of the car the thieves were driving."

"That's Pa's old car," Fagan said.

Marlow stood up. "Where's your coat?"

"In the hall closet, but why—"

The deputy went to the closet and pulled out the coat. "Put it on, Fagan. You're coming with us."

"No!" Fagan cried, and began trying to explain. "No, you can't! I'm turning my life around. See? I cleaned up the house and the dog pens, and I'm gonna start going back to church like we did when Mama was alive."

"You might have cleaned a few floors and windows," Linc said. "But it takes more than that to clean up the lies you've lived with. The lies that sent me to prison for a crime I did not commit."

"I don't know anything about that!" Fagan insisted. "I swear. That was all Lucy and my brothers. All I did was call in a fire. You can't blame a man for calling in a fire. If you're gonna take me, go open the gate to the dog pen so they can go in and out. I don't want them penned up in there and left to starve."

Marlow nodded at Eddy, who went out the back door. As soon as he was gone, Marlow started in on Fagan again.

"Out of curiosity, how did you come to learn there *was* a fire?"

Fagan was still trying to bluff his way out. "Wendell and Prince had been out running the dogs. They came home and said they saw it burning when they drove past. They drove home to make the call."

Linc remembered the voice in the trees behind him yelling at a dog to shut the hell up. So Prince and Wendell had their dogs with them that night. "But they didn't call it in, you did," he said. "Where were they while you were on the phone?"

Fagan was beginning to shake. This was serious business, and they weren't letting up.

"Uh...they drove on back to help fight the fire, I guess. I never left the house. Mama was sick that night, and I stayed home with her."

Linc poked a finger in Fagan's chest as Marlow put him in handcuffs.

"Too damn convenient," Linc said. "Everyone who could alibi you is dead. I think you stole money and Dad found out. Did he threaten to go to the police? Is that why you killed him?"

Fagan was crying again. "I didn't do it! I swear to God I had nothing to do with it! It was my brothers. They said he found out and told Lucy he was going to the police. She called Wendell and told him it was his fault, that he was bringing shame down on the family, and to keep it quiet, they had to get rid of your dad to shut him up. They did it on her order. It wasn't me. It was *them*."

Linc was shouting now. "You're talking now, but you sat in the courtroom and let people tell lies about me. You knew all of this, and just sat and let a seventeen-year-old kid take the blame. That kid was me, you bastard, and you *did* steal something. You stole my life and everything that mattered. You're a thief, Fagan White—the worst kind of thief. You're the coward who watches while someone else pulls the trigger. Damn you. Damn all of you to hell and back for murdering my dad."

Linc walked out of the house, so mad he was shaking, and slammed himself down in the front seat of the cruiser. He had to put distance between himself and White, and while this wasn't nearly far enough, there was no way in hell he would be sitting in the back beside that bastard on the way down.

They brought Fagan out in handcuffs and put him in the backseat with Deputy Eddy. Marlow got behind the wheel and then stared Linc down.

"Are we good here? You're not gonna fly off the handle on the way back and cause a wreck?"

Linc's voice was deceptively quiet. Once again, he maintained a calm he did not feel.

"That's an insult, and I'm sick of your insults. Just don't talk to me again. I'm not the fool in this car who might be tempted to get away. No wonder I went to prison. I was too young and dumb to fight back," he snapped.

Marlow hit the main lock. "No one's going anywhere," he muttered, and started the car. "I know you were done wrong, but I'm doing my best to make it right."

"Granted, you weren't party to putting me there, but you have been no better than everyone else since I came back. You haven't believed a thing I said since you drove up on my property the night of my arrival. Not even when I told you who was stalking Meg. As for helping me clear my name, if it hadn't been for me, Meg and Quinn, you'd still be sifting papers at your desk. You never would have figured this out."

Then Linc turned around and pointed at Fagan. "You better hope they put you in jail when this is over, because if you walk away from it a free man, I'll kill you myself."

Fagan gasped. "You heard him! You both heard what he said!" he screamed.

Eddy elbowed him. "Stop shouting. I can't hear a damn thing for all the noise you're making."

Fagan curled up in a ball and huddled against the door. He turned his face to the window as they drove away. He couldn't bring himself to look back. It would likely be a long damn time before he saw the mountains again.

Marlow glared at Linc, but he didn't have the balls to call him on his behavior, and he understood the anger. What had happened to him was unforgivable, and he would do everything in his power to make it right.

Seventeen

Detective Kennedy was at his desk, writing up the last report he'd taken from Lucy Duggan. Even as he was typing he kept remembering what she'd said the night of the attack. She and her husband were separated. And once they found out her husband had been shot, under any other circumstances she would have been their first suspect. But they'd taken her appearance and her story as a plausible alibi. Still, he couldn't stop thinking that they were missing something.

It was impulse that made him pick up the phone and call the hospital where Duggan was a patient. After being placed on hold a couple of times, he was finally put in contact with the business office. He identified himself and then asked for the name of the person responsible for Wesley Duggan's affairs, and was given the name of a lawyer.

He thanked them and disconnected. So Duggan had a lawyer in charge of his affairs and not his wife, which made Lucy Duggan's little fuss with her husband a bigger thing that she was willing to admit. He wondered what else she wasn't telling, and decided to run a few questions by the lawyer and see what popped up that didn't jibe with what Lucy had told them. He quickly put in a call to the lawyer.

"Simpson and Coyle, partners at law. This is Rhonda."

"This is Detective Kennedy with the Mount Sterling P.D. I need to speak to Mr. Simpson."

"One moment please," she said, and put him on hold. He got an entire verse of "Bridge Over Troubled Water" before his call was answered.

"This is Dwight Simpson."

"Mr. Simpson. I'm Detective Kennedy with the Mount Sterling P.D. I'm calling about Wesley and Lucy Duggan, who I understand are your clients."

"Well, technically Mrs. Duggan is no longer my client," the lawyer said.

Kennedy smiled grimly. Looked like Lucy's "separation" might be a little more than that. He took a shot. "In the divorce, you mean?"

"Yes. I will be representing Mr. Duggan, so she has been instructed to look for other representation. I'm sorry, I thought perhaps you were calling about the other matter."

The other matter? Interesting. Kennedy decided to push a little further. "Oh. I didn't realize you would be handling the..." He paused, hoping Simpson would fill in the blank. He was not disappointed.

"The admission of perjury. Yes. We're expecting the local D.A. to reopen the case, and my client is expecting that he and his estranged wife will both be charged. All the same, he's very much hoping his testimony will clear the name of that boy—well, he's a full-grown man now. Eighteen years is a long time."

"Holy shit," Kennedy muttered. He hoped Simpson

didn't catch the surprise in his voice. Apparently not, because the lawyer went on without missing a beat.

"That's pretty much what I thought when I first heard about it. I have to be honest. When I got the news that Mr. Duggan had been gunned down, I assumed his wife was behind it. Then I learned she was also attacked, and now I don't know what to think."

"How is Mr. Duggan, by the way?"

"My last report from the doctors was that he was holding his own. And how's Mrs. Duggan?" Simpson asked.

Detective Kennedy frowned. "It's a bit hard to say at this point, but I'm not feeling as sorry for her as I did before I called. Do me a favor and let me know when Mr. Duggan is well enough for visitors. I'd like to talk to him."

"Yes, I will make a note," Simpson said.

"One other thing. This kid who went to prison…what happened to him?"

"Oh, Lincoln Fox? He went back to Rebel Ridge just a few weeks ago to clear his name. I'm told he's working with a Sheriff Marlow in Boone's Gap toward that end."

"Thanks. I'll get in touch with Marlow for further info there. I appreciate your help."

"Sure thing," Simpson said, and hung up.

Kennedy looked at the report he'd just typed and hit Save without sending it to file. He wasn't even close to being through with this case. Then he picked up the phone again and called information for the number of the sheriff's office in Boone's Gap, Kentucky.

Meg was nervous as to what Linc might do when they went to talk to Fagan, and when she was bothered about anything, the best thing she could do was work. As soon as she got home she let Honey out and then moved through the house, fluffing pillows, sweeping ash from around her fireplace, and then sat down at her desk and wrote out checks for the bills that were coming due.

Once she'd finished with that she meandered through the house, unable to focus on anything but what Linc was going through. The place felt different, but she couldn't put her finger on why. Maybe she was the one that was off today. Lord knew she was definitely unsettled.

She went into the kitchen and thought about what she would make for supper, then poked around in the pantry, looking at what she had on hand, but couldn't make a decision. Later she went to get herself a snack, but she couldn't decide what she wanted, so she abandoned that idea, as well.

It wasn't until she went into her workroom to quilt that her anxiety settled. There was something intrinsically calming about putting the tiny, repetitive stitches into the layers of fabric and batting, turning plain cloth into usable works of art.

As she worked, she thought of the years of lies and deceit the White family had practiced. If Linc's theory proved correct, the depth of damage they had caused was irreparable. The only positive things about the past couple of days were the renewal of her relationship with Linc and the news that Prince White was dead.

She worked at the quilt frame until her neck began to ache and then stopped. It got dark so early that she decided to go put up the chickens and feed Daisy. She put on her old coat, wound a red wool scarf around her neck and grabbed a sock cap to keep her ears warm. She was putting on her work gloves as she went outside to do the evening chores.

There was an odd gray cast to the sky, and, from the appearance of the gathering clouds, they were in for another round of bad weather. The air was sharp—cold enough so that when she took a deep breath it made her throat burn—and the wind was getting stronger. Her steps lengthened as she and Honey went to feed and water the chickens; then she gathered the eggs. She took them back to the house and set them just inside the door before heading off to the barn to tend to Daisy. She needed to throw some extra hay into the stall tonight. If a storm was moving in, plenty of food helped the animals to stay warm.

The old cow mooed, then head-butted her as she entered the barn. Honey yapped once, as if to tell the cow to back off.

Meg laughed and pushed the cow aside.

"I see you," she said. "I'm not late, and there's no need to be all insulted. Come on, old girl. Let's get you into a stall where you'll be nice and warm. Extra hay for you tonight, and if you don't butt me again, I might toss a little ground feed into your trough, as well."

Honey smelled mice and began nosing around inside the granary as Meg scooped feed into the feeder and tossed some extra blocks of hay into the manger in Daisy's stall. There was plenty of water in the trough, but there was a thin film of ice over the top. She broke the ice, and then realized she'd left her pitchfork in the granary and went back to get it, laughing at Honey's antics as she moved in and out among the sacks of feed with her nose to the granary floor.

With the pitchfork in one hand and the feed bucket

in the other, Meg backed out of the granary, right into the barrel of a gun jammed into her back.

"Drop the pitchfork," a man said.

She screamed.

Honey came running toward the doorway in attack mode.

"Shut the damn door or I shoot her," her attacker said.

Meg slammed the door in the dog's face and then groaned when she heard Honey's frantic barking.

"Turn around, bitch."

Meg took a deep breath, and just like that her panic morphed into rage. She turned slowly, her fists doubled and her feet slightly apart as if braced for a blow, and recognized Prince White.

He smiled. "Good evening. If you hadn't been so damn unfriendly, we could have done this a different way."

"Why aren't you dead?"

His smile widened. "Because I'm smarter than the cops."

"So shoot and get it over with, or state your business. It's too damn cold for chitchat."

Prince blinked. This was an attitude he hadn't expected. Why the fuck wasn't she crying and begging him not to hurt her? He shifted his stance and took a firmer grip on the pistol. He should have known she wouldn't be easy.

"You have some information I need," he said. "If you cooperate, you and I can go our separate ways and no one gets hurt."

Her mind quickly putting the pieces together, she asked, "Is that what you said to Wesley Duggan before you shot him?"

Prince blinked again. "Don't meddle in my damn business," he muttered. "I need you to tell me where Bobby Lewis buried his dog, and then you and me are gonna take a little ride to his place and you're gonna show me the spot.

Meg stared back, furious at fate for dumping shit into her life just when it was starting to get good.

"I already told Fagan I don't know where the dog is buried. As for meddling in your business, you're also meddling in mine," she fired back. "So either shoot or get the hell off my place."

He swung the butt of the gun toward her face so fast she didn't see it coming. One second she was on her feet, and the next she was on the ground and blood was coming out of her mouth.

Prince was dancing now from foot to foot, getting off on the sight of her in the dirt at his feet.

"Not so smart now, are you, bitch?"

Meg raised a leg, as if she was about to get up, and then launched herself toward him, kicking him right in the groin with the heel of her boot.

He shrieked several octaves above his normal vocal range. When he grabbed his crotch, he dropped the gun.

She bolted to her feet. The gun was on the ground between his legs—too far out of reach for her to chance it. Before he could pick it up, she was gone—running out the back of the barn and heading for the hills as fast as her long legs could carry her.

He fumbled for the gun as he tried to run, but he couldn't move fast enough because of the pain rolling through his balls. He shot at her three times in rapid succession but knew he missed, because the last sight he had of her, she was flying.

"Son of a bitch," he moaned, and doubled over, still clutching his crotch. It took another minute before he could move, but when he did, he took off after her. He needed to know where that damn dog was buried. Once he had the twenty thousand dollars Bobby Lewis stole from Wendell, he would be gone. Lucy'd gotten herself into this mess. For once she could get herself out—or not. He didn't really care.

Meg was running in an all-out sprint, desperate to put as much distance between her and Prince White as she could. She knew the minute he could walk, he would follow.

At first she stuck to the trail, because she could run faster without having to wade through heavy underbrush, but she knew he would see her footprints and she would be easy to track. She needed to get farther away; then she could double back and head for Linc's house. It was the only place she could think of that felt safe.

The rapid slap of her feet against the ground marked the distance she was putting between them, but the sound was soon drowned by the frantic pumping of her heart. The farther she ran, the higher up she went. When the trail began to get steep, she stopped and then took off her sock cap to listen. For a few moments she heard nothing, and then all of a sudden a large buck burst out of the trees and ran past her. Something had spooked it—most likely Prince.

The anger she'd felt down in the barn was gone now, replaced by a growing panic. She stuffed the cap into her pocket and started running again, going farther and higher, straight up Rebel Ridge. She prayed that Linc would come back before dark. When he got to her place to reclaim his truck and found her gone, he would know something was wrong. He would come looking. Of that she was sure. But she couldn't count on him coming in time to save her, so she kept on running until her side was aching, her chest was burning and her vision was blurred with tears.

Please, God, don't let me die, she thought over and over like a chant that would keep her safe.

After a frantic glance over her shoulder, she finally left the trail. It was less than an hour before nightfall. All she needed was a little more time. Prince wouldn't be able to find her in the dark—she hoped.

She moved slower now, needing to stay as quiet as possible. Sound carried a long way in the mountains, and running through brush, snapping limbs and moving through dry leaves on the forest floor would lead Prince right to her.

One minute she was leaning against a pine to catch her breath, and the next second it was as if God had turned out the lights. All of a sudden she looked up and it was pitch-black, with a sky so overcast she couldn't see stars.

"Sweet Lord," Meg moaned. Too late to double back now and virtually impossible to see where she was going no matter which way she headed.

She didn't know whether to curl up beneath this tree and pray to God Prince didn't find her or keep moving. It was the fear of facing Prince and that gun again that made her choose the latter.

As she felt her way through the dense growth her eyes slowly adjusted until she could see different values of black. She continued to feel her way through the trees, hoping to find a place to shelter.

Something cold fell onto her cheek, then her lips, and then her eyelids. She moaned. It was beginning to snow. She lifted her hand to swipe a lock of hair from her eyes and looked up.

The next step she took was off the side of the mountain. All of a sudden there was nothing but air beneath her feet.

She screamed, and then...impact!

All thought was gone.

Prince heard the scream from somewhere above him. When it ended abruptly, he cursed. He didn't know what the hell just happened to her, but he knew when to cut his losses and run. Either she'd fallen off the mountain or she'd walked up on some cougar that had taken her out.

This wasn't the way he'd planned for it to end, but he still had Lucy's gun and he was still breathing, which was more than he could say for the bitch.

He started back down the trail at a steady clip, with the beam from the penlight he always carried safely lighting his way.

It was nearing dusk as Marlow drove up to Meg's house to drop Linc off.

After threatening Fagan's life, Linc hadn't spoken another word to anyone. He knew Fagan White's confession had cleared his name and that two lawmen had witnessed it. But until everything went through the courts and he saw the paperwork clearing the slate, he wasn't counting on anything.

His pickup was parked behind Meg's car, and he half expected her to come out, or for Honey to show up from around the house, barking as she ran.

But neither one of them showed up.

The dog must be in the house with Meg, he thought, and started to get out when Marlow stopped him.

"Look. We'll be in touch. I'll make this right, Lincoln. I promise."

"Make sure you read him his rights and whatever else it takes these days to arrest a perp. Don't fuck this up and give some lawyer a way to get him off," Linc said, then got out, but as he did, the hair suddenly rose on the back of his neck. He heard the frantic barking of a dog in the distance—just like he'd heard the night his father was killed. The ground rolled beneath his feet. He grabbed onto the patrol car to keep from falling.

Marlow jumped and reached for the door latch. "What the hell, man? Are you all right?"

Linc lifted his head, breathing in deep drafts of cold air to clear his mind. He wasn't back at his old house, he was at Meg's, and the dog barking was Honey.

"That's Meg's dog!" he said. "Something's wrong!"

Marlow pointed at his deputy. "Stay there and guard the prisoner. I'll be right back."

Linc was already running toward the house. The front door was locked. When he circled to the back he found the house unlocked and a small bucket of eggs on the floor just inside the door.

"Meg! Meg, honey, are you in here?"

She didn't answer, which meant she must still be outside. Honey's frantic barking was coming from the barn. He headed there on the run, with Marlow behind him, scared of what he would find and scared that, once again, he'd come too late.

As he raced into the breezeway he saw a bucket and a pitchfork on the ground, and Honey's barking sounded even more frantic than before, yet neither she or Meg was anywhere in sight.

"Meg! Meg! Where are you?" he yelled, then stopped in midstep when he saw what looked like the imprint of someone's body in the dust—and blood drops on the bucket and the handle of the pitchfork. All of a sudden he heard a thud against the door behind him, and then a wild, frantic yelp.

"What the hell?" he muttered, then grabbed the granary door and yanked it open.

Honey leaped out into his chest, teeth bared, ears back, and ready to fight.

Linc jumped aside, calling her name as he reached for her, but by then she had her nose to the ground, circling, circling, and then all of a sudden she lifted her head and bayed.

Marlow ran up behind him just as the pup howled. "She's picked up a scent," he said.

"It has to be Meg," Linc said.

Before he could grab her, Honey took off, following the trail with her crooked little lope, baying as she ran.

"I'm gone," he said.

"Well, hell," Marlow said. "I need Eddy to take White on to jail and lock him up. I'll call for backup at the house and be right behind you. Here…take my pistol and my flashlight. I've got spares in the cruiser. I don't know what's going on, but don't go unarmed."

Linc grabbed the gun and light, put them in his pockets and was gone, leaping a water trough and then running past the corral and up the mountain, desperate not to lose sight or sound of the dog on Meg's trail.

He knew within minutes of entering the woods that someone else was following Meg. The trail was fairly clear, the earth undisturbed except for the recent prints. He recognized the tread of Meg's work shoes, but there was another set of prints that periodically overlapped hers—a small man's boot prints. Between that and the blood trail he'd found in the barn, he was scared to death. He took the cell phone out of his coat as he ran, pulled up the number Quinn had given him earlier and hit Call. Whatever was going on, her family needed to know.

The phone began to ring just as the first flakes of snow landed on his face. Damn. That was only going to make things worse. His mind was in a panic when Quinn's voice yanked him back to the present.

"Quinn Walker."

"Quinn, it's me, Linc."

Quinn heard the thud of footsteps and the breathy sound of Linc's voice, and knew he was running.

"What's wrong?"

"Not sure. I was with the sheriff. Meg came home alone. We came back, house unlocked, Honey shut up in the barn, and it looked like there'd been a fight. Blood." Then he stopped a second and bent over to catch his breath. "I let Honey out, and she took off like a bat out of hell up the mountain. Something bad's happened. Gonna need all the help we can get. I'm following Honey, but it's dark. Starting to snow. If Meg is hurt and holed up and hiding, I gotta find her before she freezes."

Quinn felt helpless. "What the hell? I thought all this was over when Prince White drowned."

"Have they found his body yet?" Linc asked.

Breath caught in the back of Quinn's throat. "Oh, hell. No. Keep going. I'm bringing Mariah and her dog. He's good at tracking. We'll find you, and we'll find

Meg. You have to trust she'll find a way to take care of herself."

Linc dropped the phone back in his pocket and took off again. The brief respite had revived him enough that he took off sprinting, running now with a sense of desperation, praying that whatever was happening was not somehow connected to why he'd come home.

The farther he ran, the steeper the climb became. He didn't know how far behind him Marlow was and couldn't stop to wait. All he could do was follow the sound of Honey's yipping and pray to God he found Meg in time.

Eighteen

Prince felt the snowflakes. He wanted to be off the mountain before it got bad and was moving much faster down than he had going up. He was thinking he should start over somewhere warm. All he had to do was knock off a liquor store or some Quik Stop along the way. They were always easy pickings. He could grow his beard and hair longer and rob his way south, then cross the border into Mexico. It sounded like a plan that would work, and he needed for something to go his way, by God. So far, the past month had sucked eggs.

He'd been hearing a dog barking for some time now, the way they did when they were on a hot trail. He smiled, remembering how he and Wendell used to run dogs, hanging out over a campfire and drinking their daddy's homemade wine while the dogs treed their prey. Those were good times. He missed them, and he missed Wendell. His daddy, not so much.

Prince was lost in thought as he came over a little crest on the trail when suddenly he heard something running in the dark. He stopped, cocking his head to one side as he listened, but all he could hear was a panting, whining sound that made the hair crawl on the back of his neck.

"What the fuck?" he muttered as he swept the area in front of him with the tiny beam. He caught a glimpse of glowing eyes, and then something large and furry, growling as it ran. He thought, *Wolf?* and was fumbling for his gun when it leaped at him, growling and snarling, its breath hot and foul. He screamed and stumbled backward with the animal's saliva dripping onto his chin as he fell. The gun went flying as he began trying to fight off the creature. It lunged at his face, and he began flailing his arms, trying desperately to keep it from tearing out his throat.

Pain shot throughout his body as teeth ripped through his cheek. "Help me!" he screamed. "Oh, God…help me, help me!"

He was punching and rolling, and the animal kept riding him, leaping on his back, biting at the base of his neck, then through his coat to the flesh beneath.

He kicked and momentarily dislodged it, but in the dark he still wasn't sure what it was he was fighting. All of a sudden there was a ripping sound, followed by a pain so sharp that it rolled through his thigh all the way up his groin. The beast had clamped down on the inside of his leg, pierced his jeans and locked its jaws into his flesh.

Trapped on his back by both pain and the weight of the animal, all he could do was scream and keep screaming. No matter how hard he kicked, or how frantically he was alternately beating at it and pulling away, he couldn't knock it free.

Linc was still guided by the sound of Honey's yipping, and then all of a sudden she fell silent. Before he could panic he heard a man scream, and then the sounds of a fight, man against beast. Whatever was going on, Honey was in a fight to the death. With a last burst of energy he bolted toward the sound, moving too fast for the flashlight lighting his steps to be any use in guiding him past whatever lay ahead.

He burst upon the dog and the man rolling down on the ground. He swept the beam of his flashlight across the melee, saw Honey with her teeth locked in Prince White's crotch, and Prince beating at Honey's back and head. Between the snarls and the screams, he couldn't tell who was winning, but he knew who was going to end it.

He grabbed Honey by the collar and began pulling her off and calling her to heel. When she finally let go, she was trembling and covered in blood. He couldn't distinguish which one of the two was bleeding worse, but he could tell that she would have fought until one of them was dead.

"Good girl," he kept saying.

Prince White had passed out, giving Linc time to assess Honey's injuries. He kept praising and stroking her, then knelt beside the man's body. He swung the light toward the dog. When he saw her crippled paw, and that she'd run on it until it was raw and bloody and then kept going, rage washed through him.

Prince came to, moaning. "It killed me. I think it killed me. I'm bleeding all over. My face…my leg… I'm gonna die."

"She didn't kill you, but I'm going to," Linc said, and then put a hand on the dog's head. "Stay, Honey. Stay."

She dropped, trembling in every muscle, as she began

licking at her crippled paw, cleaning the raw flesh bleeding through her fur.

Linc swung the flashlight around the area, retrieved Prince's gun and dropped it in his pocket, then yanked him up and slammed him against the nearest tree.

Prince's head popped hard against the trunk.

He groaned.

"Where's Meg?" Linc asked.

"I don't know," Prince moaned.

"Wrong answer," Linc said, and slammed him against the tree again, and then again.

"My God! You're killing me! I don't know where she is."

Linc put both hands around Prince's neck. "Move and I'll break your neck where you stand."

Prince was shaking so hard he didn't think he *could* stand.

"I'm hurt too bad. My legs won't hold me," he whined.

"Then you'll hang yourself if you drop, because I'm not gonna let go. I'll ask you one more time, and I'd better get an answer I like."

Prince was crying and begging for mercy when Sheriff Marlow finally caught up. He was out of breath and staggering from exhaustion, but he had a big searchlight in one hand and a rifle in the other. He couldn't believe what he was seeing.

"Don't kill him, Fox! Don't do it! We've got Fagan. Now we've got Prince. Let the law do this right. Please! Let the law do this right!"

Linc wouldn't let go. "For the last time, where is Meg Lewis?"

But Prince's focus was elsewhere. "You got Fagan? What did he do?"

Linc's fingers tightened around Prince's neck.

"He confessed to everything, you bloodsucking bastard. You're going down for my father's murder. Now what did you do with Meg?"

"I couldn't ever catch her," Prince whined. "Her legs were too long and she ran too fast."

Linc flashed on the day he'd fallen in love with Meg Walker, watching as she crossed the finish line at the track meet with her head back and her arms up in the air. It was the first thing Prince had said that he believed.

"When did you see her last? How far up were you?" Linc said.

Prince was bawling, and fumbling at his face and the wound on his inner thigh. "Sheriff...you gotta help me. I'm bleeding to death here. The dog tore me up something awful."

"Help is on the way. Now answer his question," Marlow said.

Prince moaned. "I don't know how far up, damn it. It got dark. I guess it was about fifteen minutes ago, maybe more, maybe less, when I gave up and turned back." Then he looked up into Lincoln's eyes with an expression of cold satisfaction on his face and grinned, revealing a mouthful of bloody teeth. "And I stopped, because I heard her scream. One long scream that ended sudden...like something had cut off her breath. You ask me, she's dead."

Linc hit him on the jaw.

Prince dropped.

"He's all yours," Linc said. "How far behind is your help?"

Marlow turned the light onto his watch. "Fifteen minutes...maybe less. Why?"

Before Linc could answer, his cell phone rang. "What?"

"It's me. Mariah and I are on the trail below and coming fast. We can see your light. Did you find Meg?"

"No. Just Prince White."

"Oh shit, oh shit," Quinn mumbled, unaware he'd even spoken aloud.

All of a sudden a woman was on the phone.

"Lincoln. I'm Mariah. I take it Meg's still missing."

"Yes. Prince said he heard her scream. When the screaming stopped, he turned back. Don't know if he's telling the truth or not, but I don't know where to look next, and Meg's dog is bleeding too bad to go any farther."

"Ten minutes. Give me ten minutes and we're there. I have Moses. He'll find Meg. I promise. He'll find Meg."

The line went dead in Linc's ear. He pocketed the phone, then dug White's pistol out of his pocket and handed it to Marlow, along with the gun Marlow had given him.

"I won't be needing these anymore," he said.

Marlow pocketed them, then rolled White onto his belly and handcuffed his hands behind his back.

"This is one hell of a thing," Marlow muttered as he rolled White back onto his side so he could breathe, and then kicked the bottom of the man's shoe in frustration. "Sorry bastard. I had Eddy radio my reserve deputies and some medics when he was taking Fagan down to jail. They should be here soon."

"She's not dead," Linc said.

Marlow felt sick. He'd doubted everything this man had told him from the start. He felt shame.

There was a burning inside Linc's chest that was

coming up his throat. He wanted to scream. He wanted to rage. But he held it back, because it would be giving in to the fear that Prince was right.

"She can't be dead."

Marlow sat down on the ground because his legs were shaking too hard to hold him up any longer. He was way too out of shape for what he'd just done.

Linc walked over to where Honey was lying, then sat down on the ground and pulled the lanky dog into his lap. She probably weighed a little less than thirty pounds, only half the size she should be, and yet she'd taken down a full-grown man. She whimpered but licked his fingers, as if giving him permission to touch her. He began running his hands all over her body, feeling for broken bones or open wounds.

She whined as Linc touched her ribs, and with Marlow's floodlight aimed their way, he saw blood coming out of one ear. Her crippled paw was a raw, bloody mess. But it was the look in her eyes that broke his heart.

"Brave girl," he said softly. "Brave, tough little girl. You've done enough for one night. You caught the bad guy. You took him down like the giant you are, and now help is on the way and we're gonna find Meg. That's a promise. We are gonna find our Meg."

Within minutes Linc could hear Quinn and Mariah coming. Their dog yipped once, alerting on their presence. Linc's stomach knotted. The snow was coming down a little heavier now. Time was crucial. Everything hinged on Moses being able to find Meg before it was too late.

"Here! We're here!" Marlow yelled, and then stood up, waving the floodlight down the path.

Seconds later Mariah's dog loped into view, followed

by Mariah and Quinn. Linc stood up with Honey still in his arms. She lay limply against his chest.

And that was Mariah's first view of the man who loved Quinn's sister—a bloody giant with tears on his cheeks, holding an even bloodier pup. Moses smelled the other dog and went straight toward her. Mariah followed.

"Is she hurt bad?" Mariah asked.

"I can't tell. White was beating her when I arrived, but she had her teeth in him and wouldn't let go. Her crippled paw is a mess. I have no idea how serious her other injuries are, but she took White down on her own."

Quinn was stone-faced and edgy as he approached. He was in full search mode, with a backpack and a huge length of climbing rope thrown over his shoulder.

"Damn, but I hate the dark."

Mariah gave his arm a quick squeeze. It was a left-over fear from when they'd been trapped in a mine cave-in. He was living with it but far from over it.

Quinn saw Prince White lying handcuffed against a tree, and then eyed Marlow and Linc.

"We let down our guard when we thought he was dead...just like he expected. And when she was the most vulnerable, he struck. Linc, you called it when you asked if the body had been found. We should have been more cautious, just in case."

"What's done is done. We can't take it back," Linc said, then turned back to Mariah. "So how does this work? How will your dog know to hunt for Meg?"

"I have a shirt that belongs to her," Mariah said. "Are you ready?"

"Waiting here was the longest ten minutes of my life. I'll be right behind you." He handed Honey to Marlow. "Don't let anything happen to her."

Quinn paused. "Sheriff, Jake Doolen and his boys are about five minutes behind me. He said there's a squad of searchers coming up on ATVs. He can hear them coming."

"Those will be my men," Marlow said as he patted Honey's head, then turned to Linc. "I'll make sure we get her to a vet ASAP."

"Thanks," Linc said.

Mariah held the shirt under Moses's nose. "Hunt, Moses, hunt."

The dog leaped forward, straining against the leash, and Mariah started forward at a jog, with Quinn and Lincoln right behind her.

"Will the snow affect Moses's ability to track?" Linc asked.

"Yes, if too much falls."

"Well, hell," Linc muttered. "Can we go faster?"

"I can turn Moses loose," Mariah said. "But the danger is in losing track of him in the dark."

"I followed Honey halfway up the mountain in the dark. If your dog barks like she did, we can follow."

Mariah knew time was not on their side and didn't hesitate. "Moses. Stop!"

The big hound stopped immediately. Mariah reached down and unclipped the lease from his collar.

"Moses. Hunt."

The dog took off in a lope. Linc jumped out ahead of the others. With his long legs and steady stride, aiming the flashlight down at the ground in front of him, he slowly but surely began to outdistance the others.

Up the mountain they went, running headlong into the dark while the snowflakes got heavier and the path was slowly obliterated.

Five minutes passed, then ten. Moses continued to track, barking intermittently as he ran. Nearly fifteen minutes into the run Linc's side was burning, his legs were shaking and he was as close to physical exhaustion as he'd ever been. It was frightening. He kept praying they would find Meg somewhere along the trail, but it didn't happen.

And then all of a sudden Moses veered off to the right.

Linc called out, "He's turning east!"

"We see your light!" Quinn yelled back.

Linc was in the thick of the forest, ducking branches and stumbling through underbrush, when all of a sudden Moses bayed. The hair stood up on the back of his neck. Did this mean that the dog had found her?

He swung the flashlight across the ground in front of him and caught a glimpse of the dog. Moses was sitting, looking back, as if waiting for everyone to catch up, but Meg was nowhere in sight

Linc's heart was hammering against his chest. He was afraid of what lay ahead in the dark, terrified it was something that couldn't be fixed.

He dashed forward, only to have Moses suddenly stand up and charge him, barking to keep him back. It didn't make sense.

He took the light and swept the ground again, and that was when it hit him. All he could see in front of him was dark and falling snow. No trees. No brush.

No ground.

"No. No, no, no," he moaned, while a pain in his chest began to spread.

Two more steps and he was standing beside the dog. He could hear Quinn and Mariah running up behind him, but he had to look. Even if the flashlight didn't shine far enough down, he had to know if he was right.

He swung the light down into the void and saw nothing but snowflakes spiraling into darkness.

He dropped to his knees, defeated by an inevitability he couldn't face, and threw back his head. The roar of pain that came up his throat echoed across the canyon.

Mariah grabbed at Quinn's hand, but he kept running, unwilling to accept the despair he heard in Linc's voice.

They saw Moses first, and then Linc on his knees. Quinn took one long step forward when Mariah suddenly grabbed him by the arm.

"Stop! Don't go any farther!" she screamed.

Quinn spun. "Why the hell not?"

"It's a cliff. Linc's on the edge of a cliff."

Quinn froze. "Meg fell off? God, no!"

Mariah was crying as she slipped off her backpack. "Give me the big searchlight."

He slipped off his own backpack and dug out the light.

Mariah grabbed it, crawled up behind Linc and hit the switch. A blast of light with a million candle-watt beam cut through the dark, past the falling snow and down to a ledge about forty feet below. She could see something red, and then the sole of a shoe beneath the snow cover, but it was enough to know that there was a body there.

She grabbed Linc by the shoulder and shook him. "She's on that ledge! She didn't fall all the way! Look, Linc! See her foot? And her red scarf?"

Linc grabbed the light out of her hands, then got down on his belly and scooted forward. As he angled the light down he saw the ledge, the boot and the flash of red. It *was* Meg. He scooted back and then jumped up.

"Quinn! Meg's on the ledge! How do we get her off?"

Now the ball was in Quinn's court. He tried to make a phone call, then pocketed the phone in frustration.

"No signal," he said. "We'll have to wait for the search party to catch up."

"No!" Linc cried. "I waited long enough for you two to catch up. The snow is falling heavier, and the wind is rising. I'm not waiting again. If there's a chance in hell that she's alive, we need to get her off this mountain *now*."

"But—"

Linc pointed to Quinn's rope. "How long is that?"

"Nearly two hundred feet of heavy-duty nylon."

Linc pointed at Quinn's backpack. "Do you have any climbing equipment in that thing?"

Quinn took a step back. "Oh, hell no, you're not climbing down the face of a cliff in a snowstorm."

Linc grabbed Quinn's arm. "You don't understand. My life isn't worth much without her. I'd just as soon risk it doing this than stay safe and healthy and find out she died from exposure and injuries before we pulled her up. Look at me. I'm big, but I'm also damn strong, and I have rappelled down a cliff face before. It's not that far, so tie the damn rope off or whatever you have to do, or I'll do it myself."

Mariah stepped between them, her hand on Quinn's chest.

"Don't deny him this," she said. "Ryal said the same thing to me when I told him I was going in after you. I couldn't have lived with myself without trying. It's not your place to tell Linc he can't try. This is his decision."

And just like that, the discussion was over.

Linc quickly shed his coat as Quinn dug a chest harness out of his pack, then let it out as far as it would go. It fit Linc, but barely. After that the prep and hookup went quickly. Linc's eagerness to get down there was tempered by his fear for Meg's condition. He wouldn't let himself believe God would save her from falling to the bottom only to let her die when she was within reach.

As soon as his climbing gear was in place, they helped him put his coat back on and fasten it up. Quinn took off his sock cap and put it on Linc's head, then handed him a pair of leather climbing gloves, slipped a handheld radio in one pocket and made sure he had his flashlight in the other.

"We'll belay you down. I've got another radio. We'll be able to communicate once you're there. Mariah... give him that blanket in your pack."

She ran toward her pack and dug out a blanket.

Quinn tied it to Linc's harness and then slapped his shoulder.

"Godspeed, brother."

A look passed between them, and then Linc headed for the drop-off. He stopped at the rim and pulled hard a few times to test the rope, made sure Quinn was ready, adjusted his grip and then turned his back to the void.

"All my contact info is at my place. Aunt Tildy will know what to do."

Before they could comment, he stepped off backward into space.

"Lord have mercy," Mariah muttered, and angled the spotlight downward. It was her job to keep it on the ledge where Meg had fallen, and she wasn't going to fail in her duty. What Linc was doing was crazy, but she understood the need. Denying Linc the same chance she'd had would have been the height of hypocrisy.

Quinn was feeding out the rope, but the pull from Lincoln's weight was greater than he'd thought. When he finally heard Jake Doolen and his boys coming up, he called out, "We're here. Hold the dogs back."

Moments later the others burst onto the scene. Moses was familiar with both Jake and his dogs, and wagged his tail in welcome as they tied their dogs off next to him.

"What's going on? Where's Meg? Where's Lincoln?" Jake asked.

"She fell off the mountain. She's on a ledge about forty feet below. Linc is rappelling down," Quinn said. "Grab hold, boys. He's damn heavy."

Jake was horrified. Their sweet Meg... If the law didn't put Prince White in prison for life, he would be waiting for that SOB when he got out. He said a quick prayer for Linc and then headed toward Mariah, as Cyrus and Avery fell in behind Quinn to help belay the line.

The farther down Linc went, the stronger the wind became. There was a whirlpool effect going on in the space between where he was and the surrounding mountains, turning the falling snow into icy shards coming at him from every direction.

He wasn't thinking beyond his next step and the rope in his hands. It was the umbilical cord keeping him in this life and bringing him closer to Meg. His shoes were not meant for climbing, but they were holding up to the task. Only once did he slip and go crashing into the cliff.

Up above, Mariah gasped.

"What happened?" Quinn shouted.

"He slipped, but he's okay. He's got it. He's back on track!" she yelled.

"You okay?" Jake asked. "If you need me to spell you, I can."

"I'm good," she said.

She wasn't moving. Being able to see what was happening was the only way to keep from freaking out. The tension alone made the hair crawl on the back of her neck like it had when she was still on active duty and could almost feel the insurgents somewhere nearby.

She and Jake watched the snowfall swirling below them like a white tornado, with updrafts and downdrafts continuing to buffet Lincoln's body.

"Good thing he's got body mass on his side. He's holding his own in that wind," Jake said. "Have you seen Meg move?"

"No."

Jake turned sideways to keep his face from taking the brunt of the icy snow. "We got any medical help on the way up?"

"Marlow has a team on the way," Mariah said.

He nodded, his gaze fixed on the man at the other end of the rope.

"God help them," he said.

Lincoln continued moving down. He checked his progress only when he needed to judge the distance left to go, and he wouldn't look at Meg, too afraid of what he might see. When his foot finally touched firm foundation, his heart skipped a beat.

He'd done it! He was down!

He gave the rope two quick shakes to let them know he was there and then dropped to his knees. Still holding on to the rope, he was able to see the extent of the ledge they were on. It was bigger than it had looked from above—maybe twelve feet deep at its widest point.

He crawled to where Meg was lying and brushed the snow from her face. His heart sank. It was like looking at a mannequin. She was pale and still, and the blood that had been running down from her hairline had frozen to her forehead.

He yanked off a glove and pressed his hand to the side of her neck. Her skin was chilled, but the flesh was still supple, and he could feel the pulse in her throat. He looked up—straight into the spotlight Mariah was holding—and gave her a thumbs-up.

Mariah screamed. "She's alive! Linc said she's alive!"

Quinn tied off the rope, and then he and Jake's sons rushed to the rim.

Down on the ledge, Linc was praying to see even one small sign of consciousness from Meg. He had his flashlight trained on her, trying to check her condition through the spiraling snow. His size was something of a windbreak, but as fast as he pushed the snow off, it came back in a swirl of ice and wind. He was scared to move her for fear of causing permanent injury, and though he talked to her, he knew that it was nearly impossible for her to hear him in the maelstrom. He bent over, his mouth against her ear, hoping she could hear him above the wind's mighty shriek.

"Meg…Meggie, sweetheart, it's me, Lincoln. Can you hear me? You had a fall. Can you tell me where you hurt?"

She didn't answer.

He angled his flashlight toward her face, then tried to part her hair to see how deep the wound was, but her hair was so frozen it felt brittle. He began digging through her pockets, found a sock cap and carefully eased it on her head. A person lost a lot of body heat through the top of the head, and he needed to keep her as warm as possible until the rescuers arrived.

He ran his hands along her body, feeling her arms and legs for signs of broken bones, then slid a hand beneath her coat to check for injuries. Feeling her smooth midriff and flat belly was a blessing in itself, although he had no way to tell if she was bleeding from within. After checking her as thoroughly as he dared, he pulled out the radio and keyed it on, yelling to be heard over the wind.

"This is Lincoln. Over."

Quinn fired back. "Quinn here. What's her status?"

"Obvious head injury. Bleeding has stopped, probably because of the cold. No open fractures. Can't tell about internal injuries, but I'd bet on cracked ribs from the way she hit. I can feel her breath. She's not in distress, like she would be if a lung was punctured, but it's too damn slow. She's still unconscious. Have no way to tell where she hurts. I'm going to cover us up with the blanket and hope that warms her up. If I get her to wake up I'll let you know. Over."

"Roger that," Quinn said. "We'll let you know when the search team arrives. And, Linc…thank you. Over."

"No thanks needed. It's what you do for people you love. Over and out."

Linc put the radio down in front of him, then untied the blanket and began trying to unfold it. One side of the blanket was made of Mylar, which he knew would hold in body heat. The wind was battering them, trying to yank the fabric out of Linc's grasp, but he held fast as he scooted right up to Meg, then flattened the blanket over her as best he could and rolled under it, tucking it in lengthwise beneath him, then pulled the excess over their heads, anchoring the other side by tucking it beneath her back. He held on to the top with his right hand and the bottom with his feet, cocooning them inside the makeshift shelter and still leaving one hand free to keep tabs on her pulse.

Even though he could still hear and feel the wind, the blanket made a decent tent, and he was hoping the Mylar would capture enough of their combined body heat to warm her up. Now that they were secure, he switched on the flashlight, angling it so that if she came to, the first thing she would see was his face.

Nineteen

Precious minutes passed as Linc waited for a positive sign. When he realized the bruise on Meg's cheekbone was the same shape as the butt of the gun they'd taken off Prince White, he was heartsick at what she'd suffered. Her mouth had obviously been bleeding even before she fell, and it was swollen to the point that he wasn't sure she could talk if she tried. That injury was most likely the source of the blood they'd found in the barn. He couldn't quit thinking about how scared she must have been.

He kept rubbing her hands, trying to get the circulation flowing while waiting for Quinn to key up the radio and let him know help had arrived.

But the airwaves stayed silent, exacerbating his fear.

In the back of his mind he knew the rescue team should have been there by now. What if they'd gotten lost? He needed to do something positive, if for no other reason than to take his mind off how this might end, so he started talking to her as if she could hear and understand.

"Hey, baby...guess what? Honey caught Prince White

and took him down all by herself. She chewed him up good before I got there and pulled her off. She was absolutely amazing. When I let her out of that granary, she took off running and didn't stop until she caught him on the trails. All we could do was follow. You would have been so proud of her. She's waiting for you to come get her. We need you, Meggie...please, sweetheart... please wake up. There are so many things I want to tell you." His voice broke, but he kept talking. "Fagan White confessed to everything. Wendell and Prince killed my dad on Lucy's orders. The sheriff and his deputy heard the confession. They have Fagan and Prince in jail. My name will be cleared and they'll go to prison for Dad's murder."

A sudden blast of wind hit his back, popping the ends of the blanket so fiercely he had to take a tighter grip to keep it from flying away, and yet in the midst of the madness, Meg lay as if dead. Tears began to run down his cheeks as he touched the side of her face. It felt warmer than it had when he'd first found her.

"Come back to me, baby. I don't want to be in this world without you."

Like the answer to his prayer, Meg's eyelids began to flutter, and then she moaned.

Elated by the first positive sign he'd seen, he clutched her hand.

"Meg. Open your eyes, sweetheart. Open your eyes!"

Meg was waking up in increments. She was cold—so cold—and kept thinking she needed to put another quilt on her bed or turn up the heat. There was a loud roaring in her ears, which confused her even more, and she kept hearing a voice but couldn't make out the words.

The more cognizant she became, the greater the pain, until it ultimately engulfed her. She thought she was screaming, but all she heard was a moan. Something brushed across her face, and she could hear someone crying.

It made her sad, but the roar in her head was so distracting she couldn't think. It kept getting louder and louder. She needed to get up. Something was happening—something bad.

Linc was holding her hand and wasn't letting go, convinced it would be the anchor she needed to find her way back. She was showing signs of regaining consciousness. All she needed was to focus on his voice.

"Wake up now, Meggie. It's time to wake up. I need you to tell me where you hurt. You fell. You need to wake up now." Then his voice broke. "Please, God, please, give her back," he said, then laid his cheek against her hand. From that angle he was looking straight into her face. All she had to do was open her eyes.

Meg's eyelids fluttered again, and this time he saw her try to take a deep breath. As she did, she moaned again.

He frowned. Broken ribs? Internal bleeding? God in heaven.

The wind was whipping the blanket so hard he could barely hear himself think. What if she couldn't even hear his voice?

In desperation, he yelled, "Open your eyes!"

And she did.

Linc swallowed a sob. "Hi, baby…hi, Meggie. It's me, Lincoln."

She blinked in slow motion.

"Can you hear me?" he asked.

She blinked again, "Cold."

"Yes, baby, it's cold. You fell off the mountain. It's snowing, and we're on a ledge waiting for the rescuers to get here. Do you remember what happened?"

Her lids went shut, but there was a frown between her brows. "Running," she finally said.

"Yes, from Prince White. We caught him. He'll never hurt you again."

A tear rolled out from beneath her eyelid and down the side of her nose.

"Hurt."

His stomach was in knots. This was what he'd been waiting for, and now he was scared of what she would say.

"He hurt you, didn't he? But he can't hurt you again."

Another tear rolled.

"Meg...you need to help me now. Can you tell me where you hurt? Does your head hurt?"

"Hurt."

"What about your back? Can you move your legs?"

"Hip."

"Okay...your hip hurts?"

"Hurts."

Little by little he questioned her, until he was fairly certain that he had a grasp of where the worst of her injuries were. He grabbed the radio and keyed it up as she drifted back out of consciousness.

"This is Lincoln. Over."

"Quinn here. Over."

"She came to. Her head and hip hurt. She can feel her legs, but she won't move because of pain, and I'm thinking her hip might be broken. She has feeling everywhere, and she flinched when I pinched her leg. She could move her fingers, but she didn't try to lift her arms, and I don't want her to move for fear she's got a back or shoulder injury. Where the hell is the rescue team? Over."

"They just got here. We're rigging up a line to drop the basket for Meg. Over."

"A basket? Hell, no! The wind is too strong now. No matter how tight I strap her in, her weight will roll her out when it tilts. Over."

Quinn was shielding his radio with his body and still had to shout to be heard.

"No. It has a top and a bottom. Locks together like a wire casket. Sending a backboard and a neck brace with it. Attach neck brace first. Then put the backboard against her spine and roll her faceup. The board will stabilize her body. Strap her to it, then lift her into the basket. There are extra blankets. Cover her head to toe. Lock down the top. We'll haul her up on your cue. Over."

Linc was so cold he could feel himself growing lethargic. It would have been easy to just lie down beside her and quit. He had to get her out of there before hypothermia set in.

"Let's get this done. Over."

He put the radio back in his pocket and then patted Meg's hand. Her eyelids fluttered.

"Meg, honey…help is here. We're going to take you off the mountain and get you to a hospital. Do you trust me?"

He watched her nostrils flare slightly, and then she opened her eyes. For a heartbeat she saw him.

"Love," she whispered, and then closed her eyes.

There was a knot in his throat. "Oh Lord, Meggie…

I love you, too," he muttered, and brushed a kiss across her forehead.

He was scared out of his mind that moving her would make things worse and then was reminded that, short of death, things were never as bad as they could be.

His radio squawked, then he heard Quinn's voice.

"Lowering the basket. Over."

Linc answered immediately. "We're ready. Let's do this. Over."

He lowered the blanket and looked up. The wind was an instant blast against his face, but the snow was waning. Thank God for small favors. He kept looking up until he could see the basket descending. Watching the wind swinging it from side to side was a preview of how Meg would go up. He would rather have moved the mountain they were on than take this chance, but the decision was out of his hands.

"I love you, Meg. God help us," he added, and he pushed the blanket aside and then tucked it under his knee to keep it from blowing away.

The wind was so strong and so cold it took his breath. He could only imagine what it was doing to her, and once again he used his size as a bulwark to shield her against the blast.

When the basket finally reached them he let his mind go blank and began doing what Quinn had instructed him to do one step at a time—like following a blueprint on a jobsite.

First the neck brace, then the backboard.

She moaned when he began to turn her.

"Sorry, sorry, sorry," he muttered, and kept the motion slow and smooth as he rolled her over, then fastened the straps across her body, battling time and the elements. She was crying, but he didn't think she was fully conscious. Before, he'd wanted her to wake up, and now he wished to God she would pass out.

"Here we go, honey. Up and over," he said, and lifted her into the bottom half of the basket. The shriek that came up her throat was loud enough to be heard over the wind's wicked whine. He wouldn't let himself go there and kept working. The faster he moved, the sooner she would be on her way to safety.

He began tucking blankets in around her. The Mylar blanket was the last he put over her, and when it was secure, he pulled it over her face. There was nothing left to do but fasten her in. He pulled the top down and flipped the locks, then tested it several times to see if he could pull it open. It held tight. He grabbed his radio.

"Lincoln here. Pull her up. Over."

"Roger that. As soon as she's up, we'll pull you up. Over."

"Understood. Over and out."

He kept his hand on the basket until they pulled her out of reach, and even then he never took his eyes off the cage until it disappeared into the spotlight. It gave him a chill, watching her ascend like a spirit going into the light, and he had a sudden sense of panic that he'd just given her up to God.

In the midst of his horror, calm suddenly washed over him. What was he thinking? He'd already given her up to God. It was up to God to give her back. It seemed like an eternity, but in reality it was only a few minutes before his radio squawked again.

"Quinn here. We've got her. Over."

The relief that went through Linc was brief. He still had to get off this damn ledge, and they had to get *her*

off the mountain before an evaluation of her injuries
was even possible.

His radio squawked again.

"On your feet, Linc. We've got your line. Over."

"On my way. Over and out."

Linc was on his feet and braced, waiting for the rope
fastened to his body harness to go taut. The second it
lost slack he leaned back, tightened his grip and started
the brutal climb, fighting the buffeting winds and icy
shards.

About halfway up a gust of wind blew him sideways,
slamming him into the face of the mountain with such
force that he hit his head, cut his cheek and bit his lip.
The salty taste of his own blood was in his mouth as he
swung back into position and resumed the climb one
miserable step at a time.

By the time they pulled him over the rim onto solid
ground his legs were trembling. He dropped to his hands
and knees, and when he finally looked up the headlights
of two ATVs were illuminating the clearing and heading down the mountain.

Quinn came out of the darkness, dragged him to his
feet and then threw his arms around him and began
pounding his back.

"You did it! You by God did it, Lincoln Fox! Our
family owes you forever! All you have to do is name it,
and it's yours."

"All I want is Meg," Linc said, handing Quinn the
radio. Then, despite the cold and the wind, he dropped
his coat and shrugged out of the harness.

Quinn began packing it up into his backpack as
Mariah quickly helped Linc back into his coat.

Linc's vision was blurry from the battering cold, but

it was obvious the searchers up top hadn't had it much easier than he and Meg had down below. Even though Mariah's snow gear had a hood, and she'd wrapped a thick scarf around the lower half of her face, what he could see of her dark hair and eyelashes was almost white with ice.

"You're bleeding," she shouted as she snapped him back into his coat.

He felt the blood on his head and cheek and promptly ignored it. "Where is she? Where's Meg?"

"They're already on the way down with her. That ride is yours," Mariah said, pointing to a four-wheeled ATV with a passenger seat on the back.

He nodded. His legs felt like rubber, but he wasn't going to admit it. "Where's Jake?"

"He left with Meg. Once the search party got here and realized you'd found her, he sent Cyrus and Avery back with all the dogs. He said to tell you they're taking Honey to the vet tonight, even if they have to drag him out of bed. There's one more ATV for Quinn and me. We'll meet you at the hospital."

Linc's legs felt wooden as he headed for his ride.

Linc's driver was in the seat, the engine idling. As soon as Linc's butt hit the seat, the driver put the ATV into gear. He pulled the sock cap tight over his ears and grabbed hold. The ride was rough, the trail bumpy, but knowing he didn't have to take another step was nothing short of a blessing. There wasn't an ounce of strength left in his body.

Deputy Eddy was waiting at Meg's house when Marlow came down off the mountain with his prisoner. Prince was so battered he was barely able to move, and when they put him into the backseat of the warm police cruiser, out of the wind and cold, he passed out.

As they started back to town, Eddy began filling him in on the latest.

"A Detective Kennedy from Mount Sterling P.D. called to inform you that Lucy Duggan just admitted her brother wasn't dead, and that he was the one who assaulted her and tried to kill her husband. According to the story Lucy told, Prince came back for money to get out of the country and found out Duggan had cut her off. She said he flipped out, beat her up, stole her gun and tried to kill Wesley."

Marlow frowned. "That doesn't make a lot of sense."

"Yeah, that's what Kennedy thought. He's already digging deeper, but he wanted you to know about Prince."

"Too bad we didn't know about this sooner. It might have saved Meg Lewis."

Eddy gasped. "Is she dead?"

"Hell if I know. The last thing I heard was that they'd found her on a ledge about forty feet down the mountain."

"Oh, man. I hope she's okay. She's a really nice woman."

Prince moaned from the backseat. Marlow looked over his shoulder at the sorry excuse bloodying up his upholstery and frowned. "Don't stop in Boone's Gap. Just drive straight on into Mount Sterling. I've got to take this one to the doctor and notify Kennedy his missing shooter has been found. We'll let the county worry about keeping him in jail until they figure out what to charge him with first."

* * *

Linc knew Meg had been taken straight to the hospital in Mount Sterling. By the time the searchers got him there for treatment, as well, she was already in surgery. They x-rayed his back and shoulder, and sewed up the still-bleeding wounds on his head and cheek. As soon as they released him, he headed straight for the waiting room in the surgical wing.

He hadn't expected his reunion with Meg's family to be in a hospital waiting room, but that was what he got. Dolly and Jake. Ryal and Beth. James and Julie. Even Quinn and Mariah, who were still wearing their search gear, had arrived.

When they saw Linc walk in, they all stood up and, before he could say a word, surrounded him, hugging and shaking hands, and all talking at once.

Finally Jake stepped in. "Hey, let him sit, people. He looks like he's on his last legs."

"What about Meg? What did they tell you?" Linc asked.

"Jake is right. Come sit down," Dolly said, and took him by the hand and led him to a chair.

Linc didn't have to be told twice. He took off his coat and dropped. His head was throbbing, and the left side of his body was getting stiffer by the minute.

Dolly sat down in the chair beside him and then clutched his hand. There were tears on her face, but her voice was firm.

"Meg has a dislocated hip, a hairline fracture in one arm, a torn rotator cuff, a concussion and broken ribs that fortunately didn't pierce anything vital. They took her into surgery about an hour ago."

"Did they say anything about brain swelling or damage to her spinal cord?"

"They didn't appear to be concerned with either of those issues," Dolly said.

"Thank God," he muttered. "It scared the hell out of me when I had to move her." He wiped a hand across his face and closed his eyes, struggling to maintain his emotions as Dolly gave his hand a quick squeeze.

"Meg believed in you from the start and never stopped. We are forever grateful for your presence in our lives and hope you'll learn to forgive us for not being a better voice for you when you were young. God bless you, Lincoln. Forgive us for every slight you ever felt. No matter the outcome of your investigation, you have a place in our homes and hearts forever."

Linc glanced at Jake. "You didn't tell them?"

Jake shrugged. "Didn't hear enough of the facts to start spreading rumors."

Linc sighed. "Too bad there weren't more like you when I went to trial. So here's the scoop. Fagan White confessed that his two brothers killed Dad on Lucy's orders. It's a long story, but the bottom line is that they killed him to hide another crime they'd committed. Dad found out what they'd done and was going to turn them in. Lucy didn't want the embarrassment of all her friends finding out her brothers were thieves, so she told them to kill Dad so he couldn't tell. She committed murder to save herself embarrassment. I wish they still hanged people here. I'd pull the lever on her myself."

"Oh, dear God," Dolly said, and then started to cry. "You were railroaded, and we all let it happen. Why didn't we question more? Your grandfather and Tildy kept saying it wasn't so. I'm sorry. I'm so sorry. Can you ever forgive us?"

Linc shrugged. "There's nothing to forgive, ma'am. You didn't convict me. It was Uncle Wes and my step-mother's testimony that did it."

Dolly frowned. "That's the last time I ever expect to hear you call me ma'am. It's Dolly or Mom, like the rest of my brood."

Linc felt like crying all over again. He'd been on his own for so long that being accepted back into the family he'd thought had forsaken him was too good to be true. But none of it would be worth a damn if Meg didn't pull through.

"Did they say how long the surgery would take?" he asked.

Dolly shook her head.

Ryal looked at the time. It was nearly two in the morning. From the condition Linc was in, he looked like he was fading.

"Hey, Linc, when was the last time you had anything hot to eat or drink?"

"I don't know…at noon with Meg, I guess." And then his eyes really did fill with tears. "Damn. That feels like a century ago."

"How do you take your coffee?" Ryal asked.

"Black."

"I'll be back in a few." Ryal walked out of the waiting room with Beth at his heels.

A little while later they returned with several cups of coffee and an assortment of chips and honey buns.

"This will make you feel better," Ryal said, and handed Linc a cup of coffee and a sweet roll.

Linc took the food gratefully and allowed himself

a few minutes to relax. The other food was distributed among the family. After that, they all nursed their coffee in silence, looking up only when they heard footsteps out in the hall in hopes it would be Meg's surgeon. The footsteps walked away, and they all returned to their individual thoughts. Linc had never been good at waiting, and this suspense was a living hell.

As more footsteps approached they looked up again. Sheriff Marlow walked in, and headed straight to Linc and Dolly.

"Any news on Meg?" he asked.

Dolly shook her head.

"Where's Prince?" Linc asked.

"Down in the E.R. I think they're going to have to operate on his leg to repair some muscles in his thigh. That dog of Meg's did a number on him. Mighty fine dog. She's got heart, and more guts than good sense. If you ever breed her, I want one of her pups."

Jake beamed. "She's out of good stock."

"So which charges does he answer to first?" Linc asked. "Murdering Dad, stalking Meg or attempted murder on Wesley?"

"It's up to the district attorney."

Linc's eyes narrowed. He didn't like the ambiguity of that answer.

"No, by God, it's not. You have a duty to correct the wrong that was done in your jurisdiction, and there's proof to do it. This is exactly why I don't trust anyone with the so-called law on their side. If I have to, I will get an attorney and shove this down your throat via the media. If you can't do what's right on your own, then the fear of not getting reelected might do the job."

Linc got up and strode out of the waiting room, too angry to sit there and talk anymore.

Marlow frowned. "Damn, I didn't mean to upset him."

Quinn snorted softly. "Upset him? Hell, Sheriff, considering what happened to him, don't you think he's got a right to be upset?"

"Yes. I'll talk to the D.A. myself. I won't let this be swept under the rug."

"And neither will we. You can count on that," Dolly said.

Marlow frowned. He didn't like having his word questioned, then realized what Lincoln Fox must have felt like, having truth on his side and knowing it still wasn't enough.

"So, I've got to get back to Boone's Gap. I need to take care of Fagan. He's going to jail, as well. Just because he wasn't in on the actual acts, he can be charged with abetting due to his silence. He's going to be charged right along with the rest of them."

Linc was pacing the hall, trying to come down from the adrenaline surge. He was shocked at himself and his lack of emotional control. The construction business was a daily grind of adjustments and frustrations, and he'd never lost it like this. This had only begun happening after he'd come back to Rebel Ridge—when he'd come face-to-face with the people who'd abandoned him. Obviously he had some issues to address. Even though he'd been betrayed as a kid, he was a grown man now, and he was coming off like some grudge-bearing maniac.

Marlow walked up behind him. "Sorry, man. I didn't mean to imply that your case would be shoved to the back burner. It's just that things are so convoluted, I'm not sure what the D.A. will want to address first."

Linc sighed. "Yeah, I'm sorry I lost my cool. It's been a long night."

"I totally understand," Marlow said. "And for what it's worth, after what you pulled off, I think you're about as close to a damn superman as a mere mortal can be."

"There's one thing about this whole mess that still doesn't make sense," Linc said. "Why was Prince White so set on stalking Meg? It doesn't fit the rest of what's been happening."

Marlow frowned. "You know what? I hadn't thought about it like that, but you're right. I'm meeting with Detective Kennedy tomorrow. I'll see what I can find out."

Linc shoved a hand through his hair and winced when he accidentally hit the stitches. "This is a hell of a thing…Lucy and Prince, even Meg…all here under one roof. It's giving me an uneasy feeling, like Meg's still not safe as long as they're this close."

"Just so you know, there's a guard on Lucy's door. At first he was there to keep her safe. She doesn't know it yet, but he's there now to make sure she doesn't bolt. There's also a guard on Prince's room, and he's handcuffed to the bed."

Linc watched the sheriff walk away and was heading back toward the waiting room when he saw a man in scrubs approaching.

"He's coming," he said as he entered.

When the doctor walked into the room, they were all on their feet.

"Margaret Lewis's family?"

"Yes," Dolly answered.

"She came through surgery just fine. We'll keep her

in ICU tonight, and if there are no surprises, we'll move her to a room tomorrow."

"When can I see her?" Linc asked.

The doctor eyed the crowd. "Visitors are allowed for ten minutes at the top of the hour. Two at a time. There are a lot of you. You'll have to figure it out."

"Her mother goes first," Linc said.

Dolly's eyes welled. She knew how much it cost Linc to say that. "And you'll be with me."

Linc backed up to the nearest chair and dropped. The others were still talking to the doctor, but he'd heard all he needed to hear.

The surgery was over, and she was alive.

Twenty

It was nine o'clock in the morning, and Linc was asleep on a couch in the ICU waiting room. He'd spent the night there, waking every hour on the hour when the alarm on his watch would go off, just so he could get an update on Meg's condition. He'd sat out three separate visitations so that her brothers and their wives got a chance to go in and see her. And one by one the brothers and their wives went home, leaving Linc, Dolly and Jake. After Dolly made her second visit, Jake had taken her to a nearby motel to get some rest, and Linc was finally alone.

When the alarm went off again he was standing up almost before his eyes were completely open. He reeled on his feet, wincing at the soreness in his body, and headed for the bathroom. He'd quit looking at himself in the mirror, because his appearance wasn't getting better. His head and cheek were turning purple and green around the stitches, and one eye was slightly swollen from the impact with the cliff. It had occurred to him that even if Meg did wake up, she might not recognize him. He was a wreck. After washing the sleep out of his eyes and using his fingers to comb his hair, he headed for the ICU.

By now the nurses all knew how the patient in bed six had been injured, and knew the hunky giant who stood in line to see her was the man who'd saved her life. When he was finally admitted, Linc walked in quietly and stood by Meg's bed.

At first glance she didn't look any different. Still hooked up to machines that beeped, her shoulder and arm bandaged from the surgery, and the leg with the dislocated hip in traction. He sat down on the stool at the side of her bed and gave her fingers a soft squeeze.

"Hey, Meg. Good morning, honey. It's time to rise and shine."

She stirred, and his pulse kicked. This was the first time she'd responded so quickly to the sound of his voice.

A nurse came by and paused at the foot of the bed.

"She's been trying to wake up for a couple of hours now," she said. "Let us know if she opens her eyes and speaks to you."

His hopes rose as the nurse moved on.

"Your mom left to get some rest. She'll be back around noon. Your brothers all went home about daybreak. It's just you and me, babe."

Meg sighed. Her eyelids fluttered, reminding him of that moment on the ledge when she'd first opened her eyes and seen him.

He watched her nostrils flare slightly, saw her trying to shift position and guessed she was in pain.

"Are you hurting, baby?"

She licked her lips, then squeezed his hand just enough to let him know she'd heard him.

"I'm so sorry, Meg. So sorry. Hang on and I'll go get a nurse."

She clutched his hand tighter, silently asking him not to leave, and so he stayed.

Her eyelids fluttered again, and then opened. Not much, but just enough that he could see tiny slits of green.

"Hi," he whispered.

A frown immediately shifted her expression. She lifted her hand toward his face and touched his cheek right below the stitches.

"Wha...?"

"War wound. It's nothing."

Her lids shut, but her lower lip trembled. When a tear suddenly rolled down her cheek, Linc groaned.

"No, baby, no. Don't cry for me. With you safe and getting well, everything is perfect."

She clutched his hand and gave it a slight squeeze.

"Over?" she whispered

"Yes, baby, everything is over but your healing. They operated on you several hours ago to fix what you broke when you fell. Prince White is in custody. Your family has been here all night and left just a short while ago. Your mom will be back around noon."

She blinked to indicate she understood.

"Fell?"

"Yes, you fell. Scared the hell out of all of us. I thought you'd fallen all the way down, and then Mariah saw your body on a ledge."

A frown knitted between her brows. "How...get up?"

He stroked her cheek with the back of his forefinger. "I went down after you," he said.

She squeezed his hand even tighter.

"Hero. Love."

Tears blurred his vision of her face. "I love you, too. Hang on, baby. I promised the nurse I'd let them know if you woke up. They need to examine you."

He waved down a nurse and then stood aside as they began talking to her. He could tell they were trying to get a handle on brain function and her ability to move her limbs.

As soon as they finished, he slid back onto the stool. Meg was drifting in and out of consciousness again. He didn't care. They'd said enough. She loved him. It was all a man could ever want.

Detective Kennedy was getting an earful from Prince White. For two people connected by birth and blood, Prince and Lucy's stories couldn't be more diametrically opposed.

Even though the surgery to repair Prince's leg had been successful, he was having some post-op issues they hadn't expected. Infection had set in, and they were pumping large doses of antibiotics into him intravenously.

As a kid, Prince had been the kind to talk and walk in his sleep. When he got sick and the fever was high, he rambled nonstop, muttering, even crying out from time to time. Kennedy had heard a lot of interesting facts by the time they had the infection under control and was curious to know if Prince would admit the same things while awake that he'd confessed to in his feverish state.

As for Lucy, she was on the same floor as her brother but didn't know it. He wanted to keep it that way and had already told the nurses not to talk.

Sheriff Marlow was bringing the other White brother

to Mount Sterling today, and he'd asked the sheriff and his deputy to swing by the hospital with Fagan before they took him to jail.

He'd finally figured out that the separate stories he'd been getting from Prince and Lucy were mostly bullshit, and he wanted to see what happened when he got all three of them together. It would be interesting to see who pointed the finger of guilt first, and see who they named.

There was one last person involved in this mess who he wanted to meet, and that was Lincoln Fox. He was curious to see what kind of man he'd turned out to be after being incarcerated as a kid, and was toying with the idea of having him present, too. That might just be the trigger that would blow the top off this family conspiracy.

Ryal and Beth had done the chores at Meg's house, then picked up a change of clothes for Linc from his place, along with his truck, and brought them to the motel where Jake and Dolly were staying.

Linc was there, waiting, when they arrived. He'd already showered and shaved after Jake and Dolly returned to the hospital, and he was grateful for his truck and the change of clothes that Ryal and Beth brought.

"I sure appreciate this," Linc said as Ryal handed him the keys to his pickup and the clothes he'd requested.

"My pleasure," Ryal said. "I have to tell you, that's one heck of a fixer-upper job you did on that old bomb shelter. You should do that for a living."

Linc grinned. "Thanks. I'll give it some thought."

"Oh. Got a phone call from Cyrus. The vet has Honey all patched up. Broken ribs, some serious contusions on her head and back, and her crippled paw is raw, but he says she'll heal. The boys are keeping her up at their house for the time being. She's familiar with everything, and they'll make sure she gets plenty of attention."

Linc frowned. "Good to know. I've been worried about her, too. I still can't get over what she did. Despite her handicap and size, she's got the heart of a lion."

Ryal chuckled. "Like her owner, and speaking of which, we're headed up to see Meg. So we'll see you soon." He ran back to the car where Beth was waiting.

Linc dressed quickly, packed up his dirty clothes, put on his good coat and boots, and slogged through the snow to get to his truck. The streets were snow packed, but the main roads had been sanded, making travel a little easier. He was pulling into the parking lot when he got a text from Ryal.

Meg in room 335.

Great news. No more waiting for a brief glimpse once an hour. He hurried through the lobby and up the elevator, then down the hall to room 335.

At first he couldn't see her for the number of people surrounding her bed, and then Beth stepped back just as Meg turned her head toward the door.

Their gazes locked.

She smiled a crooked smile, wincing from the pain of her swollen lip.

Linc slipped off his coat and laid it on the back of the chair in the corner.

Dolly saw the look on her daughter's face and took charge.

"We've all had our visit, and if you're okay with Beth and me taking your quilts to the show, we'd love to do it for you."

"Yes, thank you," Meg said.

"No thanks necessary. We love you, Margaret Ann, but you'll get better quicker without all this fuss. We'll be in and out, have no fear."

Dolly winked at Lincoln as they filed out of the room.

Ryal closed the door behind them, leaving Lincoln and Meg alone.

Linc pulled up a chair beside her bed and slid his hand beneath hers as he sat.

"I'm sorry I wasn't here earlier. I was waiting on Ryal and Beth to get here with my truck and clothes. Was it a rough move?"

"Bad enough," she said, and threaded her fingers through his. "Mom said you saved my life."

"We all did, baby...but we wouldn't have gotten the chance without Honey. She led us straight to Prince White and took him down, then Mariah came along with her dog and picked up the trail."

"Jake said Honey got hurt."

He nodded. "Yes, but she'll heal, and as far as I'm concerned, she's the one who deserves all the praise."

But Meg wouldn't let go. Her voice was shaking. "You climbed down a mountain...in a blizzard." She took a slow breath, easing past the pain of broken ribs to say what she needed to say. "I remember cold...and your face."

"I was so scared that you would never wake up."

She closed her eyes. Her thoughts were already drifting away.

Linc could tell the move had exhausted her. "Sleep, baby, just sleep. I won't be far. I will never be far away from you again."

"Lincoln..."

"What, sweetheart?"

She blinked, and for a few moments her eyes were open. "Love you forever." Then she drifted away again.

Linc patted her hand, then slid it under the covers, and leaned over and brushed a kiss across her cheek. Finally he whispered in her ear, "Forever and ever, 'til death do us part."

A slight smile tilted one corner of her mouth as she recognized the line, and then she slept.

Linc sat in the quiet knowing that no matter what else happened, he was already blessed.

Almost an hour passed, and then he felt his cell phone vibrate. He got up and walked down to the waiting room to take the call. "Hello?"

"Lincoln Fox?"

"Yes, who's speaking?"

"Detective Kennedy with the Mount Sterling P.D. Do you have a minute?"

Linc frowned. "Yes. What's up?"

"Sheriff Marlow gave me your number. I'm calling to ask you a favor."

"Like what?"

"Would you be willing to be present in the room when I question Lucy Duggan and her brothers, Prince and Fagan White?"

Linc didn't have to think twice. "In a heartbeat. When?"

"Where are you?"

"Right here in Mount Sterling, at the hospital," Linc said.

"That's handy. I'm standing outside Prince's room, and since he's not ambulatory, I'm having Lucy brought here. The sheriff is in the parking lot with Fagan. What I need is your assurance that you won't try and break their damn necks, even though there are those who would argue you've earned the right."

Linc smiled. He liked the man already. "I promise I will not touch a hair on their heads. However, I hope you don't mind if my presence scares the shit out of them."

"Actually, that's what I was counting on. I need to get this mess unwound, and as long as they're all telling a different story, I can't figure out who gave the orders and who carried them out. They continue to point a finger at Wendell, who I understand is long dead, making him a far too convenient scapegoat."

Linc had an idea. "Do you mind a suggestion?"

"I'm listening," Kennedy said.

"Right at the start, if there's a way Fagan can overhear what the other two are saying to you without them knowing he's there, you might get to the truth quicker."

"Why's that?" Kennedy asked.

"I think Fagan is guilty by blood and silence only. He knew what was going to happen but wasn't a part of it, and after it was over, he never told. And he intimated to Marlow and me when we heard him confess, that Lucy is probably the brains behind most of it."

"You're saying Fagan may be the trigger that blows the lid off their lies?"

"Between my presence and what he hears the other two say, I'd say the odds are good that the whole lot of them spill their guts before it's over."

"Then I'll see you soon?"

"Where do I meet you?"

"Come to the fourth floor, room 416. Wait out in the hall until I come for you."

"I'll be right up, and thank you."

"Son, it'll be my pleasure."

Prince was begging his nurse for pain meds when he saw Detective Kennedy arrive. He remembered the man being in his room before, and watched as Kennedy paused outside the door to speak to the guard and then walked in.

He was surprised to see another cop follow and quickly move toward the far corner of the room, where he began setting up a tripod. When he popped a video camera on it and then turned it toward the bed, Prince felt a surge of panic. What the hell?

He had already come to terms with the fact that he was going down for stalking Meg Lewis and knew from questions the detective had asked him that they were all being questioned about Marcus's murder, but that had to be it, right? His own sister would never finger him for assaulting her and shooting her husband, because she had to know he would turn right around and finger *her* for arranging it. If they all stuck together, they could bluff their way out. Couldn't they?

"How is he doing?" Kennedy asked a nurse who had come to hover in the doorway, drawn by the activity.

"His fever is down."

"Good. The sooner you get him well, the quicker he's mine. We need some privacy now, please."

Prince's gut knotted. He didn't like the way that sounded.

Kennedy waited until the nurse was gone, and then sent a text.

"What's going on with all the mystery?" Prince asked.

"Considering the fact that you're going to be behind bars for a really long time, I thought you would like your reunion with your family to be recorded for posterity."

Prince's eyes bugged. The only family he had was Fagan and Lucy, and he couldn't fathom why they would be coming to visit. Fagan hated his guts, and Lucy was a snake. He didn't want to see her any more than he guessed she would want to see him.

"What the hell? Why are you talking to me like that?"

Kennedy shrugged. "How else would I address the fact that you tried to kill Margaret Lewis?"

Prince glared. "I never once told her I was gonna hurt her."

"Just because you didn't say it means nothing. You stalked her, broke into her home, shot at her, assaulted her, then chased her up a mountain and caused her to fall to what could have been her death."

Prince frowned when he heard she wasn't dead. "That's not what happened."

"Don't bother trying to deny it. Facts talk," Kennedy said, and then walked to the door.

He saw Lucy being wheeled from one end of the hall, and when he turned to his left he saw a very large man coming from the opposite direction. Since he'd been told Lincoln Fox was on the tall side, he was guessing that was his man.

"Are you leaving?" Prince asked.

"No. We've been waiting for your company to arrive, and they're here.

All Lucy knew when she left her room was that they were taking her downstairs, she assumed for some tests. Her hair was sticky and matted, and she felt naked without her makeup, but her face was still too swollen to consider it. Wesley had always referred to her makeup as war paint, and she used to giggle about it, but since she'd tried to have him killed, she didn't think it was prudent to fall back on fond memories of their time together. Like life and seasons, things changed. As far as she was concerned, he had betrayed her, giving up his rights to her loyalty. And she was a bitch when it came to keeping score.

The orderly was wheeling her briskly down the hall, but when they passed the elevator, she pointed.

"Hey, you missed the elevator. Aren't we going down to the lab?"

"No, ma'am," he said, and kept rolling.

"Then what on—"

She let the question go when she saw Detective Kennedy step out of a room just a few doors down. He seemed to be waiting for her, which made her nervous. When she saw a tall, dark-haired man turn a corner at the other end of the hall and come toward them, she panicked. It was Lincoln, and when Kennedy stopped him and shook hands, she panicked. Why did this feel like an ambush?

She wouldn't look at Lincoln, but she felt his gaze. The old saw—if looks could kill—had never been so true. And then the orderly wheeled her past the men and into the room. When she saw the patient in the bed, she gasped.

Prince saw the shock on Lucy's face and realized something was up. She was just as surprised to see him as he was to see her. When Lincoln Fox walked in behind Kennedy, it was obvious they were about to be fucked. He just didn't know how far over he would have to bend.

Kennedy was watching the siblings and their body language. What was most telling was that they had yet to meet each other's eyes, let alone speak. His phone buzzed. He scanned the text and stepped out into the hall. Marlow and his deputy were coming down the hall with a handcuffed man between them. The last family member had arrived. Time to get the party started. He waited until they were standing just outside the door, raised a finger to his lips to caution them to stay silent, then stepped back into the room.

"So, Prince...Lucy...this isn't the greeting I would have expected," Kennedy said. "Prince, I would have thought you'd want to apologize to your sister, seeing as you tried to kill her and her husband."

Lucy's gut rolled.

Prince frowned at Lucy. "What the hell? I didn't try to kill you, and you know it."

Linc eyed the detective, curious as to what he was thinking since Prince had essentially just admitted the attack on Wesley by not denying the accusation. He waited to see what else the bastard gave away.

"That's not what *she* said," Kennedy said.

The shock on Prince's face was obvious. He looked at Lucy in disbelief.

"Lucy! Is that what you told them? That I tried to kill you?"

Lucy had one chance to talk her way out of this, and she wasn't going to blow it. She turned on the tears and shrank back in the wheelchair, as if she was afraid he would jump out of the bed and start hammering on her again.

"I know you told me to lie," she said, and started to tremble. It was a skill she'd perfected back when she was a kid and her daddy would get so mad at all of them that he would start beating the first one he could catch. "I know you told me to say it was a heavyset, middle-aged man with a salt-and-pepper mullet, but I couldn't lie. I couldn't lie to the police."

Prince snorted. "Since when? You been lying all your life."

Lucy started to sob. "Oh, Prince. You tried to kill my sweet Wesley and now you're blaming me? I didn't think I could be any sadder, but I was wrong. You have broken my heart."

Prince was desperate and turned to Kennedy. "No, Detective. That's not how it went down at all. It was her idea to off her old man. She wanted him dead before he filed for divorce. Fagan knew it, too. She told him. Hell, maybe it was Fagan who did it."

Linc's heart skipped a beat. *Here it comes.*

Lucy wailed.

Prince was cursing.

And then Fagan walked in, and once again the siblings were shocked into silence.

Fagan was obviously pissed, which was what Linc had been hoping for. Earlier he'd seen Fagan trying to distance himself from the actual crimes, and he guessed that was what was about to happen again.

"I can't believe the crap coming out of your mouth," he said.

Lucy sniffed and mopped at her eyes. "I know, baby brother. I was shocked, as well."

Fagan snorted. "I was talking to you, Lucy."

Lucy gasped. "How dare—"

Fagan pointed at her. "You. Don't talk." Then he

glared at Prince. "You are a mean bastard, Prince, and whatever happens to you, you have coming."

"Shut the hell up!" Prince yelled.

Linc froze. He'd heard that voice and that phrase outside his house just before it blew.

He moved to the end of Prince's bed. "You're fond of that phrase, aren't you?"

Prince frowned. "What do you mean?"

"Oh, just that I heard you say it before, but you weren't talking to your brother, you were yelling at your dog   just before my house blew up. I know because I heard you."

"You didn't hear shit," Prince said. "You were already uncon—"

Linc's heart skipped a beat. Prince looked like someone had just stuck a cattle prod up his ass.

Linc kept pushing. "What? You didn't finish what you were going to say. Were you about to say that I was already unconscious? You bastard! You stood outside that house and watched it burn. Who killed Dad? You or Wendell? Oh, wait…let me guess. Neither one of you had the balls to stand up to him face-to-face. But you are fully capable of being the shit who distracted him while Wendell came up behind him and bashed him in the head with my baseball bat."

Prince's lips went slack, and then he started trying to explain his way out of the gaffe he'd made.

"We didn't kill your dad. Why would we? He was family."

Sheriff Marlow had been standing in the doorway, keeping an eye on his prisoner, but this was when he honored his promise to Lincoln. He cleared his throat and moved into the room.

"Sorry, Prince, but that's not true and you know it. What you *don't* know is that we have identified you and your brothers as the men who robbed a bank in Lexington over eighteen years ago. It's a done deal, so don't argue about it. Fagan confessed. What you don't know is that Fagan also told us that Marcus Fox found out that you boys were the ones who stole the money. When he told Lucy, she called Wendell and told him Marcus knew. She was mad at all three of you, because if you got arrested it would embarrass her. She told Wendell to kill Marcus to keep him quiet. She didn't care about being a widow, because she already had a lover waiting in the wings to pick up the slack. She wouldn't have to move back into her mama's house. Not when Wesley Duggan was waiting for her to move into his."

Lucy screamed and kept on screaming until Linc took a step toward her. She choked on a sob and covered her face.

Prince's mouth dropped. When he regained the use of his voice he shouted, "Fagan!"

Fagan glared. "What? I told you I was sick and tired of being dragged into your messes. I told Lucy the same thing, and now you both know I meant it. I'm done. Whatever happens to me for not telling sooner is gonna have to happen. My sin was keeping silent, and I'm done. I cleaned the dirt out of my house, and now I'm cleaning the dirty lies out of my soul, just like Mama would have told me to do."

Prince glared. "You are no Goody Two-shoes, little brother. You are a worthless drunk who smokes more of the weed you grow than you sell. I have always stood up for you! I didn't throw you out in the cold. That's what *you* did to *me!*" Prince yelled.

"And you know why, so shut your mouth," Fagan muttered, then began talking to Kennedy. "There's no love lost between me and Prince, but to be on the fair side, there's no love lost between me and Lucy, either. She's a nasty mean bitch. She can order a hit like she's ordering one of her fancy damn coffees, but she thinks if she doesn't pull the trigger, she's lily-white. So Prince and Wendell killed Marcus like she asked. And then she got in trouble again when Lincoln Fox came back and told Wesley that he'd lied on the stand. It opened up a new can of worms when Wes found out she'd lied to him. He told her he was going to divorce her and confess to perjury. She was pissed and asked me to get rid of Husband Number Two. I believe her actual request was to 'make her a widow.' I told her no way in hell."

Kennedy eyed Lucy curiously. "What do you have to say to that, Mrs. Duggan?"

She cringed, glanced up at Linc and then looked away. "I didn't say that," she muttered.

Fagan snorted.

Prince sighed. "Do I get a court-appointed lawyer?"

"Yes, but you'd better come clean now," Kennedy said. "It will go better on you in the long run."

"I'll come clean, all right. What Fagan said about Lucy is the truth."

Lucy shrieked. "You liar!" She stood up from the wheelchair and grabbed Kennedy's arm. "He's lying. I swear."

Kennedy shrugged out of her grasp. "Sit down, Mrs. Duggan."

Lucy dropped.

Prince laughed.

"After Fagan turned her down, she asked me to kill

Wesley. She didn't know he'd already filed for divorce and confessed to the perjury that sent Lincoln Fox to jail. I showed up at her house a couple days later and found her drunk off her ass. Long story short, I cleaned her and her house up, hid the empty booze bottles in the neighbors' trash cans, and then we had ourselves a little family brawl to explain why I had the gun that I was supposed to use to kill her old man. Only he's not dead, so you can't charge me with his murder."

"No, but we can charge you for Marcus Fox's murder, which we will. Got anything else to say?" Kennedy asked.

Prince's shoulders slumped. "Truth is, me and Lucy had bigger fights for less reason when we were all still living at home. She's just mad at me cuz I missed Wesley's heart."

Lucy moaned.

Fagan spoke up again then, throwing another twist into the story that took the last load of guilt off Lincoln's shoulders.

"Oh…I'm not done cleaning my house," Fagan said. "Don't forget about Prince stalking Meg Lewis. That had nothing to do with any of this other shit. Her ex, Bobby Lewis, killed Wendell a couple of years after the trial. He's been in prison ever since. When he learned he was dying of cancer, he had his brother, Claude, ask Prince to come see him, said he would make it worth his while. Just mention the word *money* and Prince would kiss the devil's ass, never mind the man who killed our own flesh and blood. So Prince goes to see Lewis, finds out that when he killed Wendell, he stole the money off Wendell's body and hid it. Something like twenty thousand dollars. Anyway, Bobby didn't tell Prince where it was buried, said it was where he'd buried his favorite dog, Ike, and that his ex wife would know and to ask her." Fagan was so mad he was shaking. "But did my brother go ask her that simple question and leave her the hell alone? No. He plagued her and stalked her and scared her half to death, then told me as soon as she told him what he needed to know he was gonna slit her throat. That's the kind of people I'm related to. Deviants. Fucking deviants!"

Linc was shocked. Finally the truth about why Meg had been targeted, and it had nothing to do with him.

Lucy was weeping loudly. Fagan turned on her.

"You better cry now and get it out of your system, sister, because where you're going, no one's gonna care. You wanted Marcus dead and Wendell did it. You wanted Wesley dead and Prince gave it his best shot. You need to be taken out of circulation before someone else pisses you off and you want them dead, too."

Before they could stop her, she launched herself at Fagan, screaming at the top of her lungs.

"I spent my life trying to live down being kin to you. It's not my fault, it's *yours!* I begged Marcus not to tell, but he wouldn't listen. He said it wasn't right that they'd taken someone else's money because they were too lazy to work. I couldn't let everyone know I came from criminals. I didn't want to be tarred by that brush."

Lincoln had had enough. He shoved the wheelchair against the backs of her legs. She fell into it with a plop as he turned her to face him.

"You are a murderer, Lucy *White*—" He used her maiden name just to insult her. "And you're even worse than your brothers. You keep talking about them dragging down your name and reputation, but you're as dirty as they are, right down to the bone. You're a killer *and* a coward. You pointed the gun and let someone else pull the trigger, then you blamed it on me—a *kid,* damn it! You were willing to sacrifice my life just so yours would stay perfect."

Linc's fingers were curled into fists, and he was so mad he was shaking.

"Detective, if you're finished with me, I think I'm done here."

"We're done here, too," Kennedy said. "We've got everything on video, loud and clear. Thank you for coming. Hell of a road they put you on. You know the justice system. This will take a little time, but you'll get your day in court and a clean name to go with it. I'm making it my business to see that your record is expunged and that you are completely vindicated."

Too moved to speak, Lincoln nodded once, then walked out of the room without looking back. The worst of his past was over.

He had a woman to see about the rest of his life.

Epilogue

After three weeks in the hospital Meg had come home to a house decorated for Christmas, and a man and dog waiting for her on the front porch.

After that, they marked the winter off in increments.

The day Prince, Lucy and Fagan White were charged with multiple counts of perjury, theft, arson and murder.

The day Meg took her first step without a walker.

The day Wesley Duggan testified in court and was jailed for perjury. Lincoln's first Christmas with Aunt Tildy and the Walker family.

Meg and Lincoln ringing in the New Year in his bed, making love on a Storm at Sea.

The day Lincoln appeared in court, and was pronounced cleared of all charges and his record expunged.

The day they were married in their old country church.

The day Lincoln showed her the blueprint for the house they were going to build.

The night she and Lincoln made the baby she was carrying.

The day they leveled the grade to begin construction on their new house.

By the time spring came to Rebel Ridge they were well into the first year of their new life.

Meg often felt as if the past eighteen years she'd spent alone had been to prepare her to truly appreciate the joy of the life that now lay ahead. She and Lincoln had gotten a very late start on the life they'd planned so many years ago, but as he said, they were wasting no time catching up.

The first time they'd gone to Dallas she'd been taken aback by the size and the noise. They'd been numerous times since, and she was learning to like hot Mexican food and cold beers.

They would be in their new house on the old Fox home place long before snowfall—the new house with a room big enough for quilt looms and shelves for fabrics, and a large cutting table to lay out her designs. It was to be next to the nursery and across the hall from their bedroom.

Three vital rooms in her house that formed a triangle binding her life as perfectly as the triangles she sewed into her quilts.

Only now and then were they reminded of how close they'd both come to dying, but that just reinforced the fact that they had surely lived for a reason.

As Meg's belly grew bigger, the house grew closer and closer to completion.

The night before they were set to move in, Linc took her up to the building site.

She was standing on the wraparound porch and looking up into the night sky with his arms around her shoulders, his chin resting on the crown of her head.

"Look! A falling star!" she said, pointing toward the east and the flash of light streaking across the blue-black sky.

"I saw one of those the first night I came back here," he said. "At the time, all it did was remind me of my fall from grace."

"What do you think of now?" she asked.

Linc stroked the swell of her belly, then kissed the side of her neck right below her ear.

"I think of how many nights we will stand on this porch looking out onto this land like our people did before us, and watch stars burning out that began falling long before we were born. I think of infinity, Margaret Ann, because that's what you are to me."

Meg was so full of love for this man that she could hardly speak. Her vision blurred as the star burned out above them, but she didn't care. There would be others, for as long as they lived, 'til death—and then forever again, because theirs was a forever kind of love.

* * * * *

REQUEST YOUR FREE BOOKS!

2 FREE NOVELS
FROM THE SUSPENSE COLLECTION
PLUS 2 FREE GIFTS!

YES! Please send me 2 FREE novels from the Suspense Collection and my 2 FREE gifts (gifts are worth about $10). After receiving them, if I don't wish to receive any more books, I can return the shipping statement marked "cancel." If I don't cancel, I will receive 4 brand-new novels every month and be billed just $5.99 per book in the U.S. or $6.49 per book in Canada. That's a savings of at least 25% off the cover price. It's quite a bargain! Shipping and handling is just 50¢ per book in the U.S. and 75¢ per book in Canada.* I understand that accepting the 2 free books and gifts places me under no obligation to buy anything. I can always return a shipment and cancel at any time. Even if I never buy another book, the two free books and gifts are mine to keep forever.

191/391 MDN FVVK

Name	(PLEASE PRINT)
Address	Apt. #
City	State/Prov.	Zip/Postal Code

Signature (if under 18, a parent or guardian must sign)

Mail to the Harlequin® Reader Service:
IN U.S.A.: P.O. Box 1867, Buffalo, NY 14240-1867
IN CANADA: P.O. Box 609, Fort Erie, Ontario L2A 5X3

Want to try two free books from another line?
Call 1-800-873-8635 or visit www.ReaderService.com.

* Terms and prices subject to change without notice. Prices do not include applicable taxes. Sales tax applicable in N.Y. Canadian residents will be charged applicable taxes. Offer not valid in Quebec. This offer is limited to one order per household. Not valid for current subscribers to the Suspense Collection or the Romance/Suspense Collection. All orders subject to credit approval. Credit or debit balances in a customer's account(s) may be offset by any other outstanding balance owed by or to the customer. Please allow 4 to 6 weeks for delivery. Offer available while quantities last.

Your Privacy—The Harlequin® Reader Service is committed to protecting your privacy. Our Privacy Policy is available online at www.ReaderService.com or upon request from the Harlequin Reader Service.

We make a portion of our mailing list available to reputable third parties that offer products we believe may interest you. If you prefer that we not exchange your name with third parties, or if you wish to clarify or modify your communication preferences, please visit us at www.ReaderService.com/consumerchoice or write to us at Harlequin Reader Service Preference Service, P.O. Box 9062, Buffalo, NY 14269. Include your complete name and address.

SHARON SALA

32792	TORN APART	___ $7.99 U.S.	___ $9.99 CAN.
32785	BLOWN AWAY	___ $7.99 U.S.	___ $9.99 CAN.
32677	THE RETURN	___ $7.99 U.S.	___ $8.99 CAN.
32633	THE WARRIOR	___ $7.99 U.S.	___ $7.99 CAN.
31264	BLOOD TIES	___ $7.99 U.S.	___ $9.99 CAN.
31241	BLOOD TRAILS	___ $7.99 U.S.	___ $9.99 CAN.
31342	DON'T CRY FOR ME	___ $7.99 U.S.	___ $9.99 CAN.

(limited quantities available)

TOTAL AMOUNT	$ _____
POSTAGE & HANDLING	$ _____
($1.00 for 1 book, 50¢ for each additional)	
APPLICABLE TAXES*	¢ _____
TOTAL PAYABLE	$ _____

(check or money order—please do not send cash)

To order, complete this form and send it, along with a check or money order for the total above, payable to Harlequin MIRA, to: **In the U.S.:** 3010 Walden Avenue, P.O. Box 9077, Buffalo, NY 14269-9077; **in Canada:** P.O. Box 636, Fort Erie, Ontario, L2A 5X3.

Name: _____

Address: _____ City: _____

State/Prov.: _____ Zip/Postal Code: _____

Account Number (if applicable): _____

075 CSAS

*New York residents remit applicable sales taxes.
*Canadian residents remit applicable GST and provincial taxes.

HARLEQUIN® MIRA®
™ www.Harlequin.com

MSS0413BL

Edited by *New York Times* bestselling author

SANDRA BROWN

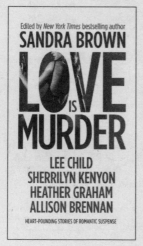

Prepare for heart-racing suspense in this original collection by thirty of th hottest bestselling authors and new voices writing romance suspense toda Bodyguards, vigilantes, stalkers, serial killers, women (and men!) in jeopard cops, thieves, P.I.s, killers—these all-new stories will keep you thrilled an chilled late into the night.

"A slam-dunk collection of the best the business." —Steve Berr
New York Times bestselling auth

Available wherever books are sold.